SATURDAY BLOODY SATURDAY

SATURDAY BLOODY SATURDAY

ALASTAIR CAMPBELL
AND
PAUL FLETCHER

ORION

First published in Great Britain in 2018 by Orion Books,
an imprint of The Orion Publishing Group Ltd
Carmelite House, 50 Victoria Embankment
London EC4Y 0DZ

An Hachette UK Company

1 3 5 7 9 10 8 6 4 2

A CIP catalogue record for this book is
available from the British Library.

ISBN (Hardback) 978 1 4091 7453 0

Typeset at The Spartan Press Ltd,
Lymington, Hants

Printed and bound in Great Britain by Clays Ltd,
St Ives plc

MIX
Paper from
responsible sources
FSC® C104740

www.orionbooks.co.uk

To Ed Victor,
without whom this collaboration would never have happened.
He was so much more than an agent – great friend,
great mind, great man.

And in memory of Jack Windeler, who took his life aged 18.
With sincere thanks to all supporters of Jack.org
and the great work they do in mental health.

We are indebted, for various different aspects of the research and publication of this novel, to Dame Anne Begg, Darryl Broadfoot, Rory Campbell, Tommy Docherty, John English, Jim Fleeting, Johnny Giles, Ron Harris, Martin McGuinness, Lucinda McNeile, Alan Samson, Ken Sharp, Ray Simpson, Nicola Thatcher, Dave Thomas, Colin Waldron; and above all to Fiona and Sian and our families for their love and support, and their tolerance of our football and banter addictions.

CONTENTS

Prologue

MARTHA

---

13 January 1961

When he thought about next Saturday, he began to sweat. It would come around soon enough, his rational mind knew that, but right now it seemed so far away. Six days, five hours, ten minutes, so much time for things to go wrong, no matter how low he lay, no matter his attention to detail. But if he got through the week, then six days, five hours, ten minutes from now, he could be on his way to unparalleled joy, his ecstasy. It was a bad habit, he knew it, but it was one he had no intention of giving up. Never mind the material goods he gained from his habit, that was not why he did it. It was the excitement. And to get there he had to endure mundane days like today.

Across from him, her eyes half-closed, her hands caressing the familiar glass ball, was the most wrinkled face he had ever seen. He guessed she was in her eighties now, an age few reached where he came from. The full-length black mesh dress and her long, heavily varnished burgundy fingernails added to the theatre of the moment. Her prayer-like actions told him she was now communicating with someone who had passed to the other side. In a gargling voice that made no sense to him, she asked the ball another question.

Dermot, with friends who would laugh if they saw him now, sat quietly, awaiting enlightenment, calmed by the smell of the incense that fogged the darkened room. He was thirty-nine and so proud to call himself Irish. He was only here because he knew his mother, a true believer, would have wanted him to be. Sitting in this grubby parlour on the Blackpool seafront was a way of showing his loyalty to her. He had cut down the visits to Madam Martha, but in the aftermath of the accident, he wanted to ask this 'great psychic' why she hadn't foreseen the motorbike that knocked down his mum as she crossed Belfast's Crumlin Road. He bottled it. He wasn't scared of much. But he was a little bit scared of Madam Martha. His mum used to say she trusted the tea leaves more than she trusted Dermot's dad, and he knew she wasn't alone in that. Dermot didn't really believe that this stooped old crone could predict his future, but as the gargling and the mumbling intensified, he was less sure of his own uncertainty.

He didn't seem to get as many trips to Blackpool as before. But whenever his work took him there – today it was with a group of pensioners from Yorkshire – he always looked up Martha, and she always managed to squeeze him in for a reading.

Laughlin's Coaches had gone from a small family firm to one of the biggest coach companies in the north of England in the twenty-odd years he'd worked in this family concern. Their bread-and-butter business was still school trips, work outings, race days, weekends in London or at the seaside, sometimes France and Spain too. But the contract that put them into the big league was the work they had with one of the country's top-flight football clubs. Every away game, often with an overnight stay, Laughlin's would take them, and Dermot loved his work for the football club more than any other part of the business.

Martha let out a few more disturbing guttural moans, her eyes rolled, she faked a ghostly shiver, and he knew she was ready to predict his future once more. He wondered if she kept notes of their past encounters, so she made sure she was constant in her predictions. As he waited, Dermot studied the pattern on the thick velvet curtains that were blocking out the Lancashire sunshine. Then – this was a first, he was sure – she murmured, her voice croaking even more...

'Give ... me ... your ... hand.'

Nervously Dermot did so, sensing her disapproval at the mild nicotine stain on his first two fingers. She grasped his hand between her own white, ice-cold bony fingers, turned it slowly to see his palm, and as her index finger ran over it, she leaned over so her nose was just inches from his lifeline. More mumbling. More silence. More mumbling. More running of that finger across his hand. He felt a shiver.

This was so different to his previous visits. There had been the time she said he would get an unexpected windfall, and when he won a premium bond prize six months later, his mum told him, 'You see, I told you to listen to me.' He treated her to a new fridge with the proceeds. There was the time he was going out with that girl Moira from Tralee, and Martha had said he needed to avoid big arguments and days later he and Moira had had the mother of all rows and she was gone. There was the time he asked her, as a joke, who she reckoned would win the All Ireland Hurling final, and she told him 'the colour closest to red', and Cork only went and won it. But this was a very different Martha to the one he thought he knew. More mumbling, more gargling, more stroking of his hand, and he could feel the drops of sweat forming beneath her touch. Then she jerked up her head, stared coldly into his eyes, and said . . .

'The Lord said, "Thou shalt not steal." If you do . . . *you will be broken into small pieces.*'

With that she rose with a speed and a force that belied her age. It was as if she was being levitated. As she stood, looking down on him with what he sensed was a mix of anger and scorn, that bony hand swooped down onto the table and scooped up the crumpled ten-shilling note he'd placed alongside the glass ball. Without another word, she floated angrily from the room, through the door marked *M*.

1

GORDON

Monday 18 February 1974

Monday. He hated Mondays. The only day of the week he didn't set the alarm, but still he woke before six, reached over to a woman's body that wasn't there, felt the regular stab of loneliness, cursed that final large tumbler of Scotch that had tipped him into hangover territory, and rolled over in the hope that more sleep would come. It did, too much of it, and it was closer to nine than eight o'clock when he dragged his aching footballer's knees to the bathroom. He leaned over the sink, stared at eyes looking so much older than his fifty-one years, dipped his head, and spat. Five days till Saturday, and his next game. Right now, he hated Saturdays even more than he hated Mondays.

Five days, six hours, ten minutes to kick-off. Assuming he made it. He knew managers on better runs of form than this who had still been sacked. He knew there were one or two on the board who felt he was already well past his sell-by date. The paper talk had started. He'd made the mistake of picking up the *Sunday Mirror* from the bar when he popped into the Rambler's Inn last night. Straight to the back page, as always. 'HOW LONG HAS GORDON GOT?' He didn't read the story, but what with the picture of a group of fans by the team coach with their 'GORDON OUT' placard, players trooping sadly in the background, he didn't need to. Then he had got into the car, and they were talking about him on the local radio too.

'We need to keep it in context, Paul,' the reporter was telling the anchor. 'This is a small group of fans who have formed a protest group. But there is no doubt this is a bad run, relegation is a real prospect now, and the question is whether the board thinks "stick with him" or "make a change and try to kick-start the rest of the season". Only time will tell, and later we get the draw for the sixth round of the FA Cup. The good Cup run we are enjoying might be the only thing that saves him now. We shall see.'

Gordon knew Don Robinson, the reporter. Not a bad guy. But these journalists, he said to himself, they just go with the flow. If the blood is there to be tasted, they all want a bit. He was grateful when they changed subject and went back to the general election, Prime Minister Ted Heath and Labour leader Harold Wilson seemingly neck-and-neck in the latest polls, with just ten days to go to polling day. Gordon would be voting Labour, as always, though he knew he was in a minority at the club. It wasn't just poor results that were causing the tension with the chairman, but with the election so close, politics too.

Only last week, Stan Moffitt had said to Gordon it would be a 'fucking disaster' if Harold Wilson came back as Prime Minister, and was visibly annoyed when Gordon said the club's supporters were 'getting screwed rotten by the Tories'. Moffitt was the owner of one of the town's largest textile factories and his business was going through a bad time because – in his view – of over-powerful trade unions. So when he saw the manager of his football team making donations to the miners and openly supporting them in any industrial action, he resented it, though he knew it made Charlie Gordon more popular with the fans, and so much harder to sack, even if he wanted to. Moffitt was a total free marketeer, felt businesses had to be able to operate free of the restrictions of militant unions and the regulation of government. He employed people in the town. He paid them the wages to enable them to live, eat, drink and see their team on Saturdays. Why did they need unions?

Even football matches were being affected by the miners' actions. A midweek game against Manchester City reserves had recently been switched from a 7.30 p.m. kick-off to lunchtime, because of the limits on the use of floodlights. 'This is what happens when unions call the shots,' Moffitt told the local paper, prompting Gordon, unknown to his chairman, to send off another cheque to the miners; unknown, that is, until he wrote about it in his programme notes. That really infuriated Moffitt, even if he knew the reason for Gordon's politics – the lack of generosity of the mining firm which owned the Fallin Colliery, which had taken his father's life.

My God, he sighed to himself as he stared at the tired face he was about to shave, I wonder what Mum and Dad would have made of all this. Actually, he only really cared about what his mum would have thought. He was sure he would have loved his dad just as much, but the recollections he had of him were inspired more by photos than actual memories. He was only eleven at the time of the pit accident.

Shaved, washed, dressed, feeling half-human at least, he couldn't face breakfast, but downed a cup of instant coffee and took another one in a Thermos for the drive to the training ground. At least he hadn't vomited this morning. That was a good sign, surely. He had been throwing up too much in the mornings of late, and you didn't need to be a doctor to know why. How much had he had last night? Couple of pints was it? Four maybe? He didn't have much at the Rambler's, because he was driving and anyway there were fans in there and they can be a pain. So what was it, three Scotches? Then how much when he got home? Another four or five? It wasn't that bad. He'd got himself to bed. He could remember that much.

Don Robinson was right. The good Cup run was keeping him afloat. Saturday's victory at Manchester City had put them in the hat for the sixth round. Pray for a home draw, I guess, especially with Lincoln City still in the tournament. Mind you, lose that and I'm a goner, he thought. So maybe pray for an away draw against a bigger club – win that and you're a hero again. Oh fuck it, he said to himself. What was it his mum used to say? Only bother about the things you can affect yourself... he could have no influence on the draw whatever. Doris Day was spot on...

'que sera, sera' ... so stop worrying about what you can't change, and worry about the things you can. Like getting Stan Moffitt and the rest of the board to cough up for some new players.

There was still frost on the ground as he drove. February is a funny month, he thought. Some days sunshine, some days snow. It was the time of year he inevitably seemed to lose a couple of players to the common cold. He remembered another of his mum's little sayings – 'don't cast a clout, Charles, till May is out'. He never knew what it meant – he thought a clout was what his dad gave him when he'd done something stupid. He'd long left home when he finally learned, from a Geordie physio treating him for an injury, that a clout was a warm winter vest.

He missed her every day. She was the only person in the world who ever called him Charles. At least she is not here to see me getting all this crap in the papers, he said to himself. He'd noticed how the headline writers who used to call him 'Charlie' were more and more referring to him as 'Gordon'. At least she's not here to nag me about my drinking, he said to himself as he steered the car onto the main road out of town. He'd had enough of that from the women in his life down the years. He tapped the little quarter-bottle of Bell's in his inside pocket, and drove on, silently pleased that it was well past nine o'clock and he hadn't even been tempted yet. Bad news – late in for work. Good news – still not touched a drop.

On the one occasion Gordon had seriously tried to stop drinking, when he went to a meeting of Alcoholics Anonymous, two and a half years ago, the mantra he kept hearing was 'one day at a time'. He was now living 'one week at a time', match to match, and he knew he couldn't survive too many more defeats.

He only did that first – and last – AA meeting. As George Best once said having tried AA, 'How can you be anonymous when you're George Best?' Charlie Gordon was not as world famous as George Best. But even though he had driven sixty miles to the meeting, worn a hat, and not said a word, most people in that room recognized him, several asked for his autograph at the end of the meeting, and as he left, he said to himself, What the fuck were you doing going to that? Any one of those people could go to the press and tell them Charlie Gordon was at an AA meeting. To be fair, none of them did, or if they did, the press didn't believe them. Either way, he never went again.

Losing his mother twelve months ago, after several horrible years of decline into full-blown dementia, during which not a day passed that he did not feel guilt at how infrequently he visited her, was still eating away at Charlie. She knew he had a busy life, and latterly she'd barely recognized him anyway. But after all she did for him, he should have done more for her. Not just in childhood either, bringing him up as a single parent. When Gordon's wife Florence finally walked out on him, as he struggled to adapt to life without playing football, it was his mother who took him back home and finally persuaded him to go back into football coaching and then management.

By then, he and Florence were childless, their only daughter Alice having died of meningitis aged seven. He'd been a player then, during that brief spell at the club he now managed, but it drove them apart. They couldn't cope with each other's grief. It exaggerated the traits they already had – in him an obsession with his football, in her a desire for money, and being seen as something in her own right. The press had covered the tragedy, so her photo had been all over the papers for a few days, sufficient for the head of a model agency to ask her to join his books. Within nine months, having first made sure to get the house, and a good slice of Gordon's savings, she had moved in with her new boss.

Charlie was not the first player to see a wife move away as his playing days came to an end. He actually got over the separation quickly. But he never got over the loss of Alice. He had a recurring dream, in which, all dressed in white, she ran towards him as he left the football field after winning a match, and he bent down to greet her and whisk her up in his arms, but then there was a pitch invasion, and she was lost in the crowd.

So Florence, gone, and good riddance. Alice, gone, and he would never get over it. His mother Ethel, gone, but the guilt about the final sad years of her life remained. He recalled the time he went in to see her in the soulless care home just outside

Newton Mearns and she would immediately recognize him and her ageing face would light up with joy. But then he would go for a pee, or out to make a phone call about a transfer, and when he came back in, her face would light up in exactly the same way, forgetting he had been there five minutes earlier. The last time he saw her, he might as well have been Denis Law or Bobby Charlton for all she knew.

He still missed her stoic advice often delivered in threes, he missed her calling him Charles, and the loss was without doubt another factor in his growing relationship with the bottom of a glass. But he was glad she wasn't there to have the neighbours telling her how badly they were doing in the League, how hard the press were kicking him. But the reality was simple – for a club expected to challenge for titles, the bottom half of the table was unacceptable. He knew that. It had to change or something had to give – probably his job. It is what you sign up for. Bigger and better men than him have found out the hard way that cold, sharp truth. The dreaded R-word – relegation – had not been in anyone's thinking as the season had started. None of the football writers had put them in their list of relegation contenders. Insofar as Gordon and his team appeared at all, they were up there with the big boys, not languishing with Norwich, Birmingham City and Southampton.

Seven years he had been at the club now. Lots of wins. Lots of promise. Two FA Cup quarter-finals. A fifth place in the League. A League Cup final, which to this day he felt was lost only because the referee missed a clear foul in the box on Jules Pemberton as he rose to head a corner. All forgotten now by virtually everyone but Gordon. Seven OK years. But no titles, no trophies. And now the R-word was beginning to form on people's lips, and when that happened the S-word – S for Sack – might well form on the lips of the chairman too.

That was the main reason managers didn't like February – so many lost their jobs around then. There was no science to it. Only last week, Ray Plater had been booted out at Wolves, and he was three places higher in the League than Charlie. Then there was Lenny McAlpine, who played with Charlie at Hearts in the mid-1950s, who had taken Carlisle down two divisions, and he was still there. If he had to put his money on it, Charlie mused as he switched on the windscreen wipers to brush away the dots of rain, he would not make it to the end of the season. But Robinson was right, with a good Cup draw and a bit of form in the League, he still had a chance of survival. But shit, he whispered to himself, this is tough.

Of course he knew he couldn't show any of these anxieties when he got to the training ground. Not when he had a Number Two who was after his job, and players who, as he remembered from his own time, always expected the manager to be strong, upbeat, on top of everything. He smiled at that one, feeling as he did weak and hung-over, downbeat and depressed, the tasks of the day turning his head into a cacophony of worry and insecurity. As he picked up speed, away from the last set of lights before the turn-off to Summerton Manor, he wondered if he might be heading for two of life's worst of evils: a cold, and the sack.

2

WINSTON

The days at Summerton Manor training ground more often than not began with a laugh, usually at the expense of one of the players. Today, everyone stayed quiet as the clock on the dressing room wall ticked its way towards 9.30 a.m. Only when the second hand showed there were ten seconds left did the chanting begin.

'*Nine – Eight – Seven – Six – Five...*'

All but four or five of the players joined in the countdown hoping that club captain Wilf Moore would again be late and have to cough up another £25 fine for Charlie Gordon's charity fund. First-team coach Ronnie Winston stood, arms folded across his dark-blue tracksuit top, just inside the dressing room door. As happened most days, Winston had been first in, partly to prepare the detail of the training session, partly to set an example which all too few of his charges followed. He was used to reporting Mooro's unpunctuality back to the manager. Captains are supposed to lead by example, he would say. What example does it set to be late as often as Mooro is? Gordon got the message, or the subtext of it. 'You are losing your grip. There is no respect.'

The first-team players changed in a small, airless dressing room, just big enough for fourteen or fifteen of them, plus a couple of apprentices who were at their beck and call. The reserve team changed in a room even more cramped, served by one apprentice. A mixture of mainly plastic chairs was scattered round three sides of the room, with hooks hammered into the walls above them. Dominant in the centre of the room was a battle-worn green leather-topped treatment bench, with synthetic white stuffing seeping through a few small cracks on the sides. In one corner, a door led out into the shower and communal bath area. Across the other side of the room, another door led to a small medical room. The team doctor used to say that if three players got injured, it was bad luck for one of them, standing room only. In the centre of the ceiling a light bulb shone brightly dimmed only by the frame of a damaged lampshade. The floor was covered with cheap cord carpet stained with mud, black boot polish and chewing gum.

The apprentices had the job of keeping the place clean, so the full-time pros weren't too bothered about how messy they made it. Also, there was a carpet shop in town whose owner was a big fan, and he provided a change of carpet free of charge to the club every other year. He also did deals for the players' own homes. It didn't take long for players to sus out the supporters who cut hair, had a butcher's shop, a furniture business or a clothes shop. Also, thanks to chairman Stan Moffitt's friendship with car dealer Val Dougdale, who ran the local Ford dealership, the top players all had courtesy cars of varying age and quality.

Just as the countdown reached *four*, Mooro breezed through the dressing room door, looking as immaculate as ever, whistling 'Ride a White Swan'. He was wearing tight bluestone Levi jeans that he had seen T. Rex lead singer Marc Bolan wearing on TV, a pale blue denim shirt, a soft brown leather jacket, and fawn Hush Puppy slip-ons. He'd left a scent of Paco Rabanne in the corridor, as he was a follower of the Spanish fashion designer and collected his after-shave lotions. Blond hair, blue eyes, six feet two inches tall, club captain, on the verge of an England call-up – could life get any better?

'You're late,' Ronnie Winston said as he came through the door. 'What's your excuse this time, Mooro?'

'Hold on, Ronaldo, I heard the countdown and made it with

a few seconds to spare. I was delayed because the dog ate my car-key,' Mooro replied in his thick Cushie Butterfield accent.

By this time Ronnie Winston was halfway down the corridor, annoyed, on his way to tell Gordon that his team captain was taking the piss. Mooro raised his voice so the coach could hear him: 'And I've been following the little fucker around the house since 7.30 this morning, waiting for it to have a crap.' With this he accepted the laughter from the dressing room and quietly turned to Dougie 'Jinkie' Jones to whisper, 'It's the wife again, Jinkie; three times in the night and twice on the kitchen table. Second time I nearly dropped my bleedin' toast.'

'Yeah yeah yeah,' said Jinkie. 'Skip,' he added, 'that perfume you're wearing is fucking horrible.'

Goalkeeper Jock Johnson, whose peg was next to Mooro's, and whose seniority and Scottishness had led Gordon to make him vice-captain, was less worried about the skipper's perfume than his piss-taking of Ronnie Winston.

'You could be calling him "gaffer" before long, you know. So be careful.'

'In his dreams.'

'Exactly. That's where ambitions start... as dreams.'

'He's not a fucking manager, Jock. He's hit his level. Good coach, that's it.'

'Aye maybe, but he doesn't know that, does he? He sees an older man failing and he thinks he could fill the gap.'

'No chance.'

'Have you not noticed the change in him since we went on this fucking Cup run?'

'What? All that "first in last out" shit?'

'And the rest... have you not noticed his little digs at the gaffer when we're training, and his arse-licking with the directors when they pop by? He's on manoeuvres, no doubt about it.'

'Yeah well, if Moffitt thinks Winston is a manager, he's even thicker than I thought he was. The gaffer's forgotten more about football than Ronnie Winston will ever learn.'

'Well, you've been round long enough to know that football chairmen and sensible decisions don't exactly go together.'

*

Winston walked down the corridor to Charlie Gordon's office. A brass-plate with the single word 'MANAGER' was screwed into the middle of the door. He imagined it was a cost-saving exercise – keep it general rather than having the expense of engraving every manager's name every time one got sacked.

He tapped at the door. There was no reply, so he pushed the door and walked in.

'Gaffer?' he said, forcefully, thinking Charlie might be using the bathroom in the corner of the room behind his old wooden desk. No reply. 'Late again,' he said to himself, and almost certainly hung-over again too.

He left the door open so he would hear Gordon coming, and took a look inside the desk drawer where he knew he had one of his little booze stashes. He had often thought Gordon was too trusting, and the fact he left his office open to all and sundry, while displaying an openness that the manager believed was important to a healthy club culture, was a mistake Winston would not make, should he ever become a manager himself. There alongside the half-empty bottle of Scotch were copies of players' contracts, an old club tie, a referee's whistle; and on the desk the files on upcoming opposition, Everton, Leeds, West Bromwich Albion. By the telephone a bowl of mints, and a wireless.

Winston was thirty-five now, so if he did get the call he would be among the youngest managers in the whole country, let alone the First Division. He had only been a coach at this level for four years, and until recently had imagined he would be into his forties before he could reasonably even think about going for a manager's job. But week by week, day by day, he had seen Gordon struggling to get the best from the team, or the results he had promised at the start of the season. More importantly, he had noticed Stan Moffitt, and director Matthew Stock, taking more of an interest in him. Might they be sizing him up for that chair behind the desk, with its NB initials carved into the top? Was it disloyal to think, and hope, that might be the case?

He had been a player, though never to the level Gordon had

reached. The office walls provided plenty of evidence of the manager's superior record on that front. There was Gordon signing
professional forms at Ibrox Park, a handsome-looking, dark-haired
seventeen-year-old, with Rangers' manager Bill Struth looking on
like a proud uncle. There was a huge, framed circular montage
of Gordon in the colours of all the different clubs he had played
for: Rangers, Preston North End, Wolverhampton Wanderers,
Leeds United, Aston Villa, Arsenal, his brief spell here, and finally
Heart of Midlothian where a knee injury ended his career aged
thirty-two. And at the centre of the circle, a photo of Gordon
eleven years earlier, winning the first of his thirty-four caps for
Scotland. He looked the part, you had to give him that. Charlie
Gordon had been your typical 'big strong centre-half'. Six feet
two inches tall. Eleven stone twelve was his ideal weight. But
there was more to him than size and strength; he also had the
key essential that all quality centre-halves possessed, *speed*, in his
case speed of thought and speed of foot.

He also had real skill on the ball for a central defender, rarely
gave it away, and could make the kind of long direct pass normally associated with midfielders and attacking full-backs. But
above all he was a superb reader of the game. That's why nobody
was surprised when, still in his late thirties, he took his first
managerial position, a caretaker post at York City, the club where
he was coach when the manager was sacked. Three straight wins
later, he was sitting in Frank Mellor's office. So, Winston mused,
he couldn't really complain about me occasionally wondering
whether I might one day inherit his position. Could he?

He wondered whether this stunning collection of photographs
was there less to remind Gordon of great memories than to
remind Winston, and anyone else who might think they were
up to the manager's job, that they were inferior football beings.
That is certainly how he felt when he looked at Gordon's playing
career. And Winston knew that though thirty-four caps may not
sound a lot, Gordon's time as a player included the years of
the Second World War, prior to which the four Home Nations
refused to recognize FIFA and so did not play in three World
Cups, and after which Scotland chose not to compete even

though technically they qualified, an act of national madness
that burned inside Gordon throughout his career, and about
which he had bored Winston and the rest of the coaching staff
on many an away trip night out. Winston never got anywhere
near an England call-up, and the biggest club he played for was
a brief spell at Southampton. But a manager's playing record for
club and country surely counted for nothing when relegation was
likelier than the promised top six finish. To Stan Moffitt and Co.,
and the club's supporters, these photos of yesteryear were a lot
less significant than the League table of today.

He scribbled a note – 'gaffer, give us a shout when you're in . . .
Mooro late again . . . let me know if you're coming out for the
session. RW' – and headed back to the dressing room where all
but the real laggards were now all kitted and ready to face the
rain.

'Right lads, out you get and just do a gentle run twice round
the pitch. Mooro you lead it and no fucking about. I'll be out
once the gaffer is in.' Jock Johnson smiled knowingly to Mooro,
who shook his head, then clapped his hands together and shouted
'OK, let's go . . . last one out has to sing two verses of a Beatles
song in the centre circle.' Winston smiled at the stampede that
followed, then lit himself a cigarette and folded his arms as he
awaited the arrival of his boss.

Despite the cold outside, with the heater full on, and his nerves
starting to gnaw at him the closer he got to the Summerton
Manor training ground, Charlie Gordon felt little rivulets of sweat
beginning to trickle down from just below his temple, down the
side of his face, then slowly into the fold of his chin. He loosened
his tie, and undid the top button of his lucky matchday shirt. It
hadn't brought him much luck of late so he had put it on this
morning, hoping it might help deliver a good draw in the Cup.
Was there any group of people in the world, he wondered, more
superstitious than footballers? Every game he ever played, he
used to warm up, then get back in the dressing room, remove the
laces from his boots, then replace them, left boot with his right
hand, right boot with his left hand. He knew that Jock Johnson,

who had read about this particular ritual in a profile of Gordon in one of the old *Charles Buchan's Soccer Gift Book* annuals, now did the same. 'Legacy,' he snorted dismissively to himself.

This season had been a nightmare right from the start. Home to Norwich City, and 'an easy two points', thought the fans and the press. Nil-nil. Away to United. Lost four-one. Two home draws, then two away defeats. Seven games before the first win of the season, then the second, but the Christmas period went badly, then suddenly it's February and they're in the bottom half of the table. OK, they'd just beaten Manchester City in the fifth round of the FA Cup but Gordon wondered whether Malcolm Allison had put out a weakened team so he could concentrate on the League.

He could feel his throat tightening a bit, and he could sense his nose was about to run. He remembered that time at Aston Villa, when he was on top of the world, Player of the Season, and he had the dressing room in hysterics taking the mickey out of Villa left-back Dickie Dorsett who had just been run ragged by Charlie Mitten. 'Hey up, Dickie,' Gordon shouted, 'your fucking nose was running faster than your legs today.' His teammates laughed back then – apart from Dickie who flicked him a V sign and threw a discarded sweat-drenched shirt at him – but he wondered which of his players would be making the joke about him today. He wasn't stupid, and nor were they.

Wiping away the sweat forming below his Adam's apple, he told himself it was crazy to think a shirt could help. It was more a sign of his desperation right now, he knew that. But every little helped, surely. If a superstition did no harm, then might it mean that just maybe it did some good? Win the sixth-round tie, and you're in the semi-finals, a big moneyspinner on a neutral ground, the chance for 45,000 fans to have a great day out. Win that, and you're in the final at 'The Twin Towers' of Wembley, the greatest football stadium on earth, 100,000 people, the country glued to the box; win that one and you're talking open-topped bus tours and a town hall reception and not a 'Gordon Out' placard in sight. Three games for a place in history. Forget about the poor League form. Come on, Charlie, think positive, we can do this. And if we keep the Cup run going, the League results will pick up too.

As the yellow-coated security man raised the barrier to let him into the training ground, he could see the first-team squad already out warming up, running half-heartedly around the perimeter of the main training pitch. Mooro was out front, Jock Johnson and Wally Graham alongside him. Jules Pemberton and Clutch Dyson were at the back, laughing. He looked for DD Marland, their record signing from Tottenham Hotspur. That DD was a talented footballer was not in doubt, but Gordon didn't like his own future being so dependent on the success or otherwise of a player about whom he continued to have doubts, and whose transfer fee and salary were yet to be matched consistently by performance. He parked up to get a better look at his squad as they jogged. Marland was at the far side of the group, ostentatiously alone like the 'big-time Charlie' he was, looking like he would rather be anywhere else. And there was Nuts, as honest and hard-working a player as you could ever hope to find, and he was having to drop him to make way for the chairman's pet signing.

There was no sign of Ronnie Winston. He had sent the players out with George Brady and Charlie Sinclair, first-team trainer and kitman cum general factotum respectively, who were laying out cones and sorting bibs into piles. Doubtless Winston would be waiting inside, ostensibly to discuss the training session, in reality to emphasize that Gordon was late in, and make him feel even worse. He thought about inventing a medical appointment, but worried Winston would see that as an added vulnerability to exploit.

That he was feeling vulnerable, on so many levels, was not in doubt. It's why his mother kept floating into his mind. 'Charles,' she used to say to him, 'we can live our lives for seventy-odd years, but you'll only have three life-changing moments.' She recollected her three: when she first met his dad; when Charlie was born; and when his dad was killed in the Fallin Colliery explosion in 1934. Her lifetime-trilogy all involved a father he didn't really know.

So what were his three? Signing as a professional with Rangers in 1940? Marrying Florence in 1945? But no, that was all over, so how can you count that? Maybe it was his dad dying? Or his mum. Or was it becoming a manager? Maybe, just as all of his mum's were about his dad, all of his were about football. Signing pro? His first Scottish cap? Becoming a manager? No, there was no doubt at all about his biggest one. It was an event from which, even if the pain did not come in the giant waves it used to, he would never fully recover. Losing his daughter.

So much for positive thinking.

He parked in his usual spot, tapped the bottle inside his jacket, once again resisted the urge, and felt better for it, rewarding himself with a triumphant little smile. Fifty-one was not old to be a manager, he said to himself, finding from somewhere a sudden burst of energy as he grabbed his bag from the passenger seat and got out of the car. The thing is, it has nothing to do with age. It is all about whether people think you're doing a good job. And there is only one metric that counts. Points. Age didn't matter. Manners didn't matter. How you dressed didn't matter. Your relations with the press didn't matter. The state of your marriage didn't matter. Religion didn't matter (outside Glasgow maybe). Your place in the League table was the only thing that mattered. Stay high, and you stay put. Fall low, and you're in trouble, and youth becomes more attractive as an option. It was no different to the phrase that kept popping from the mouths of Labour politicians as they fought to oust Ted Heath and his Conservatives... 'time for a change...' It was the obvious response to failure, and he was failing right now, way worse than Heath, even if the Prime Minister's problems might seem more serious, what with the economy on the slide and the IRA on the rampage. Politicians can argue about the stats in a way that football managers can't. A defeat is a defeat and he had had too many. That's why the players were winding back on the respect and Ronnie Winston was winding up on the ambition. It went with results. Get the team to the top of the table and you can drink three bottles of whisky a day and nobody bats an eyelid.

Winston was hovering outside the first-team dressing room.

'Give me two minutes, Ronnie,' he shouted amiably down the corridor. 'Just going for a quick pee and I'm with you.'

'OK, gaffer.' Was Gordon being paranoid in detecting a whiff of irony in the deadpan manner with which Winston said the word 'gaffer'?

He dumped his bag on the floor, went to the bathroom to splash cold water on his face, dried himself, then sat briefly at his desk to collect his thoughts. He had to be careful not to signal his worry about Ronnie Winston to the man himself. He felt the rest of his coaching and support staff were on his side, still giving their all for him, still believed he had what it took. But Winston, not him. He was lying in wait, for sure. He really had to watch him, knowing however that if he made it too obvious he was worried about him taking his job, it would be like the common cold – inevitable because you're thinking about it too much.

At least he still had his playing reputation to fall back on. That counted for something in football, surely, didn't it? Or was he kidding himself about that too? Of course the players would look and sound impressed when he talked them through the photos on the wall, and gasp in awe at the kind of crowds today's footballers could only dream of – over 115,000 at one of those Scotland games – but deep down, were they acting impressed because they were genuinely impressed, or because he was, for now, the gaffer? If a picture of Ronnie Winston's promotion-winning Bradford City side was up there, replacing Gordon in a Villa shirt holding the FA Cup aloft, would they feign the same level of respect and admiration for such lesser deeds?

'You coming, gaffer?' he heard Winston shout down the corridor. 'They're getting restless out there.'

'One minute.' He opened the drawer, took out the bottle of Scotch, quietly opened it, and just as quietly took a small, comforting sip, before putting the bottle away, and taking a handful of mints from the bowl in front of him, popping one into his mouth, and the others into his pocket. Hurriedly, he changed into a tracksuit and boots, threw on a club-crested training coat and a Rangers bobble hat, and headed out.

'Right, Ronnie,' he shouted, 'let's go.'

'You coming out to do the session, yeah?'

'Aye.'

'That's good.'

'Hope so, eh?'

3

TRAINING

Willie Buchanan waited until the first-team session was well under way, double-checked that Charlie Gordon was out there with them, then sneaked into the manager's office to make a phone call. He knew that Catriona would be at work now, and though they had spoken last night, when he had called her from a phone box close to his digs, he was missing her, and missing home so much, that he was close to giving up.

It was a sign of just how desperately he wanted to hear Catriona's voice that he was prepared to risk being caught at the manager's desk, using his phone. He knew he would have to be brief. He also knew, after another fretful night behind him, that he was getting ever closer to breaking point.

Catriona worked in the accounts department of a new four-star hotel that had been built to meet the needs of the army of oilmen who had been attracted to Aberdeen by the discovery of oil in the North Sea. As a colleague went to find Catriona for him, he felt his heart rate rising, out of excitement that soon he would be speaking to her, and out of fear that Charlie Gordon could walk in on him at any moment. He would say he had heard it ringing, and thought it might be important.

'Willie, what's wrong?'

'Nothing. I just wanted to speak to you.'

'Och, you had me worried there. You've never called me during the morning before, apart from weekends.'

'Yeah, well, I am missing you.'

'What, even more than last night?'

'Even more than last night.'

There was a pause, and he sensed that perhaps she was with company, and so couldn't talk freely.

'Are you not training?'

'Not yet. I have to do all the chores first, then clear up after the first team finishes, then we'll train this afternoon.'

'So that is something to look forward to, eh?'

'Aye, I guess it is, but there is hell to go through before that, believe me.'

'Hell? What on earth are you talking about, Willie?'

This time it was his turn to pause the conversation as he heard footsteps outside. He got ready to end the call and make his excuse for being in there, but then saw two of his fellow apprentices rush by in the corridor.

'Panic over. I thought the manager was coming.'

'Willie, can you tell me what is going on? You've got me worried.'

'It's a guy called David Brown,' he said. 'He's making my life hell.'

'Who's he?'

'He's a player in the first team, and I don't know why, but he just has it in for me.'

'Can you not tell the manager about him?'

'Everyone just seems to think it's normal, that the top players pick on the kids and then one day we will be players and we do the same.'

'Well, I hope you will not, Willie.'

'Of course I won't. But I am not sure I can deal with this.'

There was another long pause, then Catriona's voice became sterner. 'Willie, you have been given the chance of a lifetime. You have to take the rough with the smooth.'

'This is rough, Catriona, believe me.'

'You can handle it, I know you can.' She then whispered, 'Now listen, I have to go, my boss is here, I can't do personal calls at work. Phone me tonight, and dig in. You'll be fine.'

He replaced the receiver as quietly as he could and walked to the door, stopping to study a remarkable photograph of Charlie Gordon heading the ball off the line in a game for Scotland against Sweden at Hampden Park. What was remarkable was the sea of cloth-capped humanity in the background. Had Gordon, he wondered, ever been the victim of the kind of bullying to which he had been subjected since moving down from Aberdeen? But no, look at him. Tall and strong, whereas Willie was tiny, even for a footballer. Small, quiet, young, homesick and Scottish – could David Brown ever have dreamed of a better target for his bullying?

He'd signed at the beginning of the season as one of seven apprentices. The train journey south was only his third trip out of Scotland. It was a journey that just seemed to go on and on, with two changes of train, and with every hour that passed his doubts about whether he was making the right move had grown. When he finally arrived, there was no one to greet him, he'd simply been told, 'Jump into a taxi, ask for 48 Parrish Drive, get a receipt and bill it to the club.'

At just after midnight he knocked on the door of the spooky old house and Mavis Archibald was there to greet him. The old place was warm and friendly though smelling a little musty, but Mavis was happy to make him a cup of tea, have a brief chat and then show him to his room.

When he awoke the next morning the train journey was long forgotten and all he could think about was football. He couldn't wait to get to the club and meet his new teammates and mix with some of the well-known star players.

His hero was a fellow Scot, Eddie Gray of Leeds United, and like Gray he could do things with a football that few others could even think about. Willie's ball control was what had first alerted scouts from most of the big clubs to his talent. But also his movement was delicate and instinctive, and though he was small and slight his stamina was exceptional. He could run, tackle and score goals with either foot and he was also a good header of the ball, so the coaches saw his potential as limitless. He was even being compared with another Scot now at the other end of his career, Willie Morgan, who spent eight years with Burnley and was into his third season with Manchester United. Willie

Buchanan's legs were like two white matchsticks, the way he wore his shorts making it look like he was wearing a nappy. He was seventeen but looked fourteen. Then someone would throw him a ball and he looked thirty. Once he had it at his feet no one could take it off him. That's when the laughing stopped and the admiration and amazement grew.

But all that was months ago and now he was simply trying to find his way at the club, and his game was starting to crumble under the unexpected dressing room pressure from people like David Brown. Brown saw nothing wrong in what he did. He had shrugged it off back in his day; why couldn't today's kids do the same?

Gordon had told the Scottish papers that he knew they were lucky to have landed young Buchanan when Spurs, Arsenal, Liverpool and Preston had all been trying. He was a real star in the making, and had chosen this club partly because Charlie Gordon was a Scot, and he had travelled north to see the young starlet and his family face to face; but also because of the club's reputation for bringing on young players. But nobody had warned him about the sarcasm, the stitch-ups and the dressing room banter and bullying he would have to endure.

The pressure was so immense he cried himself to sleep some nights, and he couldn't believe how much he missed Catriona. They'd met at school when he was fourteen, she was his first and only girlfriend, they were near neighbours, and though she had been supportive of him moving south, he was beginning to realize how much he had counted on her to get him this far. But he had meant it when he said he was worried he was reaching breaking point. He really wasn't sure he could take much more of David Brown, or the way the other players just looked the other way. If things didn't improve by the weekend, he would tell Catriona this evening, he was jumping on a train back home to Aberdeen and never coming back to this godforsaken place. He was sure Celtic or Rangers would both have him, and if they didn't, Aberdeen definitely would. If he was as good as everyone said he was, he would never be short of a club to play for.

*

They still know who's boss, Gordon said to himself, as he and Ronnie Winston strode towards the first-team squad, now running through routine drills under George Brady's direction. The players nudged each other and looked over approvingly on seeing him emerge onto the pitch. He could feel Winston shrinking a little alongside him.

'OK lads, gather round, will you?' He asked Charlie Sinclair, his namesake loyalist, for a bottle of water and took a few gulps before throwing the bottle to the ground between his feet.

'Now, before we get going ... Light training today, and no tackling. I don't want any more stupid fucking injuries. And stock up on Vitamin C after. It's cold and flu season. I don't want any of you catching it.' The irony of the loud sniff that followed was lost on none of them.

'Secondly, I want you all to give yourselves a fucking big round of applause.' Gordon clapped his hands loudly together, once, twice, then on the third clap his backroom team followed suit, then slowly the players joined in, several laughing as they did so. As the applause died down, once again led by Gordon, now holding his hands together in front of his waist, he said: 'That was for Saturday. You did well, and I was proud of every one of you. Man City away in the Cup ... not many teams come away from there with a two-nil win. And for any of you who read in the papers how lucky we were, fuck the papers, they know nothing ... you make your own luck in this game. So City hit the bar a couple of times ... well, last time I checked the bar doesn't count the same as the net when it comes to totting up goals ... So they had twice as much of the ball as we did ... only twice as much? It felt like more where I was sat.' On cue, the brighter of the players laughed. 'And that is why we are going to work on counter-attack today ... because I'll tell you something ... when we have a goalie as good as Jock, a defence as tight as the one Mooro marshalled on Saturday, a midfield that gets up and down that pitch like a fucking yoyo on steroids, and strikers as good as Jules and DD and Nuts, we can take on anyone.

'Now the League is the main thing, we know that, but we are going to enjoy this Cup run, and we are going to take the success

of Saturday's win into the games in the League. And finally, I
want you all in my office later so we can listen to the Cup draw
together, as a team. OK?'

'Is it the Cup draw?' asked Frank 'Dipper' Temple.

'For fuck's sake, Dipper, where have you been? Do you ever
read papers or watch the telly?' said Jock.

'Who've we got?'

'That is the fuckin' point of what the gaffer just said. In his
office for the draw to find out.'

'OK, keep your hair on, baldy.'

Gordon let Winston take most of the session, in which they
went over the same four moves again and again... 'One more
time, Ronnie, one more time, I want this one absolutely hammered
into every fucking brain cell.' He stood on the touchline, hands
deep in furry pockets, shouting encouragement and criticism in
equal measure. 'Good lad, good lad... that's a ball... good lad...
oh for Christ's sake Mooro, you're not with fuckin' Hartlepool
now... better, good... oh Jesus help me, Killer, tuck in, tuck in...
better, boy, better... what the fucking hell was that...'

He'd felt it important to be out there today. Perhaps his closest
ally at the club these days was his head physio Ralph 'Magic'
Rowland, who had tipped him off that some of the players had
taken to calling him the Invisible Man. He could hardly blame
them; some weeks he didn't see them between Monday, when
he gathered them for the post-match inquests, and then Friday
and Saturday, when he'd go through tactics and his pre-match
team talk. No wonder Winston was moving in.

The players seemed a lot chirpier with him out there for the
whole of the session, and as they trooped in to get showered
and changed before lunch, the mood had lifted a little, Gordon's
included. Athletes were always happier after their bodies had
been worked hard.

A 1970s football club dressing room, like a hospital, had a smell
all of its own, a combination of Dubbin, boot polish, wintergreen, Sunlight soap and sweat, making Mooro's Paco Rabanne
incongruous.

Players who had come from other clubs around the country saw Summerton Manor as one of the better training grounds. Only DD Marland, constantly seeking to make claims for the superiority of the south over the north, seemed determined to view it as a dump, even though his former Tottenham team-mate Dipper Temple had told anyone who would listen that Summerton was better than what they had at Spurs. The previous chairman had purchased the seventy-acre site for a song ten years earlier and it had been turned into the closest thing England had to a footballer factory, an assembly-line production, followed by a conveyor-belt sale, of young players to big-city clubs. It kept the club afloat, especially as crowds had fallen in recent months. It was a battery farm, scouts finding the kids, then the club developing them (or junking them) as they progressed from school team to B team, to A team, to reserves; a few were then finally elevated to the first team and a professional football career secured. The rest were either laid off or, more likely, sold. It was a pretty good business model, for which Stan Moffitt and Matthew Stock vied to take the credit.

As for the ones who made it to the first team, the perception was that they were made for life. In reality, they had an average of about seven years as a professional player and there were many obstacles to success along the way. A loss of form; loss of speed; loss of favour; a serious injury or illness; or on occasions self-inflicted problems would soon open the door for the new players queuing to take their place. Gambling and drink problems were commonplace especially for those nearing the end of their career and certainly for those who had actually reached the end.

At thirty-four, Jinkie Jones was the second oldest player in the squad after goalkeeper Jock Johnson, and had played in the First Division for thirteen years, the last six here. Jinkie, one of the brighter ones, would say to the young players, 'Enjoy it while it lasts, because this is the best life anyone can have, and it will be gone before you know it.' He knew he would be lucky to get his contract renewed at the end of the season. He had no idea what he wanted to do when his playing days were over; he'd decided to worry about that when it happened.

This was in stark contrast to Morgan 'Taffy' Rees, who intended either to stay in the game as a coach, having taken his FA coaching badges, or join his father-in-law's business back in Wales. He'd also methodically put some of his earnings away for the rainy days that might follow his retirement if he failed to make it as a coach. Very few players had the foresight to do that. They lived for the moment, and thought this life would never end. He knew it would.

Unlike Dipper, mocked mercilessly for not knowing the Cup draw was today, Taffy Rees was considered something of an intellectual by his teammates. He often had his head in *The Times*, and not the sports pages either. He was one of maybe just two players who had an interest in politics, and had an uncle who was a Labour MP, Merlyn Rees, the shadow Northern Ireland Secretary. He'd chatted to him at a family gathering only last Sunday about all the bombs going off in London. He'd warned the family that if Labour won the election, and he was made Northern Ireland Secretary, then the next time he saw them the sniffer dogs would have to come ahead of him, and he'd have twenty-four-hour police protection. Taffy thought it sounded exciting, but he could tell his uncle was a bit anxious about the whole thing.

In recent weeks Taffy had been trying to get a bit of political debate going in advance of the election, but with the exception of Walter Graham – nickname the Prof because he was always reading books – the debate never got much beyond why Ted Heath wasn't married, whether Harold Wilson wore his Gannex coat in bed, and – above all – what the outcome meant for income tax levels. Every week Taffy had his local Welsh language paper posted to him. Because he played for the club, there were regular reports of their matches, and he would have a lot of fun translating the reports, but embellishing them to suit himself.

'What's it say about me, Taffy?' Clutch Dyson would ask.

'Says you looked off the pace, your touch was shit and your arse is fat.'

'You lying bastard.'

'I'm telling you it does,' and he would read it out in Welsh, then happily mistranslate. 'As last week, Taffy Rees was again man of the match, and must feel badly let down by his less-skilful teammates, who may have more energy in their legs, but have a lot less between their ears when it comes to understanding the game.'

'Who writes this shit?'

'He used to play for Wrexham and Wales.'

'Fucking sheep shagger,' said Clutch.

'Yeah, it's a rugby country is Wales,' joined in Jock Johnson. 'They know nothing about football.'

'And fucking Scotland does?' asked Rees.

'Try telling the gaffer we don't,' retorted Jock.

'Have they got that story about the sex-mad Welsh farmer in there?' asked Graham 'Smudger' Smith.

'What story would that be?' asked Taffy, despite knowing he was setting himself up for the punchline.

'He died in his sheep,' said Smudger, prompting hysterics from some, shakes of the head from others.

There was never a day, let alone an hour, that wasn't peppered with this kind of dressing room banter. Most outsiders would just turn away, thinking they were among a bunch of overgrown kids. If you drove it out – even if you could – Charlie Gordon believed you wouldn't be able to build the team spirit you need to win at the top level. These guys have to gel together, and humour and fun are in their own way just as important as fitness and skill. It was also a test of psychological strength, so important to sporting success. Some players couldn't handle football's psychological demands and used it as an excuse for not making it, saying, It wasn't my fault, I was a great player but my face didn't fit... The real reason, if they were being honest with themselves, was that they just couldn't hack it, either on or off the field.

A dressing room, Gordon reflected, was the sanctuary for a group of fantastically fit, comparatively wealthy, sexually driven and often poorly educated, sometimes even stupid and immature young men, all spending every day – and some nights – together, nine months of the year. When Jinkie was at Cardiff City before coming here, his nickname there was 'Brains' because he had two O-levels. In football he was a rarity.

As the laughter at Smudger's joke subsided, left-half David Brown shouted across the dressing room through the still-open door, so that his voice echoed down the corridor.

'Young'un! *Young'un!!!*' It was one of the young apprentices who he was targeting. 'Buchanan, get your arse in here *now*.'

Brown knew that Willie Buchanan would be in the boot room with another couple of apprentices checking the rows of boots that hung from the pegs on the walls, and waiting to clean the full-time professionals' boots after this morning's training session. An apprentice's life, once you took away the coaching, training and playing, was a dog's life. There were rituals they had to perform, countless tasks to complete for the senior players, errands to run; and for some, horrific humiliations to endure. For the new arrivals, some little more than children, there was next to no preparation for what to expect and in every dressing room there were always established players who thought nothing of making an apprentice's life a misery. David Brown was one of the worst offenders. He had been abused as an apprentice when he was at Manchester City, so he passed it all on.

'Go easy on the lad,' Jock Johnson suggested as Brown called in Buchanan for his latest humiliation.

'Oh, get the Jocks all sticking up for each other. If you don't like it, you can always fuck off back over Hadrian's Wall.'

'I just said go easy on the lad.'

'A bit of stick from the pros never harmed me, and it won't harm him,' he replied in his thick Scouse accent.

'*Yooouunng'uunnnnn!*' Brown's voice grew louder the more he picked up on his teammate's disapproval.

One of the tasks Charlie Gordon had given to Buchanan was responsibility for kit in the first-team dressing room. In addition to looking after the boots, that entailed putting out the training kit before the players arrived, collecting it after they had finished training, then sending it to the club laundry and getting any repairs done quickly. It meant he had to arrive at Summerton Manor at 8 a.m. every morning and he was lucky to get away before four in the afternoon. The only part of the day for which he retained any pleasure at all was the two or three hours in the late morning and early afternoon when he trained with Ronnie Winston, who often doubled up as youth-team coach. When he was playing or training, he felt alive. For the rest, it was a misery. Gordon had told him that dealing with the first team's kit was a superior position to the ones he gave to the other apprentices, like mowing the pitches or sweeping the terraces at the stadium, but he hated it. Because of that, and especially because of Brown, he was beginning to hate everybody associated with the club.

But this was exactly what manager Charlie Gordon had expected; if Willie Buchanan was going to make it as a professional footballer he had to learn to swim – so Gordon had thrown him in at the deep end. Buchanan needed to understand and accept life in the dressing room as it was and as it always had been; it was a crazy game, which needed tough people to play it well. The rigours and the taunting were character building, part of the apprenticeship.

'*Younnnnnnnnnng'unnnnnnnnn!!!!!!* How many times do I have to shout for that little Scottish twat?'

After finally getting the message from Charlie Sinclair that Brown was calling for him, Willie sprinted down the corridor, arriving in the first-team dressing room out of breath, and quickly explained, 'Sorry Brownie, I was looking for some socks for Mooro.'

David Brown froze for a moment, stood upright, put his hands on his hips and peered down at Willie.

'Sorry, what did you say?'

'I said I was looking for socks for Mooro.'

'I thought you said that. I thought you called me Brownie. Fucking *Brownie*... some socks for fucking *Mooro*! Who the fuck are *Brownie* and *Mooro*, you little Scottish shit? From now on it's Mr Brown and Mr fucking Moore and when you've won six fucking Scottish caps, which combined are worth one English cap whatever the gaffer tells you, you can then start to call us *Brownie* and *Mooro*. Is that crystal fucking clear, Willio?'

David Brown stood almost a foot taller than Willie, who felt humiliated and scared. 'Yes, Mr Brown, I'm very sorry. Won't make that mistake again. What is it that you want?'

David Brown appeared to calm down as he sat below his peg. He knew that all the players were watching him, so the theatre began. He knew his part well.

'OK, young'un, now I've got a question for you. What the bloody hell is this on my fingers?' Brown held out his hands in front of him like a schoolboy waiting to have them checked by the teacher.

Willie's heart sank when he looked closely and saw the thick black stains.

'Looks like black boot polish to me, Mr Brown.' He'd no idea how the boot polish had got there but sensed he was about to get the blame.

'Egg-fucking-zackerly, Mr fucking Jocko. And can I ask where you think it came from?'

The other players, used to Brownie's sarcastic rants, now continued with their own changing routine, quietly chatting away, all knowing what the outcome would be. Young Willie Buchanan hadn't experienced anxiety like this before; he wasn't sure what he'd done wrong or what he could do about it. He sensed that Brown's previous bullying antics had been but a warm-up to this.

'Has it come off your boots, Mr Brown?'

'Not a bad guess, Mr Sherlock fucking Buchanan, but you are about two inches out. This black shoe polish has come off the laces, not the bloody boots. So don't ever again put my boots out before checking that the bleeding laces are clean, is that fucking crystal?' Willie nodded. Brown tapped his cheeks. Willie turned to leave.

'Oi! Where are you going, Buchanan? I haven't finished.'

Willie, who thought he had got away lightly, turned and faced the second barrage from David Brown full-on.

'So who cleaned my boots, Willio? Who left black polish on my fucking laces so now it is all over my fucking hands?'

Willie was shaking now. He was trapped: he could either say he didn't know, which wasn't true; or say that he did, which meant squealing on Charlie Sinclair.

'Er, we have a rota for the boots, Mr Brown.'

'Do you now, Mr Buchanan? And whose job was it on the *row-ta* yesterday?'

Buchanan stood silent. Brown grabbed his ears and began to twist them.

'I'll find out, so you may as well fucking tell me. Was it you?'

'No, Mr Brown.'

'So who the fuck was it? Who was on the *row-ta* for boot-cleaning yesterday?'

'Sorry Mr Brown, it must have been Charlie Sinclair, I think.'

He couldn't have said anything worse. He heard three or four of the players audibly tut-tutting. Charlie Sinclair was everybody's favourite, a club player in the 1920s and 1930s, and then trainer, then kitman and now at seventy-two he just wanted to stay in touch with a club that meant so much to him. He even lived in club digs, like the apprentices. Everybody loved Charlie Sinclair.

'OK, Mr Buchanan, so now I know the real culprit, it's Charlie Sinclair. This is what I want you to do. First, pick up that phone and dial 201 and say this:

'"Charlie, get a fucking duster and get your lazy, fat arse down to the first-team dressing room sharpish and clean Mr Brown's fucking boots and in future make sure there's no black polish on his fucking laces."'

Brown paused, stared at Willie hard and then continued with his face pressed close to the young player's nose.

'And be sure you repeat what I said word for fucking word... and press that button that says "speaker" so we can all hear you.'

'Come on, Brownie, enough,' said Jock Johnson.

'Almost done, Jock,' he whispered. 'Your fellow Jocko here needs to learn a few lessons if he is going to swim with the big boys.'

The dressing room conversations had now quietened. Unlike Willie, most knew where the story was going. He tentatively picked up the dressing room phone, pressed speaker, dialled 201 and said as forcefully as his young, wavering Scottish voice could...

'Charlie?'

'Yep.'

'Er, get a duster and get your fat, lazy fucking arse down into the first-team dressing room and clean David Brown's fucking boots. And in future will you please make sure there's no fucking black polish on his laces.'

By now, a number of the players had turned to face their pegs and started to hang up their clothes or rearrange their shoes so that Willie couldn't see their faces collapsing in laughter.

'Who is this?' said a gruff voice that was not, Willie realized instantly, Charlie Sinclair's, but Charlie Gordon's.

Answering for him, Brown faked a Scottish accent and said, 'It's Willie fucking Buchanan – why, who's that?'

'You know full well who it is, it's the manager; you get yourself up here straight away.'

Willie wanted to throw up. He felt like crying. And all around him grown men were laughing and patting David Brown on the back. Only Jinkie Jones, he felt, Jock Johnson, Wally Graham and Frank Temple were looking on with a little sympathy, shaking their heads and tutting, Temple mouthing the words 'Scouse wanker' to his teammate across the way. Taffy Rees, on the other hand, was laughing so much he said he was worried he would piss himself.

These were grown men, Willie thought to himself, senior players. Several were married, with young kids. They were football stars, the kind of people he had looked up to, until he met them; last night one of them was interviewed live on TV, and now he was rolling around the floor, on his back, holding his stomach. Tommy Dyson started to chant, 'Got-ya, got-ya, got-ya,' and everybody seemed to join in. Willie stood there, still holding the phone, more determined than ever to get home as soon as he could, as early as today if he could get a train ticket.

David Brown jumped naked onto the top of the massage

table, cast an imaginary fishing line into the dressing room and pretended to reel in a big fish.

'I've landed one, move me to the top of the list, I've landed a fucking monnnnssssttttttterrrrrr!!!!!!'

Graham Smith, often David Brown's partner in crime, was quick to join the party. 'Brownie,' he shouted, 'what a belter, hook, line and fucking sinker. You had him in the palm of your hand – what a great got-ya!'

It was now team captain Mooro who took pity on Willie, thinking possibly that this particular prank had gone just that bit too far, and he suggested to him that he'd better get himself along to the boss's office. Willie did as he was told and left the room as a fresh wave of laughter unleashed behind him. Outside in the corridor he was close to tears but at the same time felt a deep rage. There was no way, no matter how stern Catriona got with him, that he was staying in this place.

He made his way to Gordon's office door and knocked. There was no reply but he could hear the manager was on the phone he had been using earlier so he waited patiently but at the same time apprehensive of the bollocking he expected to receive.

Inside, Charlie Gordon ended the call and Willie knocked again. No reply. Yet he knew he was in there. Was this all part of the same prank, he wondered? Was Gordon, one of the legends of Scottish football, no better than those English arseholes who had just tried to destroy him? Willie sat outside in the corridor on one of the two wooden spindle-backed chairs, one each side of the door. He noticed that one of the chairs had the initials NB carved into the armrest.

Eventually, he heard footsteps behind the door. He stood as it opened and Charlie Gordon filled the frame.

'Come in, son,' he said, neither friendly nor unfriendly.

Willie followed in behind his manager.

Although they were both from Scotland, even the words *come in son* underlined just how different this tough West of Scotland manager was to the young, softly spoken Aberdonian boy he was trying to shape into a man.

He closed the door behind him and followed Gordon's nodded

instruction to sit in the worn leather chair with curved wooden arms in front of the manager's desk. Gordon then made him wait a while as he finished reading through a scouting report; he could just make out the words 'Leeds United' scribbled on the front cover. Willie glanced around the office, thinking how much more trouble he would be in if Gordon knew he had been there earlier, borrowing his phone. He felt a little comforted to see the framed Scotland shirts amid the sepia photographs he had been studying earlier, of Gordon in his playing days. As he ran his fingers over the arm of the chair he wondered who NB was, as he noted the initials again carved into the wood on the front of the manager's desk.

Charlie Gordon finally pushed his report to one side and looked up at his young fellow Scot who was sitting there like a schoolboy waiting for a caning. Willie decided to get in ahead of him.

'Boss, I am so sorry. I didn't know 201—'

But Gordon had other ideas. He was an experienced manager and he knew just what to say and how to say it. He had to do what he could to settle this young man down, to get him to realize that this was all part of his football education; that it might well seem cruel and heartless, but it had gone on long before any of those old photos were taken, would continue to do so, and no one could stop it.

'Woah, young Willie, no need to apologize, my son. I know the score.'

'But—'

'No buts. You were set up ... was it Brownie?'

Willie had learned his lesson about grassing.

'I'd rather not say.'

'Good lad. Right, now you forget all about it. But learn from it. It's stupid, right, but you just have got to get used to the dressing room banter. I'm afraid it is all part of being a professional footballer. You have to learn how to handle it.'

Willie nodded.

'Tell me,' Gordon went on, 'no names no pack drill – I know

it was Brownie by the way, it is his party piece – but they didn't all join in the piss-taking, did they?'

Willie thought of Jinkie and Jock, Mooro who had brought the thing to an end, and Dipper who had just sat on his chair shaking his head. 'No, sir.'

'OK. That's a start. You know they might be minded to look after you, or to be a bit more serious than the Brownies of this world. You're a serious lad, I can see that. You want to do well. You want to make it here.'

'But—' Willie was desperate to tell Gordon he was heading home.

'Hear me out, son. Some of these players are stupid. Some of them are hard. A lot of them are nice deep down. But they are all experienced first-team players and every one of them – especially the midfielders and the wingers and the forwards – they want you to fail.'

Willie looked taken aback by that one.

'Think about it, son. They've seen you training. They know what you can do. You've more skill in your big toe than Brownie has in his whole fucking right foot. So work it out for yourself: there are eleven players in Saturday's team and if *you* make it into the squad, it means one of them is on his way out. It's nothing personal, it's just a numbers game.

'How old are you, son?'

'Seventeen. Just.'

'Can you imagine being thirty-four?'

'I don't know, boss.'

'Well when you are, you'll feel like some of them are feeling right now. When some kid who hasn't even been born yet suddenly arrives out of nowhere, and people start to say "Oh, there's the new Willie Buchanan," what are you going to feel?'

Willie nodded, silently, but then surprised himself.

'I'd train harder,' he answered. 'I'd work harder. I'd fight for my place.'

'Good lad, good lad. But you'll have spent seventeen years in dressing rooms by then. You might just decide to make the little fucker's life a misery, mightn't you?'

'I hope not.'

Gordon sat back in his chair, and smiled.

'I wish I was your age, Willie. And I wish I had been half as talented. But can I tell you a little story? I was an apprentice once. I was at Rangers. And if you think Brownie is bad... in my day if any apprentice made a mistake they had their balls painted with whitewash and they'd be chased naked round the ground in the pouring rain. I've seen apprentices have their heads pushed down a toilet then taken out and hosed down with freezing water, when it's snowing, then locked out without their clothes.'

'So you're saying I got off lightly?'

'I'm saying it's always happened, it always will, but actually it is getting better. But I'm also saying you need to understand why they are doing it. It's envy in all this especially in your case because you've got such talent. You've trained with the senior players, when we do the eleven against eleven in the final session before a match, right?'

'Yes, boss.'

'And how was that for you?'

'Good.'

'Too right it was good. You ran rings round some of them. And the five-a-sides, do you enjoy that?'

'I do, yes, I do.'

'And do you think Tommy Dyson enjoyed it when you nut-megged him last Wednesday?'

'I didn't know you were there, boss?'

'I wasn't but I hear what goes on, son. And you nutmegged a twenty-nine-year-old England A-team player and then went back and did it again. That's some balls.'

'Should I not have done it?'

'Of course you should. But here is the thing, Willie. You have skill, ability, bravery in a tackle, the right attitude in training, and you've got mental toughness in competitive games. But experi-ence comes only with time. And what happens off the field is just as important as what happens on it. How you handle what has just happened to you is important. Those players need to see you can play the game, all aspects of it – do you see what I'm saying?'

Willie had been rehearsing in his mind how to tell Gordon he wanted to go home to Aberdeenshire but now, with this Scottish football legend in front of him, and his advice ringing in his ears, the words wouldn't form on his lips. He sat in silence, and nodded slowly.

'You see those pictures, Willie? You see that one there, just over the door? That's me. Scotland against Northern Ireland, Belfast, October 1949. Do you know what the score was?'

'No, boss.'

'We won eight-two. Henry Morris of East Fife scored a hat-trick and because of the idiots who ran the game, he never got picked again.'

'Wow.'

'Yeah, wow. You see that shirt, up there? That was from our next game, Wales at home, two-nil, Linwood and McPhail. Here's a picture of the celebrations, son. Look at that crowd, seventy-four thousand.'

'Amazing.'

'Have you heard of George Graham?'

Willie thought it must be a trick question. 'Yes of course, everyone has. Portsmouth now, ex-United, ex-Arsenal, Scottish like us.'

'Correct. But you've not heard of the other George Graham? He had more influence on Scottish football than the one you see on the telly, son. And he was a fucking idiot.'

'How so?'

Now Gordon stood, and he led his young starlet to another picture, of Scotland and England teams lining up with a vast sea of people behind them.

'What was the crowd that day, boss?'

'One hundred and thirty-four thousand. Can you imagine that? One hundred and thirty-four thousand.'

'My God.'

'Big game. You see, because we supposedly "invented" football, the Home Nations never much liked FIFA. So we didn't play in World Cups before the war. I could live with that. I was only sixteen when the war broke out, so I wouldn't have made it. Then after the war FIFA were desperate to get us in. So instead of making us qualify like all the other teams in the world, they said two of the four Home Nations could go through. But George fucking Graham, he was the secretary of the Scottish FA, said Scotland would not go as runners-up of the Home Nations, only champions. England had beaten Wales too, and Northern Ireland, so this was the decider, son. There's me there. Good team that. Cowan in goal; Young, Cox, Gordon, Woodburn, Forbes, Waddell, Moir, Bauld, Steel, Liddell. We should have won.'

'Who was the manager?'

Gordon laughed. 'You won't believe this. We didn't have one. The team got picked by a committee of fucking suits like George fucking Graham.' His mother came into his mind. 'Sorry, son, too much swearing. But it still makes me angry, to this day.'

'So you lost.'

'Williams, Alf Ramsey, Aston, Billy Wright, Franklin, Dickinson, Tom Finney – bane of my life, that man – Mannion, Mortensen, Bentley and Langton. Bentley scored the only goal.'

'So they went to the World Cup?'

'Yep. George Young was our skipper, Billy Wright was England's skipper, and they both begged the SFA – change your mind, for God's sake, this is the World Cup. But Graham wouldn't back down. Unbelievable. You'll meet a lot of stupid people in football, Willie, but never forget George Graham. He took the prize.'

'Georgie Best has never played in a World Cup.'

'That's true. But his team never qualified. Ours did, we could have gone, and a numpty in a blazer stopped us.'

'What a story.'

'Yep. So listen to me, son. One day, I am telling you now, you are going to be a big player. I'll tell you something else. You see those games I played in, there is hardly any film footage of any of them. That's why I love these pictures so much. You're going to be a top footballer in the television age. You're going to make a lot more money than I ever did. More important though, you are going to play for Scotland in World Cup finals. And I am going to be there. I am going to be in the stands, and I am going to share your pride when "Scotland the Brave" starts up and we'll both have tears in our eyes.

'And you're going to remember this conversation. And you're going to say to yourself, "I wonder if David Brown is watching on live TV right now? And I wonder if he remembers the time he pranked me and I ended up in Charlie Gordon's office expecting to get a bollocking, and he told me one day I would be here?"'

There was a few seconds of silence as they stood and looked at each other. The teacher and the pupil; the has-been player and the will-be; the old legend and the young pretender.

'Thanks, boss. I appreciate it. I appreciate it a lot.'

'So next time Brownie comes at you, you laugh it off, or you fight back.'

He walked over, put his hand on Willie's back, and directed him to the door.

'And now, you are going to go back in that dressing room, and the players will all have got dressed in their fancy clothes, and you are going to tell them to take those fancy clothes off, because the gaffer has told you he wants all first-team players in his office for the draw, all in their club tracksuits, for a picture. OK?'

'OK boss, yeah.'

'And, son, when they are all in here, you take these, and you get a little bit of revenge on Brownie, and if he so much as says a word, you send him to me, like he sent you to me.'

As if his day couldn't get any stranger, he found Charlie Gordon handing him a pair of scissors, with the words, 'Cut out the nipple area of his shirt, and the bollock area on his trousers. He'll know who sent you when he finds out.'

As Gordon had said they would be, the players were all either dressed or getting dressed when Willie returned. He made a point of speaking as he walked through the door, first clapping his hands and then whistling.

'Just back from the gaffer's office. Sorry to do this, seeing as how you're all dressed, but he says there will be a photographer in for the Cup draw, and he wants everyone in club tracksuits. Everyone.'

It sparked the inevitable tirade, but Willie stood his ground. 'I am just the messenger. You lot do as he tells you, and let me get on with tidying this mess you've left me.'

Once the players were changed back again, and had been led by Winston and Mooro to the manager's office, he took the scissors Gordon had given him, found Brownie's size ten dark brown brogues, and cut off the laces. He looked up at the peg to see Brownie's favourite Carnaby Street shirt, all pink and yellow and green and purple, and he snipped off the buttons and then, as Gordon had suggested, scissored two large holes where his nipples would be. Then he found Brownie's underpants, and cut out the area where his balls would hang. Then he took out a pen from the inside pocket of Brownie's jacket, found a piece of paper in the waste bin, and scribbled a note which he left sticking from the breast pocket.

'Please call extension 201 to find out who ordered this assault on your lovely clothes.'

And with that, he walked back to the boot room, dreaming of the sound of bagpipes leading him out for his full Scottish international at Hampden Park, in a World Cup qualifier against England.

4

TROUBLES

Monday 4 February

For four months now, every day, Monday to Friday, making sure never to use the same shop or street seller twice, Colleen Connor had bought the *London Evening Standard* and carefully read through the personal section. Today she bought it from a red-faced old man with a stall outside Charing Cross Station. It was soon speckled with rain, but Colleen rarely bothered with the front or back pages. Her only interest focused on the last few pages, where births, deaths and marriages were recorded alongside all manner of messages placed by ordinary members of the public. She walked down to Embankment Station, got onto the Underground, randomly took a Northern Line train to Edgware, and, for the God knows how many times now, she read through every line.

Finally, finally, it was there, in 8-point Times New Roman script, '*Happy Birthday grandma, 65 years old today, all our love, Peter and Pamela.*' Only she, the man who had placed it, and two others knew what it meant, and as she read it, she allowed herself a little smile. At last. She wanted to cross herself she was so happy, but the key to her work was to avoid unnecessary attention. She folded the paper, and put it into her coat pocket.

Colleen had rehearsed what had to happen now so many times in her head, over and over again until of late she had even been dreaming about it.

And so, tomorrow morning, just before seven o'clock, she knew she would be leaving her sparsely furnished, rented two-bedroomed terraced house in Chiswick and making her way to another safe house in Woodville Road in Ealing. She decided to stay on the train all the way to Edgmware, and wait a while before heading back to Chiswick. She found a café close to the Tube station, ordered a tea and some toast, and looked once more at the message that had put a song in her heart. There it was, sandwiched between a golden wedding and the tenth anniversary of the death of a teenager. '*Happy Birthday grandma, 65 years old today, all our love, Peter and Pamela.*' This was, for her, a moment of history, one she believed would define her and her country's future. In that simple little announcement was confirmation that she was now a fully fledged member of an IRA Active Service Unit. It was the greatest moment of her life. So far.

Colleen was the youngest of Frank Connor's girls and her child-hood, growing up in Belfast, had been defined by the Troubles. That was hardly surprising with her father halfway through an eight-year sentence for terrorist offences, and her uncle Gerry one of the masterminds of last October's escape from Mountjoy prison when three IRA men were whisked out of the exercise yard by helicopter, an act of daring immortalized in the Wolfe Tones' hit 'The Helicopter Song', which topped the Irish charts. Her favourite uncle's role, though he was never charged with anything, was one of the reasons her father was transferred from Crumlin Road jail in Belfast to the high-security Maze.

Colleen was twenty-four, five feet ten inches tall, with thick, unruly, shoulder-length dark hair. The large scar on her left cheek was a lasting reminder of a rifle butt she received from a British soldier when she was eighteen. She and some boys were only throwing stones at the police vehicles when the young Para knocked her unconscious. She woke with a depressed fracture of her cheekbone and a two-inch gash, which needed nine stitches. After a couple of days in hospital she went to the police to say she'd been assaulted and would like to press charges. The laughter on the other side of the counter merely served to reinforce her hatred of British soldiers and Ulster's policemen.

'I'm scarred for the rest of my fucking life,' she told the desk officer.

'Sure, those streets are a dangerous place, pet. Probably best to stay at home eh, watch the telly, do some ironing?' One day, she vowed, someone would pay the price for what that soldier did to her.

The flow of courtiers slowed after that. Though her looks were not exactly destroyed, the damaged face was less of an attraction, more a sign of the Troubles of which she was part. That men might find her less attractive mattered not one jot to her. Her politics had been fired, by her background and by that experience. Not for her the squeamish worries in choosing between bomb and ballot box. And if she had to choose between a life of active service, or the life her mother had chosen for herself, looking after home and family, there was no choice at all. If she wanted to have sex with someone, she could, and from time to time she did. But she saw a life of marriage to an organization and a cause opening up ahead of her.

She'd been sent to London four months ago, given money for the house, but told she should try to find work while she was there, and despite the network at her disposal, she had struggled, save for a couple of cleaning jobs. She was sure people were put off by the scar every bit as much as her thick accent. Now at last, the ad finally having appeared, she could hopefully focus on the real job she had come to do.

Colleen had been on a number of small-scale operations, but if this came off she would be in the big league, and one day would follow in her father's footsteps into a senior position, possibly even the organization's top woman, an ambition she had long held. Jail was of no consequence, a badge of honour. Hundreds had been jailed or killed in a struggle for freedom that had gone on for centuries. As far back as 1867, her dad told her when she was barely out of nappies, the Brits killed twelve after an unsuccessful attempt to spring a jailed Irishman from Clerkenwell prison. When she was in her teens, her uncle Gerry gave her for Christmas a book about the United Irishmen Rebellion of 1798, when Republican revolutionaries inspired by revolution in America and France rose up unsuccessfully against British rule. So far as the Connor family was concerned, British soldiers and police just liked killing the Irish – always had, always would. This was not simply a struggle to get the troops out, and work for a united Ireland; for Colleen and her close relatives it was also about revenge.

She binned the dampened newspaper at a bus stop outside the café, took the train back south, changed for Chiswick, and arrived home just before six o'clock. As she pushed the door to, she threw her wet coat over the armchair, made herself a cup of tea, then turned on the TV to catch the news. It made her heart sing a little more as she heard newsreader Kenneth Kendall read out the main story.

'Twelve people have been killed and fourteen injured in a bomb explosion on board a coach carrying British soldiers and their families from Manchester to RAF Catterick in North Yorkshire. Among the dead were eight soldiers and four civilians, including two young children. In a separate incident, a postal device exploded at the offices of the Daily Express *newspaper in Fleet Street. Nobody was hurt. The Prime Minister returned from a visit to Cardiff to make a statement in the House of Commons.'*

Colleen sat and watched in wonder at the shots of ambulances racing to the scene, bodies being lined up in shrouds on the hard shoulder of the recently extended M62, miles of traffic bottlenecked, then police and politicians queuing to say what they always said at times like this. 'Cowardly' – that was the one that got to Colleen the most. Cowardly my arse. The bravery and courage of the volunteers who did this matched anything ever shown by soldiers with their fancy uniforms and the medals they handed out like confetti and the Queen and all those other hangers-on riding around on horses calling themselves heads of regiments. A small dedicated group of men – maybe helped by someone like her – had taken out a military bus. That took guts galore. Men whose identity would hopefully never be known until the war was won, when their names would be sung for centuries to come – heroes every one of them.

Even the fact that Edward Heath had to cancel a trip to

Wales to head back to London and be seen to take command, and utter all the usual platitudes, that alone showed the impact these mainland bombings were having. Colleen smiled to herself when she heard the Prime Minister say, 'This will not change anything, and we will all carry on with our lives.' 'So why have you just done a U-turn on the M4 then?' she said to the TV. And when the plummy-voiced reporter outside Parliament said the situation was 'particularly delicate for Mr Heath in light of the general election', her smile turned to a chuckle, as she muttered to herself, 'Got the bastards on the run...'

She went to the fridge, took out two eggs and a slice of bacon left over from the morning, and as she cooked her tea, she wondered if her dad knew any more than she did, about the operation in which she was about to take part.

'I am going to make you so fucking proud, Daddy,' she whispered beneath the sound of the bacon sizzling in the pan. 'Whatever it is we are doing, I'm going to make you so fucking proud.'

5

DRAW

Buoyed by his chat with Willie Buchanan, and encouraged by a call from one of his more reliable scouts that Leeds midfielder Johnny Giles was struggling with a thigh strain, Charlie Gordon treated himself to another tiny tot of Scotch and a mouthful of mints before the players joined him for the Cup draw. Lincoln away. That was the one he dreaded most. Lincoln City. How the hell had they got this far? One thing for sure though, even if he beat Leeds or actually won all his League games before the sixth round, defeat to Lincoln was the end. Fact. Non-defiable football gravity. Please God, he muttered, don't let it be Lincoln fucking City. He tried to remember if he ever played there. Was it Lincoln they beat in the third round in 1950 when he was with Aston Villa? Or was it Luton? He was always mixing up his memories of matches played. He had talked for years, at club dinners and testimonials, about the only goal from outside the penalty area he ever scored – nearly all of his goals were headers from corners and free-kicks – and he always said it was against Leicester City. But then someone found film footage of it, and it was against Everton. 'I knew they played in blue,' he said, laughing it off. But it worried him how little he remembered sometimes, and how much he thought he did.

Sometimes he would flick through the piles of scrapbooks his mum had kept. God she loved him, didn't she, to keep all that stuff? Photos, thousands of press reports, match programmes, his original contract with Preston North End when he was paid £12 10s 6d a week. But how different he looked now. Still tall, yes. But heavy – OK, fat – two chins were fast becoming three. He had lost that sleek, athletic look that had made him popular not just with the male fans for his footballing skills, but with their wives, girlfriends and daughters too. Again, he was not Georgie Best. But he didn't lack for female attention and company, and he took full advantage at times. Back then, his three-times broken nose made him look rugged. Now, it just added to the sense of an ageing, broken man, the wrong side of sixteen stone, jowly, a belly hanging over a belt on its final notch, his once shiny dark hair now thin and salt-and-pepper grey; knees which had helped carry him thousands of miles in training and in matches, often helped by cortisone injections, were now in near permanent pain, and the more he walked on them, the more the pain spread to his lower back, the more he felt an urge to stoop – but he knew the minute that happened, Winston would be in for the kill. Ageing, that is how he felt as he summoned up the energy for yet more bonhomie with the players who he could hear gathering along the corridor.

More and more often, Charlie Gordon was looking at Ronnie Winston and wondering why he had appointed him, let alone given him all the encouragement along the way. He'd never once thought he would become a threat, until now. When Winston had to retire early with an ankle injury, Gordon had been one of the first on the phone to say, 'Get your badges done, you're a born coach.' He did, and when Winston read in the press that Gordon was being linked with the top job here, he dropped him a line, almost formal in its intensity, saying he would love to be involved in some capacity with him. Gordon filed it away and when Gerry McLeod left him to take the Number One job at Kilmarnock four years ago he told him to apply. He interviewed four others, but chose Winston. He was the brightest by far.

More than that, on that same evening, before he had made the final decision, he mentioned to his mother in one of their phone calls that he had been interviewing people for the job, and she said something that at first he thought was just a little crazy. 'When assessing a new employee, you only have to look for three things, Charles: his car, his watch and his shoes.'

Charlie laughed. But she was deadly serious.

'The car will tell you how he is doing in life, and the store he puts on first impressions. His watch will tell you how seriously he takes time management, and whether he values personal possessions. And finally, and most importantly, his shoes. The cleaner the shoes, the keener you should be to hire him. Remember this, Charles: never trust a man you meet for the first time who is wearing shoes that aren't clean.' It was always threes with Mum.

He hadn't seen Winston's car, he hadn't noticed his watch. But his shoes were unquestionably dull, but very clean. He was probably going to appoint him anyway, but his mum clinched it for Winston. It was only later that he learned he drove a 1965 Ford Anglia in permanent need of a wash; and his watch face was scratched, with most of the gold plating having worn off leaving a greenish stain on his wrist.

The buoyancy had suddenly gone. He took another little sip from the bottle, hoping it might bring it back. Instead he could feel himself dipping somewhat, through sadness and into self-pity. Who would really miss him if he got the sack?

The board would thank him for his service, put out a statement full of hypocritical praise for all the great things he did for the club, then move on, just as their wives would move on, the ones who had flirted with him and on one occasion much more than that, because, as she said, 'I can't believe I've just had sex with a real life football manager.' He was sure Ronnie Winston would perform better than he had on that front. He still looked like a player, could still do a turn in the five-a-sides.

Never mind football and fitness though – it was more Winston's developing political skills that were troubling Gordon. Charlie also knew that football was a two-day wonder. If you lost on Saturday there was lots of complaining from the directors and the supporters but by Tuesday everyone started to concentrate on next Saturday's game with the defeat soon forgotten. The real fear was a combination of defeats, a lowly League position, and paper talk about a new manager as an undercurrent to the next game.

In readiness for this, Winston was also developing his board-room skills too, Gordon had clocked that. After matches, the two of them would wander up to the boardroom where the directors entertained their guests, and as Charlie posed for pictures and signed autographs for sponsors and their kids, he noticed Winston spending more and more time, not hanging back as he used to, but talking to the directors, nodding respectfully as they gave him the benefit of their wisdom.

'What was Moffitt saying then?' Gordon would ask when finally they escaped.

'Nothing much. Usual bullshit, telling us where we're going wrong. How we got the tactics wrong second half. All that crap.'

And Gordon so wanted to ask, 'Did he say anything about me?' But he knew if he did, Winston would know he had him.

Like most managers, Gordon, as a football man, had little time for directors. He saw them as a necessary evil. They were businessmen who, because they were in the business of football, thought it meant they knew about football. He accepted it was their money he spent on buying players and paying their wages, but it wasn't as though they got nothing in return. Successful local business people are ten a penny. Being a director, let alone a chairman, gives them something special. They go on the local radio and talk about matches won or lost, players bought or sold. Fans stop them and ask them their views, invite them to supporters' group meetings and (provided the team is doing OK) they thank them for all they do for the club. At away games, they and their wives sit with all the millionaires who own the big clubs, and the famous people who support them, and enjoy the food and drink on offer. But it doesn't matter how many games they watch, Gordon thought, they still know next to nothing about professional football or how to win matches.

If chairmen knew nothing, their relatives usually knew less, and it was Moffitt's son-in-law, of all people, who had been the one pushing hardest for them to sign DD Marland. Two weeks on from signing him, for a club record £132,000, Gordon remained unconvinced, despite his debut goal. The press could go on about how he was tipped to become the next England regular, but Gordon hadn't fancied him much when they played against Spurs, and his London scout had told him Marland was 'dodgy on the character front'. But he was a marquee signing, the fans were excited by him, Moffitt was willing to sign the cheque, so he went along with it. He had no choice.

DD had had a good start, though with a penalty miss in his second match, he too, just like his manager, was having to put on a brave face clouded by the mask of failure – even if he did it rather better than Gordon. He was living in the Tudor Manor Hotel, the only four-star hotel within a twenty-mile radius of the club, while his wife Lucy was still alone in Waltham Abbey with their black Labrador. The arrangement was not helping DD's on-field performance, or his stamina. He'd boasted to his new teammates that he'd been through all the waitresses and bar staff and was now moving onto senior management.

'At least you're scoring somewhere,' Jock Johnson had said when DD reeled off a list of his conquests. Magic briefed the manager on what happened next.

'What's that supposed to mean?' DD snapped back at the goalkeeper.

'Next time you steal the ball off Dipper to take a pen, hit the fuckin' target, eh? Maybe if you slept more and shagged less … you know what I'm saying?'

'Fuck you lot with your boring wives and your two-point-four kids in your four-bedroom Wimpey homes,' DD snarled across the dressing room.

Mooro, the team captain, didn't like that. 'DD. Never ever cuss players' wives again,' he said, all vestige of banter gone. He was serious.

DD shrugged. 'OK, fair enough. But I'll shag who I like. Thing is these poor northern lasses say you shrivelled northerners can't give them what they want … so they need a nice big Cockney cock like mine.'

'Enough,' said Mooro.

'You fucking big knobhead,' echoed Jock.

'Exactly,' said DD.

Gordon was beginning to see why Tottenham had been keen to let him go without putting up too much of a fight. But deep down he still believed that if he could get the best out of him, he had a star player.

Once the local photographer had arrived, and been shown in, Ronnie Winston led the file of players into Gordon's office. It was just about big enough to squeeze everyone in, and the photographer quickly took control, asking Gordon to sit on the corner of his desk, closest to the radio, Winston beside him, and all the players gathered round. Mooro was visibly irritated when the photographer asked if DD could stand right next to the manager.

BBC commentator Kenneth Wolstenholme was presiding, and as he began to speak, Gordon and Winston said 'shush' loudly, and slowly the banter and the backchat calmed down. The players at the back had to strain to hear, and Gordon made a mental note to bollock Magic Rowland. I told him to get a new transistor for this, he cursed to himself.

By way of preamble, Wolstenholme ran through the eight clubs left in the draw, giving a potted account of how they had got this far, focusing mainly on Lincoln's incredible 3–1 win against Liverpool in the previous round. And when Gordon's name came up, it was in the embarrassing context of Wolstenholme referring to this morning's press speculation that Winston was favourite to succeed him if he left the club, 'which seems inevitable if the current run in the League is not reversed'. Everyone heard, and pretended not to.

By then – and for once Gordon was thankful for a childish prank – there was a nice little distraction drawing the players' attention away from the temptation to look at their somewhat beleaguered boss and his ambitious deputy alongside him. While left-back Michael 'Killer' Kilbride had been in the shower, Tommy Dyson, once voted *Shoot* magazine's 'hardest man in football', and who resented Kilbride's nickname, thinking he ought to have it, had smeared a fingerful of Deep Heat on Killer's underpants which would touch the delicate parts of his balls and backside.

Most of the other players had seen him do it and so were keeping an eye on Kilbride to spot the first signs of awkward squirming. Then the teeth-clenching, then the jumping from one foot to another, then the 'Which bastard has done my pants?' as he finally realized he had become the latest victim of one of football's most common pranks, then the falling about of all the players apart from Dyson, who was putting on his best innocent face.

A football squad, Gordon once told a room full of schoolkids, when he went back to do the prize-giving at Fallin Primary School, is a group of grown men with a fourth-form sense of humour. Banter and practical jokes, he said, were equally part of the fuel that drove them and the glue that held them together. And provided the banter didn't become serious bullying, and the practical jokes didn't cause injury, he didn't mind. These guys saw more of each other than they saw of their wives, girlfriends, parents, kids and friends. They trained together, ate together, spent long hours travelling together on coaches and trains and shared rooms in hotels together. They even spent Christmas with each other because if they had an away game on Boxing Day, that meant training or travelling the day before.

They had their fall-outs of course, and part of the manager's job was to keep an eye out for the relationships that risked damaging the team spirit. They didn't have to love each other. But there had to be respect and trust. They didn't even have to like each other – and how can you expect a couple of dozen randomly assembled people, all ambitious for themselves as well as their team, not to fall out from time to time? – but they did have to understand there are certain lines that cannot be crossed. Deep Heat on underpants was not one of those lines. Charlie Gordon put on his best avuncular smile as Killer Kilbride danced around, Clutch Dyson slipped to the back of the group, and the photographer tried to work out what was going on.

By and large this was a good set of players, and Gordon was going to have to rely on that in the coming days and weeks. Ultimately it was what they did that decided whether he would have a pay cheque next month. He could coach, cajole, plan, he could train them, organize them, shout at them, praise them, plead with them, but if they didn't deliver, if the other team played better, they were not the ones whose name got plastered on placards and then got handed a P45.

'OK, enough,' shouted Winston. 'Here we go.' Silence fell once more. Out of the radio came the unmistakable sound of the black, synthetic resin balls, numbered one to eight. Tom Finney was shaking the balls around the velvet bag for dramatic effect. Sometimes Charlie wondered if the draws were fixed by heating up one of the balls, either to create the most exciting – and lucrative – ties, or to help a team whose success-hungry chairman or manager had paid a bribe. It happened in other countries, so why not here? But no, he thought, no way would Tom Finney OBE be involved in anything like that.

God, what a player he'd been. A one-club man, Preston North End, small and slight – you wonder how he survived the clattering footballers got in the fifties. Today's players wouldn't know what had hit them if they were taken back in time to an era when you had, more or less, to put someone in hospital for a fortnight before you got a caution. Gordon had played both with him and against him, and he knew which he preferred. The time he played against him, Finney had been moved from the wing into the centre when Eddie Brown went off injured after a clash of heads with Gordon, and really made him pay. He gave him a lesson time and again, whipping the ball away from him just as he was about to slide in; even out-jumping him when the ball was in the air. Gordon's aerial power was often cited as his greatest strength. Not that day.

As he heard Finney chatting with Wolstenholme, Charlie smiled on hearing that gentle voice. It sounded a little older now, but it was the same voice that spoke so warmly to Gordon after that game, which Preston won 3–2. 'Well played, Charlie, and well done last week against Portugal. I heard you were Man of the Match.'

'Not today though.'

'You did fine. We got a bit lucky with the third goal, that's all.' *Gentleman Tom*, he was one player whose nickname fitted him perfectly.

'Number 2,' announced Finney as he pulled the first ball from the bag.

'Aston Villa,' said Wolstenholme.

'Will play Number 5.'

'Tottenham Hotspur.'

'Please not Lincoln,' Gordon repeated to himself.

Having changed back into his suit, his shirt collar was now soaked and he could feel a line of sweat running down into his armpit. I don't need all this pressure, he thought. Why didn't I get a normal job? Even driving the bloody team coach for a living would be better than this. He looked around at the players surely thinking, no doubt not for the first time, that the gap between them and him was now cavernous. They were young and fit and vital and he was this ageing, broken fifty-one-year-old dying for a quick shot of Bell's to calm himself down and ease the stress, just a little, just for a moment. He couldn't though, not in a room full of his players.

If they felt the gap with him, he felt it with them too. He tolerated their juvenile pranks and listened with an increasing disdain to their fatuous conversations about women and horses and the things they bought with their wages. When he was a player, football teams looked like Army platoons, smart, short-haired, disciplined, respectful. Look at this lot with their flared trousers and floral shirts, their big bushy moustaches and permed shoulder-length hair, which had become all the rage. In his day, you jumped into a communal bath after a match and you shared a bar of soap. This bunch had their own little wash bags full of combs, brushes, hair products, deodorants, shampoo, conditioner even, and a mirror. Wilf Moore even had a nail file.

He felt the eyes of some of the players on him. Appearance meant everything in his line of work, and sweat is not good, unless you're playing. Managers must never show weakness; he was supposed to be mentally tough and in control at all times, whatever the circumstances. If only they knew. One thing he knew – he had to get out of here, or else they would know.

'Oh shit,' he said, leaping from the desk. 'I knew I'd left

something in the car. I'll be back in a minute. Clutch, write me down the draw when it's done.'

'He can't write,' said Jock Johnson. 'Shall I do it?'

As he walked past his assistant, he couldn't help but notice a little smirk on Ronnie Winston's face. He was a good coach, no doubt about that, and it was only recently that Gordon had begun to doubt his loyalty. But could he blame him? If he can't even last the course of a Cup draw without running out of the room in fear of a meltdown, why shouldn't a fellow professional have doubts about his ability?

As Gordon rushed out to fetch an imaginary something from his car, he saw the look of concern on Wilf Moore's face, and felt a mix of shame and fear that he knew would only ease when he downed the Glenfiddich he kept in his glove compartment exactly for moments like this.

He returned to his own dedicated parking space at the back entrance to the training ground offices and changing rooms, and took refuge in the car. It was a beautiful setting, rolling hills far into the distance, up towards the Lake District where sometimes he would go for a drive just to get away from it all. He felt like doing that now. Instead, he wound down the window and took three deep breaths.

He liked this place, even if the job was so pressured. Like most footballers, he lived a fairly nomadic life, having played with a number of different clubs. But this town felt the nearest thing to home he had ever felt since his childhood. It wasn't pretty, even if the countryside was. And as Stan Moffitt was always keen to tell anyone who would listen, keeping those textile mills going was not easy. The area's only pit had gone now. But the people were strong; they reminded him a lot of the people back home in Scotland. He felt an empathy with them. But he knew if he didn't turn things around soon, his empathy wouldn't mean a bloody thing.

He leaned over to the glove compartment, and fished out a small bottle of Glenfiddich. It wasn't even a quarter-bottle, more a large miniature. He stroked open the top and took one big slug, then another, and it was gone. He sighed loudly, nodded to himself as he felt the glow inside his chest and his stomach, and sighed again, only then noticing that one of the groundstaff was watching from the fence that separated the club complex of pitches and buildings from the beautiful landscape beyond.

'Hi, Phil, how ya doin'?'

'I'm fine thanks, gaffer. How are you?'

'I'm OK. Nothing a win at West Brom wouldn't put right.'

'Yeah, could do with that.'

Phil smiled, but Gordon could sense there was unease and embarrassment there.

'It's a little superstition,' he said.

'Sorry, gaffer?'

'A superstition – I always sit in the car for a Cup draw.'

'Ah, yeah. I see. Anyway, better be getting on.' And off he went, Gordon worrying that word of his drinking in the car would spread fast. Should he call him back, and tell him not to breathe a word to a soul? Or might that make it more likely that he would? He didn't know him well, but he always worried that people like Phil, paid a pittance to do a job that had to be done, wouldn't have much time for managers or players who earned so much more.

Charlie Gordon had not been a big drinker as a player. He liked the occasional blow-out, maybe four or five times a year, but he was a lightweight compared with some of his teammates for both club and country. But since becoming a manager, partly because the physical requirements were less intense, and partly because of the stress, he found himself drinking more regularly, and more heavily. When he had a medical a few months ago, the doctor asked him how much he drank, and like most people, he lied. He said a couple of glasses of wine with dinner, maybe a couple of Scotches at the weekend. The doc filled in his form, and only later did Gordon reflect that he could not remember the last day when he'd had as little as that.

It showed in his face, which is why he hated looking in the mirror. He looked bloated at times, especially first thing before he had managed to get his head and his eyes in gear. The scars on his forehead, reminders of a courageous career as a centre-back,

never scared to go into any duel, were now accentuated amid
the wrinkles.

That time he went to AA, he did a bit of reading beforehand,
and it made him wonder whether there had been an exact
moment or period in his life when he had become dependent on
drink. Was there a tipping-point moment, or was it incremental?
Had he fallen into it as though into a pool, or had it crept up
insidiously, like the rain still falling now? He didn't know. But
he did know that drink was one of the first things he thought
of when he woke, and one of the last things he did before he
went to bed. He did know that he was now drinking heavily, and
had been for some time, every day. He knew it was adversely
affecting his work – as he had just displayed to the entire fucking
squad – and his health and it had already adversely affected his
marriage and other relationships. Whether that all added up to
a drink problem, let alone alcoholism, he didn't know. There
were plenty of worse cases at the AA meeting, for sure. But it
wasn't great.

In the football industry, drink, usually free, was part of the
fabric of management anyway. Most managers liked to have a
drink together after a game. You drink to celebrate a win. You
drink to commiserate after a defeat. Drink flows through the
chairman-manager relationship too. Stan Moffitt always poured
two large Scotches when they met for their little chats in the
boardroom. And Gordon drank with the journalists who covered
the club. He met them a couple of times a week and he was
convinced that one of the reasons they didn't put the boot as
hard into him as they did to some other managers was because
he always had a few bottles of Scotch, gin and vodka in his
desk drawers and cupboards, and they knew they could rely
on him for generous helpings of it all. Away games were booze
opportunities too. The players were not allowed to drink on a
Friday night before a game, and he liked them to be tucked up
in their hotel beds by ten, but the manager and his staff could.
And he insisted they did. It was good for morale, he convinced
himself, and God help any coach who tried to get off to bed
before he did.

He closed his eyes, wondering if the draw was done, then wondering how his players had reacted. Why couldn't they just be better than they were? He knew they could be, because some of them had been so much better last season, when they finished sixth in the League. So what had happened since, what had gone wrong? Was it them, or was it him? If only those players, who were no doubt larking about in his office right now, could have seen him in his heyday. He'd told them often enough he'd been a real player, there was the odd bit of film, most of it old and grainy, which is how he felt right now.

Just accept it, he told himself, old medals and caps counted for nothing to these new players. He'd been in his prime before most of them were born and it might as well have been a hundred or a thousand years ago for all they cared.

If only we could get a win on Saturday, away at West Brom, he reasoned, then something at home to Leeds United; surely that is not beyond us. Four points out of six, which is 'safe against the sack' territory, even with Moffitt hovering. Then get a good Cup draw, maybe away, take it to a replay, and the money comes in, everyone's happy. Do all that, avoid relegation, and he would keep the job and be able to survive to the end of the season. 'Then,' he said, quietly but with a certain force and anger, 'I can get rid of half of this useless bunch of wasters and start to rebuild for next season.'

It was cold, and again he could hear his mother's voice gently chiding him and his dad when they were going out in the cold. 'You two, if you wear a coat you can always take it off. If you don't take a coat you can never put it on. Now take your coats!' He smiled. There was a brief moment of sunlight, then heavy, scudding clouds blotted it out and a torrential rainstorm came down as he peered across the football pitches.

Maybe that was one of his life-changing moments? The day we signed a dud named DD. No, he said to himself. Don't let that little no-mark be one of the defining figures in your life.

Inevitably, there had been so many times in the last forty years when he wondered how different his life might have been with a father. He was not a bad footballer himself, and played at a good level as a left-back for Alloa reserves. His dad could see Charlie had a special talent, even as a child, and while his mum encouraged him to work hard at school, and make sure he got a trade, his dad always pushed him in the direction of football. When he made his full international debut, for Scotland against Ireland at Hampden Park, and the photographers picked up a tear falling down his cheek during the national anthem, the commentator remarked that young Charlie Gordon – he had only just turned twenty – might be overwhelmed. But he was crying that his dad was not there among all the Gordons who were up in the stand to cheer him on. Scotland ran out 2–1 winners, and he won the tackle against Davy Walsh that started the move that led to Jock Dodd's winning goal with eleven minutes remaining. He knew how proud his dad would have been that he had listened to him, and gone for his dream of being a footballer. He knew too how happy he would have been that he had never had to set foot inside a pit cage.

He had been so excited that horrible day of the accident, because he had played in a Scottish Schools Cup tie for Fallin Juniors against Cumbernauld Juniors, won 7–2 and he had scored three of them – he was a centre-forward back then, and only became a defender when he began to outgrow everyone else. Then the second he pushed open the door of their home, about half a mile from the Fallin Colliery in Stirling where his dad had worked for years, and his father before him, he knew something was wrong. It was his auntie Sheena who greeted him, in tears.

'It's your dad, Charlie. He's at the hospital.'

She was in floods of tears now, and it turned out her brother Jim was also in hospital too. Jim lived. Charlie's dad and Malcolm McIntyre, a colliery fireman who tried to rescue them after the gas explosion, did not.

So if Alice dying was the biggest of his three life-changing moments, was his dad dying runner-up? And maybe the sack was the third; it just hadn't happened yet.

So for now, perhaps it was the injury that ended his playing career. As he turned thirty-two he was as fit as ever, never missed a game all season, a Scotland regular too. Then came Boxing

Day 1954. He'd been kicked, head-butted, elbowed and even bitten by the hardest and dirtiest players in the game, but his career-ending injury was self-inflicted. Away to Celtic and Hearts sat third in the table. The snow had threatened the game but hundreds of bales of hay, spread by the groundstaff and fifty volunteer supporters on Christmas morning, then swept away at 9 a.m. on Boxing Day, had persuaded the referee to give the game the go-ahead.

At 4.10 p.m. Charlie Gordon was commanding the back four as only he could and Hearts were winning. Strangely he heard the click in his right knee before he felt the pain. Bobby Collins was yards away, ready to crunch him, and he probably heard the click too. Things seemed to be jumbled from then on. Referee's whistle, stretcher, doctor, knee locked, ambulance, sirens, hospital, operation, infection, crutches. The report in one Scottish paper said he might never play again. They were right, he never did.

Although he worked hard, seven days a week with the club physiotherapist, after six months it was clear that the tearing of his cartilage in his right knee would bring an end to a wonderful career. Many days he sat there alone at home waiting for someone to ring and say hello. The club only contacted him to say that his contract was being terminated and they intended to claim the insurance they had taken out on him. He mentioned a testimonial; they said they'd get back to him. They never did. For the last sixteen years he had been in a team, in a dressing room, on a coach, on a club tour, with a bunch of very talented and humorous characters. And now he was all alone.

As luck would have it after twelve months he was invited to a football coaching session arranged by the Professional Footballers Association (PFA) and he was then offered a job by an ex-Hearts player as junior coach at Luton Town. From B team to A team to the reserves, he quickly developed a love of seeing young players break through to become full-time professional players. This apprenticeship for him lasted over a decade at a handful of Division 4 teams, one promotion at York City, two relegations. Then his good friend and fellow Scot Jimmy Milne asked him to join him as assistant manager at Preston North End in 1967 and although he still carried a prominent limp, he was on the ladder.

Just one more season, that's all he needed. Most people thought it was a privilege to manage the team you once played for. It is, he guessed. But Gordon also found it added to the burden of responsibility. He had been loved as a player. Not many defenders have their names sung as often as strikers, but he did.

> He's big, a Scot,
> The best of all the lot,
> Charlie G,
> Charlie G...

That was his favourite. English fans celebrating his Scottishness. He loved that, especially when he had family and friends from up north in the stands, which he did most weeks.

Then there was the one they still sang – or did until recently – to the tune of 'When the Saints Go Marching In'...

> Oh Charlie Gor—don's wonderful,
> Oh Charlie Gordon's wonderful,
> Full of boot, full of clog, full of tackles,
> Oh Charlie Gor—don's wonderful.

He loved that one too, and provided he was nowhere near the ball, he used to give a little thumbs up to the fans, and that made them sing it even more. He tried to remember the last time they did.

The rain lashed down harder, bouncing off the bonnet of his pale-blue car which, like the rent for his five-bedroomed house on the far side of the hills in front of him, was provided by the club. He liked his car. He loved his house. Two more reasons he was desperate to survive in the job. A third was that he knew what a bastard negotiator Moffitt could be, and he really didn't look forward to haggling over his pay-off. Then he was a younger man on his way up; this time he was an older manager on his way down and Moffitt would hold all the cards.

His mother, wife, girlfriend, daughter and most of his money were all gone; his deputy was after his job and he felt the only true friend he had in life was a brown liquid living inside a bottle. He sucked out the last drop of Glenfiddich, then threw the empty bottle back in the glove compartment.

'Boss, boss...' Magic, the head physio, and one of the few people he felt he could really count on, emerged through the doorway.

Magic's real name was Ralph Rowland, but even in the club programme he was always listed as 'Magic Rowland, Head Physiotherapist', and he was widely reckoned to be one of the best in the League. A widower, he was a workaholic, always there last, always trying to find one more player to work on, first team, reserves, kids, he didn't care, he loved his job. He liked a drink too which is why Charlie called him 'the best physiothera*pissed* in the League'.

He had earned his Magic nickname a few years earlier when he had worked day and night to get Wilf Moore fit for a Cup match against Newcastle. Mooro had pulled a hamstring in injury time against West Brom the Saturday before and everyone knew a torn hamstring took at least three weeks to repair. Mooro was back and fit after seven days, and scored the winner with two minutes to go. He was interviewed by a gaggle of reporters as he headed for the team coach, and he said it was all down to the 'magic hands of the club physio, Ralph Rowland'. That was the headline, and it became the nickname.

Magic had both thumbs up in the air as he headed towards Gordon's car. What did that mean, he wondered? Was it Lincoln City? Did Magic imagine that a lower-division club was an easy draw? If so, he was wrong. No, he wasn't daft, it must be a biggie, that's what he means, a big Cup tie, one that will get the fans excited and up for it. But who?

Magic was pale and breathless by the time he reached the car. Gordon wound down the window as far as it would go.

'I've been looking everywhere for you, gaffer. What the hell are you doing out here?'

'Please, Magic, not Lincoln. I don't want Lincoln fucking City.'

'No, boss. It's Chelsea.'

'Home or away?'

'Away, gaffer, Stamford Bridge, the ninth of March! Brilliant, eh?'

'It is,' said Gordon, sighing audibly with relief. He tapped his lucky white shirt and gave Magic the same double-handed thumbs up. Then he noticed that, miraculously, the rain had stopped.

6

MARLAND

Getting a high-value transfer over the line was becoming more and more complicated and DD Marland's move from Tottenham had been more complicated than most. One hundred and thirty-two thousand pounds was a lot of money for a footballer. So DD Marland was pricey, for sure, and the price tag created an extra pressure on him to deliver, and an even bigger pressure on Charlie Gordon to make sure he did. Gordon had been clear with the chairman, Stan Moffitt, that if he had six figures to spend he would prefer to use it to strengthen the defence, maybe get a new right-back for £30,000, a back-up centre-half for even less, and a couple of young midfielders to blood from the lower leagues.

'We have to think about next season, Chairman, not just this one.'

But Moffitt wouldn't be shifted. He was set on Marland, which is why Spurs chairman Sidney Wale drove such a hard deal. And Gordon knew that even if Marland was not a perfect fit for what he was trying to do, he did have a lot of talent. Alfie Ruse, a former agent who was his main London scout, had played with Gordon in his brief spell at Preston North End thirty-odd years ago, and had been clear Marland was not an easy player to handle. Even the whole DD thing – his name was Daniel, for heaven's sake, but his middle name was David and 'call me DD' had stuck and it meant the headline writers loved him. Why use the seven letters of Marland in a headline, when two will do?

Gordon also knew that having cost so much, he would have to play him, and that meant dropping Norman Nulty, who had not been firing, certainly, but who was popular with the fans and his teammates. So now Gordon's future rested in the hands of a player he rated but didn't like, DD Marland, and a centre-forward he liked but didn't totally rate, Jules Pemberton, who worked like a Trojan but lacked the finishing qualities you need in that key position.

Marland's arrival had certainly gone down well with the fans. His goalscoring record, first at Colchester, then at Spurs, was good. He was another one following in the Willie Morgan footsteps. Morgan was one of the first footballers to have his own fan club, when he moved down from Alloa to Burnley, and Marland had his too, the DD Club, his mother dealing with all the fan mail and the demand for photos and autographs that came through amid the occasional booking for a paid public appearance, which were the ones that really interested the Marland family.

DD had shoulder-length blond hair, dark green eyes and a curving scar around his temple – these scars were a badge of honour for centre-forwards, proof they were prepared to put their head in when the boots of dirty big centre-halves were flying. He had managed to keep his nose intact though, and was a good-looking guy, Gordon had to give him that. He was also one of the first strikers to have his own goal celebration, running to the crowd, then writing a D in the air with his left forefinger, another one with his right forefinger, then standing there with both arms raised waiting for the other players to come and congratulate him. Gordon, who was more of the 'shake hands and get back into your position' school of celebration, found it all too showy. But he understood that football was becoming an entertainment industry, and the showmen were going to thrive. DD Marland was one of them.

As the closing of the deal neared, Moffitt and Wale sat in one corner of the boardroom ironing out the money side of things. Marland was sitting in the opposite corner flicking through the sports pages of the *Daily Express*, while Marland's father and the team doctor Joss Partington, who was also a director of the club, were going over the various medical reports that had been assembled. Marland had had a knee injury last year and Gordon had insisted on fresh X-rays being done.

Parents were so important in football, and Marland Senior was not just his dad, he was looking after his son's financial interests too, and the papers had speculated he had managed to secure what was the biggest goal bonus in the League. Gordon was sure Marland Senior, Tony, had planted the story, because he had let slip in his conversations with Moffitt that he was thinking of becoming a full-time football agent, and not just for his son. So having other players think he could screw more money out of hard-bitten owners and managers was good for his business ambitions, never mind DD's deal. Doing it before the deal was even done was always a way of showing a bit of confidence and aggression. Some chairmen hated that. But they did tend to ·respect strength.

Gordon knew he had to keep the dad onside to keep the boy onside, and he was laying it on thick. 'This is a good move for your boy, Tony. I know this is not the bright lights but that could be a good thing.'

'Yeah, no distractions up here, eh?'

'He'll do well, I am sure of it. And I promise you that if any clubs come in for him, offering more than £200,000, we won't stand in his way.'

'I'd like him to play abroad some time, maybe Italy.'

DD pulled a face – a happy face – behind his father's back.

'Like Denis Law, eh?' said Gordon. 'He was at Torino before he went to United.'

'Yeah, yeah, Italy. Could be good,' said Mr Marland.

'Anyway he is in safe hands, we will see him and you right. It is a good day all round.'

Even as he said the words, though – and put to one side his own doubts about DD's character – Gordon knew any signing was always a gamble. Football was littered with expensive sign-ings that looked good on paper but turned out to be duds on grass. He remembered in particular Alun Evans joining Liverpool a couple of years earlier for a reported £100,000 fee and never really establishing himself in the team. Marland ticked a lot of the boxes, but he had to settle in, adjust to a new set-up, new team-mates, a new playing system – Gordon's style was very different to Bill Nicholson's, Tottenham's long-serving and recently retired manager. And to Terry Neill's, who had just taken over. It might take him several games to get accustomed to this new set-up; not to mention Gordon's sometimes strange training methodology and complex matchday strategies, about which Smudger Smith, who had been in the England squad with Marland, had already warned him.

So even as Charlie Gordon promised Tony Marland his son could go if a bigger club came in for him and DD wanted to leave, Charlie knew this might not be the case. The moment that DD signed his player registration the club could do anything they liked. It wasn't slavery as such, but once that name was on the paper, the club owned the player to all intents and purposes. That much was clear from the way Moffitt and Wale were talking about him on their side of the boardroom, like a piece of meat. Also, Gordon knew he could well be gone before Marland. So it was better for him to make these promises, then Moffitt and a new manager didn't have to break them in future. The warmth of the rhetoric was important to the settling-in process though, and even Moffitt would recognize Gordon was a master in the art of buttering up players and their families.

Before getting down to the final details, Moffitt and Wale were having a good old bitch about some of their fellow chairmen, especially Burnley's Bob Lord and Leeds United's Manny Cussins. These were the two fiercest opponents of allowing TV to cover matches live (and also the two fiercest opponents of each other). They were convinced TV would stop the fans from wanting to pay their money to come through the turnstiles.

As they gossiped, and chatted about the election – both were hoping for a Tory win – above them was a huge framed photo of one of the club's great figures of the past, Nat Broadbent, a player from the 1930s and 1940s who in the year before war broke out scored fifty-two goals in one season, a record that would probably never be beaten. Broadbent had left his mark in so many ways, not least by carving his initials all around the stadium, in the dressing room, in the ticket office, on seats in the ground, on benches in the press box, on one of the (now replaced) goalposts. He was like a one-man graffiti artist but NB was the only thing he ever carved. Commercial manager Pete Leadbetter staged a weekly tour of the stadium and training ground to trace the twenty-three sets of NB initials. Nat Broadbent had left two legacies, top goalscorer and celebrity carver.

Gordon, like everyone else at the club, was always on the look-out for new ones to find, and he showed his latest discovery to the Marlands, an NB on the side of the wooden plinth on which stood a replica of the Player of the Season award Broadbent won in his record goalscoring year, and told the story behind it. Marland Senior looked vaguely interested. But he could see DD thinking that NB ought really to be DD, and the letters should be bigger. It annoyed Gordon how little players seemed to care about the history of the sport and the clubs they played for.

With the fee for the player still not entirely settled, and his voice now almost a whisper, Stan Moffitt continued the negotiations.

'Listen, Sidney, even if I wanted to I can't find one penny more than £105,000 and that's final. It's my own bleedin' money I'm spending as all the other directors claim they're broke, so please don't give me a hard time. One penny more and I risk the bloody club going under. On the other hand if you'll *guarantee* me that DD will score us fifteen goals by the end of the season, I'll up our bid to £120,000. And that's final.'

Sidney Wale gave the appearance of carefully considering the offer. He knew there were early signs of arthritis in DD's right knee and hip but fortunately the London doctor had offered a clean bill of health. He also knew that since Bill Nicholson left and Terry Neill came in, DD had gone 'Billy Big Bollocks', as he liked to put it, and he was not sure he and Neill would get on. He was getting in the gossip columns almost as much as the sports pages and becoming all too regular in some of the fashionable London nightclubs. So he wanted him out. He'd tried to get Chelsea to go for him, knowing Marland would love the move, and knowing they had shown an interest in him when he was at Colchester. But back then Chelsea had a tough, un-compromising Scottish manager in Tommy Docherty – so many good managers came out of Scotland – and he took one look at Marland and decided he was not for him.

Sidney Wale whispered back to Moffitt: 'Stanley, Stanley, my good friend, please be reasonable. I've got other clubs telling me they would go to £150,000, and I tell you, anything less and the fans will hang me from the flamin' goalposts. The boy is our top goalscorer, and yes, that is his dad over there, but he is like a son to me too. He's in bed at ten every night, he goes to church every Sunday morning and his wife, who is also a bloody angel, is a pottery painter. They are the perfect couple.'

'You sure? Gordon told me he was a serial womanizer.'

'No way, Stanley, no way. This boy is a home-loving boy.'

He stared sympathetically into Moffitt's eyes, hoping his oppo had not seen the *Sunday Pictorial* a month ago, which albeit in coded terms suggested that DD had been caught in bed with the wife and the sister-in-law of his commercial manager.

Sidney Wale then tried his final card. 'And another thing, Stan: so far DD's not played in any of our Cup matches – he's either been injured or suspended – so he won't be Cup-tied for your fifth-round match against Manchester City. He could end up taking you all the way to Wembley.'

It took two more glasses of sherry – Gordon hated the stuff but said 'I won't say no' when Moffitt came over with the decanter – before finally the deal was done. They met somewhere close to the middle: £125,000 was the agreed fee, plus Marland's five per cent signing-on fee, total around £132,000. It was exactly where both sides imagined the meeting would end when it had begun ninety minutes earlier.

Now Moffitt went to the bar and took a bottle of champagne from the fridge, sending the doctor to call through club secretary Stewart Finley to sort contracts. Finley, another Scot, was grey-haired, taciturn, lived apart from his wife and loved his cricket, which Moffitt always felt was strange given his club secretary came from Perthshire. He had been Moffitt's finance director at Moffitt Textiles for fifteen years, but when Moffitt became chairman, he sacked the previous football club secretary, who had been very close to his predecessor Percy Summerton, and brought in Finley.

The son of a Presbyterian minister, Stewart Finley always wore a collar and tie which looked fine around the office but he had been the butt of much of the players' banter at the end of last season, when the club went on a holiday tour of Spain and Finley had worn his suit and tie even on the beach in ninety-degree heat. He was something of a tortured soul. Raised to believe, he tried to, but reading Darwin's *On the Origin of Species* hugely influenced him. He began to put reason ahead of faith, it put him at odds with his parents, who had always hoped he too would become a minister, and he moved south. But he had retained an integrity and a straightness that Moffitt relied on. If he did the dodgy deal, he could rely on Finley to deliver it straight.

He gathered Marland Junior and Senior together, sat them down at adjacent chairs on one side of the table, and he and Gordon sat on the other. 'Right, son,' Finley began, 'you are the most expensive player we've ever signed, so congratulations. Here is a contract to match. It's a two and a half year agreement with a two and a half year option. The fee that has been agreed is £125,000 and you will get a five per cent signing-on fee. OK?'

What he didn't say, however, was that this signing-on fee of £6,250 would be spread over the five years of the contract and after income tax it would be worth less than half by the time DD had received it all. Fortunately, Moffitt clocked from the corner of the room, neither of the Marlands stopped to query it. They smiled and nodded at each other.

'Your basic wage will be £115 a week for the rest of this season, £125 a week next season and £140 a week for the season after. Bonuses for the first team are £65 a point this season, £75 next season, then £85 in season three; and for each year you stay with us you'll earn a £1,000 loyalty payment. In addition, all first-team players get an £80 appearance fee per match and there's a schedule in the contract showing you how much you'll earn for each round of the cup competitions. For the first six months we'll pay the hotel bill for you and your family at the Tudor Manor Hotel and when you move house we'll pay your removal expenses up to £1,000 as a tax-free relocation fee.'

Finley paused and took a sip of water to let all of this sink in.

'What about the goal bonus?' asked Mr Marland.

'Yes. For every goal you score this season you'll get an additional £250 bonus – this has been added in by the manager this morning, he says it will *motivate you*. We would be grateful if you didn't broadcast this too widely in the dressing room, OK?'

'It's been mentioned in the papers,' said DD.

'Just say the papers got it wrong if anyone asks you,' said Gordon.

Finley went on: 'The contract is of course renegotiable on occasions. Oh, and also, finally, I forgot to mention, you get two new pairs of boots of your choice every season; if you need more you pay for them yourself. We give you a chit and you take it to Miller Sports in town and he'll sort you out. It's Alan Miller's shop and he's a member of the first-team squad although he's injured at present.'

DD was beginning to lose interest and in any event it would be his father who would double-check everything. Tony was a bookmaker from Chatham in Kent. He had struggled at school, but he had a head for figures. As he listened to Stewart Finley going through the deal in a version of Gordon's Scottish voice, he had been calculating the accumulative contract value. He was delighted. His son was now on close to double the deal he started with at Tottenham and with careful handling of the money he would probably never have to work again when he was finished with football. No more investments in London nightclubs; Tony felt that his son had learned that lesson.

At the far side of the room Tilly Foster, Stewart Finley's smartly dressed, smiley and busty secretary, was hovering with paperwork. She smiled even more – albeit like a teacher might smile at a naughty boy – as DD took a pen from her hand and scribbled on the back of the papers she was carrying, 'You know where I'm staying… I'm in the Halliday suite.'

Tilly had a completely innocent yet highly seductive habit of reaching inside her blouse to replace the bra strap that continually slid off her shoulder. DD was sure she was sending him a signal, and he decided that would be seeing her later.

'So that's basically it,' said Finley.

'What about a club car?' Tony Marland asked. 'He has a car at Spurs.'

Stan Moffitt flashed his eyes angrily at his right-hand man. They had developed something of a love-hate relationship since Moffitt brought him into the club. In his textiles firm, Finley just got on with it and held the whole thing together. Here, the big public profile of a top football club created added pressure and tensions, and they spilled out into most of the key relationships at times. But Moffitt knew he could not dispense with Finley the same way as he could a manager or a player. Finley really did know where all the bodies were buried. He could look himself in the mirror and say *he* had done nothing wrong when the Stan Moffitt Stand was being built. But he knew also that Moffitt had done things that he certainly should not have done, not least the bribes and the kickbacks that he took from the builders with whom Finley was doing the deals, and who made the mistake of assuming that Moffitt had brought his club secretary in on the deal. Not to put too fine a point on it, with Finley's near anal attention to detail, and his hoarding of all and every piece of paper that came across his desk, and the personal notes he wrote at the end of each day, he had enough in his safe at home to send Mr and Mrs Moffitt – Gloria was more involved in the club than the average chairman's wife – to prison. It was not something he would ever want to do. But Moffitt would be silly to think it was something his loyal lieutenant was incapable of doing, should the need arise.

'I'm so sorry, Mr Chairman, I completely forgot to mention to

DD and his dad about our agreement with Dougdale's Motors in town. So – our top players each get a Ford Cortina 1600E which can be changed every year. There's an unlimited petrol account at Dougdale's and you get it serviced, taxed and insured for you, all free of charge.'

'Do I get the missus on the insurance?' asked DD.

'Yes, you do. Val Dougdale is a big, big fan of the club and anything else you need car-wise he'll sort for you. In return all you have to do is attend one of Val's works' parties every year and say hello to his staff. It's a bit of a pain as they are all massive fans of the club, but it only lasts a couple of hours.'

He looked around the table.

'So that's it. There's about ten copies to sign. Is everybody happy?'

Amid the nods and the handshakes and the backslaps, DD picked up the silver Parker pen that was lying on the mahogany boardroom table and twirled it between his fingers, his eyes never once leaving Tilly's cleavage as she leaned over to set out the contracts on the table.

Just before he signed on the dotted line he looked up at Stewart Finley. 'What about membership of a golf club?' he asked. 'I play off seven.'

'I'm sure we can advise you on the clubs likely to want to offer you free membership,' said Finley. 'But we won't hold this up for that. OK. Now, sign here ... Oh, and Tilly, Don Robinson from the *Courier* and his photographer are downstairs in reception. They must be bored out of their minds by now. Bring them up.' He also signalled to her that the top two buttons of her blouse were undone, and she might consider doing them up. She did, then trotted downstairs.

Gordon did most of the talking with the *Courier*, DD just saying he was really pleased, and he hoped he could score the goals that reignited the club's season, and then they all headed to the car park where a small crowd of fans had gathered. It was extraordinary how they always seemed to know when something big was happening. Magic Rowland was there too, hovering in the background just in case the boss needed him.

Gordon explained to DD that he would like him to come up to the training ground later so that he could meet his new team-mates and be there for the scouting analysis meeting on Everton.

'Is that my debut?' asked DD.

'We're away at Goodison on Saturday. So we'll see you this afternoon at Summerton Manor, two o'clock sharp. Tomorrow morning, be at the club at nine thirty prompt to meet all the staff and if you are a minute late, there's a twenty-five-pound fine, which we give to a local charity. I'll see you this afternoon at two o'clock, DD, and again, don't be late.'

'He'll be there, gaffer, don't you worry,' said Mr Marland. Gordon smiled, though he hated it when anyone but his players and staff called him 'gaffer'.

The fans, maybe two dozen in number now, clapped as the car drove off and DD waved at them. Gordon signed a few autographs and went back inside. He had an office here at the stadium too, even smaller than the one at Summerton Manor. He went in, took the bottle of Scotch from his drawer, and poured a large serving into his Rangers mug. He always drank from his mug at work. People might misunderstand if they saw him with a glass of Scotch on his desk when they came in. It tasted so much better than the sherry or the champagne he had downed in celebration of the deal being done. He sat at his desk, onto which were Sellotaped the season's fixtures. He marked on the score and their League position week by week.

It was early February and they were just below mid-table. Winning the title, no chance. Top four or five, unlikely but not impossible if they went on a good run. Mid-table finish, probable. Relegation – not impossible. But surely a goalscorer of DD's quality would help them push for a top position, he thought. He liked him even less having spent a bit of time with him. But the chairman had yet again put his hand in his pocket and it was now up to him to make it work. If he didn't, he knew what the outcome would be. It was very much a Moffitt signing. But Moffitt was not the one who would get the blame if the goals didn't begin to flow.

*

At least the signing added a bit of spice to an otherwise dull Tuesday, with pressmen hanging around the gates at Summerton Manor once word got round. Ronnie Winston had taken a light training session in the morning, but then Gordon wanted them out again in the afternoon, DD included. Most players hated Tuesdays. This was the day to work on stamina and fitness, hard work in the gym or long runs over the hills that Gordon loved and most of his players dreaded. Some Tuesdays, they wouldn't even see a ball. But today they needed to see how DD fitted in. You couldn't do that without a ball.

Everton away was not an easy place, though a couple of hours later DD was quick to tell everyone the last time he went there he scored.

'Yeah, but it was only a pen,' said Taffy Rees, who was an Everton fan when not playing against them.

'Only a pen! Are you kidding me? Penalties are the ultimate test of skill under pressure. Only a pen ... fuck me ... no wonder you lot are struggling if that is your attitude.'

Bad start. Players don't like having their attitude questioned.

His first day at the club. Three days to matchday. Not long to get DD used to his new teammates. He already knew winger Frank 'Dipper' Temple, who had played briefly with DD at Spurs. Dipper was now twenty-nine and he'd been at three other clubs since but DD was pleased to accept his invitation for a bite to eat before the afternoon training session which had been specifically arranged for DD's benefit.

The El Greco café, Bridge Street, was on the edge of town, a couple of miles from Summerton Manor. As they placed their order, a couple of excited teenage autograph hunters came over for their signatures.

'What's your name, son?' DD asked the first one.

'Walter,' he said. 'Walter Barton.'

'Well, keep that, Walter, because that is the first signature DD Marland signed for your club. It could be worth a lot one day.'

'Thanks.'

On the radio, the recent Number One hit by the New Seekers, 'You Won't Find Another Fool Like Me', was playing, cause for

DD to tell Dipper about what he would like to do to singer Lyn Paul. And when Suzi Quatro came on next, he moved from nice gentle things he would like to do with Lyn to rather more aggressive sexual activity with the Queen of Leather.

Then from behind the counter came the cheeky-looking serving girl, nervously carrying a menu. 'Mr Marland, can you write "lots of love to Sandra" on this?'

'Course I will, Sandra.'

'Oh no, Sandra's my mum. She's a Spurs fan.'

'Ah, and what about you?'

'I don't go to football, but I basically support whoever George Best plays for.'

'He's nearly finished, love. This'll be his last year at United, mark my words. You want to support a proper team like ours.' And with that he tossed the menu, his name scrawled illegibly upon it, across the table.

Yannis, the café owner, had heard who was there and came over from his house a short drive away, quickly telling Sandra that DD and Dipper were not to be charged for their coffees and cheeseburgers.

'He's got us training again this afternoon,' said Dipper. 'Not sure about a cheeseburger but anyway.'

'It's not going to be a proper session, is it? It's just to give the telly some pictures of me arriving.'

'I guess.'

DD was not exactly hiding the fact that he was the big shot now. And as though to remind Dipper Temple how he had overtaken him, he asked him straight out: 'So what happened to you when you left Spurs? Everybody said you were heading for one of the big three.'

Temple thought for a few seconds before answering.

'To be honest so did I. Tommy Doc had come in for me when he was at Man U because Morgan was getting on and slowing down a bit. Then next minute Morgan signs a new contract; the Doc ends up in a big scandal with the physio's wife and I end up at Newcastle. I'm meant to be the man sending crosses over for Malcolm Macdonald, who they'd just bought from Luton. But my wife just couldn't settle up there, so I asked for a transfer, went to Stoke, and I'd barely been there five minutes when this lot came in for me, eight months ago.'

'And?'

'Good club, DD. We're way better than the League table says.'

'League table never lies.'

'There's no way we are worse than Wolves. If we can just pick up a few points in the next few games, I still think we can be close to the top, then really be in the hunt for trophies next year.'

'What's Gordon like? I can hardly fucking understand him and he's a scruffy git.'

'He's all right. Knows the game inside out. Tactically spot on. Drinks too much I reckon, but who can blame him? Big pressure here. Sandra's little girl might not be a fan but I tell you, I've never known a place like this. I thought Geordies were passionate. This lot think they fucking own you. I'll give you a word of advice. When your missus comes up house hunting, get one a good way out of town. I missed a sitter against Villa last year. I had a fucking delegation outside my door first thing Sunday morning. I've got my little lad in my arms, he was only four months old, and they're all there giving me that "we pay your wages" shit.'

'Does Gordon do the sessions?'

'Bits and bobs. Mainly it's Winston.'

'Used to be at Bradford?'

'Yeah.'

'What's he like?'

'Smart but slimy. Mooro reckons he is after the top job.'

'Right. Interesting.'

They both fell silent for a while as they ate, then DD asked: 'So come on, Dipper, talk me through the squad. Talents, heroes, villains, shaggers, churchgoers, wankers, who's who?'

'To be honest, DD, all I can say is that they're all *a great bunch of lads.*'

'Oh fuck off, Dipper, everyone says that.'

'No, honest, of all the clubs I've been at, this is the best, easy.

Sure, there are some total pricks, but honestly, there is a great mix here.'

'OK, go on then, convince me. Who's in goal? What's his name? Johnson. Used to be Scotland keeper?'

'Yep, Harry Johnson, everyone calls him Jock. He's thirty-nine, oldest player in the First Division, still got it though. And he's the first Scottish keeper I've come across who doesn't have dropsy and in five-a-side he loves playing outfield and I better warn you he kicks the fuck out of everybody. Married, three kids, serious guy. Bound to be his last season, and I reckon he's already sorted with a two-year contract back home. Ayr United, that's where he started. Says he wants to play till he's forty-five if he can. His dad's an estate agent in somewhere called Troon, so when he's finished with football it looks like he'll join the family firm. So that's Jock.'

'Right-back? Is that Dyson?'

'Yeah. Dyce to his face, Clutch behind his back. Don't call him Clutch whatever you do. He is fucking hard. Don't wind him up in training, no point. Let him win a few tackles or he'll have you. He's a fucking nutter basically, but if he likes you, he's a good lad. If he's in a bad mood, just leave him be. He nearly killed George Best two seasons ago. Bestie was taking the piss, beat him, then ran back and beat him again, nutmegged him, whole of Old Trafford was laughing. "Oh shit," I thought, the best player in the League is about to get done. So Clutch goes for him next time, Bestie jumps over him, and Clutch follows through so hard he takes out a fucking cameraman behind the goal; the guy ends up in hospital with a torn kidney. So worth keeping onside with him, believe me.'

'Why's he called Clutch?'

Dipper laughed. 'He was reversing his wife's car into the garage and he got his size eleven stuck under the clutch and wedged on the accelerator. He went right through the back of his brick garage, ran over their dog and ended up in his neighbour's fishpond.'

DD spluttered out a mouthful of coffee, laughing, and Dipper joined in.

'Honestly, DD, forget I told you. Do not ever mention it to Clutch – I mean Dyce.'

'Have you still got that nancy-boy Kilbride at left-back? I fucking murdered him last year.'

'Yeah, Killer.'

'Killer? Are you kidding me?'

'It started as a joke. But he took it seriously, and to be fair it's hardened him up a bit. You're right, we all thought he was a big softy when he came from Birmingham. He's got curly blond hair, pretty-boy blue eyes, five feet six and nine stone wet through. Also he walks a bit, you know, *poofy*. He's worked out because he looks like a nancy he can get away with more than a Clutch or a Chopper Harris. I reckon he has taken out more wingers than Clutch this season.'

'I'll believe it when I see it.'

'He's also a chain smoker. Forty a day. Smokes in the fucking team bath. And if you splash his fag, watch yourself. Clutch and Brownie are the only ones who dare.'

'Is he married?'

'Yeah, two kids. Barbara. She's taller than him.'

'Right-half?'

'Taffy.'

'Welsh, yeah?'

'Taffy Rees. Sixty caps for Wales.'

'Anyone can play for Wales. Just got to have a granny or been there on holiday once.'

'No, he's a player. Workhorse type. Scores goals though, eight last season from defensive midfield. If he had a bit more pace, he'd be a United or Arsenal player. Big pisshead though. Big.'

'How big?'

'I've seen him when he can't remember his own fucking name. But if he has a skinful, he comes in early and runs it off before the gaffer's here. Thinks he can sing too. Once sang in a school choir so with a few beers in him he thinks he's Tom fucking Jones. Coach journeys back from away games, "Delilah" if we win, "Green Green Grass of Home" if we lose.'

'Then Mooro at five, yeah?'

'Yep, Wilf. Capitano, Mr Smooth, Geordie and dedicated follower of fashion. I wouldn't like to see his clothes bill. Never wears the same thing twice. Good player though, good skipper.'

'What's a good skipper do?'

'On the field he makes sure we are doing what we're supposed to. He is a leader, leads by example. Off the field, he makes sure any cash we make from outside appearances gets properly shared, and he makes sure the gaffer knows how people are feeling about life, without ever dropping us in it. The gaffer rates him, big time. He hates all the clothes and the hair shit but he loves him as a player. I think he reminds him of himself.'

'Was Gordon much of a player?'

'Fuck's sake, you serious?'

'Yeah, why should I follow fucking Jocko football?'

'He was a top player, make no mistake.'

'Fair enough.'

'Six is Brownie, David Brown. Got to be honest, I think he is a total arsehole. He's the only one who objects to Mooro's "all share the spoils" policy on outside stuff. Massive gambler, massive. Horses, football, you name it. I reckon he bets on our games sometimes, including to lose. Horrible to the kids and the junior staff. We put up with it because he can still play. He's thirty, maybe thirty-one now, but still got a bit of pace, great first touch, quick, good with both feet, excellent header of the ball and has an engine on him that can't be matched by anyone else. As a player, good. As a human being, twenty-four-carat total cunt. Hate him.'

'Do you want another burger?'

'No, better not, don't want to be chucking up.'

'OK. Hey, Sandra's girl, Mrs Best ... get us another burger, love.'

'So, who's left?'

'Well the most important thing is ... who am I replacing?'

'Not me, I hope. You know all about me – fast, skilful, great reader of the game, fantastic crosser and dead-ball player, all-round good guy.'

'And caps for England?'

'Not my fault. I tell you, if they had picked me ahead of Dave Thomas, we'd have qualified for the World Cup. Looks like it's Norman Nulty who's going to get the chop now that you've arrived. Did well last season but this year the goals have dried up.'

'Yeah, sure, don't worry, it won't happen to me. Who's nine?'

'Jules Pemberton nine, Jinkie Jones ten, Smudger Smith eleven.'

'Smudger? Is that Graham Smith who came through the youth system here? I thought he went to Leeds.'

'Nearly yeah, but Don Revie fell out with the gaffer over it. Smudger is an out and out left-winger, can't play on the right to save his life thank God, so the gaffer says to Revie, "Why do you want another left-winger when you've got Eddie Gray?" And he worked out Revie was buying him to stop him playing for us, and he was just going to dump him in the reserves. But Moffitt is smelling the pound notes and they start at seventy grand then get up to ninety-five but then the gaffer says bollocks to this, I am not selling a player we have built up from his schooldays to sit on the fucking bench for that bent bastard Revie. So he called it off.'

'Mmm.'

'See what I mean about him – he fights for you if he thinks you're being done in.'

'And what's Smudger like as a bloke?'

'Tight as an arsehole. Never spends a penny on anything. Scrounges a lift every morning with whoever will pick him up and he has never bought a drink in his life. He's also fallen under Brownie's spell. Whenever they get the chance they go to the races together.'

'When have we got Leeds next?'

'Three weeks on Saturday.'

'Home or away?'

'Home. Could be your debut. Jack Charlton or Norman Hunter kicking shit out of you, which do you prefer?'

'Saturday's my debut, don't worry about that. What about Pemberton, he any good? Gonna make me any goals?'

'Good header of the ball, good at running in behind... yeah, he should do. Not the brightest, but he works hard. Thing is, the gaffer tries to keep it simple. He's obsessed with analysing where goals come from. Honestly, he couldn't give a shit whether it looks good. Leave that to your Uniteds and your Chelseas. He just wants to win, and that means goals. So what he's after all the time is the ball going out to me and Smudger and we are meant to get the ball into the box, far side of the six-yard box, close to goal but not close enough for the keeper to come and get it, and we're looking for Jules every time and his job is to knock it back towards the penalty spot for one of the midfielders, or back across the box to Nuts, or you, or whoever. If we cross well, and Jules heads it down into the box, and none of the midfield guys or the non-crossing winger are there, Gordon goes fucking ballistic. But you'll learn more about this later when you're spewing up that second burger!'

'So Jules is my main man?'

'I like to think me and Smudger might be too, but yeah, Jules is going to be putting the ball on a plate for you.'

'And what's he like as a bloke?'

'Total hypochondriac; he spends more time on the treatment table than any of us. Always feeling niggles and stuff. But he always makes a miraculous recovery every Friday afternoon, just in time for Saturday's game.'

Dipper looked at his watch and suggested that they'd better get going to avoid a fine.

Yannis came over and told DD he would be welcome any time, free of charge, and would he mind having his picture taken and would it be OK to send it to the local press? So they posed for a few snaps, first Yannis with DD and Dipper, then with DD, and Yannis made him promise that if he scored on his debut he would say it was down to the cheeseburgers.

'Yeah, sure, no problem,' said DD.

As they drove to Summerton Manor the chat continued in the car; they had plenty of time, as it was only 1.45 p.m.

'Come on then, Frank,' said DD, 'I'm guessing these lads are all asking you about me, like I'm asking about them, so what are you saying, eh?'

'You want the truth?'

'Course.'

'Big ego.'

'Yep. Good start.'

'Fancies himself a bit.'

'Spot on.'

'Top player, bags of self-confidence, great speed, can shoot with both feet, eye for the goal, and a pin-up for all the teenage female fans.'

'Just a cross I have to bear, Frank.'

'What about me then?' asked Dipper. 'Come on, what would you say?'

'Sound as a pound. Solid. Reliable. Good crosser. And ugly as sin.'

They laughed, then Dipper told DD about Gordon's approach to game management.

'He has a system of *setting up his team*, as he calls it. First he briefs us all together, then he gives each player three or four key requirements for each game and then he goes through them with you quietly on Monday mornings if you don't deliver. It's a novel system but it works for us.'

'Not been working this season, has it, or else he wouldn't have broken the bank for me.'

'The table's lying.'

'Bullshit.'

When at Spurs, DD normally played golf on Tuesday afternoons, a two-ball foursome, him and Pat Jennings against Alan Gilzean and Phil Beal. He would miss them, and as they drove through the outskirts of this rather sad-looking town, he knew he would miss the south too.

A new club provided a great sense of personal expectation but he knew it would take time before he was as settled here as he had been at Spurs.

'You've got a small squad then,' he said as Dipper turned his Cortina into the tree-lined lane that led to the training ground.

'*We've* got a small squad, you mean? You're here now, not Tottenham bleedin' Hotspur.'

'So what happens when there's an injury?'

'Oh yeah, the gaffer likes to play a settled side, but we have enough squad players. There's Walter Graham, he's usually sub. He's had a number of clubs and looks like he might retire in a year or two. The Prof, we call him, because he does crosswords in the big papers, and he reads books about history and stuff, kings and queens, ancient Rome. He's nearly thirty-three now but he can play anywhere. He scored a great header at Upton Park when Jules came off injured and the boss stuck him up front. Strange, talks with a lisp and has never married. He's the only player the boss didn't bring to the club.

'Dusty Miller gets the odd game too if there's an injury or suspension. He's been at the club ten years and played maybe just ninety or a hundred times. The fans love him though, sing about him even if he's not playing. Blackpool were after him, promised him a regular first-team slot, but he's local. This is his team and he just loves it.'

As they neared the security barrier and the 'no members of the public allowed beyond this point' sign, Dipper slowed the car and the dozen or so autograph hunters crowded round the passenger side window. DD obliged, then passed the books and programmes over to Dipper. They all had little words of gratitude and encouragement for their new star player. Dipper noticed that DD didn't look at any of them, and didn't reply to their questions.

Then as Dipper restarted the engine, a burly steward in a luminous yellow jacket lifted the barrier, welcomed DD with a big smile and let the car through. DD was impressed by the view that opened up before him, beyond a river trickling its way downstream. Six full-sized pitches and one red shale floodlit all-weather pitch for use in wintertime.

'Seven pitches? Nice.'

'What were you expecting? A bog, and whippets running around?'

DD nodded appreciatively, wound down his window to get a better look, and heard the sound of birds and running water.

As they stepped out into the light rain, and Dipper locked his car, he remembered one more player worth a mention. 'Oh yeah, there's a young apprentice who tidies up the dressing room. Now this lad is a threat to me, for sure. He's tiny, comes from Aberdeen; they reckon he's going to be the next Jimmy Johnstone. He is as good a crosser as I've seen. The boss takes apprentices on the odd away trip to get them blooded so it won't be long before you'll see him joining us on a trip somewhere. He's a sensitive kid and Brownie's at him all the time. Gordon has told Mooro that he wants us to give the lad a hard time to see if there's any fight in him off the field. I'm hoping there's not or I'll be looking for another club next season.'

'What's your contract say?'

'Runs out this summer. From what I've seen of him in training he's probably good enough to replace me now. His name is Buchanan, Willie Buchanan.'

7

SUMMERTON

Same day, 5 February, p.m.

It was Percy Summerton who created what many saw as perhaps the best training ground in UK sport. Nevertheless, Stan Moffitt always ensured that he took most of the credit, with the Moffitt Textiles hoardings, and his constant mentioning of the club's investment in the training ground in his interviews and sessions with supporters' clubs. But Summerton, long gone, was the mastermind, and it was a big part of his legacy.

In 1961, he made two visionary moves that would have a long-lasting impact on the success of his football club, and on the game more generally. Firstly, though it meant him ceding some of the power he held, he decided that a football manager should be appointed and made responsible both for recruitment and for team selection. An ex-player, who understood the game, would surely know more about football than the mill owners, builders and accountants he had on his board.

This was at a time when the board had a major say not just in who was signed, but who was picked on a Saturday. It was a nonsense, but it took Summerton to have the guts to say so. What experience did they have, these butchers, bakers and candlestick makers who would go to matches, evaluate players, decide who they fancied, negotiate with the selling club and then select their players in the team?

His second visionary move was to insist that a professional

football club needed professional training facilities. Not long after he became chairman he went to see the players train, and left shocked and bemused that these professionals, who at weekends would play in front of as many as fifty or sixty thousand people, were training in local parks alongside gawping kids and antisocial dog walkers who would think nothing of their dog chasing the ball, or crapping in the makeshift goalmouth. Quietly, without fanfare, he spent months looking and waiting for a piece of land that would provide a suitable 'training ground', as he called it, for the exclusive use of his team.

The negotiations were long and complex, but when they were done, he purchased seventy acres of National Trust land for £4,398 and immediately gifted this to the club on the sole condition that it would, while in the club's ownership, always carry his family name. This isolated rural location, set in the middle of forestry that had to be felled, and split down the middle by the picturesque River Trenton, provided a superb resource for the first team, reserves, A, B and C teams, the youth development squads, and any school teams the scouts wanted to check out. Percy Summerton passed away ten years later, but he left behind a legacy important even to those, like DD Marland and younger fans of the club, who thought Summerton was a place, not the name of that rarity – a football chairman with real vision and foresight.

At five minutes to two, the rain falling more heavily now, DD Marland and Frank 'Dipper' Temple ran down from under the sheltering trees that lined the car park to the entrance of the changing rooms. Ronnie Winston was waiting to greet DD at the front door.

'Welcome on board, big man,' he said, holding out his hand. 'I've been pestering everybody for six months to bring you to this club and finally you're here. There's a great future for you here, son, and that begins today. Come on in, and I'll show you around.'

DD followed in behind Winston, who had completely blanked Frank Temple. Dipper had been looking forward to introducing his old friend DD to his new teammates, but this was typical

Winston behaviour. Mooro was right, he was after the main chance now. By the time Dipper had gathered his thoughts, and calmed his temper, Winston and DD were at the far end of the corridor, outside the medical room, shaking hands and saying hello to people. Dipper walked down and followed them inside. Magic was giving a back massage to Jules Pemberton who had a slight strain following Saturday's match, and was asking to miss the extra training session that afternoon. But Jules was quick to jump off the treatment table to say hello to his new striking partner. They'd played against each other on a few occasions, but never really met.

'Hi, DD. How's it going?' Jules asked as he reached over to shake hands. 'Looks like we might be spending some time to-gether in the odd penalty box.'

'You knock that ball down, Jules, and I will put it in the back of the net.'

'And vice versa, DD. I can score too, you know.'

'Yeah, yeah, course.'

'How was that bastard Mike England when you left?'

DD laughed. England was in the Clutch school of defenders. 'That dirty sod kicked me all over White Hart Lane last season and then after the match, we're in the players' bar, and he comes over and asks if he can buy me a bloody drink.'

DD had a big smile on his face as he replied, 'Ha ha. That's typical Mike England. He's an animal on the field and a gentle-man off it.'

Winston, clearly agitated that he was being cut from the con-versation, stepped between them and brought over Magic to be introduced to DD. 'This is Magic Rowland, the finest physio in English football. If you have an injury you're in at nine o'clock prompt and two in the afternoons. If you're a minute late there's a twenty-five-pound fine and it doubles up every time you're late till you're fit again. The money goes to some hospital charity the boss has chosen.' And with that he strode out of the room, first telling Magic to 'sort out Jules for Saturday', then telling DD to 'follow me . . . first-team dressing room next'.

As they walked slowly down the cream-painted corridor, DD

tried to take in some of the framed quotations in giant letters on the walls. He assumed, the first one being from Celtic manager Jock Stein, that Gordon had selected them. He knew Gordon was a Rangers man at heart, but he had read that he saw Stein as the greatest manager alive, and no doubt shared the view of the Celtic boss that *'There is no excuse for a professional footballer not to be 100 per cent fit.'* Then there was one from the American football coach Vince Lombardi: *'Winning is not a sometime thing, it is an all the time thing. You don't do things right once in a while, you do them right all the time.'* There was a picture of England's World Cup-winning manager Alf Ramsey, and the famous quote he delivered to his players after the end of ninety minutes in the 1966 final against Germany: *'You've won it once. Now you'll have to go out there and win it again.'* Then another from Stein, whose Celtic team was the first British club to lift the European Cup: *'We don't just want to win the European Cup. We want to do it playing good football, to make neutrals glad we won it, pleased to remember how we won it.'* And finally, Benjamin Franklin: *'Fail to prepare and you're preparing to fail.'*

'Who did Benjamin Franklin play for, Ronnie?' DD asked.

'Fuck knows, but knowing the gaffer, I'd take a guess at Queen's Park or Stenhouse-fuckin'-muir. I tell you what, DD, if you want to get onside with him, you should think about wearing a kilt.' They laughed together, and strode into the boot room.

Winston again took control. 'OK, you're on peg eight and your kit number is eight too. Any problems with kit just see Charlie Sinclair. He's been at the club since before football was invented, and he spreads Dubbin on his toast of a morning to keep himself alive.'

Willie Buchanan was standing in the corner, putting kit just back from the club laundry onto the shelves, and looked both dumbstruck and starstruck to see DD Marland.

'You OK, son?' said DD. Willie's silent nod indicated to the new signing that the young apprentice was a fan.

'Where is Charlie Sinclair, young'un?' Winston asked.

'He's in town, Mr Winston, picking up some boots for Mr Rees. He said he'd be back at two thirty so he won't be long.'

Ronnie Winston nodded – no thank you, no introduction to DD, nothing.

Winston led DD to the first-team dressing room where the rest of the squad were waiting. He took him round the players individually. DD recalled his duel with Mooro at White Hart Lane last year, when he won a penalty by forcing the big defender into a clumsy challenge. He bantered a bit with Clutch Dyson telling him Alan Gilzean was still looking for him after that foul in the same game, and he told David Brown that Pat Jennings told him not to try shooting from thirty yards again. All good-humoured stuff. The only moment of tension was when Winston introduced him to Norman Nulty, who understood as well as anyone that DD was likely to take his place. He did his best to smile and not look churlish, but it was obvious to everyone he was hurting inside, and Winston didn't help when he said, 'Chin up, Nuts, we've all been there.'

It was always a strange time in a dressing room when a costly new signing arrived. Each player understood that one day their legs would go, or their nerve would go, and it would be their turn to be replaced. So there was a modicum of sympathy for Nuts, but it was a fact of life that he had averaged a goal every three games last season, and this year it was working out at one goal for every five matches. He knew it wasn't good enough, and his work rate and confidence had taken a hammering. Seeing DD Marland stroll in with his expensive clothes and his cocky manner wasn't going to help the confidence one bit. It wasn't just pride at stake either. The loss of appearance money and win bonuses wouldn't go down well at home, where in Naomi he had one of the more expensive wives of the team. And if it became clear he was never going to get back in, that meant finding another club, probably taking a drop in wages and another house move, just as his two daughters, aged seven and five, were settled in their first school. Naomi would kill him if they had to move on again. Players had next to no control over which team they joined next. The manager would simply call them in and say, 'We've just sold you to Plymouth, they're expecting you first thing in the morning. Bye.'

Naomi was a real character. The other players liked her because she had worked in fashion, and she now ran a little sideline making novelty ties, and most of the players had bought some. They especially liked the ones with their own pictures on them. Mooro had a dozen of those. She was a big spender though, and her earnings were not going to keep her in the manner to which she was accustomed. Nuts had to fight for his place now, but his teammates sensed it was a losing battle from the start.

Winston told the players to get changed into their kit, said it would be a light session; the TV cameras would be there for the first part, 'so the gaffer will want to be there for a bit'. This time, Mooro was not alone in detecting the clear dig. To be fair to Winston though, he knew exactly how Gordon would want to run the session, to show DD in particular what was expected of him, and in preparation he had already been out to lay out the cones and markers.

Trainer George Brady, Number Three in the coaching hierarchy, had driven the boss down to Summerton Manor from the stadium and they had both arrived kitted out in club tracksuits at 1.30, giving Gordon a little time to prepare his thoughts and his words.

Winston knocked and burst through the door, both at the same time. Fortunately Gordon had not opened the miniature whisky in his hand and he carefully slipped it back into the top drawer of his desk.

'Everybody's ready, boss. Shall I get 'em out and warm 'em up?'

'No, not yet, Ronnie, I need a private chat with someone first.'

'DD?'

'No, Norman Nulty.'

Winston headed back to the dressing room and, as if Nulty wasn't feeling low enough, he dragged him even lower.

'Nuts, get a move on. Boss wants to see you. In his office. Now.'

Everyone stopped talking. They knew what the conversation would entail. Black humour was always the best way to puncture a mood like this one, and David Brown was usually the first to react. 'Take a phonebook and stick it down the back of your shorts, Nuts. You're in for a spanking the way you've been playing.'

Jock Johnson's jibe was less amusing, a lot more biting and sarcastic, and evidence that Winston's undermining campaign was working with the players. 'More likely he'll say as you're not needed to play now, can you go down the offy and get him a bottle of Scotch?'

Although Nuts was about to lose his place in the team, he hadn't lost his banter skills.

'Well, he sure wouldn't ask you, Jocko, 'cos he knows given your form you'd fucking drop it.' Cue clapping and shouting of 'Jocko Jocko what's the score? One-nil to the Nuts.'

As he walked down the corridor to Charlie Gordon's office the motivational statements he had seen so many times meant little to him right now, though the one that stopped him short was Jock Stein saying there was no excuse for a lack of fitness. Was it fitness, or form that he had lost? Either way, he knew what was coming.

He tapped on the door.

'Come in.'

He pushed open the door. Gordon rose from his chair and motioned to Nuts to sit down. He sat, and noticed the NB carving on the front of Gordon's desk, telling himself that right now they stood not for Nat Broadbent, but Nulty Bollocksed.

'That's it, Norman, sit yourself down. Do you want a mint?' Gordon asked as he took a couple from the bowl ever present on his desk and popped them into his mouth. Nuts shook his head. Gordon had a soft smile on his face, and he looked Norman straight in his eyes.

'I won't beat around the bush, Norman. You're a senior player, a grown man, and I am not going to insult you with bullshit. You know as well as I do, things are not going well for you this season. Some of it is bad luck, but when your job is to score goals and the goals aren't coming, I have to do something. You understand me?'

Nulty nodded sadly.

'So the bottom line is, I'm leaving you out for the Everton game.'

'Yeah.'

'But,' Gordon said with heavy emphasis, 'I still want you to travel with us. You won't be substitute, but I want you to feel you're still part of my team. And if we win or draw I'll make sure you also get the match bonus.'

'Thanks. Thanks, boss, yeah.'

'Nuts, let me be frank, you've now got a clear choice. You can either plod around the place with your chin on your chest and blame the world for your bad luck... or, you can come out fighting and dedicate yourself to winning your place back. That means going to bed an hour earlier, getting here first of a morning, staying back in the afternoons for extra training and in simple terms working your bollocks off till you're back in the team and not allowing *any* obstacle to stop you. You understand me?'

'Yeah.'

'You're not a bad player, Norman, or else you wouldn't be here. You're a good player going through a bad patch and only you can get yourself out of it. DD is a good player, but he's not Kenny Dalglish or Joe fucking Jordan. You can win your place back but not by sulking, not by going on the piss or going off the rails, or by hoping he breaks his leg when Norman Hunter's on him, but by hard work, effort, showing me and everyone else you've got a bit of fight, a bit of resilience. You understand me?'

'I do, gaffer, yeah. I'm sorry I've not done it for you this season. I really am. But I'll give it a go.'

'Good lad. OK. Tell them I'll be through in five minutes when I've had a pee.'

That is why the players still like him, Nuts said to himself as he walked back. He's basically just fired me. But I don't feel like I've been fired. Fired up maybe. Not fired. How fitting was the quotation closest to Gordon's office, from someone called Joe Kennedy, who he assumed was a Scottish footballer or manager of yesteryear.

'When the going gets tough, the tough get going,' it read. That had to be his mantra now, or else he was done.

Inside, a fire was starting to burn and he was thinking, 'I'll show these bastards who can score goals at this fucking club . . . and nothing's going to stand in my way.'

Brownie was the first face he saw and the first voice he heard.

'So what was it? The cane, or a new contract?'

'Neither, Brownie, he was just trying one of his riddles on me.'

'What you on about?'

'He just asked me, "How do you keep a dickhead in suspense?"'

'So what did you say?'

'I'll tell you later.'

The laughter rang around the room. Mooro and Dipper went over to pat Nuts on the back.

'Now, you lot,' Nuts said, 'the gaffer told me to tell you he wants you all in the team room, now.'

8

COLLEEN

Colleen Connor had eaten her bacon and eggs in front of the telly, read for a bit then gone to bed for an early night, and slept as soundly as she had since moving to London. This is what she was made for, she knew it. The cold didn't bother her, the creaky bed and the irritating nylon sheets didn't bother her, the stupid gas meter that guzzled her coins, none of it bothered her, because all of it was necessary for what she was there to do. She had dreamt of home, and her mother bent over the fire as she walked in to surprise her, and she rushed to give her a hug, then the dog jumped up at them both, and her mother asked if she was eating well, because she looked so thin, and her dad was sitting there stern-faced, and simply said, 'You know not to ask these kind of questions.' She smiled to herself on remembering it as she brushed her teeth, her eyes as always focused on the scar that moved around her face as the brush did its work.

As she went to buy her cigarettes in the corner shop close to her house, her mood was lifted even further by the front pages of all the newspapers and their pictures of yesterday's carnage, and headshots of the dead and dying. She then made her way to Ealing Broadway, glad for the light rain which meant she could wear a large hat, the rim down almost over her eyes, and her hair tucked in tight. She walked first into a record shop, and browsed, then out and into the electrical goods store four doors down, where she half-heartedly looked at a few lights, irons and kettles, one eye always trained on the door. Then, as rehearsed once a fortnight since she had been living in London, she left by the rear exit, stopped and waited for two minutes to ensure there was nobody following her out.

She then caught the No. 65 bus to the High Street and strode the five hundred yards to Woodville Road, retracing her journey several times. She was also thinking ahead to her next visit, when an entirely different route would be needed.

When she arrived at 61 Woodville Road, at exactly ten past nine, she lifted the large green plant pot concealed behind a dustbin, and found the Yale key she had been told would be there. She let herself in, pleased that the front door had been repainted dark blue – the emerald green of old was a tiny risk, but no risk was too tiny now. There was very little furniture in the house, and no people, but it was here that she was to meet Peter and Paul. Her own name was now Pamela, and the codename for the whole exercise was 3Ps. They didn't need to know each other's real names. They didn't need to know anything about each other at all, just that they had been chosen. They were soldiers in an IRA Active Service Unit, not friends.

At bang on quarter past nine, she heard another key going into the lock, and the door opened, closed, and then a man came through to join her in the bare, uncarpeted front room. Colleen went over to shake his hand. 'I'm Pamela.'

'Yeah, right. And mine is Peter or Paul or some fucking thing. Fucking silly codename bullshit.' He walked past her, avoiding her hand.

He was tall, maybe six feet, but skinny, weighed little more than nine stone. He was in his early thirties probably, but bald. Colleen placed the accent closer to Derry than Belfast. She guessed this was the engineer she had been told would be part of the team, reckoned to be one of their best new bomb-makers. Colleen wondered if he had had anything to do with yesterday, but didn't ask. It seemed odd, given most people in Britain were talking of nothing else, that neither of them mentioned the M62 coach bomb in the few minutes they had together. She sensed that he didn't like the fact that a female was part of the team.

Her new colleague was badly dressed, in shabby torn denims and white Puma trainers that had seen better days. The collar on his red checked lumberjack shirt was worn. He needed a shave and had an odour that he left in his wake.

'So what have you done to deserve being here, girl? Or are you just around to make the tea or perform a few tricks if the mood takes us?' He sniggered without looking at her. She said nothing.

'Is there a fucking kettle in this dump?' he asked.

'Yeah. Let me get you a cup of tea, seeing how you think that is my job.'

'That's fuckin' good of you – milk, three sugars.'

'I'm not sure there is any milk. We'll need to get some.'

'Black is fine. Four fuckin' sugars though.'

'So Pa-me-la,' he asked, mocking her codename as Colleen went to fill the kettle. 'Do you reckon I'm Peter or Paul?'

'You're Peter.'

'Yep. I wish they had given us names that didn't make us sound like a bunch of fucking budgies. Pamela, Peter and Paul, fuck me, couldn't they have made it Pete, Paddy and Pussy?' Again, he laughed at his own crudeness.

'Might be a bit obvious. Like the green door.'

'Yeah. Who chose fuckin' Tory blue though? That you, girl? Or would you like it painted pink?'

'No. I just said I thought green was stupid.'

'Can you get them to fix the fucking heating in here too? It's fucking freezing.'

'So where is Paul?' she asked, fervently hoping the third of the Ps would arrive soon.

He laughed, then said, 'He's always fuckin' late, except when it matters. Do you want to know his real name?'

'Not unless he wants me to.'

So they did know each other, thought Colleen. They were veterans. She was the novice. But they were novices once, she told herself. No need to feel inferior.

She found a couple of chipped mugs in a cupboard above the sink, which was also chipped and cracked around the plughole.

She wondered if the IRA actually had any houses that people might want to live in. The Formica worktops were scratched and badly worn. But the kettle worked well enough, there was a box of Tetley tea bags, and once she found the sugar, she was in business.

There were four chairs in the kitchen, two armchairs and two straight-backed wooden chairs with cushions tied on, but 'Peter' chose to stride around the room as he slurped his tea noisily, not taking his eyes off her when he slowly sat down.

'Fucking tea without milk is fucking shite,' he said.

'Yeah, sorry about that.'

'Yeah. Don't suppose it's your fault.' It was a rare sentence from her new housemate without the word 'fuck' or 'fucking' in it.

'What the fuck is that on your face, girly? Looks like you've been in a fucking car crash, or did you just cut yourself shaving?' He laughed as he took another loud slurp of his tea.

As he laughed she grabbed her mug, smashed it against the fireplace and dived at him from across the table. She grabbed his throat with her spare hand and brought the broken cup to his eye socket. As they fell to the floor the chair leg snapped and she landed on his chest, pinning him to the floor with the broken cup now inches from his eyeball.

She bent forward and whispered in his ear, 'Now listen carefully, you streaky piece of shit. Don't – fuck – with – me. I won't say this again. If you call me "girl" just one more time, it might be the last time you ever see. Is that clear?

'We are here to do a job, and if you mention fucking again, when I'm within earshot, you might find that you'll have nothing to fuck with. Is that also clear, you slimy, smelly twat?'

She slowly climbed from his chest and quietly sat back at the table as he looked up not quite believing what had just happened. A few seconds later, still shaken, he got to his feet and without a word he too sat back at the table next to the broken chair.

'Now drink your tea,' said Colleen, 'and let's start all over again. OK?'

His gaze was frozen as he now looked at her face not her body, and he nodded hesitantly and took a sip from his mug.

'Hi, I'm Pamela,' she said, extending her hand.

He took it, shook it limply and said, 'I'm ... Peter.'

'There,' she said, 'wasn't so hard now, was it?'

9

TEAM TALK

Ronnie Winston, acting in his self-appointed role as manager elect, sat in the chair facing the group, and told them of his impressions of Everton when he had gone to see their recent game against Blackburn Rovers. Vulnerable at set-pieces, that was his main point, one he was making for the third time as Gordon walked in. Winston quickly vacated the seat and retreated to the corner of the room, saying, 'Right lads, quiet now. Over to you, boss.'

Gordon was not looking good. Half of his shirt was hanging out at the front. His suit seemed too small, especially the trousers around the stomach. His jacket was stained and creased and it was a good job his mother wasn't there to see his scuffed shoes caked with the mud that had formed in the short sandy lane that led from the car park.

As he began, it was his mother who popped into his mind again, another of her little trilogy homilies – '*in any workplace there are always likely to be three people who hate you*'. Who were his three? Winston was Number One, he was becoming more and more certain of that. But his mum had ended the advice by saying, 'You'll never find out who they are, so just get on with it.' So he did.

'Thanks, Ronnie. Now, gentlemen... gentlemen... gentlemen. Can I begin with a warm, warm welcome to Daniel David

Marland – you didn't know that was his name did you? Nor did I till I saw the contract, but I am very pleased he signed it. He is a top player and we now have, I believe, one of the strongest squads of players in the division. So come on, let's hear it . . . round of applause.'

The players clapped with varying degrees of enthusiasm, and once DD had nodded his appreciation in all directions, and they settled down, the real business began. His tie may have been askew, his left shoelace undone, his jacket stained and his hair a mess, but Gordon was on top form. They were listening, no doubt about that.

'Gentlemen, at the start of the season I predicted that by now, early February, we'd be in the top six. I was wrong, wasn't I? We find ourselves in twelfth place, just below mid-table. There is just one reason for this – a lack of goals. Nothing else. If I've said this once over the last seven years, I've said it a thousand times, and I will keep saying it until I am inside a coffin and on my way to my maker. It's only GOALS that matter.'

Gordon paused as his eyes scanned the group in front of him.

'What's our sport called, DD?'

'What?' asked Marland, taken aback suddenly to be asked a direct question in front of people he hardly knew.

'The game we play, what's its name? Not a trick question, son. Begins with F.'

'Football, boss.'

'Correct. But you know something? Whoever called it *Football* in eighteen-whatever-it-was got it badly wrong. The game should be called *Goals*. Or OK, if they are determined to mention the ball part of it – *Goalball*. Why? Because you can play the best bloody football on the planet and some rough-arsed bunch of thugs from Leeds or Sheffield can watch your glorious display, applaud your brilliance, be mesmerized by your talent, be under siege for eighty-nine minutes and then break away and score one goal more than you, and you've lost the match. Does that ring a bell, Mooro?'

'It does, gaffer, Sheffield Wednesday, last month. Battered them, and lost.'

'Exactly. Jock, you've been around a few years. Which is a better team, us or Sheffield Wednesday?'

'We are, boss.'

'And where are they in the League, Jinkie?'

'I dunno. Eighth, ninth.'

'Seventh. Sheffield fucking Wednesday, several places higher than us. And why? Anyone?'

'Goals, gaffer,' said Taffy Rees.

'Goals, Taff. Goals. So we are better than some of the teams above us. But if we don't score the goals that show it, they stay above us. Simple, lads. Simple. It's a very simple game. Crazy, oh yes. It's a crazy game, drives me crazy every day of my fucking life. But it is simple. It's just Goals, Goals and Goals.

'And before any one of you half-wit defenders starts moaning *"What about us, boss, don't we have a job in the team?"* I'll remind you I was a defender, I know as much as the next centre-back that defending matters, but here's the thing: in every game there are two types of goals, the ones you score, and the ones you concede.

'So the reason we have meetings like this, when you'd rather be running around a field, and you have to sit there and listen to an old has-been like me who never earned more than twelve quid a week when he was an international player, is to remind you cash-rich superstars – in your dreams – that it's only *goals* that matter, and nothing else. So come on, Brownie, remind me – what are the two types of goals?'

'The ones you score, and the ones you let in.'

'Correct. So when we work through the plan for Everton this afternoon and welcome DD into the team, I want us all to concentrate on those two things alone – how we score goals at one end, how we stop goals going in at the other. The fancy bits in between can take care of themselves.'

He was then back to talking to DD again. 'So, DD, I've made you feel good, now you make me feel good. So far, is this a better team talk than you got under Billy Nicholson?'

'Way better, gaffer,' said DD, loudly, and the players cheered.

'Good. That is what I want to hear. Now, let me tell you how

this magic is achieved. To score goals we need three sets of players. Firstly we need thoroughbred, athletic, instinctive, brave and
majestic *forwards*, now becoming known as *strikers* you may have
noticed. These are the golden boys who will win us the game.
Beautiful women drool after them and throw their knickers in
their path out of pure lust and wonder. Hands up if you think
we have our share of these, especially now DD has joined.'

Up went virtually every right arm in the room.

'So they score goals. Now, Smudger, what do we need to do
at the other end?'

'Stop the ball going in our net.'

'Correct. And for that we need a good goalkeeper for sure, but
we also need big, stupid, child-eating, low mentality, horrible,
nasty and ugly *defenders* to kick lumps out of the other team's
strikers, in such a way that the referee doesn't notice.

'White-haired old ladies lie awake at night dreaming that one
of these will come into their lives and push their wheelchairs.'

The forwards were now pointing at the defenders and laughing.

'So do we have some of these big, stupid, child-eating, low
mentality, horrible, nasty and ugly *defenders*...?'

'Less of the ugly,' shouted Mooro above the din of most of the
players yelling their agreement with the question.

'And finally,' Gordon went on quietly, almost whispering for
effect, 'to make all this possible we need some oil in the engine,
some grease. Everything good in life needs a bit of lubrication,
whether it's a good hinge, a good car or a good shag. And our
grease, gentlemen, comes from short-arsed little midfield players
who in between working their bollocks off fetching and carrying
the ball for the golden boys, need to be in the opponents' box
to score goals themselves, and then they must run like hell back
into their own box to assist their Goliath defenders to stop *goals*
going in.

'Middle-aged women with varicose veins, bulging arses and
sagging tits are attracted to these box-to-box boys, and never
feel threatened in their company.'

'Bullshit,' shouted Taffy Rees.

'Not at all, my little Welsh friend. This is the simple truth about our crazy game. So, so simple, and we are going to keep it that simple from now on. Big bad defenders battering their forwards, box-to-box midfielders, and forwards doing what we know they have to do, sticking the ball in the net so we have a ... Jules, what do we get if we put the ball in the net?'

'A goal, gaffer.'

'Correct, and what do goals do, Prof?'

'They win games, gaffer.'

'You see? Prof is the brainy one, and he gets it. Goals win games. So let's fucking do it, shall we? DD, you now have the philosophy. You have just heard my scholarly and erudite explanation regarding the science of football. You all now know what is expected of you, and you all now know very clearly your position in this team. So let's get out there on the field and show Mr Daniel David Marland what this plan is all about, and why it is going to see us climbing up that table, starting with a win at Goodison "Toffee" Park.'

And with that, as he leaned against the wall, he was touched to see Wilf Moore start a round of applause that was far louder than the one for DD earlier in the meeting.

'Enough, enough,' protested Gordon, putting his hands up. 'Any questions?'

Jules Pemberton was first to shout up.

'Can we go and train?'

'Fuck me, that's a first,' said Magic Rowland.

'Yes, Jules,' said Gordon. 'We can go and train. Let's go.'

As they filed out, Mooro found himself alongside Ronnie Winston.

'He's still got it, eh Ronnie?' he said. Winston nodded, unsmiling, then jogged ahead, into the rain.

With the buzz from the Glenfiddich wearing off, Gordon made his way across the first-team pitch alone. Thinking that the game was getting much too complicated for an old pro like him, one day, he supposed, it might be possible for someone who had never played at the top level, like Winston, to become a top manager. But managers need their players to respect them. And the one thing they all at least knew about Gordon was that he had been a decent player. He won his first cap for Scotland at twenty-one but, thanks to George Graham's small-mindedness, played for them just thirty-four times, and never played in a World Cup.

In the main, players liked training in the rain, even when it was falling as fast and hard as now. It kept you cool, it softened the ground and quickened the game. It was wind they hated. As Clutch Dyson once poetically put it, 'rain is rank but wind is wank'.

To start the session Charlie Gordon took the forwards and three midfield players, while Ronnie Winston set up a session for the defence at the other end of the field. It was important that DD understood the manager's game plan. He had already learned that team talks here were different. He was now learning that training sessions, and Gordon's game plans, were too.

Once everyone had moved into their positions, Gordon took control, shouting from the centre circle.

'OK, Brownie, you feed the ball down the wing to Smudger; Smudger, it's your job to move down to somewhere between the eighteen-yard line and the dead-ball line, then float the ball over *past* the far post. Jules, when that ball comes over you should know just where to be and I want you to head it as near as possible to the penalty spot, where you'll find Jinkie, Taffy Rees or Dipper, just waiting to smack it in. Jink, Taff, Dip, you've got to be on your toes and predict where Jules is going to head the ball. I don't mind if you miss the target, but if you are not queuing up to get a shot in, I'll run on the field and kick the shit out of you. Do you understand me?'

'Yes, boss.'

He then moved down the field to speak one-to-one with his new signing. 'DD, this is what I'm expecting from you. You are the predator; you're the one who needs to read every situation. Wherever that ball breaks in the eighteen-yard box you've got to give yourself the best chance of being on the end of it. Sometimes Smudger will hit the ball short; it's then your job to predict this and get a header in at goal from the near post. Sometimes Jules will head the ball short of the penalty spot, or past it, or their keeper might drop it; again it's your job to anticipate this and be there to smack it in. This is called instinct. I can't tell you what to do, I just know that all the great goalscorers can smell a goal before it happens; it's in their genes. As a kid you must have watched Jimmy Greaves at White Hart Lane – he was the master. On other occasions *Smudge* will send the ball short of the far post; that's when it's Jules's job to get his header in at goal. OK?'

'Yes, gaffer.'

'Right,' Gordon yelled, now addressing the whole squad, 'you all know what I'm expecting of you, so let's give it a try.'

He walked to the touchline to watch, but made sure to have another private word with DD en route.

'Son, I *can* tell you how goals are scored; but I *can't* tell you how to smell them out. All I do is set the scene. You're the one who sniffs the perfume, steals the show, marries the Princess and banks the money. Just go and make it happen.'

Time and again for the next twenty minutes, the players started from the same position, and tried to do the same thing. The first couple of Smudger's crosses were overhit, but the third was perfect, Jules met it, nodded it down, Dipper was there to hit it goalwards, Jocko saved it but failed to hold it and DD tapped in the rebound.

'Goooooaaaaaal!' screamed Gordon from the sideline. 'It wasn't pretty, DD, but it counts the same as a forty-yard volley. OK, we go again.'

And so they did, and again, and again, and again... DD converted his fair share and generally linked well with Jules Pemberton considering this was their first session together. It felt good. Gordon could tell DD knew exactly what was expected of him. He felt he had an *edge* – the manager called it *an achiever's edge* – and now he had met his new teammates properly, he sensed DD was impatient to put it into practice in a match situation. He hoped he was impressed, too, that he made a point of involving Norman Nulty in the session, as an extra midfielder, and how hard Nulty was trying to make a mark. If he was sulking at DD taking his place, he wasn't showing it. Gordon went over to Nulty at the end of the session, put his arm around him and said, 'You did well there, Norman.'

As Gordon headed inside, he spotted Willie Buchanan, who had been watching the training session through the laundry window as he fed last Saturday's unwashed kit into the Hotpoint. Gordon gave him a little wave. The boy looked a lot more relaxed.

He was then joined by Charlie Sinclair, with one of his useful bits of intelligence.

'Stock alert,' he said.

'Not again?'

'Yeah, he was watching the whole session, from behind the poplars.'

'Is he a fucking saddo or what?'

Of all the directors, Matthew Stock was the most regular visitor to the training ground, sometimes openly, other times covertly. Although everyone was polite to him, he knew he wasn't welcome. But Gordon knew this caused him little concern. Stock had a thick skin. He was one of those directors who had always wanted to be a footballer, but a lack of skill, parents who preferred rugby, and one leg shorter than the other meant he had no chance. At school, he was bullied, and excluded from playground matches.

Having realized he would never be a player, and knowing that only former players made it as managers, relatively young he had set himself the ambition of one day owning a top club, then no one would dare to make fun of him. He was well on his way, having been a director for twelve years and having built his insurance firm into one of the biggest in the region. He felt like he was more than halfway up the ladder. Gordon had little doubt about Stock's long-term game plan. One day, Moffitt would be gone, Gordon would be gone. He would still be there, and he was determined one day to be chairman. For now though, with a game looming and a new player to bed in, Gordon had enough to worry about without getting overly fussed about the ambitions or the bizarre snooping of Matthew Stock.

*

Given the nastiness of the moment, and the slight cut to 'Peter's' face, then despite the pleasantries of their reintroduction, and the shared attempt to 'start all over', Colleen could have done without 'Paul' being late.

He"d finally arrived at 9.40, over twenty minutes behind schedule, full of apologies, explaining he'd been out late last night with a pal from the football world, and then to a meeting up Kilburn way.

'Would you like me to make you a nice cup of tea?' asked Colleen.

'Yep, just what I need,' he replied, producing a pint of milk from the small black rucksack he was carrying.

He noticed the trickle of blood on 'Peter's' cheek.

'Are you OK?'

'Yep, fine, just caught myself on the cupboard door.'

'Do you want sugar?' asked Colleen.

'Just the one,' replied 'Paul'.

'Will you be wanting another cup, "Peter"?' she asked.

'No, I'm fine,' he said nervously.

'Everything OK here?' asked 'Paul', sensing an undercurrent in the conversation.

'Yeah, all good,' said 'Peter'.

'All good,' echoed Colleen.

'Good, that's good then.'

'Paul' waited for the tea to arrive, added his own milk, then said: 'So here we are, the 3Ps. Have you ever heard such a trio of stupid sounding names?'

'We've done that one,' said 'Peter'. 'Move on.'

'OK, I will... nice to see you're in a good mood... "Peter".' The tone confirmed to Colleen that they knew each other well, and there was a tension there. She was very much the new girl.

'Now,' he went on, 'remember we are not here as friends, colleagues, buddies or even workmates. We are here as a small team to do a job, and sorry for the 3Ps nonsense, but it helps if we don't really know each other's true identities. If any of us gets caught they can torture us all they want, the worst they will get out of us is a codename. So let's all stay focused on the job and then maybe we'll never see each other ever again.' Colleen could tell, as 'Peter' stared at her, that the thought seemed to please him.

'Paul' apologized again for not arriving on time, but said: 'You should be happy I'm a bit late, as I was delayed on the Circle Line because that whole Fleet Street area is still screwed up after the letter bomb thing.'

'Nobody fucking died though, did they?' said 'Peter'. 'The coach up north, that was a proper job, that was.' Colleen wondered whether he was trying to convey a little pride of authorship, have them think he had been responsible.

'Two more dead this morning,' she said. 'I heard people talking about it on the way over.'

'Hey, give us some of that milk, will you now?' said 'Peter', and Colleen went to pour him some.

Though 'Peter' liked to play the hardman, and impose himself on all around him, his false confidence had now been shattered, first by Colleen's threat, now by 'Paul's' arrival. 'Paul' was the undisputed boss of this little team. His job was to plan the mission, oversee the reconnaissance and coordinate the assembly of the bomb that 'Peter' would be responsible for making. He'd been given this job because of his success in three previous missions. He had also impressed his superiors by collating a list of possible high-profile targets, culled from a mix of public and private sources. He knew where all the top civil servants and politicians lived. He knew their car registration numbers. He knew who the main military advisers within the MoD and the Northern Ireland Office were. He knew which judges travelled by which routes to the High Court, and he had done a lot of the research unaided and without being asked to. He had even managed to get hold of the pathetic video the Home Office had made for potential targets. The advice was basically 'look under your car, and don't trust strangers who offer you packages'. He was a self-starter, Colleen could see that, and while 'Peter' shouted and bawled to show his strength and assuredness, 'Paul' just emanated it. Colleen took a liking to him as instant as the dislike she had taken to the third P, whose whole demeanour, she was glad to note, had changed since the incident with the mug.

'OK,' said 'Paul'. 'Pull up a chair. You must be "Pamela", yeah?' he added as he offered Colleen Connor a warm handshake and stared at the scar across her face, nodding knowingly.

'So "Peter" and I have worked together before. We know each other, trust each other, kind of, and when either of us asks you to do something, you do it, OK?'

Colleen nodded. 'Sure, yeah. I know my place. I'm just glad to be here.'

'This house has been used before. Good area. Good for airports. Good for key areas of London from Ealing Broadway Station. And nobody ever checks on their neighbours. But it goes without saying, we do nothing, nothing, to draw attention to ourselves. We will probably only use this place three or four times. Meantime we all stay wherever it is that we're staying now. When we are here, we leave the house alone, we come in alone. We make no noise. We play no music. We drink nothing stronger than water. And we never bring anyone back here for a fuck. Is that understood?'

She nodded.

'Peter' grunted his assent.

This tiny cell would receive funding both for all living expenses and all materials needed – and 'Paul' had a large petty cash fund to buy anything, or pay any bribes – to make the operation a success. But most of what they required would be brought to London by mainly female couriers working out of the south. They also had a network of sympathizers who worked on the ferries, trains, airports, airlines and baggage handling centres, who often got the volunteers and the couriers out of tight spots. In their last mission together, 'Paul' and 'Peter' had put together a 36lb bomb with materials variously brought in via car door panels, make-up bags, ship containers or, for the key parts, on fishing boats with midnight landings on the vast Lancashire and Cumbrian coastlines.

'OK, this is what's going to happen. At the next meeting we'll know both the date and the target. "Peter", it's your responsibility to manufacture and deliver the device. I know you've done it a few times before so you know the ropes. As at this stage we don't know all the details of the target, I can't tell you the size or the weight of what we need. You'll find that out at the next meeting. We'll also know the exact location but it's going to be a central London hotel.'

He explained that elsewhere, at another London address known only to him, a batch of gelignite wrapped in a cotton cloth, packed in sawdust inside an old leather suitcase, had already arrived via the Cumbrian route. Nitroglycerine had also arrived, and was on its way south from Barrow in a volunteer's car.

'"Pamela", once we have the location, it'll be your job to place the thing, and "Peter" will be with you to set the timer. You must both keep an eye out every day in the *Standard* for the date of the next meeting, when I'll have much more information. Today is just our first date and a chance for us to get to know each other and check out this place. Some smart arse in Belfast has given this unit the codename 3Ps and only we know that. We are going to become the 4Ps because we have another guy who will be joining us.'

'Who?' asked 'Peter', as ever suspicious of outsiders.

'He's called Paddy.'

'Real Paddy or code Paddy?'

'Real Paddy. He works in the hotel, and he is the one feeding us the info we need.'

'So why can't you tell us which hotel?' asked Peter irritatingly.

'Because I don't fucking know until I need to know, and when I need to know, they will fucking tell me, and when you need to know, I will fucking tell you. OK?'

'So what did we need to meet for today?'

'Oh, you had other plans did you? So sorry.'

Colleen spoke. 'I think it is good we got the chance to meet.'

'Exactly,' said 'Paul'. 'Also, I needed to tell you, "Pamela", to be at home at eight o'clock each morning until I tell you otherwise.'

She nodded.

'I am going to be getting a call when we have confirmation

of the hotel, and we are going to have to check out this Paddy guy from all angles. We think he stands up, but we need to keep checking, and we're going to be asking you to track him once in a while. OK?'

'Sure. Eight o'clock. I'll be there. You know where, yeah?'

'Yep, I do. OK, now, before we leave today, "Peter", clean the place up and wash the cups, we mustn't leave anything behind. "Pamela", you leave by the back door and him and me'll leave through the front door in an hour or so. Are there any questions?'

There weren't.

'Next time we meet, "Peter", you're the one who's always moaning about milk, so you bring the milk – and a few biscuits would be good?'

'Peter' snorted, and asked: 'Any idea when?'

'You know not to ask, we just wait till we hear. It could be a week or it could be a month, I don't know, but we've got momentum and something really big is going to happen very soon.'

'Bigger than yesterday?'

'Yesterday should have been bigger than yesterday. Someone fucked up with that letter bomb.'

Colleen sensed strongly that 'Paul' had also been part of the M62 bombing plan. She was struggling to hide her excitement that whatever it was she was involved in now could be even bigger.

She asked if the operation had anything to do with the election, now just a few weeks away.

'Don't know yet. Makes no fucking difference anyway. Wilson, Heath, when it comes to Ireland, they're peas in a fucking pod. That slimy bastard Wilson and his nodding-dog Rees need to know there is going to be no peace for the wicked if they win. But we may just have to bide our time, OK?'

Colleen asked if they wanted another tea. 'Paul' answered for both of them. 'No, we are nearly done for now. Keep getting the *Standard*, next time all it will say is "*Happy Birthday granddad, 75 years old today, all our love, Peter and Pamela*." Same page.

Same timings to be here. By then we will have a date and a target.

'OK, first in, first out. Any questions before you go?'

Colleen shook her head. 'Peter' stood and put on his brown khaki cap.

'"Pamela",' said 'Paul'. 'Just one thing – and don't take this the wrong way. The single biggest cause of things going wrong is loose lips. It's young men swaggering too much, saying too much to some bird they want to shag, or some bloke they want to intimidate. Just don't. Better be thought a weakling than have someone think you might be about to take out a general or a politician. Do you understand what I'm saying?'

Colleen nodded purposefully.

'So we know our roles. I'm the brains, he's the builder, and you're the gofer, OK? Don't take it the wrong way. It's important we all know what we are doing and we know what we're not doing.'

Colleen put the milk in the fridge, home to two tomatoes and a pork pie, put on her coat and hat and prepared to leave. First 'Paul' shook her hand again, and said, 'You should be very proud you're here. I know a little bit about you, and I like what I hear. But remember this is big time now. No messing, no talking, no mistakes, OK?' 'Peter' meanwhile was busy wiping down everything he had touched, including the mugs on the draining board beside the sink, but as Colleen headed for the door, she heard the shattering of one of the mugs as 'Peter' let it fall through his hands. She went back to volunteer to clean it up but 'Paul' indicated to Colleen she may as well leave him to it.

It had stopped raining but as the cold air hit her lungs Colleen almost wanted to scream with excitement. She didn't know what they were meant to be doing, but all the talk of gelignite and nitroglycerine and couriers and mules had really excited her. As she walked slowly back towards Ealing Broadway, she was visualizing Parliament with a great big hole through it, Buckingham Palace burning, trains bombed from their tracks, nightclubs and cinemas ripped apart. She felt sure her dad would know who 'Paul' was. She felt sure he was a main man. She would just love for her dad and her brothers to know, but she had got the message on that score. Better to stick with the story she had told her mum when she called her a couple of weeks ago: she was working on a market stall in Leyton selling pots and pans, and going to folk clubs in the little spare time she had.

10

DONCASTER

The Doncaster, 48 Parrish Drive, was a fine building set in its own grounds on the edge of town. Built fifty years earlier as a private home for Sir James Doncaster, a wealthy mill owner, the property then became a hotel once the prosperous days of cotton had ended. Its location and homeliness attracted returning customers, mainly sales representatives. Its black and white beamed exterior with a red-tiled roof, set amid a tree-lined, well-kept garden, added to the hotel's popularity up until the 1950s when the hard times set in. By the time Willie Buchanan was living there, the Doncaster had become the club's grandly titled Doncaster Halls of Residence.

For as long as anyone could remember, Mavis Archibald had provided digs for the club's young apprentice professionals. She used her own six-bedroomed house, and a network of houses owned by friends around town, to make sure the young players and trialists were well fed, had comfortable beds, learned how to do their own washing and ironing, and kept out of trouble.

She and her husband Cliff had run the house overlooking the town's main park as a bed and breakfast until Cliff's sudden death from a heart attack in 1954. Mavis and Cliff had been unable to have children, so they'd fostered two, eight-year-old Denise and ten-year-old Nancy, and were in the process of adopting them when Cliff died. The adoption fell through, and suddenly Mavis was a heartbroken widow running a guesthouse single-handedly.

She decided to sell up and move to the North East where her parents lived. It was Charlie Sinclair who persuaded her to stay.

At the time Sinclair was working at the club as a trainer for the reserve team, with vague hopes of one day being a manager himself. He preferred Mavis and Cliff's homely boarding house, and her fantastic cooked breakfasts, to staying in the various hotels used by the club. When Cliff died, and Sinclair began to see the extra strain on Mavis, he went to Percy Summerton and made the case that as the club was developing a reputation as a good producer of young players, it made sense to have their own dedicated housing or 'halls of residence' for apprentices and trialists. Summerton liked the idea, both for the reason Sinclair gave but also because ultimately it would save money. He bought the Doncaster and Mavis was put on a fixed annual fee to run it, to be reviewed each season, and so had no worries about whether passing custom was going to come her way. Having the young boys in her care also appealed to her maternal instincts, and helped her get over her loss. She was proud to run the place, and felt 'Doncaster Halls of Residence' gave it the feel almost of a university.

She explained this history one evening over dinner to Willie Buchanan. She had taken a bit of a shine to Willie. He was so small, with a sweet temperament, always asking if he could help her with the chores she had to do around the house. And he was so palpably missing his home and his girlfriend that she felt she needed to pay him special attention.

'So Charlie Sinclair was a trainer?' he asked. 'He hasn't always been the kitman?'

'Charlie has been at that club for half a century, starting as a player.'

'He was a player?'

'Yes. He was a good player, a full-back.'

'Wow. I never knew.'

'He is one of those souls who just gives his everything to something, never boasts, never demands. I bet he never told you he was the one who got this place sorted for the club?'

'No. He is a nice guy though. Everybody likes him. Even Brownie – and there's not many he likes.'

He had told her of the stunt he pulled with Brownie's clothes, and how the midfielder had chased him around the car park, watched by half of the first team who had been witness to his rage on returning from the Cup draw in Gordon's office to discover his clothes had been cut up. Willie was too fast for him, and as the noise of the players' cheers had grown louder, Gordon himself had come out to see what the fuss was all about, and Brown got the message whose side the gaffer was on.

'Maybe you should pick on someone your own speed, Brownie,' he shouted.

Willie got the clear message from the other players that he had done the right thing and that they – Brownie included – respected him more for it. Some of them had been impressed, too, when at the end of training they came in and he banged his boot on the wall, asked for their attention, and said: 'I notice you always just throw all your dirty kit in a heap. Would you mind putting shirts in this basket, shorts here, socks and jockstraps here. Thank you.'

But though he was feeling better about things, he told Mrs Archibald, exasperation in his voice, 'I don't understand why these grown men like all the bullying that goes on.'

'You're not the first to say that to me,' she replied. 'Some just can't take it. I've had tears at bedtime in this house, oh yes. But the worst tears, that's when the boys get told they're not being kept on. That can be tough all round. I hope it doesn't happen to you, Willie. Charlie tells me you're a rising star so hopefully it won't.'

'Do you talk to the gaffer?'

'Oh yes. He likes to know how everyone is settling in.'

'I see.'

'Don't worry, Willie, I've said nothing but good about you.'

Her house rules were sensible, strict and non-negotiable. Up and out of your room by 7.30 a.m. except Sunday, bed made; breakfast at 7.45; lunch at 1 p.m., unless eating at the training ground; evening meal at 6.30 p.m. No alcoholic drinks allowed on the premises, in bed by 10 p.m., no girls allowed on the premises, no smoking or swearing, no use of the house phone, but family and friends could ring in, no TV before 7.30 p.m. or after 10 p.m., no loud music, all washing in the wash basket by 8 p.m. and each apprentice was responsible for his own ironing. This, and the rule that everyone washed and dried the pots via a rota system, was introduced by Charlie Gordon to ensure that these young men could be self-reliant in some small areas of their life should they not make it as professional footballers, as the majority, he and she both knew, would not.

Though the rules sounded strict, there was a nice atmosphere in the house. She was also someone who didn't mind lending the odd pound or two to the boys, up to a maximum of ten pounds, and she carried around with her a pad showing the current position of all the apprentices. Charlie Sinclair still lived there, and he acted as an extra pressure on the boys not to mess around. They all knew how close he was to the manager.

'Doesn't he have a family?' Willie asked.

'He is a widower, and like me and Cliff they had no kids. His family is the football club.'

'That's a wee bit sad,' said Willie.

'Well, yes and no. How old do you think he is?'

'Sixty?'

'He's seventy-two,' she said. 'It's his love for his work that keeps him young, and since his wife died, that is all he wants.'

Matthew Stock had tried to end the arrangement under which Sinclair lived rent free at 'Auntie Mavis's apprentice academy', as Gordon called it. Summerton would hear none of it, but Moffitt was more open to the idea when he took over and began to look for savings. Gordon fought for Sinclair, and he won. The old kitman had tears running down his face when Gordon told him the news, told him he was part of the fabric of the club and 'so long as I have a job here, so do you. And if that twat Stock comes near you again, I'll take him into the car park and punch his fucking lights out.'

Willie Buchanan had settled in at the boarding house far better than he had at the training ground, and he enjoyed his chats with

Auntie Mavis. She had noticed that he was making regular trips to the phone box at the top of Peter Street.

'It must be costing you a pretty penny making all those calls to Catriona?'

'It is. But I don't spend much on anything else.'

'You must be missing her a lot.'

'I am. I really am.'

'Well, look, it is still raining. If you promise not to tell the others, why don't I turn a blind eye and you make a call now.'

Willie's eyes lit up.

'That is really kind of you.'

'On you go, I'll tidy up.'

'0-1-double2-4-6-double-3-5-9,' replied a familiar Scottish voice.

'Hi, Mrs Macintyre, it's Willie again.'

'OK, son. Let me find her for you. She's up in her bedroom.'

He imagined the scene as the black ivory handset was placed on the sideboard at 14 Forbes Street, Aberdeen, across the street from No. 15 where he had been born and raised. He and Catriona had known each other since they were kids. It was only over the past year or so that their friendship had developed into a romance, and both the Buchanan and the Macintyre parents were happy about it. Though she was taller than Willie, they seemed a perfect match. She didn't take much interest in football, but nobody was better at reading Willie's moods, boosting his confidence when it needed boosting, bringing him down to earth when he was getting a bit carried away.

He heard her coming down the wooden stairs two steps at a time, then the phone being picked up, and the excitement in her voice clear.

'I was beginning to worry you weren't going to phone. I missed you a lot today.'

'Me too. I missed you too.' He was speaking quietly lest Mavis or, even worse, the other apprentices through in the TV room heard him.

'So how you feeling?' she asked. 'Better, I hope.'

'Still raining.'

'I asked about you, not the weather. It's snowing here.'

'It's not easy. I'm not sure I can stick this much longer.'

'Stick what?'

'All the bullying.'

'This Brown guy again?'

'Yes.'

He told her the whole story, from start to finish, aware now that Mavis was listening through the kitchen hatch. At points, he felt he was on the verge of tears.

'I actually went to see the manager to tell him I wanted to go back home, but he was so nice, Catriona, I've decided to give it another week.'

Catriona laughed when he described the scene of Brown chasing him round the car park, and Gordon coming out to join the players.

'I don't know why you're laughing, Catriona. I was scared out of my wits.'

'Yes, but do you not see, the manager and the players were on your side, so you won.'

'He'll get me again, I'm sure of it.'

'He might try, but he knows the manager and the captain are watching your back. It sounds to me like a good day all round, Willie.'

'I hope you're right.'

'So why has this Brown feller got it in for you?' she asked.

'Och, if it wasn't me it would be someone else. He's just one of those people.'

'He's likely jealous of you. Can't be easy seeing someone as young and as wee as you coming in, and being better than these big old guys.'

'That's what the manager says.'

'Well, you listen to the manager. If you don't give this a go, you will never forgive yourself. And nor will I. If you come home now, they've won and you've lost. Do you want that?'

'Course not.'

'Well then... and remember, if you come back to a Scottish club, you'll still have the David Browns of this world to deal with, and you'll have half the wages you'll be on if you get a professional contract down there.'

This was not the first time she had shown him a bit of tough love. When he played for Scotland under-18s at a tournament in France, Willie tormented a full-back a good foot taller than him when training, who was dropped as a result. He never missed an opportunity for verbal and even physical abuse when he saw Willie, who was onto Catriona on the phone in tears.

She insisted that he focus on his game and take each tirade of abuse with a big smile, without response.

'You're in a man's game, Willie, so you have to be a man. So you are not coming home, you are going to stay and see it through. This is not about you, or me. It's about learning your profession. OK?'

'OK.'

'Also, Willie, there's another reason why you need to stay and make it work... I don't know how else to tell you this. But there's now three of us to consider.'

'Oh my God,' he said.

'I know. It's wonderful, isn't it?'

'But, but...'

'I know, we'll have to get married.'

'But we're seventeen, Catriona. Don't you think we're too young? We don't even get to vote in this election they're all talking about.'

'Do you imagine we will be together for ever?'

'Yes, well... I hope so.'

'So do I! So let's do it.'

'Have you told your mum?'

'No. We should do that next time you're up, tell them all together.'

As he put the phone down, he felt exhilarated, but he felt sick too.

'You OK, Willie?' asked Mrs Archibald.

'I'm fine,' he said. 'I'm fine, honestly.'

11

DRIVER

The new team coach stood dominant and gleaming in the Summerton Manor car park, its engine running as the players and management prepared for their journey to Merseyside for the away game against Everton. The mood in training had been good. Though DD Marland had rubbed several of the senior players up the wrong way, with the constant boasts about both his footballing superiority and his sexual conquests, even the cynics had to recognize he added some much needed quality in training, and merited his debut. There really was an air of optimism that had been missing these last few weeks. It was shared by the fans, and a bigger than usual away following was expected tomorrow at Goodison Park, one of Charlie Gordon's favourite grounds when he was a player. It was fitting then that Cochrane's Coaches were using their new state-of-the-art coach for the first time.

As the players milled around the car park waiting for the off, and waiting for the stragglers, George Brady and Magic were overseeing the packing of a huge array of skips filled with kit, towels, medical equipment, food and drink. Dermot Cochrane, who had been driving the team for almost as long as some of the players had been alive, knew exactly where everything had to go as he, Willie Buchanan and Charlie Sinclair filled the underbelly of the coach. Willie hated this part of the week. It reminded him that for all the training he did, and for all the talent everyone kept telling him he had, he was still a dogsbody, not a player. He was so small that Dermot used Willie to get inside the storage space and make sure every inch of space was used.

Cochrane's Coaches, which had, some time ago, changed its name from Laughlin's Coaches, was started in the late 1940s by Dermot's father, Frank Laughlin. Though the proud possessor of a sometimes incomprehensible Irish accent, Laughlin Senior was a big fan of the club, not least because he saw its business possibilities. He persuaded Percy Summerton that whenever they were playing more than fifty miles away from home, they should stay overnight, and travel in luxury. Conscious he would be able to market the connection, he offered Summerton a great deal which over time became a standard – large – contract. His firm had kept the contract every year since. Back then, father Frank drove a good old-fashioned charabanc, but when Dermot heard that rival coach company boss Fred Cochrane was selling up, he persuaded his father they should buy him out and merge.

Overnight, they grew from a small business to a medium-sized operation, then invested wisely, especially in the quality of the coaches. If DD thought the training ground was superior to Tottenham's, he was about to discover that the team coach was too, with its safety belts on every seat, a stereo, a toilet, a fridge and a coffee machine.

Dermot, known by everyone simply as 'Cockie', was a popular figure with the players, especially the handful of occasional smokers who could always rely on him to have a spare cigarette. He had an earthy sense of humour, and wasn't afraid to take the mickey out of the big names. Or the manager for that matter. Like a lot of Northern Irish Catholics, he supported Celtic, and he liked winding up Gordon, a Rangers man, about his team's recent dominance of Scottish football. He still had a strong Derry accent, though his father had moved to England when Dermot was eighteen, after Frank lost his wife to a stroke. All his childhood, Dermot had heard Frank talking about the great opportunities in England, and how Ireland was going nowhere because of the Troubles which he believed would never end. Frank was heartbroken when his wife died, but he wasted no time in leaving.

Dermot had married young, as most people did back then, but even on the wedding day itself, he worried he was making a big mistake. Jenny O'Driscoll was pretty enough, and bright, but they soon discovered a happy courtship which mainly involved heavy petting sessions down by the Foyle was hard to sustain under the same roof, slowly discovering how little they had in common. After five months, Jenny fell pregnant, but Dermot had already decided he was staying no longer. That meant getting away from Derry, a long way away, and he headed off to be with his dad.

They had barely spoken since Frank had left, but Dermot knew he had a small coach company; it wasn't hard to track him down, and his dad was pleased enough to see him, if surprised the marriage had ended so soon. Dermot did feel the occasional stab of Catholic guilt that he had left behind his young child – he heard from a friend it was a boy, and she had called him Seamus – and barely a day went by that he didn't fear her tracking him down at Laughlin's Coaches, and forcing him to confront his baby son, Seamus Laughlin.

The merger of the two coach companies provided a solution to his concern. To Fred Cochrane's surprise, Frank and Dermot Laughlin were keen to name the new bigger company Cochrane's, rather than use their own name, Laughlin's. They said they liked the fact it began with C, like Coaches. The real reason was they intended to use it to change their own names and so escape their past lives even further. So not only did Laughlin's become Cochrane's Coaches but Frank and Dermot Laughlin became Frank and Dermot Cochrane. To Frank, it was a way of sealing total abandonment of Derry; to Dermot it was a way of making it harder for Jenny to find him once he waved goodbye to the surname he was given at birth.

Frank, a heavy drinker and smoker, died of a collapsed lung in 1972, leaving Dermot in sole charge of the company. For a while he tried to stop smoking himself, not wanting to go the same way as his father, but within days he was back into thirty-a-day mode. A second failed marriage behind him, he poured his energies into his work, with twelve coaches and a pool of nine full-time and four part-time drivers, but the one driving job he still did himself was the football. He loved his weekends away with the team. He loved nearing grounds and inching through packed crowds with 'Cochrane's', his firm, emblazoned in huge letters on the side of a coach regularly seen in the press as players were snapped getting on and off, and occasionally on TV too.

Everyone called him 'Cockie' to the point that many of the players had no idea his actual name was Dermot. On overnight stays, he was very much treated as part of the team, sharing a room with Magic, joining in the late-night drinking sessions with Charlie Gordon and co. after the players had gone to bed, and sharing the lows and highs of losing and winning. Newcastle, Sunderland, Southampton, Ipswich, he had had some great trips, but it was the London trips that he most looked forward to.

Club director Matthew Stock had come to see the coach leave, having publicly taken credit for pressing Stan Moffitt to sanction the extra spending for the upgrade. Stock felt appearances mattered and that when a team arrived at an away ground, they had to give an impression of confidence and intimidate in any way they could. A big 'fuck you' coach was one way of doing that. Stock also loved these away games involving an overnight stay in the same hotel as the players. He would love it even more if, as under Gordon's predecessor Harry Ingram, the directors were allowed to travel with the players. But Gordon viewed that as a distraction, an extra pressure even, added to which they took up seats better used by players being able to stretch out and have some comfort.

Stock was clearly thinking, if he associated himself with the new coach – and he had briefed the local paper that it had been his idea and his contacts that helped deliver it – that just for the one game maybe, Gordon would let him and his wife Shelley go along for the ride. So he hopped aboard to have a good look around, tried to banter with the players about the new mod cons, but once all the players were on, Gordon stood at the front and shouted, 'OK, all but playing and backroom staff off the coach now, please. Time to go.'

Stock smiled as he passed him, but there were no words of encouragement, no wishing of good luck. 'See you there,' was all he said, as he and his wife headed to their own car and prepared to follow the coach.

Gordon knew that clubs had to have directors, but he hated having to deal with them too much. He also saw it as his role to protect the players from them. Directors loved picking the brains of the players and then passing on their little titbits to friends, colleagues and family. And even though his current board was not the most dynamic, or the brightest, just being a director was enough to intimidate some players into saying more than they should. It was Michael Kilbride who had been chatted up by Stock before last season's fifth-round League Cup tie away to Coventry. Gordon had decided he would play a couple of the youth team, including Luke Broome at left-back, and had told Killer he could stay at home for the evening. Killer mentioned it to Stock who had been hanging around the training ground, who mentioned it to a journalist who mentioned it to another journalist and by the morning Joe Mercer, Coventry's wily manager, knew; he decided to play his most experienced side possible and they gave the young kids a night to forget, running out 5–1 winners. Gordon blamed Kilbride for blabbing, but he blamed Stock for being there to make him blab.

That was the final straw that allowed him to persuade Moffitt that the team coach should be a director-free zone. He knew though that Stock had been telling Ronnie Winston that the next manager ought to reverse the ban.

As the big white barrier went up and the coach left the training ground, twenty or thirty fans were there to wave them off. Some had been there as the players arrived, either by taxi or in their own cars, and had got them to sign photos and cuttings and programmes. The number of locals who supported the club was impressive and they had a reputation for making more noise at away games than far bigger clubs. The football club meant more here than in most towns and cities. As Gordon was forever saying to the managers of clubs from more fashionable parts of the country, this was a region hard hit by industrial change, unemployment was high and social problems were growing, and the football club was something that could bring the town together and give it a bit of hope, happiness and prestige. They knew that winning the title or the FA Cup was a big, big challenge for a relatively small-town club. But what they did demand was an understanding of how much their club mattered; they demanded the players played with a bit of pride and passion.

As he settled down for the drive to Liverpool, Cockie put on the radio for any traffic reports, and moments later, the local station was talking about Saturday's match. They played a clip from Charlie Gordon's interview last night, when he said this was a huge game for both sides, and he really felt good about it. He talked about how well DD had gelled with Jules in training, how up for it they all were, and he warned Everton's central defenders Mick Lyons and Roger Kenyon they would have to be on their best form. Gordon was pleased with the clip they used, and pleased the players heard it. Even when he did a press conference, his audience was never the journalists, or the public, it was always the players. To him, the press was just one more vehicle to communicate to his players, and one way of doing that was by telling the public how good they were.

He looked around to see where DD was sitting. Players tended to want to sit in the same seat every time. So did he, and like most managers he took the two seats directly behind the driver for himself. Magic sat over from him, alongside Charlie Sinclair, who was a renowned sleeper on the team coach. Winston and George Brady sat directly behind Gordon.

The coach had been fitted out with two tables, and the players split into four distinct groups – readers at one table, card-players at another, talkers towards the front, and loners at the back. He

noticed that DD was sitting with the readers, though only the
Prof ever read an actual book. Clutch and Jinkie shared a couple
of newspapers, and football magazines – occasionally something
a bit more adult, though Gordon only allowed those on the trip
home – and would occasionally throw out soccer trivia quiz
questions. Wally and Taffy were the trivia kings.

Brownie, Jules, Smudger and Jock sat directly opposite the
readers on the table to the right, and played cards for hours on
end, often for quite big money. The big talkers – Killer, Taffy,
Mooro and Dipper – were always in between the management
and the tables. As for the loners, it was a funny one. They all
felt they had to mix in, but everyone understood that if you
went to the back two rows, it meant you didn't want anyone
to bother you. Sleep, reflection, or just getting away from the
rest of them. There tended to be more use of the loners' seats
after a game, especially a defeat, than before. But win, lose or
draw, Brownie, Jules, Smudger and Jock would be straight out
with the cards.

Gordon had never been at a club that didn't have at least one
player with a serious gambling problem. In this team, it was
David Brown. He was a lost cause, but what worried Gordon
was that he might be dragging Smudger Smith down with him.
Gamblers like to have other gamblers losing more than they do.
It was a vice Gordon had never understood. He didn't like horse
racing and had never put a bet on football in his life. He had
seen Brownie and Smudger bet on anything, from what the score
would be in the Derby County-Aston Villa game to whether
Cockie would stop at Watford Gap or Leicester Forest East on
the way back from a game down south.

The club knew all about Brownie's gambling when he joined
them from Newcastle. Gordon counted Newcastle manager Joe
Harvey as a genuine friend and Harvey had warned him about
Brownie's debts. So when Gordon signed him for £32,000, he sat
down with him and his wife Caroline and urged him to see this
as a fresh start and a chance for him to kick the gambling habit
once he had cleared his debts in Newcastle. It didn't work, and
Brownie was forever asking for a sub on his expected bonuses.

His wife finally left him at the end of last season, and Gordon let him miss the Spanish tour to try to win her back, and he succeeded. The marriage had been on-off-on-off for years. When she had dropped him off at the training ground this morning, they were rowing again; the row had been witnessed by several players as he got out of the car, and they could see she was crying.

It made for an uncomfortable atmosphere at the start of the journey, and the players knew not to provoke him.

'You OK, mate?' Graham Smith asked him quietly, as they sat down. 'Caroline looked upset.'

Brown groaned with a kind of resigned acceptance. He felt comfortable with Smudger. 'I can't kick it, Smudge, I just can't walk past a bookie's. Why did I come to a club that has a betting shop directly outside the entrance to the training ground? I get myself sorted out up in Newcastle and then I get into the same mess down here.'

'What's the damage?' Smudger asked.

'Six hundred,' Brown answered. 'It's not that bad, I've been in worse states. But the wife found out. I'd promised her I'd stopped, and she found a load of slips in my back pocket.'

'If you need any help, you just say.'

'Yeah, cheers, Smudge.'

Gordon managed to get a little nap on the motorway. It had been a good week, but a tiring one, and he had had a heavy night last night after getting home. He watched a recording, sent to him by a friend at ITV, of Everton's last home game against Leeds, and must have had four or five Scotches during the ninety minutes, on top of the wine and the brandy he'd had at a dinner with one of Moffitt's new sponsors.

As the coach slowed to leave the motorway he woke, stood and stretched out his lower back, which was where the stresses and strains on his body seemed to gather. He reached up for the tatty travel bag he had now had for almost twenty years – yet another lucky emblem that he kept even as the luck seemed to be running out. He flicked it open and pulled out a little box of mints, taking one, then offering them to his staff.

As he put the bag back up on the rack, he noticed a newspaper that had been left there. He wasn't much of a newspaper reader, but there was a good half-hour to go, so he picked it up and sat down to turn to the back page. However, the photo of the bombed-out coach on the same M62 they were now on, surrounded by headshots of the people who had been killed, grabbed his attention. He stared into the eyes of a young nine-year-old girl, Emma Ridley, whose father, an RAF pilot, had survived. Poor guy, he said to himself, he'll never get over it.

'I see your IRA Celtic pals have been at it again, Cockie,' he shouted across at the driver.

'Nothing to do with me, boss,' said Dermot. 'And nothing to do with Celtic.'

'Fucking barbarians. You see these young girls killed? I mean, what the fuck is that going to achieve?'

'Don't ask me. I'm OFD.'

'You're what?'

'Only the Fucking Driver.'

Gordon flicked over the election coverage on pages two and three – Heath talking about the jobs that would flow to the UK if we went into the Common Market, Wilson blaming the Tories for unemployment and industrial unrest, Liberal leader Jeremy Thorpe making a speech on education – turned to pages four and five, and saw more harrowing stories and pictures of the horror that had taken place on the bombed Yorkshire coach four days before. The IRA had admitted responsibility.

As he then flicked through the paper, another story caught his attention, in particular a picture on page seven. The face was familiar, then he looked at the caption, and so was the name – John Poulson. The headline could not have been clearer: GUILTY.

The report said the 'disgraced architect' had been sentenced to five years in prison for corruption after a fifty-two-day trial at Leeds Crown Court. As he read, Gordon realized this was the man who had been at the ground a couple of years earlier and in Moffitt's office several times prior to and during the building of the *Stan Moffitt Stand*! Like fraud and corruption cases often are, it was a complicated tale, and had Gordon not met Poulson, and known of his connection with Moffitt, he would never have read to the end.

The prosecution had made the case that Poulson came up with a good idea, but became perverted by greed. The idea was the concept of a 'new football club stand' at a time when many of the old ones were in danger of collapse because of age and ancient girders slowly twisting out of alignment. Poulson's concept was straightforward: that all architectural, design and building processes should not be seen as separate bodies, but as an all-in-one service. This wasn't primarily about football, and he was behind a whole wave of new buildings in Newcastle, Leeds, Bradford and Manchester. But as the web of contacts grew, he saw the opportunities in football. The new 'cantilever' stands his firm was designing were breathtakingly simple, they afforded an unimpeded view of the action to all, and allowed for other activities, such as bars, offices, hospitality rooms, in otherwise useless space beneath the stands. It was brilliant in its clarity and with Poulson clever enough to develop it, the contracts rolled in. However, in some of those early deals on shops and hotels, the police established, and the jury accepted, that he had won the huge contracts by offering a series of very large bribes.

There is no way, Gordon thought, that Poulson did not carry that habit into his work in football, which is more prone to corruption than most industries. Neither Moffitt, nor any other club chairman, was in the report. But he suspected that was because they just wanted enough evidence to put Poulson away. He stood again, took down his bag and put the paper inside. That cutting could come in handy.

'Is Finley going to be at the hotel?' he asked Magic.

'Dunno, do you want me to find out?'

'No, it's OK.'

Gordon rested his eyes and sucked on a mint. He was trying to remember when Moffitt bought the Rolls-Royce with that SM1 number plate. Then he recalled seeing the huge new barn and conservatory that had gone up in Moffitt's garden when he had gone up for a Christmas drink. Was that two or three years ago? And there was that Caribbean cruise Gloria Moffitt still talked about.

'When was the Stan Moffitt Stand built?' he asked Magic.

'Are you OK, boss?'

'Yeah, why?'

'I've never heard you ask non-football questions before, not the day before a match.'

'Seventy-one,' Charlie Sinclair said. 'The old one was knocked down in the close season. Remember we had a year when we only had three sides, and we had that friendly match with Newcastle for the official opening? Don't you recall?'

'Yeah, course,' said Gordon, closing his eyes again, smiling, and wondering if Matthew Stock was aware of just how close Moffitt was to Mr Poulson.

The closure of two lanes all day as a result of an accident meant a journey which would normally take two hours had taken closer to four. More time for Charlie Sinclair to sleep and Brownie to lose at cards. Once Gordon had parked his thinking about Moffitt and the Poulson scandal, he turned his mind once more to the match, and in particular whether he should change his defensive plan depending on whether Royle or Latchford was playing up front for Everton. Last time out at Goodison, Royle had beaten Mooro all ends up, on the ground and in the air, and he was worried it might be preying on his captain's mind. Mooro was not one to let his feelings show, not about himself anyway, but he knew he would be hoping for Latchford.

As Dermot pulled up outside the Midland Hotel and another gaggle of fans ready to greet them off the coach, scrapbooks and autograph books in hand, Gordon got his answer about whether Finley was staying over with the team. He was standing there with his secretary Tilly Foster on the hotel steps, holding a tray full of room keys.

At some clubs, players tended to have the same 'roomie', as they were called, every time. But Gordon – a habit he picked up when he was at Rangers under Bill Struth – liked to mix things up. Players fell in and out with each other. Some got on each other's nerves. Others helped each other's nerves. So far as he was concerned, *where* and *how* they slept, and *who* they slept with, was an important part of the match preparation. So when he had been dozing, Ronnie Winston had taken the list Gordon had pencilled out that morning in his office, and gone round the coach telling them where they were all to sleep. He put DD with Dipper. He put Nuts with Mooro, and Gordon made a mental note to brief Mooro on the chat he had had with his discarded striker. He was going to be hurting, whatever the brave face he put on as he drifted between the talkers and the players; though by the time the coach arrived in Liverpool, he had gone to the back to be alone.

As the players filed off the coach, DD made a point of going to collect the key for Room 212, and flashed it at Tilly Foster so she could see the number, whispering, 'Dipper can sleep in the bathroom!' She shook her head gently, smiling, in contrast to Finley whose disapproving look was something DD would get used to, as all the other players had. Finley liked football, but disliked most of the people who played it, managed it, watched it and ran it.

Gordon, like Winston, Finley and, as the only woman staying, Tilly Foster, routinely had his own room. Tonight, the hotel, clearly keen to impress and perhaps also hoping for the business not just when they played in Liverpool, but also even against the Manchester clubs, had thrown in a couple of complimentary rooms so George Brady, Ralph Rowland, Charlie Sinclair and Dermot Cochrane all had a nice surprise on arrival too. Gordon walked towards Finley who handed him the key to the Presidential Suite, explaining that Moffitt was driving over in the morning, and wouldn't be staying tonight.

'I see from the *Express* that his friend Poulson went down,' he said, and Finley virtually froze as he did so. Gordon walked towards the staircase, shouting across the lobby to Winston that he would see him in the team room for dinner.

The hotel had placed a complimentary bottle of wine, a

complimentary bowl of fruit, and a complimentary copy of the *Liverpool Daily Post* on the desk in his room, along with a letter of welcome from the manager. He found a corkscrew in the mini bar, opened the wine, a Merlot, and poured himself a large glass. He sat in a soft chair close to the window and turned to the back page, where the main headline signalled Everton manager Billy Bingham's intent: 'WE CAN WIN THE TITLE'. Everton were fourth, on a good run of form, and reading between the lines, Gordon sensed his opposite number saw his side as an easy touch for two points. There was condescension in the quotes he didn't like. 'Hard-working, organized, good at the long-ball game, we need to watch them on the break.' He also indicated that he would be playing Martin Dobson, recently signed for a record fee from Burnley, alongside Howard Kendall. What I wouldn't give to have those two in midfield, Gordon thought as he took a large gulp of Merlot.

By 5.30 p.m. Dermot Cochrane had parked his coach in the space reserved for it behind the hotel, and checked in. But there was still work to do. The arrangements he made today would set the scene for the next trip to the same hotel in Liverpool when they played at Anfield, just as, he was sure, the arrangements he made on his last trip to London's Great Western Hotel would provide an incredible adventure.

On leaving the hotel, he found what he was looking for within a five-minute stroll. He walked into the tiny, grandly titled 'Shoe Repair Emporium' and asked them to cut a copy of the key he had been given to his room at the Midland.

When back in his room, he opened his briefcase. He wrote the date, the hotel, and the room number on a tiny piece of sticky paper which he placed over a hook inside the briefcase, then hung his newly cut key alongside the others he had gathered from hotels all around the country.

He was in Room 414. The last time he stayed here he had been in Room 623. Tonight he intended to pay another visit to that room with the key he had had cut when they played Everton at the end of last season. He lit a cigarette and smiled to himself, the smile of a man proud at having kept a secret so long. He was excited, exhilarated even. It was not on a level with the excitement he felt about the Great Western Hotel in London, but it was exciting nonetheless.

12

CHOIRGIRLS

___

Tuesday 19 February

Patrizia Moretti was sitting in the back of the hired Bentley, flicking through Bella Luca's fan mail, and knowing her client would be in full whinge mode when she and her security man fought their way through the crowd and into the car. All she wanted was to do a bit of shopping. How on earth did her fans find out where she was going shopping, Patrizia wondered? Bella's own bodyguard, Tommy Keith, knew, but they both trusted him. It must be the Harrods people. Keith would call ahead to tell them she was coming. Then presumably they put the word round, and the fans gathered, and they got a bit of free publicity. It was the side of fame Bella liked least but Patrizia was more of the view that all publicity was good publicity – provided it was Bella who was getting the exposure.

Patrizia spotted Keith and the Harrods security team emerging from the front door and realized Bella had aborted her shopping trip. Their driver, Mick, had parked the silver Bentley on the pavement outside, as close to the entrance as he could get, but even with that it took a good thirty seconds for Keith to get through the throng of people, open the door and shepherd Bella into the back seat.

'I hate this shit,' she said as Keith jumped into the front passenger seat, and Mick sped away.

'Price of fame, Bella,' said Patrizia Moretti, smiling kindly, like a mother to a whining child. 'No fans, no sales. No sales, no charts. No charts, no success. No success, no fans, and round and round we go.'

Patrizia was Bella's longstanding personal assistant and general dogsbody though her business card said 'manager', and Bella's real management, Decca Records, didn't mind. If it made Bella happy to have her fellow Italian alongside her, and it made Patrizia happy to tell people she was more important than she really was. Provided The Choirgirls' records kept selling, all was fine.

Bella was the real star of The Choirgirls and like all stars she needed her own human comfort blanket, and Patrizia was hers. Now in her mid-thirties, Patrizia had never married, nor ever really had a long-term partner, and was totally dedicated to Bella and, as the group's fame grew, her fellow Choirgirls.

Patrizia was born in Sorrento and from leaving school had worked in her father's small record shop, one of the first to open on the Amalfi coast. She'd seen many young bands and aspiring musicians trawl through the ever-growing collection of records checking to see if their latest release was making progress in the music charts. She fell into management by accident when she was asked to find a band for a friend's wedding and soon she became the 'go-to' person for pop groups and singers. Patrizia was tall, with long auburn hair, a voluptuous figure and a quick wit that attracted a long line of courtiers.

Unlike some 'behind the scenes' figures, Patrizia had no desire for publicity herself. She wanted the benefits of the pop scene with none of the downsides. The one time she made something of a splash in the newspapers was when Bella was invited to the tennis at Wimbledon, and Patrizia was photographed bra-less in a see-through lace top chatting to Chelsea owner Bernie Yaakov. As the *Daily Express* gossip columnist William Hickey put it, 'The playboy multi-millionaire football club owner seemed to show more interest in the assistant than he did in the sulky-looking star.' Unbeknown to the papers, that interest developed into a romantic attachment later that evening, one which Yaakov later decided could have an impact on his football team's FA Cup run.

It was ten months since The Choirgirls had had their last number one single, 'His Kiss Is My Bliss', which had sold almost half a million copies. Bella was finding the pressure hard, and it had got a whole lot harder since the *Sunday People* had exposed the rags to riches story on which Patrizia had helped market her as something of a myth. Father killed in the war, mother took her own life four years later when Bella was just a young child, and so began a childhood moving from orphanage to orphanage, and when she was sixteen a recording agent heard her singing while entertaining her fellow orphans, went in to see her, agreed to get her proper training, and then promote her as a pop singer.

It was one of those stories where a grain of truth had been turned into a mountain of hype. It was true that Bella – born Isabella de Luca – lost her father, when she was a child. But he had never served in the war – he was a very successful business-man, and had died of a heart attack. It was also true she lost her mother, in a car accident when Isabella was in her early teens. But she and her brother were never in an orphanage. They were raised by her mother's sister, Aurora, and raised well given the money that their father had left behind. It was true that she was 'discovered' by Patrizia who happened to hear her singing by chance. But it was because her niece went to the same private school as Isabella, and she heard her sing at a school concert. 'The orphan girl singing star', however, was too good a storyline to miss. If only they had known she would become so big that every last detail of her life was going to be pored over, they – or at least Bella – might have been more careful. Bella had been living a lie in interview after interview and now that the truth was emerging, Patrizia didn't quite know how to control it.

It was another chance encounter that had taken Bella from relative success in Italy, mainly as a live performer supporting bigger names in concerts, to the fame and stardom she had now. A British record company executive, Anthony McLaren, had taken his wife to Florence for a long weekend, and saw Bella sing at a cabaret show in the hotel where they were staying. He saw immediately she had something, but not enough to make it on her own. She was very beautiful, had enormous charisma and stage presence, but he felt the voice was just two or three notches short of where it needed to be to make it as a solo artiste. But that very week he had been in a meeting at which Decca, for whom he worked, had decided to 'create' an all-girl group. When he and his wife Lisa sat down with Isabella and Patrizia later, he told them of their thinking. The real success stories of the sixties were less the likes of Sinatra and Como, but the groups The Beatles and The Rolling Stones. Also Motown was becoming more and more popular and among its successes were all-women groups like The Marvelettes and The Supremes. Why, they wondered, could they not do the same with white female singers, bring them together to create a new and unique sound on a par with the male groups taking the world by storm?

He told her they were auditioning over the next few months, and he would like her to come over to London and give it a go. Patrizia went with her, and both were an instant hit with the Decca crowd. They also loved the rags to riches back-story, which Anthony had picked up from Patrizia who, scenting a cut on a bigger deal than Italy could ever provide, had embellished even further.

Anthony McLaren was hailed as a hero at Decca. Nobody had even thought of getting a non-British singer, but Bella fitted perfectly with the whole concept of a modern, new, different approach, and they put together a line-up of two Brits, a French girl and Isabella from Italy. First they changed her name though, and Bella Luca was born.

The one worry they had was that the public would reject the idea of a 'manufactured' group, rather than one that had emerged out of geography or personal friendships, as The Beatles and The Stones had done. On the contrary, it provided an added interest for a media that was becoming increasingly keen to cover the lives of famous people. So anything that generated more attention on such famous people was a bonus. Bella quickly emerged as the one they found most interesting for her looks, her waspish sense of humour, an accent that had men in particular almost faint with desire, and above all the story of her life, which she told so often she may even have ended up believing it.

As the silver Bentley raced away from Harrods Patrizia passed her a glass of pink champagne. Bella sipped it, but it added nothing to her mood.

'It's getting really bad, Patrizia. They grab my hair, my clothes, I swear a hand went up my skirt, and when I looked around it was a young girl with a big smile on her face. It's scary. I just want to be able to go shopping and be normal.'

'Hey Bella, enjoy it while it lasts. One day they'll be chasing someone else and you'll be wondering where it all went, and you'll miss it. Believe me. Anyway, you can take the afternoon off and I'll meet you later for dinner. I have something else to worry about – how we sort out this mess about the orphanages and the rags in the rags to riches falling apart.'

Bella stared out of the window, clearly slightly ashamed of herself that she had allowed it to get so out of control. The tone in Patrizia's voice suggested it was serious. She wanted to change the subject.

'What news on the charts?'

'Number One by the weekend, nailed on.'

'That's good.'

'Yeah.'

'I'm Always Here For You' had a special significance for Patrizia as it was written at her suggestion by the established melody writer Billy Stanton.

'Billy wants to know if you have made any progress on the new song you've been working on with Stella.' Stella McCafferty helped to compose many of The Choirgirls' songs as she liaised with Decca.

'Let me work through it again this afternoon and we'll chat about it tomorrow. Where are you off to now?'

'Well, I've arranged to meet Stella about the lyrics and I'm repaying a favour for Bernie Yaakov.'

The mildly disapproving shake of the head suggested Bella

knew what kind of favour it would be. 'Don't do anything I wouldn't do,' she smiled.

'As if,' replied Patrizia.

When Patrizia first came across Bernie Yaakov he was just another rich son of an affluent Jewish Daddy enjoying the London nightlife. But he just had something about him that attracted her to him. She liked to think it was not merely the millions he would one day inherit. She liked his sense of humour, and she loved the way he encouraged her and seemed to take as much joy in her success as she did. She had ended up in bed with Bernie the first time they met, at the tennis. Even now, several months later, they were not exactly a couple, and she knew they never would be. But she loved his company, not least the fact he was not remotely possessive of her, or jealous when other men made advances. Indeed, he seemed positively to enjoy watching men mentally undress her in front of him, and far from pushing them away when they chatted her up, he seemed to encourage it.

During the last twelve months he had bought a number of London businesses and properties, the most high profile of which was Chelsea Football Club. Bernie had been raised as a Spurs supporter, but Chelsea was the only London club they had a realistic prospect of owning, and he and his father had been steadily purchasing shares and eventually had sufficient leverage to go for overall control. Patrizia had always liked football, had been an occasional supporter of Fiorentina as a kid, and going to Chelsea matches was another way of making sure she got to meet London's business elite as she was always in the directors' box with Bernie and had found a few new bedfellows there. Chelsea was a fashionable club and success was being built on the new money being pumped in by Yaakov, and a stream of new players brought in by Alfie Ruse, who had been an agent and was now helping with player recruitment.

Bernie Yaakov loved his music and in the early days had invested in Decca's new discovery The Choirgirls, who were then Number One in the charts. So as well as liking him, which genuinely she did, Patrizia felt she owed him too.

Patrizia had also arranged for The Choirgirls to sing at Bernie's brother's wedding, as a favour to him. Today she would start to repay favour number two, a rather exciting venture which he had explained when they had met last night in a Kensington hotel.

'Patrizia, it's vitally important for me that you make this happen, so I'm counting on you. Do you want me to go through it again?'

'No, it'll be fine, I know exactly what is expected of me. And who knows, Bernie, I might even enjoy it. A young, fit man and all that goes with it.'

Yaakov laughed as he sipped his champagne and straightened his Chelsea FC tie. 'And don't forget. The date to aim for is Friday March the eighth, and the instructions are to get him *tired, very tired, totally exhausted.*'

'"Shagged out" – I believe that is the expression you are look-ing for,' she suggested, and they clinked glasses and laughed.

And with that memory still floating in her mind, Patrizia wrapped a beige Pashmina scarf around her neck and put on her dark glasses and a large floppy hat. Finally she picked up the ream of sheet music from the Bentley's cream leather seat and clasped it under her arm.

Mick had been cruising aimlessly around Mayfair but as 3 p.m. approached he made his way towards the entrance to Burlington Arcade. As Patrizia stepped out of the Bentley, she kissed Bella goodbye, told her to get some rest, and then looked once more over the note Bernie had given her. 'He's twenty-six, blondish shoulder-length hair, green eyes. He is due to do a signing at Smallfield's Jewellers 3.15 p.m. Once you have made the first contact, by knocking into him and getting his attention, go straight to Peddler's Café on Burlington Arcade where Stella will be waiting for you. Good luck, and enjoy.'

Clipped to the note was a picture of the man she was tasked with exhausting the night before Chelsea hopefully made it through to the FA Cup semi-final. As the Bentley disappeared towards Hyde Park, she smiled to herself at the extraordinary turn her life had taken, from a shabby little record store to a life mixing with pop stars, multi-millionaires and, if the plan worked, a top footballer.

*

Without work to go to, for the last fortnight Colleen had been sleeping for as long as her own mind would let her, but 'Paul' having told her to expect an 8 a.m. visit at the house in Chiswick any day, she had got herself an alarm clock, and set it for 7.40.

The very next morning, as the pips on the radio signalled the start of the eight o'clock bulletin, the election and the bombings still the main news, she at last heard a firm knock at the door, and skipped downstairs.

'Who is it?' she asked before opening.

'It's me, "Paul".'

She opened the door, and he removed a black baseball cap as he came through.

'So it's not true you're always late unless it really matters, then?'

'Don't listen to him,' he said. 'The guy is bitter as fuck.'

'I got that impression.'

'But he is the best in the business when it comes to making bespoke bombs.'

'You make him sound like a tailor.'

'No, no. He is a lot more precise than that.'

She showed him through to the kitchen, turned off the radio, and put on the kettle.

'Have you had your breakfast?' she asked.

'Get you with your Irish womanly stereotyping,' he said. 'That is the first time I have ever been offered a cooked breakfast by one of my team.'

'Well? Eggs? Bacon? Sausages?'

'You got no black pudding then?'

She smiled, shook her head, and set about making their breakfast, while he sat and flicked through the book that lay open on the table.

'Fuck, is this not a bit heavy?' he asked.

'Marx? Clever guy.'

'Yeah, maybe. Fair to say I am more practical operations than political theory.' He pushed the book away.

They ate in relative silence, 'Paul' several times nodding and murmuring his enjoyment.

'Can't beat a cooked breakfast,' he said.

'Sorry about the black pudding. I'll know next time.'

'Hopefully there won't need to be one. The other thing is cooking nicely too, "Pamela". That is why I'm here.'

He told her that the plan involved a specific target who regularly used the Great Western Hotel near Paddington Station. They had a man on the inside who knew when the target would book in. 'It could be a matter of days.'

'Do we know who it is?' she asked.

'You'll know in good time. But fair to say your hunch about the election wasn't far wrong.'

'Not Wilson?' she asked. 'Not the next fucking Prime Minister?'

'Enough questions now,' he said firmly. 'Here is what we need you to do.'

He explained that Paddy O'Connell – the fourth P – had been head porter at the hotel for years. They had no reason to doubt his credentials, other than the fact that he had only in recent months helped out.

'He's a bit of a folkie, and he didn't realize that one of his regular haunts was one of our fundraising and networking joints. One of our volunteers was chatting him up a while back, and you know, a guy like that in a hotel like that, it's kind of useful.'

'Sure, yeah. So he's not a volunteer?'

'Well, he kind of is and he isn't. We had someone marking him, a woman called Margaret, and she's just slowly been drawing him in, like, and they've been seeing each other a bit at these folk gigs.'

'Is he married?'

'Yeah, but his wife's not been so good, so yeah, he ended up taking Margaret back to the hotel a couple of times and giving her one, you know, so he was maybe drawn in more than he wanted. And now he's well drawn in, and we think he is properly up for it. We have been checking him out all over the place, but we just need to keep on checking, you know.'

'Yeah.'

He took out a file from his rucksack and pulled out some photos. Several of O'Connell, who had a nice smiley face and thinning red hair, going a little grey at the edges. Then there was one of his house, the Fulham address written on the back. There were pictures of the various pubs and clubs where he went to hear his music. And one of his wife, who looked a lot older than him. She was overweight, slightly stooped.

'You can see why Margaret found him easy prey,' he said, picking up on Colleen's reaction.

'And that's even without seeing Margaret,' she said. On cue, he produced a picture of a striking-looking woman in her late forties, sandy curly hair, green eyes, an impish smile, unmistakably Irish.

As he edged nearer to her she could sense he was seeing more closely the horrific scar on her face.

'Is he still seeing her?'

'He is.'

He explained that today O'Connell was working the late shift at the hotel, starting at four in the afternoon.

'He tends to go out during the day. I don't think there is much of a marriage going on, you know. We just need him followed. He goes everywhere by public transport, mainly the Tube, doesn't have a car.'

'Am I looking for anything specific?'

'No. We just need to be sure he is not seeing people he shouldn't be seeing, doing things he shouldn't be doing. We can't afford a set-up.'

'OK. So had I better go there, like, now?'

'He was working late last night, so I doubt he'll be out much before ten or eleven.'

'What do I do if he is seeing Margaret? Will she know who I am?'

'No. We're following her too.'

'Oh, I see.'

'Can't be too careful, "Pamela".'

'No, I understand. So ...' She paused, wondering whether she was about to stray into 'too many questions' territory.

He read her mind. 'So are you being followed as well?'

She smiled.

'Assume you are. But fair to say, we know more about you than we do about Paddy O'Connell. So fret not.' He put his hand on her arm, and she felt a real sexual charge as he did so. She reached out her hand to touch his face, but he pulled back.

'Now now,' he said, 'none of that. You'd better be going to Fulham.'

'Sorry, yeah, sorry, I misunderstood.'

'No problem,' said 'Paul'. 'I will see you later.'

'You will?'

'I'll be around the hotel when he arrives for work. Maybe we could meet up somewhere near there and I can debrief you.'

'OK,' she said. 'Sounds good.'

'I'll find you.'

'Great. And sorry.'

'It's forgotten already.'

13

CHESSINGTON

Friday 8 March

Angela Chessington didn't need anyone to tell her how lucky she was; successful in business, her desire for a national profile slowly being satisfied, two lovely children and a loving husband who consented, more or less happily, to this excursion on her own. As he dropped her at Bristol's Temple Meads Station and she leaned in to blow kisses to the kids in the back of the school run Volvo Estate, he knew she would be seeing a woman later on for an annual expression of her bisexuality. 'Don't ask, don't tell' was the agreed approach, and though she knew he didn't much like it, they had what most people would see as a successful, happy relationship.

It wasn't as if she had ever lied to him. On their first date, ten years ago now, when she had hired him as the architect for one of her early care home projects, she had said to him, 'I've had girlfriends as well as boyfriends,' and he seemed to understand what she meant. It was only when they became sexually involved themselves, and then started to talk of setting up home together and having children, that it started to gnaw away at Eddie. So she agreed – no more women. But she found it hard, she still wanted that special release she felt only a woman could give her, and they came to this arrangement they had now had for five years, since shortly after their second child Pia had been born.

She was sure a lot of it was about her mum. She died when

Angela was fourteen and now, eighteen years later, she thought of her and yearned for her every day. The pain was less intense, obviously, but there were still moments when the grief would hit her as though it was raw, the deathblow newly struck. As the eldest of four daughters, she had been something of a rock, and a confidante, to her mother Avril. It had left a hole that had never and could never be filled.

Their father was a rep for a brewery, and spent much of his life in his car, driving all over the country, so Angela became something of a main carer for her three sisters, and she grew up fast. He too struggled to get over the loss, and became ever more workaholic as the only way of coping. But one day every fortnight, from August to May, was sacrosanct, namely Bristol City's home matches. Perhaps it was their way of avoiding talking too much about their loss that led to football being the thing they talked about most. She was alone among the four girls in sharing her dad's passion for the Robins, so it was very much a father-daughter thing, just the two of them.

When she was sixteen, she persuaded her dad that she and her sisters would soon need bedrooms of their own and they should think of building an extension to turn their three-bedroomed house into a five-bedroomed one. It would have the added bonus, she said, of increasing the value of the house so that when they all left to get jobs, husbands and homes of their own, he would be able to sell it, find somewhere smaller, and maybe retire early. He liked the plan.

What with being a carer and a football fanatic, she had never really excelled at school, and she decided to leave at fifteen and took on her first property project. She scribbled some drawings, found an architect, submitted plans, gained planning permission, tendered the work and project-managed the job, all within a budget agreed with her dad. Then when she reached nineteen, her grandfather died suddenly and it seemed sensible for her grandmother to move in with the family. Another house extension, paid for from the sale of her grandmother's cottage near Compton Dando, again increased the value of their home and she then had sufficient capital to speculate on a small bungalow, which she later extended and sold on for a good profit. That was the start of what became something big, and had made her regional businesswoman of the year, and the UK's young entrepreneur of the year before she hit thirty. Chessington Properties was now a multi-million-pound property empire boasting housing estates, nine care homes, three hundred student bedrooms, two office blocks and a hotel and restaurant overlooking the River Avon. She also owned a small office block in East Bridge Street, Enniskillen, which she visited quite regularly, and had recently met an interesting music producer who said she worked for The Choirgirls, the chart-topping pop group.

The awards, and the profile they brought her, had also got her onto the lucrative public speaking market. The business scene was so male-dominated that a young, female, good-looking, sexy, successful business figure became as sought after as better-known male business leaders.

Her three sisters all had roles in the company, and they had given their dad the sixtieth birthday present of his dreams – a cottage, bought for cash, with a view of the Clifton Suspension Bridge, so he could retire, stay close to his wonderful daughters and watch Bristol City play at Ashton Gate, like his father had done in the 1930s.

The only break in tradition from her father and grandfather was that Angela now watched home games from the directors' box after joining the Bristol City board in 1972, when she put in the money needed to buy some new players. The manager, Alan Dicks, had joined the club in 1967 and between them they planned to get the club promoted back into the First Division for the first time since 1911. Even though rugby was dominant in the West Country, it was ridiculous that a city like Bristol, with a vast catchment area, did not have a top-flight club.

Like millions of boys, and not so many girls, Angela fell in love with football at first sight. She was seven years old when her grandfather, Derek Chessington, first took her to watch Bristol City play.

Of their walks to Ashton Gate she remembered how her granddad would get a pint of mild in the Crown and Dove Hotel on Bridewell Street, while she was sent to buy a pie and a match programme across the street. The match programme became her granddad's bible through the following week and each day it would become blacker and blacker. He was an engineer at Bristol Cars Limited, and could never quite get the grime out of his hands. He called Ashton Gate his 'second home', and she fell in love not just with the sights and sounds of football, but with the pleasure it gave to him and to her father too. He bought Angela her first rattle, her first rosette, her first scarf, and shortly before her granddad died, she'd asked her dad if she could put these precious items in his coffin to be buried with him.

His death also got a mention in the programme – he would have loved that – because together with Harry Dolman, a fellow engineer, he had designed and installed the new floodlights at Ashton Gate in the early 1950s, which were still in use in the 1970s.

As a girl in what was still very much a boy's world, she got a childhood reputation as something of a tomboy, not least because she chose to keep her hair short, and dress like a boy, partly to blend in, partly in the hope they would take her more seriously when she talked football. It was a tradition she carried on when she joined the board. Although she dressed to express her femininity in her day job, for board meetings at Ashton Gate she preferred a pinstriped trouser-suit, shirt and tie. It felt like an important link to her childhood. Given her life with Eddie and her two children, nobody ever guessed that it was in part an expression of her still confused sexuality.

As the train sped towards Paddington, the thought alone of what lay ahead filled her with an excitement sex with her husband rarely managed. When she was with him, that made her feel guilty. When she was with her friend from Enniskillen, as she would be shortly, the guilt became a price worth paying.

14

PATRIZIA

Tuesday 19 February

A fortnight after his transfer from Tottenham, DD Marland was back in London for a short break, and also to help his wife Lucy sort out the move north. As Everton away was his first match, he had struggled to fit into the team at times, but overall it went well because he'd scored the equalizing goal. Everton centre-half Roger Kenyon had stuck with him for most of the match and, after Bob Latchford smacked in a twenty-five-yarder with only ten minutes to go, the game looked over. Whether it was Gordon's coaching plan or just good fortune, DD found himself briefly unmarked at the near post as Dipper jinked his way to the goal-line and managed to whip in a cross, well short of the penalty spot. Did DD smell a goal coming or was he just in the right place at the right time as he nipped in front of Kenyon to glance the ball past Dai Davies in the final moments of the game? This had gone down well with the fans, and with Charlie Gordon. A single point didn't of course shoot them up the League, but neither did they drop a position.

'Dream debut for DD', as the *Sunday Express* put it, a picture of DD doing his famed celebration on the back page as his team-mates ran to congratulate him. It made him even cockier on the coach ride home, and at one point the Prof asked him to pipe down as Marland threw out a number of quiz questions – the answer to all of which was DD Marland – to the team.

'Name the last player to score on his debut for this poor unfashionable club.'

'Which First Division player has scored on his debut for three separate clubs?'

'Which First Division player has scored on all five occasions he has played against Everton?'

'Yeah yeah yeah, we get the fucking point,' said the Prof. 'You're a world beater. Now shut the fuck up and let me read my book.'

'I don't know what to call mine when I write it,' said DD. '"How I Saved a Club", maybe.'

He was so over the top, some of the players were beginning to warm to him.

He had less luck in his second match, the Cup match against Manchester City at Maine Road that took them into the sixth round and the tie with Chelsea. It was indeed a real stroke of luck that, as Sidney Wale had explained when he was being signed, DD was not Cup-tied. It was an added bonus for Charlie Gordon, and away in the Cup against Man City should have been a perfect game as he tried to establish himself in the team. The fans gave him a fantastic welcome, he played well, but when Mike Summerbee, back defending a corner for City, knocked over Smudger Smith in the box, and the referee pointed to the penalty spot, DD immediately grabbed the ball, and Dipper, the usual penalty taker, let him, despite David Brown urging him to grab the ball from DD.

Marland hit it well but the ball smashed against the bar. He was less boastful afterwards, and it took goals from Jules Pemberton and David Brown to secure the 2–0 win. But once they had all showered and changed, he was back on his usual form. 'Two games with DD, unbeaten. How are you feeling, lads? Glad I came?'

'Yeah,' said Brownie, 'just let Dipper take the pens in future, OK?'

'I missed it deliberately to get you all fired up.'

Gordon had been pleased enough with him, and gave him the two days off to sort his move, but told him he wanted him to stay focused and fit, train both days, no socializing, and get his head in gear for Saturday's League match against West Bromwich Albion at The Hawthorns.

That afternoon Lucy Marland had shown the fifth set of potential buyers around their three-storey terraced house in Waltham Abbey and she was delighted to welcome DD home. For the first time in their married life, she felt, they could stop worrying about money. DD now had the comfort of a two and a half year contract with a further two and a half year option, and if he carried on the way he had started, they would be well set up.

Although he'd been well paid at Tottenham, buying and furnishing their home and the failed investment in a West End nightclub had proved expensive. His brother Darren had persuaded DD that he would triple his money in two years. Unfortunately neither had any experience in the nightclub industry and soon the club was running at a loss and Darren was back working as a plumber, once DD's finances had been drained back to zero. It had been an expensive, painful lesson. It was one he could and should have learned a lot earlier, when he went to a PFA seminar at Fulham's Craven Cottage ground some years before, where a former Fulham player, John Mitchell, had warned them of what he called 'the OPM problem'. OPM stood for 'Other People's Money', and Mitchell had explained that now they had a bit of cash they would be stalked by friends, family and new hangers-on, who would want them to fund all manner of business ideas with *their* money. 'It is great for them; very risky for you.' DD should have listened. He didn't. It took the nightclub debacle to teach him.

Lucy knew that DD was prone to infidelity, and when she first found out she had gone back to her mum's and told him she never wanted to see him again. But she went back, not least because her parents told her maybe she just had to accept that some men needed more on the romance and sex front than they would ever get from a wife. And when all was said and done, he was a special kind of guy, and where else was she going to find someone who could provide her with such a lovely home and as much shopping money as she wanted? It was not what she had expected to hear from them, knowing as she did that if her mother ever suspected her father of being unfaithful, he would be out the door. Of course once she returned, DD felt empowered to do the same thing again, and again, feeling he would always be able to get her back.

It was being a goalscorer that made him special. Gordon's theory on the three types you need in a team was deliberately simplistic, and DD knew the whole thing had just been a way of making him feel special as he started out with his new club. But it was true. These were the players adored by fans and chased by women.

Today, with Lucy being so positive about the house move, he was determined to be as loving and helpful as he could. Up early, open all the mail, settle all the bills, cancel the papers and the accounts with local stores, and all after cooking breakfast for Lucy, and taking it up to her in bed.

They'd been married for four years and they'd been trying to start a family for the last two, but now DD had stability and an element of financial freedom, maybe the tension would lift and the kids would follow. Lucy was not a typical footballer's wife. Her father was a successful Wimpole Street dentist. She had done pretty well at school, but went into modelling as a teenager and realized there was a better living to be made there than wasting several years at college. She met DD when he had come to a fashion show with a friend of his, a photographer, and he seemed to like the fact that she didn't have a clue who he was, and had little interest in football. She had learned the hard way that a lot of women did know who he was, did like footballers – or at least the men who played it at the top level – but she had decided that so long as he was a loving husband around her, and didn't humiliate her publicly, she would turn a blind eye.

Today, she expected finally to sell the house – a couple were coming for their third look – and already they had established they could buy somewhere far bigger up north, having taken Dipper Temple's advice to look at places 'way out of town'.

'So what's happening this afternoon, Dan?' Lucy shouted

through the kitchen hatch as she washed the breakfast crockery, 'Are you in or out when these people come?'

'I've got a telly interview.'

'Not here I hope?'

'No. I promised Alfie Ruse I'd do an interview about my move with some new sports channel he's getting involved with.'

'OK, love. In town?'

'Yeah. St James's Hotel, half two, then he wants me to call in and sign some autographs for this guy who has a shop in the Burlington Arcade. I should be back by five. Shall we go out for dinner? I can drive back north later tonight when the roads are clear.'

'You don't want to be tired for training tomorrow, pet.'

'I'll be fine. Early dinner then off.'

DD drove his new Ford Cortina to the station, put on a wide-brimmed hat, and caught the train into town. A couple of Spurs fans recognized him and came for a chat, picking his brains about their favourite players. They were surprised at his move.

'I went there a couple of years ago. What a shithole.'

'Yeah, but I won't be living there, and the training ground is quality. That's where I'll spend most of my time.'

'You're not going to win trophies there though, are you?'

'Well, we'll see.'

His taxi driver in London, an Arsenal fan, also wanted to talk about the move.

'Pleased as punch you went, mate. Spurs won't be the same without you.' And he laughed.

When he dropped him at the St James's, he asked DD for an autograph. DD gave him a big tip and shook his hand.

The interview went well, and he found himself talking very positively about the set-up, and also the quality of coaching. He hoped Gordon would see it. By the time he had finished, word had spread round the hotel and some of the guests and staff were lying in wait in reception to get autographs and pictures.

He made his way through the hotel's revolving doors and drew in the crisp London air. He knew then there was no better city in the world, and he would miss it. Walking across St James's Street a bus conductor spotted him, and shouted: 'Hey, DD. Get back to the Lane. Chivers is not the same player without you.' It was interesting how little he cared now about how well Spurs did without him. It cheered him up though that the fans missed him.

As he strolled down Burlington Arcade in search of the jewellery shop where he was to do a signing for a friend of Alfie Ruse, he collided with a woman hurrying in the opposite direction. She was carrying a file of papers, which fell to the ground, some of the papers flying out.

She was wearing a large floppy hat and dark glasses, but he could tell she was distressed and flustered – good-looking too – so he quickly bent down to gather together the file and the papers, which seemed to be a collection of sheet music.

'Sorry, sorry, that was my fault. I wasn't looking where I was going. Here you go. You OK?'

'I'm fine,' she said, 'just late for a meeting, as usual.'

They stood looking at each other for a moment.

'Anyway... I must rush,' she said. 'I have a meeting with one of my writers.'

'Do I know you?' he asked, and she laughed.

'No,' she said, 'I don't think so.' But she took off her hat to let him see her face, and he nodded his appreciation.

She was ten, maybe fifteen years older than him, but pretty. Her auburn hair fell down and as she tilted her head she smiled. He looked closely at the shape of her face – clear olive skin, high cheekbones and lips slightly parted. She was wearing a black jacket and jeans, and a thin cream shirt unbuttoned just enough to reveal a deep cleavage. Simple, but the height of fashion.

'Listen, thanks so much,' she said, her Italian accent less strong than when first they collided. 'I really must go now. I am meeting my writer in Peddler's Café.'

He let her go, having already noticed four sheets of paper that had blown into the door of a tobacco store. He waited till she was at the end of the arcade, then chased after her, so he was a little breathless as he caught up with her.

'Hey, hey, you forgot something.'

'Oh my God,' she said, as she caught sight of the song she

and Bella had been working on with Billy Stanton. 'Thank you so much.'

'So,' he said, 'you get the papers if...'

'Oh no, come on, I must go...'

'...if we go for a quick coffee first.'

'But I am late, someone is waiting for me.'

He put the papers behind his back, shook his head, and she started to smile.

'I can come to the meeting with you.'

'Do you know anything about music?'

'No. I only know about football. I'm a footballer.'

'Why don't I know you then?'

'Because you're Italian.'

'So what is your name?'

'One cup of coffee, and I tell you.'

She stood there feigning annoyance, but then said, 'OK, one coffee, promise, then you leave me alone. Oh, and by the way, I don't believe you're a footballer.'

But the second they walked into Peddler's she was put right on that score. First, the guy behind the counter let out a loud 'Deeeee Deeeee, I thought you'd emigrated,' and then the woman Patrizia was meeting said, 'Oh my God, where did you find my favourite Spurs player?'

'Ex Spurs now,' DD said, offering his hand.

'I just bumped into him. Literally. And he helped me pick up my papers after they went flying.'

'Sounds like a good excuse to me,' said Stella.

'Not every day you bump into a beautiful older woman on your way to a signing,' he said.

'Hey mister, less of the old,' said Patrizia.

Stella went to the counter to order some drinks, and when she came back, in a buttery Irish accent she said, 'I am Stella McCafferty, I work with Patrizia Moretti, who you've just met. I'm a music adviser and we both represent The Choirgirls.'

'And who the fuck are you?' Patrizia asked him jokingly.

DD laughed, loving the directness. Also, like a lot of foreigners, she couldn't quite master swearing so that it sounded incredibly seductive, not aggressive or sarcastic. The smile indicated he was starting to find this older woman very, very attractive.

'This is DD Marland, football star,' said Stella.

'Didi? What a silly name.'

'No, DD, as in letter D followed by letter D,' said Stella.

'Ah yes,' said Patrizia. 'I think I may have heard of you. I don't follow English football so much. So boring, but that strange name rings a bell.'

'What? Compared with the defensive crap you lot play? Do me a favour, love.'

As Stella pushed a coffee his way, DD chuckled to himself, then said: 'Patrizia and Stella – shouldn't you two be a double act?'

'We kind of are,' said Patrizia.

'I write the lyrics of the songs for The Choirgirls,' said Stella, 'but I am too old, too ugly and my bum's too big to be allowed to sing them in public.'

'You are anything but ugly,' said DD, deciding not to comment on the big bum.

'Is there any woman you don't chat up?' said Patrizia as she rose to visit the ladies and make a call on the public phone in the corner of the café.

'I just tell the truth. Always,' he said in a slightly raised voice, to her back as she walked between the tables.

'The Choirgirls, eh?' he continued. 'Quality. I love that Bella Luca. What's the chance I can get to meet her, Stella?'

'You'd need to square Patrizia for that. She's the sidekick, not me.'

'So is writing songs for The Choirgirls your full-time job?' he asked as they waited for Patrizia to return.

'No. I own a shop too – that is my main work.'

'What kind of shop?'

'Do you promise not to be shocked?'

Stella laughed, and DD guessed.

'Not a sex shop?'

'Adult emporium, I prefer to call it. Just off Soho Square.'

DD somehow managed to look both shocked and amused.

'It's not what you think,' said Stella. 'Not a dirty raincoat in sight. It's very much aimed at young couples, heterosexual or homosexual, and what they can add to their sex lives with lots of fun stuff.'

'Wow.'

'What's the surprise?' asked Stella. 'Women are into sex just as much as men, you know.'

'Yeah, I guess.'

'Give me your address and I'll send you a few samples.'

'You serious?'

'Of course, one phone call to Enniskillen and it's done. I have a little factory over there in East Bridge Street. It used to be a nunnery, but even where I come from there is a bigger market for sex toys than nuns these days.'

'I really do need to get to know you ladies better,' laughed DD. 'Listen, do you mind waiting for me if I pop out for a bit to do this signing? You can do your work and then I can come back and we can carry on, yeah?'

With that, he stood up and walked out before Stella could answer. 'Back in five minutes, ten max,' he shouted as the door closed behind him.

He managed to get in and out of the signing in fifteen minutes – a few snaps, a few dozen signed photos – and then back he went to Peddler's Café. Stella was standing, talking to Patrizia while packing up to leave.

'So, songbirds, is the next hit now written?'

'No. But the next but one is,' said Stella. 'Nice to meet you, DD. Now, do you want to give me that address for the samples?'

'You'd better send them to my new club. We're moving house soon.'

'OK. Will do. I'll leave you two to have a chat.'

She gave Patrizia a hug and kiss on both cheeks, pecked DD on his cheek, and left.

'So,' said DD. 'Just you and me now, Patt-tri-ziah.'

'I'm killing time before my next meeting. Should you not be hounding someone a little nearer your own age?'

'Well, I wouldn't say no to meeting Bella Luca.'

'Oh I see, trying to use me to get to someone more famous.'

'Not at all, no. I like women with a bit of experience. But Bella, you know…'

'Yeah, I know… Where's your next meeting?' she asked.

'I'm doing a TV interview,' he lied. 'What about you?'

'Grosvenor House Hotel. Decca rent a bunch of flats for us there when we're in London.'

'Nice.'

'It is.'

But she then explained that she was due to be leaving London next week for a series of European gigs with The Choirgirls, and wouldn't be back until the second weekend in March.

'So when do you leave London?' he asked.

'I'm off on Monday.'

'So how about dinner Sunday evening?'

'I'm not coming up north.'

'You mean you don't want see me play on the Saturday, and stay over?'

'In a word, no,' she said, standing and putting on her hat and glasses again. 'I've got a better idea – dinner. Sunday. Grosvenor House Hotel.'

He hesitated, thought for a moment, then said, 'OK, I'll be there.'

'And this better not be just about meeting Bella, Mister DD.'

He painted on a face of mock hurt and sang, badly, the line from the old Flamingos song… 'I only have eyes for you.'

Patrizia stood, smiled and left, then looked for the nearest phone box so she could tell Bernie that all, so far, had gone according to plan.

Colleen was cursing herself as she stepped off the train and headed out in search of Paddy O'Connell's little house. What on earth was she thinking of? How the hell did she so badly misread 'Paul's' gentle touch on her arm? He must think she a complete tart. But would he have touched her like that if she had been another man on the team? 'Peter', for example? She doubted it. It was a come on, and she liked him, had fancied him a fair bit the moment she saw him, and wondered just how special he must be to be in charge of a London-based unit. He had been flirting with her, for sure, both times they met. Yet he had also dropped other opposite hints in that first meeting... no loose lips, no taking anyone back to the safe house for a shag... was there maybe a rule she had transgressed? Was he testing her? More important, would he hold it against her as the operation advanced? He had been friendly enough when they parted, and she alone seemed to feel embarrassment.

'Just put it behind you,' she said to herself as she emerged from the station, her *A–Z* street atlas open at the page where she had traced the long walk to O'Connell's small terraced house in one of the quiet, tidy side streets close to Fulham FC's stadium, Craven Cottage. Take him at face value, she thought. He had forgotten it as soon as it happened. He had bigger and better things to worry about.

She had no interest in football, but the fact that she could see O'Connell's tiny front garden from outside the main entrance to the ground, where a fairly steady stream of people came and went, gave her the chance to lurk without attracting too much attention to herself, let alone being seen by O'Connell.

After an hour or so, with her concentration beginning to wane, and her legs starting to stiffen up, she wondered if he had already gone out for the day, and took a stroll up his road, on the opposite side to his house, to see if there was any sign of life inside. She could make out the form of his wife, seated, through the front window, and she could see that a fire was lit. There was no sign of him. She walked on for a few dozen yards, crossed over and walked back. This time she got a look through the front room and into a small kitchen, and she could see the back of a man washing up at the sink. That must be him.

She strolled back to the stadium office and waited. It was dull work, enlivened only by the sight or sound of any movement ahead of her, but so often it was a false alarm – a neighbour of O'Connell's moving out, a cleaner or a workman moving in.

'Can I help you at all?' The voice was neither warm nor

unfriendly, but Colleen could see from the name badge on her dark blue suit that she worked for Fulham FC.

'No, I'm fine. Just waiting for someone. I've a horrible feeling they're lost, but I've no way of getting hold of them.'

'You've been waiting a very long time.' This time the voice was less friendly, quizzical, suspicious.

'Yeah, I'm going to give it another half-hour, then go.'

'OK, I was just a bit worried, you know. We have to be very careful these days.'

That last comment provoked something in Colleen that she failed to hold back, despite momentarily telling herself she should.

'What? With me being a filthy Paddy and that?'

'I beg your pardon. I did not even know you were Irish.'

'You knew the second I opened my mouth, didn't you? And then you start giving me all that "got to be careful" stuff.'

'I'm sorry I asked. I was only trying to be helpful.'

'Well, thanks for your help. I'm fine.'

She then noticed movement over the woman's shoulder and she could see a tall man wearing a trilby hat emerging from one of the little gates. As he turned to close the gate and check the latch, she could see his face. O'Connell.

'Anyway, I'll be troubling you no more,' she said. 'I'm off.'

She walked purposefully across the road and once she was about thirty yards behind him she slowed to O'Connell's pace. He stopped briefly to light a cigarette, so she slowed a little more. He went into a newsagent's and emerged unwrapping a packet of Fruit Pastilles. He walked on to a café where he sat at a corner table and, so far as she could see from across the road, spoke to nobody apart from the waitress who fetched him a tea and a cake.

She almost lost him when he came out, started to run, and jumped onto a bus heading for Earls Court. But it was held up at the next traffic lights and she was able to catch up. She found herself turning as she boarded the bus to see if anyone else was following her. O'Connell had taken a seat upstairs. She waited downstairs until, about nine stops later, he came down, jumped off, walked for about two hundred yards, then headed into a dentist's surgery. She wondered, alarm mounting, if like her he had certain routes through shops and offices to get away from possible followers, but surely, if he wasn't even a fully fledged volunteer, he wouldn't be doing that kind of thing. He had shown no sign of concern at being followed so far. She approached the front door to the surgery, and she could see him, sitting reading a magazine. Panic over. Another wait. Christ, she thought, some people did this kind of thing full-time, though usually not alone. 'It would drive me fucking crazy,' she muttered.

O'Connell couldn't have had much work done to his teeth because as soon as he came out, about half an hour later, he headed into another café, and this time had a proper meal. Chips, some kind of pie, baked beans, toast and tea. He talked to the guy at the next table and, as he had his back to the street, she took the risk of going in and standing at the counter to read the menu, so she could pick up on any chat. She quickly realized they were two strangers making small talk. Weather. Food. Football. The election. She left and waited five doors along.

And so his day went on, dull, insignificant, uninteresting so far as she could make out, finally a Tube journey to Paddington, a detour up Praed Street to the dry cleaner's to collect some shirts, and then to work. He used a side entrance to the hotel, and when she got there herself, she realized he had needed a key to get in. She walked round to the main entrance, and just sat in the foyer, sure he would pitch up again. Indeed he did, about twenty minutes later, now dressed in tails and shiny black shoes, and clearly master of all he surveyed. He wafted from one guest to the next, one staff member to another, always smiling, always helpful. There was no way in the world that bitch at Fulham's stadium would have taken *him* for a terrorist, Irish accent or not. So far as the Brits were concerned, there was nice Irish, and there was IRA scum Irish. Colleen knew which one she looked like, with her hard eyes and that fucking scar across her face. Paddy O'Connell, now joking with an American couple as they struggled to open a folded street map, was as nice Irish as they come.

Suddenly she was startled by the presence of a youngish man right by her, holding out his hand, saying 'There's a message for you' and placing a tiny scrap of paper on the arm of her chair. He was gone before she could get a proper look at him. The message said simply 'Out, right, second left, fifty yards down, Café Europa. See you there in ten minutes, Paul.'

She decided to go ahead, Paddy O'Connell having disappeared into the lift with a couple of large suitcases and a young family he was escorting to their room. It was getting dark and cold outside, and as she turned into the street where Café Europa was located, she spotted a tiny shop on the corner selling cheap woollen scarves and went in to buy one. While wrapping it around her neck, and putting the change into her pocket, she spotted 'Paul' talking to someone on the corner of Praed Street, just a few yards from her. It was a man, and as they said their goodbyes, she gasped on seeing 'Paul' raise his hand and touch the man's face tenderly, much as she had tried to do to him earlier in the day. His friend squeezed his free hand, and she could see him mouth the words 'love you' before the man turned and headed towards Paddington Station.

15

PRESS

The relationship between a football club and its local newspaper is rarely smooth, but both at least have one thing in common – a desire for success for the team. Though it is widely believed that good news doesn't sell, the sports editor of the *Courier* had established a proven link between the success of the team and the sales of the paper. But a newspaper which was doing its job properly was bound to get into conflict from time to time, and it had happened last season, when the paper ran a front-page story suggesting that Stan Moffitt has favoured a network of personal friends from outside the area, rather than rely on local firms, in the building of the stand he named after himself. The story was essentially true, but Moffitt insisted he had simply awarded contracts according to the best value for money. His lawyers wrote to the paper's editor insisting the story insinuated impropriety and even illegality, and they demanded a prominently published apology. The editor insisted there had been no such accusation, the story simply said the main contracts went outside the area, and the big ones went to people he knew socially, therefore there would be no apology.

Caught in the middle of this was Don Robinson, who had covered the ups and downs of the club for almost twenty years. He'd had nothing to do with the story, but Moffitt decided that until an apology was published, nobody from the *Courier* would be allowed at the ground, and that included Robinson.

Though the paper initially held firm, they did decide to sit on a story they had been planning to run as a follow-up, on possible inducements Moffitt had received. That was the first step in a process that ended, a month later, with a humiliating front-page 'apology' to Moffitt, and an acceptance they had implied wrong-doing and that none had occurred. They had been forced to accept a hard reality, that without full coverage of matches, and everything else to do with the club, they would lose thousands of readers who bought the paper mainly for the football. Don Robinson was bereft at being unable to be there, and although the paper managed to get a reporter into the stadium as an 'ordinary fan' his reports lacked the insight and knowledge people had come to expect from someone who knew the club inside out.

Stewart Finley was convinced the scraps of information on which their dramatic front page had been based came from Matthew Stock, but he had no firm evidence of that. Surprisingly, Stock had been on holiday in Australia when the scandal broke.

Charlie Gordon had put two and two together and was pretty sure it made four: that Stan Moffitt had benefited from a corrupt relationship with the demonstrably corrupt John Poulson. He had sensed Finley's concern at his mere mention of Poulson's name when he had spoken of the court case on the eve of the Everton game. The Football Association had briefly examined the *Courier* story but decided there was insufficient evidence to justify taking any further action.

The *Courier* would again unwittingly cause problems for the club a few days before the Leeds game in early March. The newspaper had received a photograph taken by a freelance of Michael 'Killer' Kilbride leaving the Park Hotel in Crainton, a small village twenty-five minutes out of town. The photograph, taken at 6.14 a.m. on Sunday morning 24 February, clearly showed the player holding a cigarette in one hand with his other arm around Abigail Partington, a seventeen-year-old girl who worked part-time in the club's ticket office, a job that had been set up by her father Dr Joss Partington, a director of the club.

His smoking was hardly news to anyone, even if most people would find it strange that a professional athlete smoked as heavily as Kilbride did. But given he had two children, and his wife Barbara was pregnant with a third, an extramarital affair with a girl only just legally old enough to have sex at all was the kind of story football clubs really could do without, especially before a big game. It was Finley who was first to hear, in a call from the paper at lunchtime, just hours after the photo had been taken, the day after a 2–0 away defeat at West Bromwich Albion. The *Courier* had received the picture that morning and there had been a lot of agonizing about whether to pursue it. But they realized, the picture having come from a freelance, that if they didn't run it, another paper would, because he would sell it to them. Given he would get more money from a national, it was odd he hadn't sold it to a bigger paper already.

Don Robinson didn't like to do non-football stories, but he was worried the paper would go over the top with it, and asked the editor that he be allowed to handle all dealings with the club on this. Having been banned once, he was determined it would not happen again.

'Stew, look, I am really sorry about this, but we have a picture you need to know about.'

'What is it?'

'One of your players out on the town with a girl from your ticket office.'

'So what?'

'Well, the thing is he is married with kids, and she is seventeen.'

'So what? They might just be friends having a cup of coffee or something. You're not the *News of the World* you know, Don.'

'I know. The thing is we know he booked a room under a false name, and we know when he arrived and when he left and she was with him the whole time.'

'You don't know they did anything.'

'True, but we know they spent the night together in a hotel room while his pregnant wife was waiting at home. And the thing is, Stew, we can do the story and hopefully do it in a way that is not too damaging; or we say no and this guy goes to one of the scandal rags and it goes whoosh.'

'It'll go whoosh if you do it.'

'But we can control it, and we can make sure nobody else gets the picture. We can buy it out of the market.'

Robinson paused to let it all sink in, but then went on: 'There is one other factor here you need to be aware of. The girl is Abigail Partington.'

'Joss Partington's daughter?'

'The very same, one of your directors. And they don't have a care in the world. Him with his fag in one hand and her in the other.'

Finley had to accept it was a story. Also Robinson was right that even if the *Courier* didn't run it, someone else would.

Finley thanked Robinson for calling him and giving the club time to respond. He asked the reporter to give him a few hours to speak to Charlie Gordon and the chairman and he would get him a response – 'promise'. He was dreading telling Gordon. The manager would be furious at the stupidity of the player, and also with the distraction. Don Revie would love it.

Stewart Finley quietly placed the white ivory telephone handset on its holder as he slowly gathered his thoughts. Moments later he picked up the phone again and dialled Don Robinson.

'Hi Stew, that was quick.'

'Sorry Don, I forgot to ask. Who's the player?'

'Don't you do crosswords? I dropped the cigarette clue.'

'Six letters; begins with K?'

'Got it in one. Killer.'

He tracked down Moffitt first, and said, 'We have a situation with a player. He is about to be exposed over an affair.'

'Not DD fucking Marland?'

'No. Kilbride. But there is a complication. The girl is Joss Partington's daughter.'

'What? She is jailbait, surely?'

'Just over.'

'What does the manager say?'

'Trying to find him.'

'Well when you do, get him to come into the club. Let's meet up in the boardroom at two.'

'OK. I'll get Pete Leadbetter to come too.' Leadbetter was the commercial manager but also he had worked as a journalist at the *Courier* for several years before joining the club.

Stewart Finley had been trying to persuade Moffitt and Gordon for a while that the club needed a press liaison officer. These kinds of stories were becoming all too frequent in football and Finley did not feel confident in dealing with them. He just couldn't fathom some of the things the players did and he resented having to dig them out of their mess. He had a full-time job keeping on top of the finances and the day-to-day running of the club, and yet he seemed to have to do so much outside of that job. Football was becoming more and more high-profile, there was more and more coverage every day, and yet they had no professional support at all. To Gordon, money on a press officer was money that could go on players. To Moffitt it was just money, and he didn't like spending it unless he was convinced it would deliver what he wanted. Also, he was far from convinced they needed to hire in an expert, when Pete Leadbetter knew so much already about how the press worked.

Finley and Leadbetter were deep in conversation when the two most powerful people in the club walked into the boardroom to join them. Moffitt was still dressed in his golfing gear having been called from the course to take this 'urgent call' – he'd thought something must have happened to Gloria and half-run, half-walked all the way to the clubhouse.

'I don't know why Stewie couldn't have waited a bit,' he said. 'I was one up with three to play.'

'Can't disagree, Chairman,' replied Gordon. 'I was dozing off in my armchair listening to *The Archers*.'

'If only!'

Moffitt did not mess about. 'OK, Stewie, tell me more.'

Stewart Finley set out the facts as he knew them. Moffitt tutted loudly at regular intervals.

'Fucking Leeds at home, then Chelsea in the Cup,' sighed Gordon, shaking his head from side to side.

'How did they know he was there?' asked Moffitt. 'Have we got someone stirring against us?'

'Could be anyone,' said Leadbetter. 'The girl, someone in the hotel, a journalist who struck lucky by being there. You can go mad worrying about that. The thing is how to deal with it.'

Gordon was worried only about the player. 'He hasn't murdered anyone, she is not under age, but my worry is the problems it's going to cause him at home. Also the Leeds fans will crucify the boy. He's not the strongest mentally.'

Moffitt was livid they were even considering running it. 'We're days away from a bloody general election,' he said, 'and the *Courier* is more interested in this crap.'

'Well, the election is hardly going to be close in this part of the world, is it, Chairman?' smiled Gordon. 'Labour all the way.'

'More's the pity.'

Moffitt asked Leadbetter direct, 'Pete, what do we do?'

Leadbetter paused, and took a sip of water from one of the small bottles on the boardroom table.

'All they have is a picture. Yes, he has his arm around her, but they're clothed, there is no suggestion he was drunk, it could have been taken any time anywhere.'

'But they know he had a room there.'

'He could have had a mate in town. Listen, I know the *Courier*, and they will be bricking it. The ban hurt them, Robbo will be desperate not to get banned again, and he'll be looking for reasons not to run it. Others in there will be fighting the other way, and the editor will be blowing in the wind.'

'But Robinson said if they don't run it, the photographer will take it elsewhere.'

'He might. But in the end he is a freelance photographer. So he wants to get paid for the picture. If we stop the *Courier* from running it, then we find him and buy it off him.'

'Can you do that?' asked Finley.

'We can try.'

'So how do we stop the *Courier*?' asked Moffitt.

'We make them think the picture doesn't tell the real story.' He suggested they have a cup of tea while he worked on a draft statement in his office down the corridor. Ten minutes later, he came back and read it out.

'OK,' he said, 'this should come from a lawyer, not the club. As follows...

'*Dear Sir,*
My client would like to thank you for alerting us to the existence of a photograph of one of their players and a young lady, taken, we have been told, some time on Sunday morning. The club asked me to investigate and, having spoken to all parties, I am satisfied that no wrongdoing occurred and that any suggestion to the contrary would be actionable. The young lady in question is a friend of the player and his family. The player had visited the hotel the previous evening because a relative was staying there, at his expense. We have no further comment at this stage but we will not hesitate to act in the event of further dissemination of false suggestions about the player in question.'

Moffitt nodded, impressed. Gordon immediately saw the problems. 'What if people saw them going in the room together?'
'They were visiting this relative of Kilbride's. She is a family friend, don't forget.'
'What if they demand to know who the relative is?'
'None of their business.'
'So we are going to have to ask them to lie?'
'No, we are going to ask them to say nothing, and to agree with the broad thrust of that letter.'
Moffitt had heard enough. 'OK, Charlie, you need to speak to Kilbride and tell him what is going on. I will talk to Partington and tell him he needs to get a grip of his fucking daughter. I think Pete has given us a way out, and it's all we've got.'
'I'll call the lawyer,' said Finley.

As they set off Moffitt was left alone in the boardroom. The older he got, the more he enjoyed his own company, especially in this room. He made his way to the drinks cabinet, and poured himself a brandy. OK, he said to himself, it is a pain in the arse to be dragged off the golf course to have to deal with trouble caused by yet another over-sexed footballer, but what a wonderful position to be in, chairman of the club he had supported since he was a little kid. So many great moments home and away, lows and highs, the signings and sackings, the suspensions and injuries, the fights, the amazing array of characters from other clubs who had been in this room on matchdays. He'd seen it all, and now the stand was named in his honour. It had been a close call, as his own company was in trouble at the time, and the cost of the stand spiralled way over budget. But he'd survived. Who was it who said the strong survive and the weak are trampled on? Was it Darwin? Well, whoever it was, he was right. It had been touch and go, and yes, he accepted that the deals he did with big outsiders meant he may have pushed some of his old subcontractors close to the wall. But that was business. That was life.

He caught a reflection of himself in the glass on a framed picture of the promotion side of the 1930s; he raised his brandy, and toasted himself: 'To you, Stan. To Stan Moffitt and the Stan Moffitt Stand.'

He drove home in his black Rolls-Royce, and immediately called Joss Partington. Partington was weak, and Moffitt knew he could railroad him. He spoke quickly, explained the situation – not neglecting to mention the 200-yard drive he hit before the messenger from the clubhouse arrived to disturb his round – and then told Partington he needed to speak to his daughter 'and get her under manners'.

'Of course, Stan. I am so sorry about this. I will talk to her immediately.'

'She says nothing to nobody, and if Kilbride comes near her, she tells him to get lost.'

'I'll say all that, Stan. I'll be honest, we have been having problems with her at home.'

'Well, make sure they stay as your problems, not mine. I want this letter going out from the lawyer by nine o'clock in the morning, so call me back when you've squared her.'

He then called Gordon to check how his conversation with Kilbride had gone.

'Difficult at first,' he said. 'His missus was in the background. Anyway I got him to call me back. He's fine with that letter.'

'What did you say to him?'

'I said he was a fucking idiot.'

'What is it with these footballers, Charlie? I mean, he's got a lovely wife, kids, what on earth is he doing putting all that at risk for some teenage rebel who's just out to annoy her dad?'

'I don't know. Listen, when I was a player, I just wanted to play football. For some of these guys it's what goes with it that they like.'

'Can he keep his mouth shut?'

'I've told him I want him in tomorrow morning before anyone else has arrived. He will be scared shitless by the time I have finished with him.'

'Good.'

'What about the girl?'

'Sorted. I'll call Leadbetter and Finley now, and we'll get the letter over to the *Courier* first thing.'

'I don't feel comfortable going along with a pack of lies, but with Leeds and Chelsea coming up ...'

'Don't see it as lying, Charlie. We are telling a different truth for the greater good.'

'Aye, right, I see.'

No sooner had Moffitt replaced the receiver than the phone rang. It was Joss Partington.

'OK, Stan. I've spoken to her and I think that's fine.'

'You *think* it's fine?'

'Well, as I told you, she has been very difficult recently. She was expelled from boarding school for persistent smoking...'

'No wonder she likes Kilbride.'

'...and since she has been back here she has just been very difficult, especially with me. You know, rude, aggressive.'

'I don't know, Joss, no. But I do know if we end up with a front-page sex scandal involving one of our players with these big games coming up, I will hold you personally responsible.'

'Yes, yes, I understand, and I think I have sorted it. I'm going to give her some money and she is going to go on a little holiday in Spain for a while. I mean, if the letter to the paper has the desired effect, this will just blow over, won't it?'

Moffitt felt contempt for the desperation in Partington's voice.

'Let's hope so, for your sake.' And with that he put the phone down.

16

VINCENZO'S

The dream debut at Everton seemed a long time ago now. Though they dominated the first half away at West Brom, prompting Gordon to give one of his favoured 'steady as she goes, no need to change anything, you're all doing great' half-time team talks, DD missed a sitter from seven yards out with just twelve minutes to go. Two minutes later, Ally Brown took the lead for West Brom and his namesake Tony added a second from a corner in the first minute of injury time. After the sense that the draw at Everton and the Man City win would be a turning point, the talk was once again of Gordon's future.

DD knew he had cocked up, big-time. He trudged off the pitch head down and whispered 'sorry' as he passed a dejected-looking manager on the touchline. But once they were showered and dressed, and the kitman was wheeling all the skips out to the coach, David Brown quickly managed to provoke him into being his belligerent self. With Gordon off talking to the press, and Winston having disappeared to the boardroom for a drink, Brownie shouted across the away dressing room.

'Hey guys, quiz question. Which First Division striker today missed a chance from inside the box that my fucking granny could have scored?'

DD thought about it for a moment then snapped back. 'Thing is, Brownie, the FA decided that today only people called Brown were allowed to score, and unfortunately West Brom have two Browns who both know how to play football.'

'Yeah, yeah, yeah. Striker my arse. In fact not just my granny, my granny's budgie could have scored.'

'Yeah – why don't you all have a good moan about me on the coach home, eh? I won't be there. You see, being a special player, the gaffer's given me a couple of days off to go to London. See you, lads, enjoy the whippet racing tonight.'

He drove home, Magic having driven his car down to meet up with the squad at the hotel, and was actually beating himself up about the miss. Jules had headed the ball down from a perfect cross from Dipper, Smudger had shot from just inside the box, it came off the post, and with the goalkeeper on the ground having dived to save Smudger's shot, the ball fell right at DD's feet. He just had to dink it, but instead he blasted it low and it bounced off the keeper's midriff and was cleared. For all his bluster in the dressing room earlier, he was hurting, and reliving the moment over and over.

'Oh *fuck*!' he shouted at one point, hammering his hand on the steering wheel. Lucy knew not to fuss over him too much when he had lost, and she had heard on the radio one commentator saying, 'You will have to go a very long way to see a worse miss than DD Marland's at The Hawthorns today.' They ate a late dinner, he watched *Match of the Day*, went to bed, and though Lucy tried to take his mind off his miss by sliding her hand down to his groin as soon as he joined her, he rolled away.

Partly it was because he was tired, partly the disappointment. But also, he was already looking forward to tomorrow night, and Patrizia.

On Sunday morning she called to tell him how to reach the flat. She said there would be paparazzi front and back looking out for any of The Choirgirls, but there was a garage entrance he should use that would get him into the main hotel, and she then explained how he could access the part of the hotel with private apartments.

As he put the phone down, he explained to Lucy that he was meeting Alfie Ruse for dinner, to discuss some new commercial tie-ups that had come in on the back of his move.

'OK, love.' Lucy was always fine about him bringing in extra money from his off-field activities.

Just before he left, Patrizia called again, and once more he had to go through the motions of talking to Alfie.

'Change of plan,' she said.

'Oh, OK. What now, then?'

She explained that there were just too many photographers at the hotel, they now had all entrances covered anticipating a visit from Bella Luca, so she was worried he would be seen, and there was a risk the photographers would put two and two together and make ten. But she had booked a small private room at Vincenzo's, a restaurant in St John's Wood, and they should meet there instead.

'When you arrive, ask for Paolo and say you are meeting Constance.'

His disappointment that he would not be going straight to her flat was matched by a certain excitement that she was going to such trouble to make sure she kept her promise to see him. Either way, he made a mental note to pick up a packet of condoms on his way to the station.

Since meeting her, he had been looking at the news pages of the papers more often and The Choirgirls were mentioned virtually every day. Any scrap of a story about them would find its way into print. He guessed these photographers who stalked their every move wouldn't do it unless they were well paid for the pictures they managed to get. Patrizia was not big news like Bella Luca and the other girls, but he guessed a picture of the band's middle-aged manager out with a top footballer would still fetch a few bob. He felt quite touched that she was doing all she could to make sure nobody got it.

He arrived early at the restaurant, found Paolo, and was led up a short staircase to a small room, where a table was set for two. A bottle of champagne sat in an ice bucket on the serving table, and Paolo popped the cork and poured a glass for DD.

'Patrizia won't be long,' he said. 'I know she is on her way.'

When she arrived, she was flustered and agitated as she sat

down. 'These fucking photographers are killing me, they follow me now because they think I will lead them to Bella,' she said.

'Have a seat, have a drink, take your coat off,' DD said.

'DD, I'm so sorry, I can have one drink with you and then I need to leave. One of the girls, Millie, has thrown a total strop because she has found out Bella has a better deal on royalties than she does, and she is talking about refusing to do this European tour. So we have a meeting at nine. Honestly, I am so sorry. I was really looking forward to seeing you.'

She could tell he was disappointed.

'Honestly, I do want to spend some time with you, and if the tour goes ahead, I promise that when I get back I will make it up to you. My head is just all over the place right now.'

DD took her hand, and said: 'Why don't I book a hotel somewhere, and we can meet up when your meeting is done?'

'No, not tonight. I really can't. I'm so sorry.'

'OK.'

'I am back at the end of the first week in March. When are you in London again, DD?'

'Let me think. We're playing at Chelsea that weekend.'

'So I will see you then. I promise. Where do you stay?'

'I can check.'

'OK. Let me know – these are all my phone numbers – and I will make sure I am there. I promise.' And with that she handed him her card, kissed him briefly on the lips, and left.

He got home in time for a late dinner, after which Lucy's efforts to arouse him were more successful, though it was Patrizia, her scent, her eyes, and the body he had briefly felt against his when she kissed him, that he thought of.

17

SURPRISES

Willie walked back to his digs still apprehensive, but he was over the shock of Catriona's pregnancy. Having a baby. How in God's name? ... Well, he knew how, but they had actually not had sex that often, and only once without a condom. Once. Just once. All those jokes that Brownie made about him barely being out of nappies ... now he was going to be a father, for heaven's sake. He could tell from Catriona's tone that she wasn't even thinking about not having it. Good Catholic family and all that. But what the hell? He was now talking to himself ... 'I'm too young to be a dad. I've got enough on my plate trying to make it here. This changes everything ... Marriage. Baby.' Willie was not a great swearer, but he found himself stamping his foot on the ground, saying 'fuck, fuck, fuck'. She had sounded so happy about it. He could see nothing but grief coming out of this.

He could barely eat, and Mavis Archibald noticed. As he helped her clear away the plates, and the other apprentices went to watch TV, or up to their rooms, she asked him, 'Are you OK? You barely touched your dinner.'

He shook his head.

'What is it, love?'

Surely, he thought, he should be telling news like this to his parents first, not his landlady.

He told her anyway.

'I've had a bit of a shock,' he said.

'Don't tell me Catriona has dumped you.'

'Anything but. She's pregnant.'

Mavis clapped her hands together and squealed in delight.

'Oh, that is marvellous, Willie.'

'I'm seventeen,' he said. 'I don't have a pro contract. I don't live where Catriona does. My parents won't be happy.'

'A new baby is always good news. They might surprise you.'

'What about the gaffer? What will he think?'

'Managers like players who settle down young.'

'Seventeen, Mavis.'

'You'll be eighteen when it comes along now, won't you?'

'I guess.'

'My, what a lot of growing up you've done this week, Willie, what with David Brown and now this.'

Nor was the growing up news finished, though the third bit was more unequivocally good news.

Willie had gone to his room, and was getting ready for bed, when Mavis knocked on his door and told him there was a phone call for him.

'Catriona?'

'No,' she replied. 'It's Charlie Gordon.' He felt the blood draining from his face and his guts.

'Does he know? About Catriona expecting?'

'No, I don't think so. He said he had some good news, and he wanted to tell you himself.'

As he ran down the stairs, Mavis urging him to 'take care and don't injure yourself', he wondered if he might be about to get a call-up to the first-team squad. But no, why would he phone after ten o'clock to tell him something like that? It could wait.

He could tell straight away from the tone of Charlie Gordon's voice that whatever the news was, it had already made the manager happy.

'What is it, gaffer? I got the fright of my life when Mavis said you'd called to speak to me.'

'And what did you think might be the reason?'

'I wondered if all your wingers had gone down injured and you were giving me a go against Leeds.'

'You up against Bremner, Lorimer and Gray? You'd love that, wouldn't you?'

'Of course.'

'Well no, it's not that. But it is something pretty exciting.'

Willie could feel himself relaxing inside, that it wasn't about Catriona.

'You know of Willie Ormond?'

'The Scotland manager? Of course, yes.'

'Aye, well he called me today for a general chit chat, and we got talking about you. And he's got an under-23s game against Wales next week, and he wondered if you wanted to go up and train with the squad?'

'Yes, I'd love to, of course.'

Ormond had played his entire career in Scotland, but only won six international caps. For the first two he shared a room with Gordon, and it had created something of a bond between them. In truth, it was Gordon, not Ormond, who had suggested Willie Buchanan enjoy a little taste of international football preparation.

'I doubt you'll be playing,' he said, 'and you probably won't make the bench, but you'll learn a lot training with these guys, and you'll get yourself on Willie Ormond's radar, which is no bad thing with a World Cup coming up.'

'Wow. You don't think I could get to the World Cup squad, do you?'

'It's doubtful, but this is not a bad wee step on a very nice ladder, son. You make the most of it.'

'I will, gaffer, I will.'

He explained that the training base was in Largs, Ayrshire, and the game was to be played at Ayr United's ground.

'One more thing, gaffer. Could I maybe get home to see my parents and my girlfriend while I'm up there? I've got a bit of a situation at the moment.'

'I don't see why not. If you head off home tomorrow, you can be at Largs when they all get together the day after?'

'That's great.'

'What's your situation, son?'

Willie took a deep breath, then just told him, straight out, 'My girlfriend's pregnant.'

'Jeez-o,' replied Gordon, 'you boys will be boys, will you not? Well, so much for those cracks Brownie keeps making about you being a virgin.'

'So you don't mind?'

'Who am I to mind? These things happen. We can talk about it. But for now, son, you just get to bed and dream sweet dreams about pulling on a Scotland shirt.'

'Thanks, gaffer,' he said, quietly putting down the phone, and hoping his parents would take the news as well as his landlady and his manager had done.

On Monday morning, Gordon called DD, talked him through what they were doing in training, and asked him to do a steady half-hour run.

'OK, will do. And, boss, sorry about the sitter. I can't stop thinking about it.'

'Forget it. Ninety-nine times out of a hundred, you score. Just one of those things. But DD, when you do fuck up, put your hands up like you did to me, don't go winding up Brownie. It's not worth it.'

'Was he slagging me then?'

'Is the Pope a Catholic?'

'Fair enough. Listen, boss, one other thing – my family's asking. When we're at Chelsea, where do we stay?'

'Great Western at Paddington. Let me know if they need tickets. I can get a few more for Cup games. I'll see you tomorrow.'

'Thanks, boss. I'll go for that run now.' And he did, stopping halfway at a telephone kiosk to call Patrizia and tell her 'Great Western, Paddington. We'll be arriving late afternoon.'

While he was out, Lucy took a call to be told the deal on the house sale was done, so they decided to go out for a celebratory lunch, then went to the cinema to see the new Mel Brooks film *Blazing Saddles*. He dropped Lucy home, then set off for the long drive north, reaching the Tudor Manor Hotel just before midnight.

He slept well, but was woken by the phone. The radio clock said it was just seven o'clock. He answered groggily, and heard club secretary Stewart Finley's soft Scottish voice apologizing for such an early call. He said he needed him to be at the ground at half past eight.

'But the gaffer is expecting me in training.'

'I have told him. He understands.'

'What's it about?'

'Hopefully nothing, but we have received a suspicious package addressed to you, and the cops want to ask you about it.'

'Jesus.'

'See you at half eight.'

When he arrived at the stadium, there was a police car parked right outside the main entrance.

Tilly Foster was waiting for him in reception. Things had been a little frosty between them since the night before the Everton match, when he had given the receptionist his two compliment-ary tickets for the match in exchange for Tilly's room number, only to find when he knocked on the door that Jules Pemberton was already in there, and that he and Tilly were something of a pre-match item.

'What's this about?' he asked.

'I don't know, Mr Finley is waiting upstairs with the police.'

Chief Inspector Jeff Bailey was a big fan of the club and had been since his father took him to his first match when he was seven years old. He had made his way up the police ladder and was now in charge of all police activity on matchdays. As with most clubs, there was a hooligan element to worry about, but most of their work was very basic policing, to do with traffic management and crowd control, and he did it well. On occasions he was invited into the boardroom after a game. Bailey was a good friend of the chairman and he often helped the players and their wives get off minor offences like speeding fines.

Bailey stood to shake DD's hand, and introduced him to Inspector Peter Hubbard. DD didn't catch his full title – he just heard the word 'anti-terrorism'. DD started to feel a little faint, and poured himself a glass of water.

Hubbard tried to lighten the mood, saying he was a Chelsea fan, and he was minded to put him in the police car and take him back to Tottenham so he couldn't play in the Cup match.

DD smiled weakly.

'Now, Mr Marland,' the anti-terrorist officer continued, his tone changing completely, 'we are facing a considerable threat on the mainland right now. You'll be aware of the recent bombings, and also the IRA are pursuing a highly active letter bombing campaign. And we have intercepted a package addressed to you that is causing us concern.'

'Me?'

'A football club would be a very good target. It would generate publicity all over the world, especially this close to an election, and it would create a lot of fear, so this is probably not about you personally.'

'OK.'

'The thing is I need to ask if you have been expecting any packages from Ireland.'

'I don't think so.'

'This contains electrical goods, which is why Mr Finley very kindly alerted us to it. We can deal with this easily enough, but I just wanted to know if there was an easy explanation.'

'I just don't know.'

'Do you visit Northern Ireland at all?'

'Never been.'

'The Republic?'

'Did a pre-season testimonial there with Spurs once. That's all.'

'Are you political?'

'No. Never voted in my life.'

'Do you have anyone who might bear a grudge?'

He thought about saying 'a few husbands', but held it in. 'No, not really. I mean, there are people who don't like me – Jock Johnson and David Brown for example – but they wouldn't harm me, I don't think.'

'OK,' said Hubbard, leaning down to pull out a large box in plain brown paper from beneath the table. DD pushed himself back in his chair.

'Don't worry, there is no immediate danger. We've scanned it pretty carefully. I just need your permission for my people next door to open it.'

'Sure,' he said.

Just twenty-one days earlier he had been there with his dad chatting with Gordon while Stan Moffitt negotiated with Sidney Wale. Now he was sitting being grilled by the cops about a suspected parcel bomb addressed to him, which was now being carried through to a room where bomb disposal experts were waiting to take it apart.

Minutes later, a plain-clothes officer popped his head round the door. 'Sir,' he said to Hubbard. 'Have you got a second?'

Hubbard followed his colleague, and returned two minutes later.

'DD, can you come with me?'

'Do you want us all?' asked Finley.

'No, just Mr Marland.'

DD noticed as they made the short walk to the Broadbent Suite that Hubbard was smiling, close to laughing. As they joined his disposal team, he realized why.

Hubbard handed him a note on a compliments slip. 'DD. As promised, a bit of fun from the Enniskillen nunnery. If Mrs DD doesn't want to play, from what I gather Patrizia might. Ticking Dick is her favourite.'

'Oh fuck!' said DD. 'That mad Irish woman.'

'Mad, Irish and a woman ... we were right to be worried,' said Hubbard, now letting go of the laughter he had been holding back. His three colleagues joined in.

DD flicked through the contents of the box. The Enniskillen dildo. Mister Buzz. Tickly Tommy (batteries provided). Whips, underwear, men's thongs, massage oils, aphrodisiacs, masks, novelty condoms, videos – it was like a sex shop in a box.

'Please don't tell them,' he said. 'If the players get hold of this...'

'OK,' said Hubbard. 'Here's the deal. We tell Mr Finley it was a Dublin alarm clock company asking if you would promote their clocks in exchange for a free holiday in Ireland... and you get the four of us tickets for the Chelsea match.'

'Fucking deal,' said DD. 'You lot are stars.'

'I hope you understand why we had to take this so seriously,' said the police chief, 'what with the bombings we have had, and the election this week.'

'Yeah, sure.'

Hubbard wrote down his address and phone number, and asked: 'What do you want us to do with the package?'

'My car's downstairs,' he said.

'I'm sure Mrs Marland *will* be pleased.'

He smiled, but he was already thinking not of Lucy but of pouring the oil over Patrizia's beautiful olive shoulders, and hoping to God none of these police guys spoke to the press.

18

DIRECTORS

Wednesday 27 February, late afternoon

The following afternoon, just before six o'clock, Moffitt parked his Rolls-Royce in his dedicated space in the club's main car park, nodding appreciatively, as he always did, at the 'Chairman Only' placard painted in club colours that greeted him. There were always a few supporters around, buying tickets or checking out the club shop, and he made a point of talking to them. He didn't much like the fans, who seemed to think anyone rich enough to be chairman had a bottomless well of money on which to draw, but it was important to know what they were thinking. He positively disliked the president of the official supporters' club, Toby Wilkins, but that was less because of his agitation on behalf of the fans than on account of his homosexuality. Wilkins was 'out, loud and proud', and on the one occasion Moffitt invited him to watch a match in the boardroom, he brought along his boyfriend, an Irishman called Martin. Matthew Stock went so far as to suggest Martin should perhaps be asked to go to the ladies' lounge.

Nonetheless, Moffitt understood it was important to know what the fans were thinking. West Brom had been a big disappointment; the fans he met in the car park had clearly been reliving DD's miss as often as the player himself. But they still felt he had quality and a lot of goals in him, and with Leeds and Chelsea coming up, they were excited.

'Got to beat Leeds,' said one.

'*Dirty* Leeds,' said Moffitt. 'Must give Revie's bastards their full name.' He walked on, feeling warmed by the laughter of the fans he left behind.

It cheered him up, but he was worried on two fronts. Football, of course. But also politics. Tomorrow was the general election, and it was too close to call. He wasn't a massive fan of Ted Heath, not least because he had taken the country into the Common Market, but in his view 'a bad Tory is always better than any socialist, and especially Harold bloody Wilson'. These were certainly volatile and unpredictable times. Within days, he thought, we might have a change of Prime Minister and a change of manager.

He always saw Stewart Finley for a pre-meeting chat in advance of the board meeting, which usually took place in two parts: first the board, then a short break, and then they would be joined by Charlie Gordon for the 'manager's report'.

Finley was waiting for the chairman at the foot of the stairs that led up to the boardroom. They always met in the ladies' lounge first, knowing none of the other directors would go there. Most clubs had a ladies' room, and it was only in recent months that women had been allowed in the boardroom at all. Gloria had persuaded him he would look modern and with-it if he joined those clubs which had finally broken the ban. But some visiting clubs still liked to keep the sexes separate and so the ladies' lounge was essentially for them. Nat Broadbent had been there, one of his largest NB carvings having been gouged into the side of a mahogany table where on matchdays Tilly would always place a vase of eleven roses, one for each player.

Moffitt knew that some of his colleagues would question Gordon's position. Defeat at Leeds and Chelsea – even though these were both tough games, one home, one away – would see the pressure on the manager raised several notches. He had asked Finley to prepare a note on the financial implications of sacking him, and also a list of possible successors and their likely salary demands.

Finley made clear that the club's finances were even more

precarious than last year. Gates had fallen on average by two thousand, and the outlay for Marland, without any money coming in for transfers in the other direction, meant their pre-season planning was askew.

'You know what we need, Mr Chairman. A draw at Chelsea and a win in the replay here.'

'Yep, then win the semi-final and win the final at Wembley, simple as that. But it's not going to happen if we play like we did at West Brom.'

Finley liked to ask very direct questions of his boss.

'If we lose the next two games, Leeds and Chelsea, is he a goner?'

'Well, I think the fans will turn a bit. It's harsh because on paper you'd have us down to lose both games, but he did give us all that talk of top six, top four at the start of the season.'

'Yep.'

'So who would replace him?'

'Well, Winston would be the cheapest option for sure.'

'Gordon would go fucking ape. They've fallen out.'

'Well, whose fault is that? Listen, there is nothing more ex than an ex-manager, you know that. Once he's gone, he's gone. You can ask Winston to be caretaker for a few games and if he does OK, you give him the job full-time and meanwhile we shop around for a Plan B. But people will forget Gordon quickly enough. Three defeats on the trot. The fans will have had enough.'

'You seem harder on him than I am,' said Moffitt.

'Have you seen the way his hands shake these days?'

'No.'

'I've been keeping an eye on his desk drawer here and at the training ground. He is hitting it.'

'Well, so long as it doesn't affect his work.'

'Mmm, well, how could it not?'

'Plenty of people drink a lot and do a perfectly good job, in all walks of life.'

'Possibly,' Finley replied doubtfully. 'There's something else you need to know. He had that *Daily Express* story about Poulson in his briefcase at Everton, and he asked me about it.'

'What do you mean he asked about it?'

'Not asked maybe, but he mentioned it, and I don't know, I just thought there was a bit of a glint in his eye.'

'Was there now? OK. Anything else before we go through?'

'I suppose you should have a word with Partington, just check how the daughter is doing.'

'What a wimp he is. Can't control his own bloody daughter.'

'Listen, Chairman, money and the manager, that is all that's going to be on their minds. Just let them talk a bit.'

He was right of course. As he went through, the other directors were helping themselves to drinks and chatting. Moffitt went to his seat, ran his fingers over the scar on the table – *Percy's Gouge*, the cleaning ladies called it – which was his way of reminding himself to keep his cool no matter the provocation. The four-inch gash was created many years ago when Percy Summerton was negotiating a contract with ex-manager Billy Carroll, and got so angry at Carroll's chiselling for more and more that he smashed his brandy glass on the table.

He tapped his pen against a glass as a way of calling the meeting to order, and as the others sat down, he said: 'Gentlemen, you have all received a copy of the minutes of the last board meeting. Will someone confirm that they are a true and proper record of the event.' Several voices echoed their agreement.

They were onto the second item – club finances – when Matthew Stock asked directly: 'What is the situation regarding the manager if we lose these next two games?'

'Well, let's hope we don't, eh?' said Moffitt.

'Of course,' said Stock. 'But we have to plan for possibilities, surely. We can't be left scrabbling around if and when it happens.'

'So what do you propose?' asked Moffitt.

'I propose,' replied Stock, 'that we agree that if we lose both games, he has to go, and we make preparations now as to his replacement.'

'I think that is too black and white,' said Moffitt. 'It may be he has to go, but let's say we lose to a disputed last-minute penalty against Leeds. Is that the same as losing four-nil? Then let's say we lose at Chelsea but the players are cheered off by our fans because they gave everything, hit the bar, had a goal disallowed, lost it to a fluke goal. Is that the same as getting battered?'

'A result is a result, and we were told by Gordon if he got the support he was asking for, we would be no lower than sixth.'

'Stewart, I know you have been looking at the numbers. Kindly bring the board up to speed.'

Finley pushed a sheet of paper in front of himself, clasped his hands together and read, slowly and methodically, from notes he had jotted down earlier.

'Thank you, Mr Chairman. If you recall, gentlemen, Mr Gordon is now in his seventh season with us—'

'We know that,' snapped Stock.

'I think the context is important,' said Moffitt. 'Carry on, Stewart.'

'We were fifteenth in the League the year before he joined us, and he has kept us in the top division every year, finishing fourteenth; twelfth; thirteenth; tenth; fourth; and eighth. These finishes are broadly in line with the expectations he set out for us. This is the first season in which we are well shy of where he said we would be.'

'Top six, maybe third,' said Stock.

'Indeed, yes. We stand in fifteenth place after what was not a bad start to the season, and if we continue on current trend, relegation is a possibility. We have added DD Marland to the squad at considerable expense, and although he appears to have added something to the gate for his debut, we had budgeted for average gates of 33,750 based on the manager's predicted League position and we are averaging more than two thousand one hundred less than that, so that leaves us around three hundred thousand off target if this trend continues to the end of the season. Barclays have indicated a certain reluctance to go beyond our current borrowing limit, so we would expect to have to come back to ask the board for loans or personal guarantees. As you know, the chairman found the funding himself for the DD signing.'

'Thanks, Stewart. Has anybody got anything to say about DD before we discuss the manager?'

Geoffrey Raymond raised his hand.

'Yes, Geoffrey.'

'I understand that we are paying for his hotel accommodation. The manager tells me we might save a lot of time and effort if we put him up in a brothel.'

'He'd certainly score more there,' said Stock.

'We may not approve,' said Moffitt, 'but we are dealing with wealthy young men who we train and feed until they are superbly fit and our local girls find them extremely attractive. I don't think we should link too directly his off-field sex life and his on-field scoring. You may be aware of a Mr George Best who runs defences ragged every Saturday, despite the odd misdemeanour through the week.'

Cliff McGuire laughed out loud. 'Odd fucking misdemeanour! I'm told when they played West Ham last week, Bestie was pissed as a fart on the Friday night, shagged the hell out of a chambermaid Saturday morning, and then went and scored a hat-trick and got man of the match.'

'So maybe DD needs to drink more, not just shag,' said Moffitt.

'A Double Diamond works wonders, works wonders, works wonders…' McGuire could barely contain himself.

'OK, OK, let's settle down,' said Moffitt. 'Does anyone else have a view on this?'

Partington spoke up. 'I agree with you, Stan, that even if we do lose at Leeds and Chelsea, the mood around the manager might be positive. Even at West Brom, where let's be honest we were dreadful in the second half, the fans clapped them off. There was a small protest, literally just a handful, but there was no general mood against Gordon.'

'That is because they are all excited about the Cup,' said Stock. 'They know we have blown the League. And after that sitter, they know that DD is a dud. I warned he would be.'

'I don't recall you warning any such thing,' said Moffitt.

'There is nothing in the minutes to suggest so,' interjected Stewart Finley.

'One of the Spurs directors told me he was trouble with a capital T and I passed that on to you, Stan, you know that.'

'People say all sorts of things about other people. In the end you make judgements in the round. I don't suppose you thought that when he knocked in that equalizer at Goodison, did you?'

'So we've shelled out £132,000 for one goal, have we?'

'No, Matthew. I have. I shelled it out. And he will score plenty more goals, have no fear on that front.'

'We'll see.'

'I believe that you are also suggesting we replace the manager? And who do you think should replace him?' asked Moffitt.

'I think Winston should be given a chance,' replied Stock. 'Maybe as caretaker.'

'He has no managerial experience at all,' said Moffitt.

'So he wouldn't cost so much,' said Stock.

'I'm not sure that is reason enough.'

'We'll save on the bar bills too.'

'OK, that's enough,' said Moffitt, his hand falling on Percy's Gouge. He said he did not want anyone suggesting outside the room that Gordon was out if he lost both games, but he did agree that they would have an informal emergency board meeting if it happened.

'Gordon knows the score. But we should do nothing to pile on the pressure. Anyway, I've got a feeling we can get something out of Leeds.'

'Oh, spare me football fans and their "just got a feeling..." How many Leeds fans have just got a feeling they can put us into freefall?' said Stock.

Finley interrupted. 'Mr Chairman, perhaps I can brief you on the new advertisers in the programme, and also the travel and hotel plans for Chelsea?'

As he did so, Moffitt stood up to stretch his legs and wandered over to his favourite spot by the window, just as a bus below sent spray onto two schoolchildren walking by. Beyond, lines of terraced houses stretched out into the distance, plumes of smoke rising, and then beyond that the great tall chimneys, reminders of a once flourishing cotton industry that was now finished. Without the club doing well, Moffitt said to himself, this town is nothing. He returned to his seat to hear the directors haggling over how many complimentary tickets they should ask for from Chelsea. 'My son is at the LSE,' said Stock. 'I'd like a couple for him if possible.'

At least this board was made up entirely of real supporters of the club, Moffitt reflected. They all shared much the same accent, memories of the same players long forgotten by all but the most ardent, the same desire for the club to do well. Every one of them had been taken to their first game by a father or a big brother, and every one of them felt a desire not just for the power and status they enjoyed, but genuinely they wanted to put something back into the club that had been such a part of their lives. It made sense that Moffitt, the wealthiest by far among them, was chairman, but they all did their bit, he had to recognize that. He recognized too that they all had their own strong instincts for survival. What Stock was signalling was that when the fans turned, it was important they turned on the manager, not them. They had all seen it before, and it could be horrible, as unedifying a spectacle as those that the Prof would read about in his books on Ancient Rome, when bloodthirsty crowds gathered to watch gladiators in combat. The booing. The cruel howls being hurled from the terraces. The whistles and insults. Sometimes players got it. Football men still recalled the time Alan Ball, a World Cup winner no less, was reduced to a shadow of himself by the non-stop abuse coming from the terraces. Boards got it too. 'Sack the board!' was the cry they dreaded most. Chairmen copped it if it was felt they were not providing the cash needed for players, but with DD Marland so recently joining the club, that charge could not be levelled at Moffitt. No, if the crowd turned here, they would turn on Charlie Gordon, for sure.

Moffitt brought this part of the meeting to an end. 'I suggest we have a little break, top up drinks or teas, and then we will get the manager in. All back in five minutes.'

Moffitt took Stock to one side afterwards.

'I hear what you're saying, Matthew. But I mean it – no talk outside about him being on two defeats and out.'

'The press are already saying it, Stan.'

'There is a world of difference between them saying it and us saying it. Also, I don't want you talking about his drinking either. Until he goes, he is our manager and we support him, OK?'

'OK. Understood, loud and clear.' And with that, he turned away and walked out of the boardroom.

Then Moffitt sought out Partington.

'How is Abigail?'

'Away with her sister. All fine. Nothing to worry about.'

'Good.'

Moffitt was concerned about the League position, but not overly concerned about the manager's heavy drinking. The game was full of managers who drank too much. Some of them – Brian Clough, for example – were the best in the business. The qualities that made him a genius manager who had taken two unfashionable and poorer clubs, Hartlepool and Derby County, to unparalleled success were probably the same qualities that made him an alcoholic. He did not think for one moment Gordon drank as much as Cloughie. And just as Clough's long-suffering chairmen tolerated his abuse of the bottle and his abuse of them, provided Gordon won matches and challenged for trophies, he would take the same approach. If he won against Leeds and Chelsea, he could have Scotch on his porridge and brandy on his breakfast for all he cared.

Also, with Stock now clearly promoting the cause of Ronnie Winston, Moffitt felt a certain added empathy with his manager – both of them in the Number One position, being openly undermined by their Number Two.

This was hardly news to Moffitt. But it was the first time it had surfaced in the boardroom.

'How do I get rid of that twat Stock?' Moffitt asked Finley after they had retreated to the ladies' lounge again to assess the discussion so far. 'That felt like a full-frontal attack, not just on Gordon, but on me. And the jibe about the bar bill was a low blow.'

'You have to buy him out or vote him off.'

'How hard?'

'Not easy. He has about nine per cent in shares, and he won't give them up easily. If you got the rest of the board against him, that could work, but I'm not sure they'll go for it; they like the mix. So you'd need a seventy per cent vote to oust him before the next AGM.'

'Less than ten per cent shares? And he talks to me like that. This is the Stan Moffitt Stand, not the Matthew Fucking Stock Stand, and you know what, there is an old Yorkshire saying from when textiles was kingpin up here: "If tha name's on't chimney, tha can do what the fuckin' 'ell tha likes." It is my name on't chimney and he better know it.'

The fall-out had been a long time in the brewing. Through all the changes at the club since the Summerton era came to an end, Stock was a constant. His skill was sniffing the winds of change before they blew in, and that was what Moffitt found so worrying now: that he had dared to be so open revealed his belief that if Gordon went, Moffitt might be vulnerable too. Nine per cent was a low base, but he had allies with less courage but greater shareholdings. Cliff McGuire, nominally deputy chairman, and the second biggest shareholder after Moffitt, regularly socialized with Stock. The fans liked him too. He was the only director who would never miss a home reserves or A team game. He would always turn out at a fans' meeting. He had an incredible memory of every game he had ever seen and he could talk to the fans all night with real passion and they liked him for it. He was not to be underestimated. But in the last couple of seasons, Moffitt was developing the impression that if he proposed something, Stock would automatically oppose it. The Marland signing was but the latest example. He was leading the opposition to a new club lottery, and a new system of pricing for pitch-side advertising. He was also convinced that Stock was the source of some of the more troubling stories that had been fed to the *Courier* and beyond, which is why he had put him on notice about the 'two defeats and you're out' angle, a story that Don Robinson would manage to get on the front page, never mind the back. He was even wondering if he had been involved in notifying the *Courier* about Killer's evening with Abigail Partington.

When everyone was back in the room, he asked Finley to fetch
Gordon from his office down below.

Gordon was wearing a smart suit and a freshly laundered shirt,
with the club tie, but with the extra weight he was carrying he
had left the top button undone. He was also sucking a mint and
Finley noticed a stain on the back of his jacket as he followed
him in to join the board.

'Mr Chairman,' he said. 'Gentlemen.'

'Thanks for coming, Charlie. Can I get you a tipple?' asked
Moffitt. Gordon looked around the room, noticed that most had
their glasses charged, so said he would have a whisky. Finley rose
to pour it for him.

'So, Charlie? How are we?'

'I'm OK, thanks. Obviously West Brom last Saturday was a big
disappointment. It just shows you the fine lines in this game. DD
puts that chance away and we can tighten up at the back, easily
hold on, two points. He misses, they go up the other end, lapse of
concentration by Killer, Brown's in, we're behind. That's football.'

'I thought the ref had a stinker too,' said Cliff McGuire.

'Yeah, you expect better from Jack Taylor, meant to be the
best in the country. Definitely missed a shove on Dipper. So you
see, if he gives a pen, we're in front – what was that, fifty-eighth
minute?'

'Yes, OK,' said Stock, 'but you'd agree Kirkpatrick had a stinker
when he sent off Larry Lloyd in the Liverpool game and so a
match we were losing two-nil we end up drawing, so it's swings
and roundabouts.'

'Sure. But Saturday we really didn't have any luck.'

'We had a great chance though, and your star striker fluffed it.'

'True. Hands up to that one.'

Moffitt sat up straight, clearly not enjoying the prospect of
saying what he was about to say.

'Charlie, let me, and indeed the whole board, let me be frank
with you. We are a long way off where you led us to believe
we would be. Now there is no way you have become a bad
manager overnight but you know as well as I do, this is a results
business and the results are not good enough, especially as we

have strengthened the squad. So I am sure you understand that things must improve.'

'Of course I do. I have no excuses to offer you; I wish I had. I prepared the team in exactly the same way as previous seasons. The spirit is actually pretty good. DD is taking time to settle but he will, I am confident of that...'

'Do you think he might get his wife up here and leave the hotel staff alone?'

'I'm working on it. He's sold his house and she should be up this weekend after the Leeds game. But he is a quality player and we will get the best out of him, I'm sure. There was a time Geoff Hurst couldn't get in the West Ham team; next thing you know he's scored a hat-trick in the World Cup final. You need patience with new players. Maybe he scored his first goal too soon, and we all expect too much of him.'

He stopped for a moment to scratch his ear and take a hankie from his trouser pocket and wipe away the beads of sweat forming on his forehead.

'I'm not naïve, gentlemen. You'll be looking at the League table and thinking maybe we need a change. I understand that. But if you stick with me, I will turn this around, I promise you that.'

'And if we lose at Leeds, and then we lose at Chelsea, what would you recommend we do?' asked Stock, his eyes burning into Gordon's.

'That will be a matter for you. But nobody is doing more to prevent that from happening than I am.'

'I think we know that, Charlie,' said Moffitt. 'But clearly we have to see an improvement soon.'

'Yep. I get it.'

'Anyone else?' asked Moffitt. He looked at Stock but it was Geoffrey Raymond who spoke.

'Mr Gordon, it is not my intention to interfere with your team or your tactics, but I want to ask you a question. Football has been around for over a hundred years. Last year a company called Hewlett Packard introduced a pocket calculator and now they've developed these computer things, which allow you to do amazing mathematical calculations and formulations. In America they're manufacturing these machines on an enormous scale. I just wondered whether you saw any role for these technologies in football?'

Gordon was baffled by the question. So, clearly, was Stock. 'Mr Chairman, that is surely not a football question.'

'Well, it is,' said Raymond. 'Because I am wondering if they can be used in some way, to gather and assess information, to analyse systems. I think our world is going to change out of all recognition – we are already seeing it in business – so I am interested in the manager's view.'

'I'd certainly be up for looking into it.'

'Well, let me give you an example. My son-in-law, George, he works for one of these computer companies. George is a football fanatic. He sits at these machines all day and in his spare time he has been feeding in information about all the goals scored in our division over the last five years. And then he asks the computer to assess the stuff he feeds in.'

'Geoffrey, where is this going?' asked Moffitt.

'Bear with me, please. Now we all know a lot of goals come from corners. OK? But did you know this – if you take an inswinging corner, your chances of scoring are double what they would be if you took an outswinging corner.'

'Oh for God's sake, what the fuck is he on about?' said Stock.

'I am saying, if you measure corners taken against goals result-ing, twice as many come from inswinging as outswinging. Now if I was a manager, I would find that a useful piece of information.'

'I do, Mr Raymond,' said Mr Gordon. 'I do.'

'He has also analysed free-kicks, penalties and strikers who run at the goalkeeper in a one-on-one situation and his conclusion is that if you follow the statistical findings and *only* adopt the *most likely* option, you'll score ten-to-twelve *extra* goals each season. Those goals could mean the difference between winning and losing, and over a season the difference between fourth and first, relegation and survival.'

'Mr Chairman,' protested Stock, 'I've been at this club for nearly thirteen years and I can honestly tell you that that is the biggest load of bollocks I've ever heard from a fellow director.

Football players are human beings, not machines; you can't programme them to score goals just because of what a computer
says.'

It was the deputy chairman Cliff McGuire who intervened. He
spoke calmly but was clearly angered by Stock's rude outburst,
possibly fuelled by the fourth or fifth red wine since the meeting
had begun. McGuire was as worried as anyone by the club's slow
drift down the League table, but at the same time he had a soft
spot for Gordon and he knew how hard he worked. In addition
the term *personal guarantees* had scared the life out of him.

'Mr Chairman, on the contrary that sounds to me like one of
the most interesting things I have ever heard at a board meeting,
and I for one would like to learn more. I also recommend that
Charlie meets up with Geoffrey's son-in-law to investigate the
opportunities that this new technology might give us, and then
report back to the board. What have we to lose from doing that?'

As Stock sat shaking his head, Moffitt asked Finley to minute
Raymond's point, and thanked Gordon for coming.

'The next meeting will be on Wednesday March the thirteenth.
So let's beat Leeds and Chelsea, and by the time we meet we
will know who we have in the semi-finals, and we can hopefully
be planning a big day out at Hillsborough or Villa Park.'

'I'd take Villa Park any time,' said Gordon. 'My old home
ground.'

Stewart Finley was extremely frustrated yet again as the board
had only considered the manager and football elements. On the
agenda sent to them days ago, Stewart had listed season ticket
prices; bonus payments to staff; club shop extension; new drain-
age at Summerton Manor; and rates assessment. As ever, the
board didn't want to discuss the dull day-to-day stuff that kept
the place running. It was the high drama and the low politics
that consumed them.

Over the next fifteen minutes the room slowly emptied save
for Moffitt who stayed in his seat to clear his head. He did this
after every board meeting and also looked behind the bar to
see how many bottles of wine had gone down. Plenty. Stock
had some nerve talking about other people's bar bills. He stood

and leaned against the bar top. He loved this room. To him, it was the heart of the club, the room where decisions had been made for decades, where chairmen had shaped the fortunes of the club, where managers had been hired and fired, players had signed contracts and, dramatic though it sounded, where history had been made. That was what he loved, the making of history, the shaping of things. When he was long gone, people would still recall his name. They would see it on that stand.

Most people die and are forgotten by all but a few, he thought. His name would be there in the club history books a hundred years from now, and chairmen and directors as yet unborn would come in, look at the pictures on the wall and say, 'That's Stan Moffitt. Legend.' They would never say that about Stock, not after the way he talked to him today.

19

LEEDS

Charlie Gordon had left the board meeting feeling a lot worse than when he arrived. Though it wasn't spelled out in so many words, he got the message loud and clear – lose against Leeds and get knocked out of the Cup at Chelsea, and he was out of a job. He had gone home via The Drum and Monkey, and had two swift large Scotches, but there were too many supporters in there wanting to talk, give their advice and opinions, and he decided to head home and drink alone. He had a lot of friends in football, people he could call and talk about players, matches, old times, good times, bad times. But as he poured himself his fifth, or was it sixth, glass, and the national anthem played on the TV, and the day's programmes came to an end, he realized he had nobody, literally nobody in his life to turn to and admit the truth about his situation ... that he was drowning in drink, and his fate was in the hands of a group of players without the moral fibre he once possessed, heading for the scrapheap. He stood to turn off the TV set before the 'go to bed now' screech came on, and put on an old record of Scottish songs sung by the Alexander Brothers. When 'Nobody's Child' came on, an old favourite of his mother's, he started to cry.

He went to phone Sadie, a temptation that often came upon him when he was the worse for wear. But, as so often before, he started to dial the number, then stopped halfway through, and went back to his glass. She was a lovely woman, for sure, but she was also just another reminder that he had fucked up virtually everything in his life, certainly every relationship with a woman that went beyond a one-night stand, in large part because of drink. Sadie was the only serious relationship he had had since his divorce, the only one that ever got him close to thinking a second marriage might be a runner. She had been a nurse on Alice's ward when they met, and she was a ward sister by the time their paths crossed again some years later.

She had warned him often enough about his drinking. She once told him that the small red blood vessels on his cheeks reminded her of a map of the London Underground, as she traced her long red fingernail across his face. She didn't mean ill with it. In fact she was seducing him, and ten minutes later they were in bed together. But it bothered him then, and what was really troubling was that it didn't much bother him now. So what if he looked a bit rough. He was a football manager not a pop singer or a film star. Who wouldn't drink with the kind of pressure he was under, and the kind of loneliness he endured? It didn't make him an alcoholic, just a heavy drinker who needed occasional medicine to soothe his insecurity.

Sadie had brought him some measure of comfort and happiness; she'd always had the knack of calming him down one day, or cheering him up another. But the day came when she decided she no longer wanted to be with someone who put football first, whisky second, and her a distant third. She was, he thought, just something else to add to his list of fuck-ups.

He woke up in his chair, feeling sick. He knew he would only be able to start the day if he vomited out last night's whisky. He walked through to the bathroom, kneeled on the floor with his head over the toilet, put two fingers to the back of his tongue, and felt a warm painful rush over his throat.

'This is happening too fucking often, Charlie,' he said to himself, vowing that he would not drink again until after the Leeds game – a vow broken by lunchtime, and several times thereafter, including as he parked his car, just after noon, on matchday. Just one slug of Johnnie Walker's red label, from the quarter bottle in the glove compartment. He thought about taking the bottle with him, but then summoned the strength to put it back where it came from. A real alcoholic, he told himself, would have put the bottle in his inside pocket.

Despite his hangover, and despite the certain knowledge that defeat today would give him one game to save himself – and even that might not be enough given the mood of the board – he still managed to get a little of that special matchday feeling. It was why he was so desperate not to lose his job. How could a near empty car park feel different one day to another? But it did. The whole town felt different on matchdays. Even as he drove in from home, three hours and more before kick-off, every other person on the streets seemed to be wearing the club colours.

Scarves and flags were flying from car windows and whenever he was spotted by fellow drivers there would be thumbs-up signs to return, good luck messages to thank them for. Groups of mates were meeting up to head for a few pre-match beers. Queues were forming outside the chip shops. Sellers of scarves and badges and programmes were lining the streets and already doing business. And though Charlie hated the hooliganism that seemed to follow football like a cold that could never be shaken off, the sight of police on every street corner added to the excitement. This was a big one, Leeds at home. It was always big, but never bigger than when your own future might hang on it.

Even as a player at Rangers, or when he was winning trophies with Aston Villa, he had never quite known a town like this for the one-eyed passion of the fans. Rangers had Celtic in the same city, not to mention Partick Thistle, Queen's Park and St Mirren down the road in Paisley. Villa shared England's second city with Birmingham City, and on a matchday there he knew there were almost as many people in the city hoping the team failed as succeeded. Here it was different. This was one of the great one-club towns, and everywhere you looked you saw club colours and pride.

Gordon stopped to sign a few autographs at the entrance to the car park where a couple of stewards were mingling with the gaggle of fans waiting for the players. He always looked out for an old guy called Henry, who had a vast collection of scrapbooks. He must have signed his name for Henry a thousand times.

'Gonna win then, Charlie?' a teenage boy asked, and Gordon smiled, but thought how he would never have dared call a manager by his first name when he was that age.

'Hope so.'

'Got to get DD firing today, eh?'

'Yeah, give it time.'

'Good luck, Charlie.'

'Thanks.'

He knew that if he went after Chelsea, those fans would still be there, excited to meet the new manager who was replacing him. Managers and players come and go. Real supporters are there for ever, and though they have their memories, and their favourites, and though players like Nat Broadbent get a mention in the match programme every single time, most get forgotten. Fans matter, Gordon thought, but today I need to think about myself.

A smartly dressed commissionaire saluted as he arrived at the players' entrance, stopping to sign a few more autograph books, then he strode to his tiny office three doors down from the changing rooms. He liked to be first in. If we lose, he thought, please let it be an acceptable or an unlucky defeat. In Gordon's mind, based on his many years in the game, there were three types of defeat. There's *unlucky* – the team plays well, but twice they hit the bar, a blatant penalty doesn't get given, while at the other end their opponents' single shot on target somehow dribbles over the line. And there's *acceptable* – they play well, create chances, really fight, but against a team of expensive table-topping superstars with that extra quality, and so they lose 3–2. Or there's *unacceptable* – no fight, players under-performing, tactically outwitted, and worst of all showing no passion.

Fans hated it if the players weren't up for it. The last time was Wolves at home. Half an hour to go, and Gordon was getting berated by the fans sitting directly behind him. 'Do these lazy bastards actually train, Gordon?' 'Hey Gordon, any chance these overpaid poofters might turn up?' When things were good, he was Charlie. Bad, and he became Gordon.

For the visit of Leeds United, he had drilled home the message all week that they had to be at their best, and they had to fight like hell to dominate the game. Leeds were one of those teams whose reputation was worth a goal every game. Even watching them stride from the coach, smiling at the booing that greeted them, captain Billy Bremner waving nicely at a fan screaming, 'You dirty bastard, Bremner, I hope Taffy Rees breaks your fucking neck,' manager Don Revie head down, determined, gruff – even then, they looked scary. When they went out to warm up, they seemed to relish the abuse that rained down on them. Johnny Giles, with the innocent look of a choirboy but, Gordon had reminded his team, 'even dirtier than Bremner and harder than Hunter', couldn't resist shouting back at the fan who called him a dirty Irish bastard, 'Must be nice for you losers to have a big club here for once, eh?' Sadly, he had passed a late fitness test.

They intimidated players and referees. They even intimidated the ball boys. From back to front, from David Harvey in goal to Willie Buchanan's hero Eddie Gray on the left wing, this was as hard a group of players as you could wish for, a team and a culture entirely made in Revie's image. Winning was all that mattered. Do what it takes. Nothing else matters.

The trouble was they could play too. Reaney, Charlton, Hunter, Cherry – fuck me, Gordon said to himself as he looked at the team line-ups on the programme, what he wouldn't give for a defence like that. Reaney was a brilliant defender, a fierce competitor and very hard to get past. Cherry and Gray on the left, what a bloody combination. Bremner and Giles – how could two tiny men be so fearsome? Just seeing their names on the sheet, Bremner at four, Giles at ten, and thinking back to the damage they did last time they were here, Gordon felt his confidence sinking a little. Peter Lorimer, another hard Scot, reckoned to have the fastest shot in the League, Mick Jones and Allan Clarke up front, Gray out wide. On the bench Paul Madeley, always so composed playing the ball out from the back – he would walk into any team in the League, Gordon said to himself, and yet there he was as a sub.

Ronnie Winston had arrived, and popped his head round the door.

'OK, boss?'

'We are going to have to be on our game today,' Gordon said. 'And they are going to have to be off it.'

'Let's focus on the first, eh boss? Nothing we can do about the second.'

Then he walked off to the dressing room, leaving Gordon to ponder that his Number Two had just talked to him as though he was Number One. Maybe it was inevitable. For now, as he saw the players arriving in dribs and drabs, and then heard the fuss in the corridor as Leeds United arrived, it was time to push all negativity aside, and try to get his players up for it.

He knew from his own playing days that players do not take in too much from the final pre-match team talk. Friday's was, in his view, the most important meeting of the week. Today was all about mood, instilling a bit of confidence, reminding them of a small number of key points.

First, as always, he went to wash his hands – and clear his head. As he walked back into the centre of the dressing room, Winston with his arms folded beside him, things went quiet. The players seated on the ramshackle mix of chairs and benches, he was brief and to the point.

'I've no need to tell you, Leeds are a formidable team. It's March and they are top of the table and they've got there by bending all the rules in the book. You know it, everyone knows it. They are a bunch of bullies. So what do you do with bullies? You fight back. You outbully them, do you understand me? Their first corner, Jules, you track back, you're on Cherry, you make sure his feet don't get off the ground. DD, Norman Hunter, he's yours. He only understands one language. Make sure he hears it. Brownie, Charlton may be bigger than you, but make sure when he giraffes his way up for a corner that you won't be pushed around. OK? Dyce, Eddie Gray is to my money the best winger in the world – apart from Dipper and Smudger obviously. Just remember this – *he shall not pass*. OK? Our fans hate Leeds. I hate Leeds. You hate Leeds. We all hate Leeds. Make sure they know it.

'When they surround the ref to pressurize him, we surround them. When they kick, we kick harder. And when they know what they are up against, we play... through the flanks, ball into Jules, knock down, three into the box, DD hanging... we can do this, lads.'

They are up for it, thought Gordon, I can see it in their eyes. I'll leave them to it.

He could hear the sound of The Carpenters, 'We've Only Just Begun', playing over the tannoy as he walked back to his office, took a short slug of Scotch from the bottle of Bell's in his top drawer, then turned on the radio in the hope there was some concrete news about the election. Thursday's vote had seen Labour's majority in the town increased, and Gordon had made a point of wearing a red tie then and since, but the national result had been inconclusive. The Tories won more votes, Labour won more seats, but neither won enough for a majority. Also Northern Ireland had largely elected Ulster Unionists who were refusing to take the Tory whip. Ted Heath was trying to hang on, possibly by doing a deal with the Liberals. As the Prof had told Gordon at the end of training yesterday, it was the first election since the Second World War not to produce an overall majority. And from the talk on the radio, it sounded like Liberal leader Jeremy Thorpe was unwilling to play ball. It looked like Harold Wilson was on his way back after all. At least Gordon would have something to smile about when he saw Moffitt later, win, lose or draw.

He went back to wait at the door of the dressing room. It was one of his rituals. Wait for the referee's bell to ring, then as the players came out, just tap them on the shoulder as they went. Sometimes, saying nothing was the best encouragement you could give. He stood and waited for them to disappear onto the field. He loved the sound of studs on concrete, a sound which diminished and vanished as one by one they jogged onto the grass, and almost forty thousand voices screamed and shouted in anticipation and, not to be too romantic about it, in love.

The players ran out in front of the biggest crowd of the season so far. Leeds had a huge travelling support, filling one whole end of the ground; some had also managed to get into the home sections and the police were having to eject a few of them as scuffles broke out. Gordon walked from the tunnel to the home bench, returning the applause and cheers of the crowd, who were as up for this as for any game he could remember. He spotted Moffitt and his wife Gloria, her fur coat, bleached hair and bright pink lipstick making sure she stood out from the crowd up in the front row of the directors' box in the upper stand. He nodded at Moffitt as if to say, 'We are ready.' When Stock raised his thumb and mouthed 'all the best', Gordon nodded and muttered as he took his seat on the bench, 'Two-faced bastard.' George Brady heard him, covered his mouth, and said, 'Remember the cameras are here, gaffer. We're the main game on *Match of the Day* tonight.'

Chief Inspector Bailey strode past on his way to the police control room. 'Win-win for me, this one,' he said. 'We win and I'm happy. They win and the chances are we can get their bastard fans off to Leeds without the town centre getting wrecked.' Gordon smiled but he was barely hearing anything now. This was the moment when the all-powerful manager became virtually powerless. It was all down to his players. As he watched them, then looked into the other half and looked at Leeds, he was no longer filled with confidence.

Their dugout was one of the smallest in the League, low too, set down at pitch level, and he squeezed in with Winston, Brady, Ralph Rowland and the Prof. He had gone for Walter Graham as sub just because he had such a calm head.

He spotted Don Revie walking to the away bench. He rose to greet him. Revie pretended not to see him, pulling the collar of his sheepskin coat in tight, and went to take his place, oblivious to the chants of 'dirty Yorkshire bastard' being sung in his direction.

Wilf Moore towered above Billy Bremner as they stood either

side of the halfway line and waited for the referee to toss his coin.

'How can someone so small be so scary?' Gordon asked Brady, leaning across Winston.

'Ask Napoleon,' the Prof shouted down the line.

'You and your fucking history, Prof.'

'It's all in there, gaffer.'

Moore won the toss, and chose to kick towards the away end so they would be playing towards their own fans in the second half. Gordon reflected for a moment on what Geoffrey Raymond had said about the use of computers. Was it an old wives' tale that playing to your own fans helped you? Or was it possible to work it out, like he said you could with corners and free-kicks?

Leeds kicked off, and the noise levels went up even higher. Jones to Clarke, Clarke back twenty yards to Hunter, Hunter tapped it to Charlton who launched the ball into the opposite end of the field for a throw-in deep near the corner flag.

As Clutch Dyson waited for the ball to come back from the crowd, Gordon watched the Leeds players pushing a little closer to an opponent. Bremner, Giles, Hunter and Charlton were screaming at each other like New York cops on a drugs raid. Clutch knew that whoever he threw the ball to, they would get clattered. These guys did it in their sleep. Hunter had such a reputation, all managers hated him; but all would have him in their side at the drop of a hat.

This was the first minute of the game, and referees were always reluctant to get the book out so early. Revie knew that. So first chance of giving someone a kicking, kick them hard, that was the Leeds way. Clutch threw it long, and it was Frank 'Dipper' Temple who got the short straw. He brought the ball under control, but it had barely left his foot when he felt the full force of Hunter coming in on him, knee on thigh, and he was flattened. Hunter raised both hands in a humble apology to the referee, his body language suggesting 'Sorry, slightly mistimed my tackle.' The referee, Jack Taylor, a butcher by trade, gave the free-kick and waved Hunter away.

'Get into the fucking ref,' Gordon said under his breath. But nothing. Dipper picked himself up, Brownie prepared to take the free-kick. Psychologically, one-nil to Leeds.

Brownie floated the ball into the box, and Jack Charlton rose highest to head it away, simultaneously bringing both knees into Jules Pemberton's lower back. They fell together, but with the ref's eyes now following the ball, he didn't see Charlton's boots land on Pemberton's stomach. Jules writhed for a second or two, then ran to Taylor, but Charlton got there first.

'Fucking hell, ref, get a grip on Pemberton – didn't you see him? He made a back – I could have broken my fucking neck.'

Gordon could see it all going on. At least Jules had had a go. Marland looked off the pace, and he was out of position, probably wanting to try his luck against Cherry rather than one of the big ugly centre-backs.

'DD,' he shouted, 'stay central!' But above the noise it was impossible to be heard, and Marland drifted wider.

Charlie Gordon hated Revie, had done as a player too, but he had to admire him. Once the tone was set, and Leeds were bossing the game, they started to turn on the skill. They were slicker, smarter, faster. He reckoned they could have been just as successful without all the nastiness and the intimidation, but teams reflect the character of their manager, and Revie couldn't live without it, he was like that when he was a player. It was bred into the players, and psychologically the players needed and loved it too. Within fifteen minutes Bremner and Giles were controlling the game as though they were in a home match against Bradford Park Avenue. And as they strengthened their grip, the real skill players started to come into their own.

'HE SHALL NOT PASS ...' Perhaps it wasn't the wisest thing to tell Clutch, because Eddie Gray was making him look silly. On one occasion he beat him on the outside, and with the Leeds fans now drowning out the home support, Gray turned back on himself, ran past Clutch in the opposite direction, and did the same again. By accident, as Gray was not one of the Leeds assassins, his arm swung as he passed Dyson and smacked him in the eye. No need for the physio to come on. It would be black in the morning and Dyson was riled by Gray's apology as he jogged by.

The Leeds singing turned to laughter, Clutch raced after Gray and hacked him down. The first booking of the day went not against dirty Leeds, but Clutch. Bremner ran up to him, nose to nose, and said, 'Hey hard man, you're one tackle away from an early bath.'

Gray stood over the ball, ready to cross in for one of the big defenders who had gone up. Gordon was screaming at DD, who had let Hunter drift off to the back post. Jules was at least doing as he was told, hugging Cherry close, not letting him leap, but as the ball came over, Cherry fell to the ground and Taylor gave a penalty.

The Leeds players congratulated the defender as though he had scored a goal. Mooro made a half-hearted protest to the referee, but Taylor waved him away. Peter Lorimer placed the ball on the spot, ran in, hit it straight down the middle and Jock, who dived too early, was beaten. One-nil. All but Harvey ran to celebrate in front of the Leeds fans.

Gordon leapt from the dugout, clapped his hands and shouted, 'Come on, dig in, basics, a bit of fight,' but – one, he couldn't be heard; two, these were more cries for help than guidance. He looked at DD walking back to restart the match. The man's a fucking dud, he thought. As he turned to retake his seat he caught the eye of Stan Moffitt, who was clearly thinking the same, and he heard Revie's unmistakable voice, shouting out, 'Come on Billy, keep stoking, this lot are weak as piss.'

Leeds began to target Clutch, getting the ball to Gray any time they could, hoping the winger would draw another foul and get them reduced to ten men. He didn't, but only because Clutch was backing off him now, giving him more space to get by him. Two minutes from half-time, Gray beat him, crossed, Mick Jones knocked it down and Giles ran in to hammer it home. It was a carbon copy of the move Gordon had his players practising every single day in training. Leeds just did it better.

Charlie Gordon was now desperate for half-time. At two-nil down, there is always a chance of a comeback. Three, and it becomes impossible. He was sure Geoffrey Raymond's son-in-law George, with his computer stats, would confirm that.

'What you gonna say, boss?' Winston asked as they walked to the dressing room, the sounds of Leeds' cheers and home boos all around them.

'Fuck knows,' he whispered back to Winston. 'If I told them the truth, they'd all just break down and cry.' He found himself echoing Revie's analysis of his own players. 'Weak as fucking piss.'

He waited a few minutes before speaking. He went to his office, partly so they got the message he was angry with them, also so he could take a slug of Scotch and gulp down a couple of extra-strong mints. When finally he went into the dressing room, it was a subdued place. Before speaking he went to wash his hands and face, needing to clear his head once more.

'OK. You are all professional footballers. You know that wasn't good enough, I don't need to say anything about that. But why? Because we are not doing the things we said we would. Bully the bullies. Fight fire with fire. Intimidate the ref. Shut their fucking fans up. Come on, you're better than this, every single one of you. So we keep the same shape, we keep the same game plan, the game starts now and we have to win three-nil. OK?'

They nodded, but the optimism of just one hour ago had gone, evaporated, and it wasn't coming back.

Six minutes into the second half Lorimer scored his second, and Leeds' third, direct from a free-kick twenty-five yards out, after Gray had lured Brownie into a clumsy challenge. Gordon noticed some of the home supporters heading for the exits. Leeds fans in the home end were now openly celebrating, and Chief Inspector Bailey had to send in officers to calm things down and make more arrests. At three-nil, Leeds now delivered the final humiliation – they stopped being dirty.

Gordon sat with arms folded, silent, willing the rest of the half to speed by. On seventy minutes, Gray beat Clutch again and drove into the box, where Mooro brought him down. Another penalty. Lorimer hat-trick. Game over, the home sections half-empty as the final whistle drew near.

Giles and Bremner continued with the wind-ups, and as Giles taunted Clutch during a break in the play – 'How come you conned this lot into thinking you were a First Division player?' – the right-back finally snapped, and lashed out, his arm hitting Giles across the throat. As the Leeds midfielder hurled himself to the ground choking, the referee ran towards the incident, and immediately sent Tommy Dyson to the dressing room.

'You stupid, stupid bastard,' sighed Gordon.

'Looks like you'll be playing at Chelsea, Prof,' Magic whispered to Walter Graham.

As the referee mercifully brought the game to an end, Revie positively bounced out of the dugout, and came over to shake Gordon's hand.

'Well played, Charlie,' he said, automaton-like.

'Don't rub it in,' said Gordon, who then joined the trudge of despair as his ten remaining players made their way off the pitch, heads down, trying to block out the boos from their own fans and the taunts from the Leeds supporters. As defeats go, this was neither unlucky nor acceptable. They were destroyed by a better side, with better players, a better mindset and, he feared, a much better manager.

If it hadn't been for their win against Southampton, thanks to an own goal by Saints' centre-half John McGrath and a lucky draw at Everton, this would now be the longest losing streak in the League since promotion fourteen years ago.

Dyson's sending off meant he would be suspended for the Chelsea quarter-final, unless he appealed against the decision, which Gordon would ensure that Stewart Finley did first thing on Monday morning. In addition, Jules Pemberton, for all his hypochondria, looked like he had picked up a genuine injury, and Magic was arranging for him to go to the hospital for a scan on his thigh.

As the players got changed in almost total silence, Gordon had a little sip of whisky in his office and then went to talk to the reporters who had gathered at the end of the tunnel. The stadium was almost empty now but for the stewards turning up the seats and the apprentices sweeping the terraces clean of the piles of discarded food and drink containers, newspapers, cigarette ends and programmes dotted around the ground.

The first question came from the *Sunday Times* reporter, but it was the one they all wanted to ask.

'Do you feel your job is on the line now, Charlie?'

'A manager's job is always on the line, we know that when we sign up. But we have a massive Cup game next week and my job now is to pick them up, learn from today, be stronger next week.'

'What went wrong today?' asked Don Robinson.

'We never got going. Some days it is hard to understand. We trained well all week, we had a clear game plan, but we just didn't do it, didn't put it into action.'

'So you're saying the players didn't deliver.'

'I'm not playing the blame game.'

'Do you feel you have lost the dressing room?'

'No, but...'

Dick Kingsley from the *Pictorial* was in next. 'If you lose at Chelsea will you quit or wait to be sacked?'

'I will spend the next week focusing on trying to win.'

'I was speaking to a member of the board before the game today. He said the board was very clear – "two defeats and he's a goner" – do you accept that?'

Gordon knew full well who Kingsley's contact was. The overweight, balding veteran of the *Sunday Pic* had only last month written a profile of Matthew Stock as 'the man waiting in the wings'.

'I can't respond to every piece of gossip and tittle-tattle. I can only do my job, and I will continue to do that.'

Then came a question he hated more than any other. It was from the football correspondent of the *Yorkshire Post*, who only covered their games against Leeds and sometimes the Sheffield clubs.

'Mr Gordon, do you have any players here that you think would get in Don Revie's side?'

Gordon knew the answer. Not one.

'I have good players here, and we have strengthened the squad recently. But Leeds is done for this season. The focus now is Chelsea and I know we can give them a game.'

Moffitt liked the manager and his assistant to join him in the boardroom for a drink, win or lose. Gordon had never felt less like it than he did today. As he walked back onto the pitch, groundstaff now replacing divots, the bare centre circle, so lush when the season started, seemed to him a symbol of his year so far, and of his life.

He was pleased to discover the Leeds directors had all gone. Moffitt spotted them emerging through the door.

'Charlie, Ronnie, come in, come on over… let's drown a few sorrows?' The barman, who knew Gordon's tipple, poured a large whisky for him, neat.

Moffitt made his way over, gently navigating his way through fellow directors, sponsors, hangers-on, raised his eyes and shrugged as if to say: 'Ah well, what can we do?'

'Just better than us,' said Gordon. 'Better than us in every position, every part of the game.'

'There was no fight, Charlie, no guts. They looked beaten before we started.'

Gordon nodded. He knew. He was tired of saying it, tired of hearing it. He was losing his fight too. He wanted to say to Moffitt what a mistake Marland had been, how he should never have involved his stupid son-in-law – busy laughing and pouring another white wine – in the transfer market. But he said nothing, sighed, shrugged.

He could sense the other directors glancing at him every now and then, and he knew full well what they were thinking. Was this his last home game in charge? Would it be Ronnie Winston in here alone and in charge after the next home game?

Yesterday Magic had seen Winston talking to Moffitt and Finley in the car park and whereas a year ago Gordon would have thought nothing of it, now it fed a paranoia he knew he was justified in feeling.

Moffitt left him to talk to a business colleague he had invited for the day, and Stock filled the gap. His speech was a little slurred, and beneath the friendly smile Gordon sensed menace.

'One of those days, Mr Gordon.'

'Yep. Horrible to watch.'

'What did you say to them?'

'What can you say? They're not daft. They know how poor they were.'

'So you said nothing, is that what you're telling me?'

'I said see you Monday, we'll talk it all over then.'

'You're not minded to get them in for extra training? That's what Revie does when they play badly, so their directors were telling me.'

'Revie can do what the hell he likes. I will do it my way.'

'Mmmm,' said Stock. 'My way or the highway . . . it's not exactly going to plan, is it?'

'Next week's another game.'

'Indeed.' And he turned smartly on his heels.

Gordon felt old as he trudged back to the dressing rooms, now empty apart from the apprentices, the cleaners, and Magic and Charlie Sinclair packing everything away. If he felt old, the board must sense that. They were looking for – what was it Moffitt said when he first hired him seven years ago – an injection of vitality? Maybe he was just too tired and beaten up to give it to them, and maybe Winston could. As he watched Magic packing bandages and tubs of Vaseline into a small skip, he felt a responsibility for people like him, and Brady, and Sinclair. Winston and Stock knew they were 'Gordon's people'. If he lost his job, the chances were they lost theirs, and their pay-offs would be peanuts compared to his.

Sinclair was a good twenty years older than Gordon and had tried his hand at every job in the place; he'd even been grounds-man for a while, and was now a totally dedicated kitman and all-round good guy and friend. It would break his heart if he didn't have this in his life. He was the last point of connection with the era of winning the title and the Cup. He had been a regular in the title-winning season, and only missed out on a Cup medal because of an injury he picked up in the semi against Arsenal.

Gordon invited him into his office and poured two Scotches into two mugs – one Rangers, one Villa.

'Cheers, boss. Here's to next Saturday. Can't be worse than that.

'Do you think I should quit, Charlie?'

'No way, gaffer. Don't even go there. Tomorrow's a new day. Monday you'll get stuck into them, tell them what's what, bruise a few egos, work 'em and work 'em and then work 'em some more – and by the way, watch that Winston.'

'I know, don't worry. But if we lose next week that's it, don't you think?'

'No, I don't think. Because if you think like that, you make it happen. So just stop it, boss. You know this game better than anyone. Tonight we feel like there's been a death in the family. Next week, we have births and weddings rolled into one – one goal, that's all it takes.'

'I guess.'

'You know I'm right, boss. But if your head drops, everyone's head drops. So lift it, gaffer, lift it.'

'You're right. You're always right. Maybe you should do this job.'

'Not a chance. Remember that team talk you did when Marland arrived – everyone knew their role? I do. And I know nobody could do it better. If I was sitting where you're sitting, I wouldn't last ten minutes. Fact.'

'Trouble is people like Stock and Winston think they can do the job.'

'Don't even think about them. There are people like them in every club, in every business in the land. They're not worth worrying about. You won't change them. Focus on yourself, you're better than both of them combined.'

They finished their drinks, hugged, and Gordon made his way to the car park. A lone steward said goodnight. Gordon knew he was over the limit but felt if he drove slowly he would be fine. He tried to remember if there was enough in the fridge to make himself a sandwich. He couldn't remember, so stopped at a late-night shop to buy some ham and cheese, and then popped into the off-licence to get a bottle of Glenfiddich.

'I could do with that,' said the shopkeeper, 'after watching that rubbish earlier.' Gordon paid, nodded and left.

As he started the car, he felt an almost overwhelming sense of loneliness. No wife, no kids, no girlfriend. He thought about calling Sadie to see if she was free for dinner, but she was probably working. Also, she was probably with someone else by now.

The radio news was reporting continuing political stalemate, but the mood music was all pointing to Labour leading a minority government. Another IRA bomb had gone off in London, but no one had been hurt this time. He got home, made himself a sandwich, and poured a large drink.

Moffitt had been friendly, considering how poor they had been. Maybe Finley had told him that Gordon had mentioned the Poulson link. It was not Charlie's style to fling dirt around, but if they performed like that against Chelsea next week, playing the Poulson card against Moffitt might be his last chance of saving himself.

20

MAGPIE

To the outside world, Dermot Cochrane was a successful businessman who had turned a small coach firm into a household name in the region, its 'Cochrane' branding known to everyone as his coaches ferried schoolkids, works outings, and – the bread and butter – pensioners to the seaside. He hated the pensioner outings, all those stops for toilet breaks, and so had cut back, and now, being the boss, just gave himself the prestige job of driving the first team of the local football club to all away matches, and left the dreary work to his staff. He was so much part of the operation that he even wore the same fitted suit as the manager and players, with the club emblem on the jacket, and the club tie around his neck. He had never met another team coach driver given that privilege.

Also, it doesn't matter which part of Britain you come from, there is always something a bit special about a trip to London, even though at present there was a slight anxiety as the IRA continued a bombing campaign in the capital. With so many top teams in the city, he knew the journey from stadium to the Great Western Hotel so well, he even had a special little route from the bottom of the M1, taught him by a London cabbie he had helped get the team's autographs for his nephew.

But beneath the veneer of success, there was a dark and brooding side to Dermot Cochrane, who was forever moping and mulling over his two failed marriages and a stack of family issues he had never been able to resolve, chief among them guilt

at leaving behind a child. He was drinking too much, though –
touch wood – he had yet to be stopped when over the limit.
Chelsea away gave him the lift he needed, not least because
there were so many other things to plan around the trip. His key
collection, and what he did with it, had become his obsession.
He liked it when they visited new hotels, and he could add to
it. But when they visited the same place again and again – and
the Great Western was their most used hotel by a long way – he
collected as many room keys as he could.

By his own hand, he had modified the inside of his leather
box briefcase, which had dozens of keys hanging side by side
from hooks he'd lovingly inserted, each key with its own little
note stuck alongside, recording in microscopic writing the name
of the hotel, date, room number, floor number, and any 'special
comments'.

When they played Fulham early in the season, he struck lucky,
and was given an executive double room, as most of the standard
double rooms had been converted to twins because in addition
to the team being there, a touring Irish rugby team was also
in town. Room 427, with its own little lounge no less. Now a
perfect replica of the Yale key had joined the others in his locked
briefcase.

You didn't need to hear his accent to know that Dermot
Cochrane came from the other side of the water. Pixie-like pink
ears, freckles around his eyes and a nose giving the impression of
a cheeky smile even when he looked grim. Red, albeit thinning
hair, which he still wore longer than was good for a man of his
age – a remnant of his days playing bass in a band called 'The
BallyCats' in his youth. They were something of a fixture on the
Northern Ireland music scene, and even had a few of the London
music scouts coming over to hear them play, but one night in
Belfast all that came to an end as a bomb ripped through the
pub where they were playing. Seventeen dead, among them two
of the band, lead singer Paul McArdle and the drummer, Roddy
Lafferty. He lost his zest for music after that, and though he
and the lead guitarist Joe Albiston ran a couple of auditions for
replacements, they knew in their hearts it was over. Bombs did

strange things to people. Sometimes fired them up. Other times just drove the life out of them. Cochrane, or Laughlin as he was back then, had not picked up a bass guitar since.

In any event, a year later he was gone, off to England, leaving wife and child behind, to track down his father, Frank, who had started out as a casual driver picking up shifts whenever he could, and ended up owning the company. Like father, like son, Cochrane had a charm and a drive that ensured they got places.

When Laughlin's became Cochrane's, there was something very special in seeing his own new name emblazoned across so many coaches, parked up at their HQ. Laughlin was history now. He barely thought of his old name. He was Cochrane in business, Cockie on the team bus.

Only once had he come close to being caught in one of his hotel escapades, at the Nottingham Hilton. They had played at Notts County in a League Cup tie which ran to extra time, and stayed overnight after the game so they could all get a decent sleep and get driven straight to training the next day. He was in Room 318, got the key cut first thing before the players were up, and so when back for the League game against Forest a few weeks later, he checked the room was empty with a call from the lobby, then paid a little visit. He had barely got in when a middle-aged man came in, and Cochrane suddenly morphed into a chambermaid, turning down the bed, introducing himself as the assistant manager, bemoaning the flu which had decimated the cleaning staff, wishing him a nice stay, and legging it as fast as he could back to his own room. Fortunately, he had not begun to pack anything valuable into the sports bag he had with him, and the real occupant of Room 318 was either too bemused or too stupid to notice why he was packing a sports bag into a Marks and Spencer carrier as he left.

But he had a pretty good hit rate. It was rare that anyone staying in a hotel would be in their room all the time. He would ring the room twice. If his calls went unanswered, he would go straight there. If there was someone in the room, he would call again an hour later, but never more than three times.

Then he would go to the lobby, and if there was more than

one lift, he would hold one for himself, and send the others
to the highest floor. He would take his own lift and, once he
reached the targeted floor, send that lift upwards too. He gave
himself two and a half minutes each time. Maximum. The deadline added to the excitement. He would count in his head – one,
elephant, two, elephant, three, elephant – and never stay beyond
one hundred and fifty. Sometimes it meant finding nothing. But
more often than not there would be cash, watches, women's
jewellery, men's cufflinks, clocks, radios, nice clothes, and he
would scoop them quickly into the bag, and go. What he really
liked though was when there was nothing obvious on display,
and he would check what experience had taught him were the
favoured hiding places for valuables: under the mattress, inside a
sock inside a shoe, inside a jacket pocket inside the wardrobe, on
top of the wardrobe, behind the toilet or in the cistern. One of
his best discoveries was a wad of cash inside a pillowcase, and he
always looked there now too. Cufflinks, jewellery, clothing, shoes,
books, calculators, cash, radios, calculators, expensive perfumes
and aftershaves. He raided the room, counting away until his
time was up.

He loved the sensation of his pulse rate soaring as he got closer
to one hundred and fifty, then the calm that fell quickly upon
him as he got back to the lift or the stairs.

His only risk was a roaming porter or chambermaid, or the
guest returning to their room, but he had confidence in his own
blarney and his ability to charm his way out of any tricky corner.

He had a special place in the hold of the coach, where he
would take the bag immediately after the raid, pack it away, and
look forward to driving the coach into the yard late on Saturday
night. Then, in the early hours of Sunday morning, after dropping
the players back at the training ground to pick their cars up, he
would sit inside the hold and discover what he had managed to
steal. The thrill he felt at that point was indescribable. It didn't
matter whether it was a gold watch or a piece of tat, a thousand
pounds or a tenner, it wasn't about what he stole, it was the thrill
of the stealing. Then, at this moment, all alone in the bowels
of the coach, knowing he had got away with it once more, he

felt an elation. It was almost as exciting as the times the police would arrive at the hotel after a guest reported the theft. Only once – at Southampton – did they actually interview anyone from the football club, but not him.

Although Dermot Laughlin was involved in minor thefts throughout his childhood, it was only when he started drinking in his teenage years that the stealing developed into a habit, and only after the name change that the habit grew into the obsession it had become. It cost him his second marriage to Rebecca, a nurse at the local hospital who tried to persuade him it was an illness. She had gone to collect him from work before they were meeting friends at their favourite pizzeria, and on walking into his office – everyone else who worked there knew they had to knock – he hurriedly, in a panic, locked the door in the wall behind his desk.

'What's in there?' she asked.

'Oh, nothing. Lost property, stuff people leave on the coaches mainly.'

'Can I see?'

'No, come on, let's go, I booked the table for half seven.'

She sensed his nervousness, and made a mental note of the key he had used to open it. The next time she was in there, as he went out to deal with a problem on the forecourt, she took the bunch of keys from his desk, quickly found the Chubb which she had seen him use on the door, opened it, and uncovered a veritable treasure trove, thousands of items neatly arranged. There was a pile of watches, a stack of wallets and purses, a basket full of wigs, shirts and jackets on a coat hanger, shoes all neatly lined up in rows, radios crammed into a wooden box, glasses and sun glasses, umbrellas, towels, even children's dolls, dozens of them. And there was an old tea chest almost overflowing with cash.

Suddenly he was in the room, back early.

'What do you think you're doing?' he asked.

'All this? Lost property?'

'It's none of your business what it is.'

'Dermot, if you are thieving again, I am not staying with you.

One day you'll be caught and go to jail, and I am not being humiliated like that. You either get help, or I go.' Angrily, he stubbed out a cigarette in the ashtray on his desk and stormed out.

She went to stay with her sister, but the next day had delivered to him a long and loving note, saying he had a problem, she wanted to help, but the only way to deal with a problem like this was to admit to it. If he didn't, he was beyond help, and she could do no more. She included a note she had asked for that morning from a consultant psychiatrist at the hospital, Dr Donlan. She assured Dermot she had mentioned no names, and was 'asking for a friend' who just wanted to understand the condition. In essence, over three pages, Donlan explained that kleptomania is an impulse control disorder often associated with anxiety or alcohol or substance abuse. It manifests itself in compulsive thefts, which are not about material or financial gain but about acting out dangerous patterns of behaviour. That was so clearly him, but he didn't want to know.

Rebecca ended her letter by repeating that if he didn't get help, she was leaving him for good. He wouldn't. So she did. And the only way he knew how to deal with it was to steal even more, take even more risks.

21

BUILD-UP

For all the pain of the Leeds defeat, by Tuesday night/Wednesday morning, for players, fans and press alike, it was largely forgotten, and minds turned forward again, to Chelsea away. Despite Saturday's humiliation, there had been a rush for tickets, and Finley was able to report that they would have their biggest away following of the season. Also, as Gordon knew better than anyone, footballers are a strange breed. They can go from abject, pitiful failure one day to superhuman self-confidence the next, with nothing much happening in between.

Fans were the same. Saturday night moaning, Sunday moaning, Monday at work, all talking about just how crap they had been, Tuesday more of the same, but toned down, then by Wednesday... what's so special about Chelsea? If DD finds his game, we can beat those soft southern poofs. Soft? A team with Ron Harris in it? There are none so blind as the one-eyed football fan...

Then by Thursday those with tickets were busy planning travel, and those without were busy scrabbling around trying to find a mate with a spare, as the club announced 'no more tickets available for Chelsea away'. There were few things designed to create more excitement than that. A sell-out, and thousands travelling south.

The players didn't need to be told by Gordon how much it mattered. They heard it all week. Stopping to fill the car with petrol, fans honking their horns, thumbs up; others asking if they had any comps left. Dipper and Mooro went to play golf on the

Wednesday afternoon, to take their minds off it all, but five times during the eighteen holes they played they found other golfers coming over to say hello, wish them luck, get their score card signed, ask if they had any spare tickets. There was no escape. But this was the kind of pressure, Gordon would tell them, that good players love. It builds that powerful link between club and fans. They all want the same thing, but in the end only the players can make it happen. Not him – he trains them, he picks the team, he dictates the tactics. Not the fans – they can cheer and cajole and provide injections of adrenalin. Only the players can deliver, nobody else. That's what makes them special.

The sixth round was when the FA Cup really started to mean something. Three wins and you're heroes, your names written for perpetuity into the history of the club, your status as a legend guaranteed; kids as yet unborn would be able to recite your team – Johnson, Dyson, Kilbride, Rees, Moore, Brown, Temple, Marland, Pemberton, Jones, Smith. For a day, there would be nothing else on the BBC. The papers would fill whole pages telling their readers where you were born, what your wife was called, what your favourite food, film, holiday destination, car and colour were. You might get to meet the Queen, Prince Philip or the Prime Minister, depending which bigwig got to present the Cup. There would be an after-match party and your mum and dad, your brothers and sisters, would all get passes for it, and be treated like royalty. More importantly, so far as Gordon was concerned, losing four-nil at home to Leeds, flirting with relegation, all the mistakes and the missed opportunities, they'd all be forgotten as the town prepared for a victory homecoming parade and the streets filled with hero worship of the men with medals dangling around their necks. This was the beauty of this crazy game.

All the papers were carrying big stories on the build-up to Saturday, and for Don Robinson from the *Courier*, this was as good as it got. Back-page lead guaranteed. Two pages inside. But also news and features were asking him for pieces. He was without doubt the man of the moment, and was even given a couple of assistants to put together a special eight-page pull-out for Friday's edition. Anything the players said was news. He managed to get a couple of minutes with Wilf Moore at the entrance to the training ground. Moore reminded him of how Peter Osgood scored a hat-trick for Chelsea last season, adding, 'He wound me up big time after that. This time let's see if he is quite so cocky.' 'GRUDGE MATCH' screamed the 72-point headline with a subhead – 'Mooro throws down gauntlet to cocky Chelsea'. David Brown, a Brummie and an Aston Villa supporter as a boy, criticized the Stamford Bridge stadium, saying 'The Shed', which housed their most passionate supporters, was too far from the pitch. 'The Bridge is a dump – they don't deserve a top club' was the headline on that one, a story Robinson sold to several of the nationals. Unsurprisingly, Graham 'Smudger' Smith was a little more circumspect. He knew he would be up against Clutch Dyson, who was regularly mentioned in the same breath as Chopper Harris and Norman Hunter whenever football's hard men were being discussed. 'It'll be a tough game against a good team. Wherever you look on the Chelsea team sheet you see great players – Hollins, Tambling, Hutchinson. Ron Harris is as good a defender as I have ever played against.'

Smudger felt footballers fell into two categories. Assassins and artists. He was an artist. Harris was an assassin. Dyson was an assassin. Brown was a bit of both. The greatness of Leeds was built on having artists who were assassins and assassins who were artists. He was going to be looking to his team's assassins to protect him, and perhaps to take Harris on away from the gaze of the officials. What the referee or linesmen didn't see was not a foul.

There was a special interest for the journalists in Frank 'Dipper' Temple, who'd played for Chelsea in the 1971–72 season, and who was constantly being asked – including by his teammates – for insights into his former fellow players. Dipper was one of the brighter members of the team, and he said over the years he had realized there was something of a North-South divide in football. He told Robinson – in another interview the *Courier* man was able to sell on – about centre-half Colin Waldron, bought by

Chelsea from Bury, but he just could not settle in London. He had a nightmare few months, was widely blamed for a glut of goals conceded, and eventually manager Tommy Docherty cut his losses and sold Waldron to Burnley for £30,000. 'He's flying there now, he's club captain, plays every game, and Burnley are punching way above their weight.' Chelsea were good at playing the press game though, so when Dipper added, 'I've seen it the other way too, southerners who can't hack it in the north,' he named no names, but a canny media liaison officer at Chelsea persuaded the *Daily Express* and the *Daily Mirror* to lift the quotes and use them under headlines suggesting Dipper was taking a direct swipe at DD Marland.

The fans were also a big part of the *Courier*'s build-up. With such a demand for tickets, they were printing photos every day of fans kissing theirs. They were running stories on the lengths some were going to in order to get to the match, including a fan who worked on the oil rigs in the North Sea and was taking a holiday to be there. An exile living in Canada told why 'I've got to be there' despite the cost of a transatlantic flight and a couple of nights in a London hotel. But perhaps the best and most common sentiment was expressed by a former mill worker, Dan Southern, who told the paper, 'Me and my mates work hard all week and most of the time life is hard, the wages aren't great, and redundancy hangs over us. Also, let's be honest, this isn't the most beautiful town in the world. So it's a joyless life we lead a lot of the time; then comes Saturday and there is the chance of real joy. Come a big Cup game like Chelsea, and we have the excitement that comes from hope. Hope. That is why it means so much to me.'

A factory worker called Dave Meadowcroft, whose job was to pack clothes into boxes before sending them out to stores around the country, said he would give his right arm to be a footballer. 'Those guys are doing what we would love to do. So if they win, we win. If they lose, we lose. That's why we get so angry when they don't even try, like the Leeds match.'

The pull-out was full of pictures of matches with Chelsea down the years, including the famous game in 1938 when Nat

Broadbent scored a hat-trick of headers in a four-nil win. The article also made mention of how Broadbent's twenty-three NB carvings at the ground were now an integral and popular part of stadium tours. This all added to his legend, especially as at the time he had been heavily fined by the club for the carvings.

As Saturday neared, Don Robinson's editor put him under ever greater pressure for new angles, new interviewees, and so he came to write a column on 'The Road to the Bridge' – an interview with coach driver Dermot Cochrane, photographed in club suit as he leaned against the side of the coach. He told a few funny stories, especially about the practical jokes Mooro used to play before he became captain and had to get serious. His favourite was tying a dirty old rope, frayed at one end, to a tree near to where the coach was parked at a hotel in Southampton. As the players ate their dinner in the team room, Nuts asked a waitress if she had any raw carrots in the kitchen. Told she did, he asked her if she would go to the team coach and feed the team mascot, a Shetland pony called Bluebell, who only ate raw carrots. Then the players ran upstairs to watch the chaos that ensued as the waitress went out with the carrots, to see a rope, frayed at one end, round the tree with no pony attached to it, then ran back in to call out reinforcements who would fan out in search of a pony that didn't exist.

There were much more serious stories for the *Courier* too. For example, Robinson discovered that the police had issued a warning to all clubs about the need for vigilance amid the current IRA bombing campaign. There was nothing specific about their match at Chelsea, but a sell-out FA Cup tie, in the capital, was clearly an attractive target for terrorists whose current bombings were as much about generating publicity as killing people. He called Jeff Bailey, the police officer in charge of matchday security, who confirmed he'd had a meeting with Finley and Gordon to discuss what he called 'the one in a million' possibility. That was enough for Robinson's superiors to let their imaginations run wild, and under the headline 'Terror threat to big match' they played a dangerous game of speculation. What if the IRA preferred to target the stadium, the team hotels or

coaches, the Tube station or the motorway service stations likely
to be rammed with supporters on their way south? What would
happen if there was a bomb scare phoned to the ground at 3.15,
with the match under way? Would it be called off? Did they
have stadium evacuation plans? What would wives and families
be thinking of their loved ones trying to concentrate on football
while all this was going on?

It was, as Chief Inspector Bailey said in a statement released
after the 'terror threat' story appeared on the front page, 'ir-
responsible' to take a generalized threat and try to make it
specific. He said there was no specific threat against the team or
the match; of course people should be vigilant at all times but
that did not mean they should change their plans.

Toby Wilkins, president of the official supporters' club, echoed
the police chief's sentiments. 'This is the biggest game in years
and we should not let terrorism or inflammatory journalism put
us off from going to support the club we love.' Yet again, in this
week of big news for the town, Robinson's story was picked up
by the national press. The *Mirror* ran a back-page story illustrated
by a picture of Gordon looking grim-faced, and the headline –
from something the manager never said – 'We can beat Chelsea
and the IRA'. It all underlined the reality of the lesson the IRA
High Command had finally learned – that one bomb in Britain
is worth ten in Northern Ireland. This was terror coverage they
were getting without lifting a finger.

Charlie Gordon's general approach to the press was 'why use
one word, when none would do?' But he realized in weeks like
this he had to give the local and national journalists a fair bit of
time. He got the same questions again and again – did he feel
under pressure, did he think he would be sacked if they lost, was
he disappointed in DD Marland so far? They were not that difficult to deal with, but he had to be careful he didn't allow them
to feed the negative mindset he was desperate to avoid. Think
you're going to lose, and the chances are you will. That was what
happened against Leeds. Every single Leeds player walked out
convinced they would win. For all his Churchillian words, his
own players lacked that basic belief and confidence. Somehow

he had to get it back in them for Saturday, or else – the papers were right about this – he would be a goner.

He did his final interview with Robinson on Thursday afternoon, having told the players to rest and relax after the final heavy training session of the week. Robinson liked Gordon well enough, and knew he was under pressure. He wanted the Friday headline to be one that helped the overall game plan. He also knew, however, that his editor would throw out anything too tame or too soft. Gordon told him he expected a reaction from his players after last week's humiliation, and the headline 'Chelsea will get Leeds debacle backlash – Gordon' kept everyone happy. Now all that remained was to make sure they did.

Paddy O'Connell was at the bottom end of the pay-scale at the Great Western Hotel at Paddington Station. But it didn't stop him being one of the highest earners. He was as much a part of the furniture as the beds in the rooms and the tables in the restaurant. He was also one of the reasons guests often gave to explain a repeat booking. So what Paddy received in tips more than made up for the very low salary that came to him each month in a small sealed brown envelope.

He was always charming and helpful with first-time visitors, familiar and chatty with the regulars. He rarely forgot a name or a conversation, so that even Americans who might have a year or two between visits he would greet as long lost friends, remember their names, remember where they had visited, what their interests were. He loved his work, and he took it seriously. It was all about relationships, people skills, and he had been working on them all his life.

In the Summerton era, the team had mainly used the Langham Hotel near the BBC, but Charlie Gordon loved railway hotels. It stemmed from the times Rangers stayed together overnight before a Cup final at the hotel in Glasgow's Central Station. So one of his first decisions as manager was to say that for all London away games, he wanted Finley to book the Great Western. The regular work meant Finley could strike good deals, and of course football people talk to each other all the time, so it was partly as a result of Gordon's decision that word spread about what a good place it was to stay before a big match, and now clubs as varied as Newcastle and Manchester City, Sunderland and Leeds had stayed there. Leeds United's stay in May 1972 had got Paddy O'Connell a bit of live TV coverage too, as the team's departure for the FA Cup final against Arsenal at Wembley had been filmed live by the BBC. It was another classic Revie win, a scrappy, dirty game, the only goal an Allan Clarke header from a Mick Jones cross. It was also a game with real legacy for the fans, as the B-side of the record made by the players for the final – 'Marching on Together' – quickly became the supporters' favoured anthem, as Charlie Gordon had heard all too loudly.

It was perhaps Gordon's somewhat nomadic existence, and his travelling up and down the country so often as a player, that generated his interest in trains and station hotels. The Great Western Railway originated from the desire of Bristol merchants to maintain their city as the second most profitable port in the country with good trade routes to the US. The increase in the size of ships and the gradual silting of the Avon had seen Liverpool's attractiveness as a port grow, and with a rail connection between Liverpool and London under construction in the 1830s, it threatened Bristol's proud status. The answer for Bristol was, with the cooperation and cash of the London merchants, to build a train line of their own; a railway built to unprecedented standards, including a hotel at the start and end of the journey.

Paddy O'Connell always looked forward to visits from Charlie Gordon. The Northern Irish Catholic felt something of a bond with the Glaswegian Protestant, one cemented by the fact that one of Gordon's superstitions was the giving of a fiver to his favourite doorman cum head porter on arrival. He always did it so as many players as possible could see, so that they might think – rightly – that the warm-hearted Ulsterman would be keeping an eye on their activities, and if he saw them getting up to no good, the manager would know about it.

O'Connell was used to all manner of comings and goings. Husbands meeting other men's wives, and women meeting other women's husbands. Businessmen cutting deals good and bad.

Quite a few MPs stayed there: it was near enough to Westminster without being too near and there had been plenty of them in recent days, coming and going amid the political turmoil, which had ended on the first Monday of March with Harold Wilson being asked by the Queen to form a government. This in turn had set in train a series of events in which O'Connell had become unwittingly involved and which right now, far from making him feel chatty and lively, was making him fear for his life.

Of all the reservations for Friday 8 March it would be Angela Chessington, a young and successful businesswoman from Bristol, who would catch his eye.

Just thirty-two, a very smart dresser, with auburn shoulder-length hair which bounced and bobbed with every confident stride. On checking in, she asked O'Connell where the gym was, and he couldn't resist looking her toned body up and down. He would discover that she had won a major business award last year and had featured in a number of magazines.

She signed herself in as 'Mrs', but said she was having a night away from her husband and their two small children. Yet when he was chatting to the receptionist about her, he learned that the note attached to her booking said 'double room, preferably suite – must be double bed'. Paddy could tell – there was just something about her – that she was there for excitement or devilment or both.

'Why the press outside?' she asked Paddy.

'Oh, we have a football team staying with us tonight. They're down playing Chelsea in the Cup.'

'Staying here?'

'Yes. Who's your team?'

'Bristol City,' she said, and she told him how hard it had been as a young girl growing up every bit as passionate about her team as the boys, but she was never taken seriously, and ended up cutting her hair short, dressing like a boy, to try to be accepted.

'Well, for sure, Mrs Chessington, you look a lot better as a fully fledged woman. Mr Chessington is a lucky man.' She smiled, but seemed a little pained to hear her husband being mentioned.

She asked where he came from.

'Belfast,' he said, and she explained it was an old Irish auntie who had set her on the road to being a successful business-woman. She had persuaded her to invest in a small office block in East Bridge Street in Enniskillen, which had a small bar and restaurant below. She would visit on the odd occasion to check on the tenants and the ongoing renovations. Late one evening, a chance meeting, and for her, things would never quite be the same again...

The 3Ps operation appeared to be no further on, and Seamus, or 'Peter' as they insisted on calling him for this operation, was getting tired of waiting. He sat staring at the pile of *Evening Standards*, and opened another bottle of Guinness. He just wanted to get on with it, get on with doing what he was made for, making and setting off bombs to kill the people he blamed for his misery. He knew drink wasn't good for him, but the more bored and impatient he got, the more he drank; the more he drank, the angrier he got. The angrier he got, the more the well of revenge within him filled. Then, he just couldn't stop thinking about it, over and over again. The events of that Sunday morning played around his head. His wife Sinead bright and bubbly, as she always was. They were off to the fair, which had landed in town for the weekend and she'd promised young Tom that they'd take him on the rides. Sinead had packed up the picnic hamper and she asked Seamus if he wanted her to pack a couple of bottles of Guinness. She looked in the fridge not knowing that Seamus had drunk the last two bottles late last night when she was in bed.

'Seamus, you get Tom ready while I nip to the shop for some Guinness and crisps and I'll also pick up a paper... do you want anything else?'

Those were the last words he ever heard her say: 'Do you want anything else?' He never even replied, which was his usual way of saying 'no'. He did remember Tom shouting 'Mummy, Mummy, I'm coming too,' then he heard the front door close, he heard their excited chatter as they went to the car, he heard the two doors open, then shut, then... the explosion rocked the house, knocked Seamus unconscious. At least it spared him the sight of his wife and son, their bodies in bits strewn across the garden, their Hillman Hunter still a fireball when the police, fire engine and ambulance arrived.

He awoke in hospital a couple of days later, alone. Then a nurse walked in, followed by his priest, and he knew before a word had been spoken that Sinead and Tom were dead. He shed no tears, and never had. The grief he felt was dwarfed by anger, hatred and a desire for revenge.

22

BROWN

If there was a secret ballot asking the squad 'Which players do you dislike most?' David Brown would win by a landslide. But if the same players were asked 'Which player instils most confidence in the team just by being there?' he would win that too. Only Wilf Moore would get near. Brown was a complex, curious man, who needed enemies to thrive. During the week, his enemies became his teammates, the management, any system he was meant to conform to. But on Saturday afternoon, these all became his friends, and a bigger enemy – the opposing team – made him a formidable friend to have. The phrase 'you'd rather have him with you than against you' could have been invented for the ill-tempered, super-fit Brownie.

He didn't really like football. Fans find that thought beyond belief, but why should football be any different to any other industry? Some people did it because it was what they were good at it; didn't mean they liked it. His biting sarcasm, though directed at the individuals in his eyeline at that time, was often aimed at the game as a whole. But come Saturday afternoon, he was the one player Gordon knew would do exactly what was expected of him: box to box, tackling hard, dictating the pace of the game, playing the killer ball – he could do it all.

He had grown up in Birmingham and made his way through the junior teams, finally making the grade at Aston Villa aged eighteen when he made his first-team debut. Over the next decade he played for Blackburn Rovers and Leeds United before joining West Bromwich Albion in 1972. Brown's time there lasted only twelve months until he was transferred for £34,000.

His gambling habit ran in the family. His dad was so busy gambling, and escaping his nagging wife, that he barely ever watched him play football or encouraged him. It was Brownie's gambling that led to West Brom offloading him, the manager finding him too disruptive an influence as he sought to involve the other players in his trips to the races or the bookies, added to which he was constantly in debt to them. It had cost him his marriage and but for the horse racing scam, which, to date, had made him over £27,000, he would be in big money trouble again.

He'd operated this scam for the last four years, initially on a small scale with full-back Kenny Thompson until he had been hastily transferred to Partick Thistle. His latest partner in crime was his new best friend Graham Smith, who, since he'd established himself in the first team some months earlier, had been assisting Brownie with the sting.

As David Brown sorted the morning mail sitting by the fireplace in his four-bedroomed detached house, which looked down on the town, and from where on a clear day he could make out the floodlights of the stadium, he tore up the latest letter from Hamilton's Solicitors about his wife filing for divorce, and tossed it into the fireplace.

His affair last season with Kenny Thompson's wife Helen, though it lasted barely three weeks, had worsened his reputation in the dressing room. Having sex with a teammate's wife – there are not too many cardinal rules that cannot be broken, but that is one of them. A big part of Charlie Gordon had felt it should be Brownie who paid the price, and moved on. But Tommo was out of form, and his old knee injury was going to need another operation, whereas Brownie was often, after Mooro and Jock, his first name on the team sheet. He felt sorry for his fellow Scot, but he called in a favour from his old Hearts

teammate Archie Drew, now managing Partick Thistle, and sent
him on his way.

Since the day Kenny Thompson had found out about the
affair, the two of them had not spoken. It meant that Brown's
guiltiest secret, which had nothing to do with his sex life or
his football career, was shared with a sworn enemy. Added to
which, Tommo's wife Helen was the niece of club director
Matthew Stock, and she had not taken kindly to having to
move up to Scotland, her husband taking a drop in wages to
do so. She had phoned Brownie several times, each time more
menacingly as he tried to insist the affair was at an end, and
he had to concentrate on his football. But at the fourth time of
refusing to see her, Helen threatened to tell her uncle Matthew
what he and Kenny had been up to at the races these past four
years.

He sat staring at the empty, cold fireplace, and wondered how
he had managed to get himself screwed over by two women –
one who he knew would be pressing him for more and more
money, the other effectively blackmailing him, and threatening
his entire career, unless he agreed to resume an affair he wished
he had never started.

And though he still regularly came in first, second or third
in the weekly cross-country run that Gordon made them do
every Tuesday morning, he feared arthritis was setting in to
his right knee, and only ever larger doses of cortisone were
seeing him through ninety minutes. He had one, maybe two
years left, maximum, at this level, and he had decided after
his spell with West Brom that he would never play outside
the top flight again.

He had no desire to stay in the game at all, and pitied the
senior pros already taking their coaching badges and preparing
for the day they all knew would come, when the playing had
to stop. 'When I finish, you will never see me kick a ball again,'
he would say.

'Not even charity matches?'

'Especially not charity matches. You won't catch me playing, watching, commentating, nothing. It's a job, that's it, and when the legs go, I go.'

It meant he now saw the betting scam less as a sideline than, perhaps, his future career.

He had come across it by chance on a day out at Huntingdon races in 1970. He and Kenny Thompson had been invited into one of the private boxes on the course. At just after three o'clock he needed to make a telephone call to his bookie back home, to place a bet for the 3.30, and he asked one of the waitresses if there was a phone he could use. She took him to the catering manager's glass-fronted office on the third floor of the stand, which overlooked the winning post. He picked up the phone and dialled his bookmaker's number. As he was chatting to his bookie he watched a horse called Jolly Princess cross the winning post with Jack the Hatter in second place ten lengths behind. As this was happening he overheard over the phone, in the bookie's shop a hundred or so miles away, a punter placing a bet. 'Three o'clock, Huntingdon, Jack the Hatter, five pounds to win.'

He said nothing, but went back having placed his own bet, and shared what had happened with Tommo.

'Are you sure you heard right?' asked the stocky Scottish defender.

'Hundred per cent. The race here was finished, but they were taking losing bets on it. I promise you.'

'So maybe someone could have placed a winning bet too?'

'Exactly, Sherlock.'

Over the next couple of hours, they worked it out. The Extel tannoy system used in bookmakers' shops mainly focused on the big meetings like Ascot, Cheltenham and Goodwood, which is what most of the punters were betting on. The minor racecourses, like Huntingdon, Sedgefield and Kelso, were rarely covered either by the Extel service or the live TV coverage. So the bookies had to wait to get the result sent through by phone or via one of the news wire services.

So all that was needed was an unfashionable course not covered by the national network; a telephone in a location that overlooked the finishing line; in the event of any doubt, a runner who could relay the name of the winner the moment it crossed the line; and someone at the other end of the country with two telephones: one to take the incoming call with the name of the winner; the other, an open line to a local book-maker to place a bet on the winner. The open telephone line was essential.

It was fairly standard for regular and serious punters to have an open line. So all that Brownie and Tommo needed to do was establish themselves once and for all as serious punters. Also, as they were footballers, the bookies loved having them anyway. It did mean Brownie had to lose bets as well as win them, to avoid too much suspicion of a winning run, but that meant small bets when they didn't know the outcome, large bets when they did. Easy. One of them at the course, the other at home with his phone line open all afternoon, whistling loudly whenever they wanted to place a bet. The bookies knew the system inside out.

So Brownie would be at the course, and as the horses entered the last furlong, he would call Tommo, then, the moment the winner crossed the line, pass on the news.

'Number 5, Chasing Shadows.'

Tommo would whistle, loudly.

'Tony, put me a ton on Chasing Shadows, Huntingdon 2.30. Twenty-pound double on the same horse and number 6 in the 3.50 at Cheltenham; and twenty-pound win treble on the same two plus number 7 in the 4.10 at York. And a sneaky tenner on number one Apres Le Deluge, 4.55, Ayr.'

Then the bookmaker would lay down the phones, keep the line open, wait for the next whistle. The losing bets would help militate against detection of the scam.

With Tommo gone, Brown had targeted Smudger, first of all to establish his interest in racing, then his trustworthiness and his ability to be loyal. After six months or so, he felt he could trust him. By 1974, after four years of practice, the scam had been honed to perfection at different courses and small independent bookmakers around the country. His working hours also fitted in perfectly; after finishing training early some days at twelve noon, or on a day off, he'd be at the racecourse by two o'clock. He stayed well away from placing his bets with the large, established bookmakers like William Hill, Coral and Ladbrokes. Sometimes it would be Smudger on the course, Brownie on the phones; other times vice versa. The courses were so used to them wanting to use the phone, at Market Rasen, Towcester and Huntingdon, they didn't even have to ask. Being a footballer opened doors closed to others. And there wasn't a small racecourse catering manager or general manager in the land who hadn't been gifted a few complimentary tickets for matches.

Only twice had the bookie said, 'That one's already gone, I think,' but it wasn't difficult to feign ignorance and move on.

It was inevitable, Brownie supposed, that Tommo would have told his wife Helen about their little scam. If she told her uncle Matthew Stock, there could be real trouble afoot. Brownie, on the other hand, originally told nobody apart from Tommo. But his wife Caroline couldn't have failed to notice that he had plenty of money to spend, and a lot of it he was spending on her. So one night, after dinner out at one of the most expensive restaurants in the region, and after too much champagne, she sweet-talked him and he told her all. She warned him to be careful, but he assured her it was foolproof, their pension.

Then one night, Kenny Thompson's wife, looking for some excitement, lured David Brown to her house while Kenny was playing in the reserves and it wasn't long, after a few glasses of wine, before they were both naked in bed. Afterwards she let Brownie know that she knew all about their racecourse scam and she would let her uncle Matthew know unless Brownie visited her regularly. He went along with it, and would probably have continued to do so until the night Kenny came home early, having injured himself in the warm-up before another reserves match, and found his teammate and gambling scam partner having sex with his wife on the sofa in the lounge. Brownie legged it, Helen begged for forgiveness, eventually got it, and went off with him to Glasgow. But before long, the desire to see Brownie again had led to her calling him, and starting the blackmailing all over again.

23

TARGET

Tuesday 5 March

Finally there was some movement for the 3Ps, and they were
about to be joined by P number 4. At least getting the *Evening
Standard* every day meant the IRA team had been able to enjoy
reading the continued coverage of the recent attacks on the
mainland. Day after day, stories of angry politicians denouncing
them, grieving relatives of victims telling of their hurt, the police
looking and sounding ever more desperate at their inability to
find the perpetrators. There was the usual talk of yet more anti-
terrorist legislation being put before Parliament. There was even
a story about how the sixth round of the FA Cup was being
targeted. But more important than any of that, there it was, on
the notices page on Monday 4 March: '*Happy Birthday granddad,
75 years old today, all our love, Peter and Pamela.*' It was the signal
for the second meeting at the safe house, where they would all
learn who and what they were targeting.

'Paul', whose real name was Martin Kelly, was alone among
them in knowing the real identities of the whole team he was
putting together to pull off what would be one of the highest-
profile assassinations in the IRA's history. He still worried a little
about Paddy O'Connell, even though weeks of surveillance had
provided nothing to suggest he was working for the other side.
Seamus, or 'Peter', was a problem, as always, as he was so not a
team player. But when it came to complicated, difficult bomb

attempts, as he had shown time and again, most recently on the M62, there was nobody better. He was just brutal, totally focused, couldn't give a shit about anything apart from the job in hand – which made him so good at what he did, even if it also made him unpleasant and difficult to deal with. Kelly had been warned he had his work cut out in getting the team to gel, but the Army Council had decided these were the best people for the job, and though he sensed occasional moments of tension between Seamus and Colleen, by and large he felt they would work together fine. The story about the FA Cup game being threatened had been an unexpected and, for him at least, unwelcome surprise. His boyfriend, Toby, was chairman of the supporters' club of the away team due to play at Chelsea, and theirs was the only Cup game in the capital. Kelly had heard nothing official about an attack on a sporting event, and he was sure he would have done had it been planned. He also now knew, at last, that the target of Operation 3Ps was very much political not sporting. But he was nervous nonetheless. It was hard enough being homosexual and keeping it quiet, when Toby was so keen for them to show each other off to the world. It would be even harder if he thought the secret he kept from Toby – his real life working for the IRA, not as a plumber or a spy as he'd jokingly suggested – might prevent him from letting him know he was at risk. He didn't like to admit it, but if there was a choice between compromising an operation and telling Toby his life was in danger, he would put the operation ahead of the danger to his boyfriend.

The advert in the *Standard* appeared on the day the election outcome finally became clear. Time to head back to that grotty kitchen in Ealing. Martin got a message to Paddy O'Connell to be there. He knew the hotel porter would not be feeling the same excitement as he was, or Colleen and Seamus, but O'Connell was in too deep now. He would be there.

Martin Kelly could sense the impact of the campaign even as he travelled around London. People seemed a little less confident, a little less sure. Every time he passed a news stand, he saw headlines that could have been scripted by the IRA propaganda team. Each time it gave him a little lift. Inevitably, then, it was going to have the opposite effect on these Brits going about their business, angry that their little lives were being disturbed, never giving a thought for the fact their government and their troops were the cause of it all with their continued occupation, and their persecution of the Catholic minority.

There were times he wondered whether the bombings would do anything other than harden opinion against them, and make their goals – troops out, united Ireland – even more unachievable. He knew how hard it was for British politicians ever to be seen to be bowing to terrorism. He knew too the hatred people felt for what was being done. But on days like today, he felt like a man on the right side of history, morally superior, and happy and confident that he was about to score one of the greatest hits the struggle had ever known.

The *Standard* ad having been placed by a courier, he knew that for him, Seamus and Colleen, Tuesday 5 March, the day of their second safe house meeting, would become one of the defining days of their lives. They all felt it, for sure. They didn't have to be best friends to be looking forward to working with each other on this.

This time he was to arrive first, and he got there nice and early. He took some milk and made himself a cup of tea, and waited to see if 'Peter', arriving second half an hour later, had remembered he was to bring milk and biscuits. To be fair, he did.

Kelly knew all about his chief bomb-maker. Born at home, halfway between Derry and the border with the Republic, raised by a single mother, he was a fairly low-level operative, until the bomb meant for him had taken his wife Sinead and their young son Tom during the violence of the late 1960s, and it fired him up to be one of the true believers, possessed of a hatred of all things Unionist, all things British. Prior to their deaths he had worked full-time as an electrical engineer at a small electronics plant close to the border, and his work as a volunteer was part-time. After the killings, his priorities switched. He saw his work now as nothing more than a place to learn more about the mechanics of explosives; his real work was taking forward the Republican cause via violence. He loved the science of bomb-making, and he loved the political and human impact even more.

He had established himself as the go-to manufacturer of letter bombs, and had got particular satisfaction from one, which maimed the wife of a judge with a reputation for handing out longer sentences to Republican terrorists than Unionists. It was his favourite 'eye for an eye' moment. 'They kill my wife and boy; I get one back, and I'm happy she and her husband have to live with her scars and deformities for ever,' he told Kelly on the one occasion they socialized together. Another 'great day' was when he posted a device inside a red Royal Mail post-box in Liverpool, retreated one hundred yards, then waited ten minutes before the timer triggered an explosion that took the arm off a young woman posting a letter, and sent debris flying for twenty or thirty yards in all directions injuring four others.

Martin Kelly had twice visited Seamus's little factory in his garden shed, once to discuss the recruitment of a possible informant inside the Customs team at Dover, the second time uninvited, when he knew Seamus was away, to see how well secured it was. Not very was the answer, and it led to Seamus being visited by experts from Belfast who tightened things up. To this day Seamus was unaware that Martin Kelly had broken in. Kelly saw, however, that though Seamus might not have taken enough precautions about security – a couple of padlocks and a Chubb key were the limit of it – he had been able to gather enough materials for one hell of a lot of bombings. Inside the shed, it was immaculately clean, almost disturbingly ordered.

The time Kelly visited by arrangement, they had shared a six-pack of Guinness, and Seamus had opened up a bit about why he hated the Brits so much. But the loss of his wife and only child had fuelled another obsession, which ate away at him with much the same intensity as his hatred for the British; and that was the desire to trace his own father. It wasn't easy for his mum raising him alone, and it wasn't easy for him either; other kids could be cruel and they taunted him with all manner of stories about who his dad was, and why he had gone. 'He took one look at you and thought, "No way am I spending my life with that little runt,"' was the one that stuck in his mind.

Then one Sunday afternoon, when he was in his late twenties, he popped round to see his mum, and found her locked in intense conversation with her two sisters. It was all a bit garbled but one of their cousins had a friend who had grown up with them, Aisling Byrne, who had moved to northern England, and she'd been on an outing to see a pantomime, and she was sure she had seen Seamus's father.

His mother didn't want to talk about it, as so far as she was concerned, her husband was no longer part of their life. But Seamus asked his aunt for Mrs Byrne's number, called her, and asked her to tell him who and what she saw.

'Was it definitely him?' he asked, probably too directly, because she sounded nervous.

'I don't know, son. What I said to yer aunt is it sure looked like him, and he was Irish, I heard that sure enough.'

'So you heard him speak?'

'Yeah, he was just hanging around having a smoke outside the theatre.'

'Did you talk to him?'

'I did. I asked him if he was who I thought he was.'

'And what did he say?'

'He said no, he wasn't, that wasn't his name. He said I must be confusing him with someone else.'

'Did you get his name?'

'No, I didn't. I just left it.'

'What was he doing there?'

'I don't know. He was just having a smoke on the steps, like he was hanging around waiting for people.'

Whether it was him or it wasn't, the episode, and the anguish it seemed to cause his mother, gave birth to a desire he had never before felt to find out who his father was, where he lived, what he looked like, why he had deserted him. In his mind's eye, he saw a fatter, older version of himself. He was determined to track him down. It is partly why he moved to England. His mother had told him many times that is where his father had fled to.

Then one day, sitting flicking through a magazine in the dentist's waiting room, he saw an advert for a little charity in St Albans called Search & Reunion, which, for a fee, helped people to locate parents, siblings, children, aunts and uncles from which they had become separated. He got in touch with them, and they sent through some forms. He didn't much like all the questions he had to answer, as to get what he wanted he needed to be himself, not one of his many identities. He had filled it in as best he could though, given them the sparse details he had of his father, which came mainly from the copy of the birth certificate he had with him, and the unconfirmed sighting of him outside a theatre in the north of England. He expected to get a reply a few weeks hence telling him they had made extensive enquiries but, alas, had been unable to locate his father.

One of Martin Kelly's challenges, as 'Paul', was to try to ensure Seamus, as 'Peter', did not allow his emotions to get in the way of the mission. Easier said than done. Nobody got into terrorism without a lot of emotion pumping through them. Kelly had more than most. He was homosexual, with an English boyfriend, a football nut who knew nothing of his service with the IRA. It was a relationship that began in an underground bar in Leeds. Most football fans in the North and South of Ireland followed an English team, most commonly Manchester United or Liverpool, and Kelly's, because he admired Johnny Giles, was Leeds United. He met his boyfriend Toby who had been watching his team lose 3–1 at Leeds United's Elland Road stadium in the late sixties. A one-night stand soon became something much more serious.

Living so much of his life under cover – hiding his homosexuality from family and friends, hiding his real work from his boyfriend and all but a handful of IRA colleagues – he got a special thrill out of going north on a few weekends each year to see Toby's team play, having Toby introduce him as 'my other half', watching football together and having a time away from the Troubles. It was the one risk he allowed himself.

When Colleen arrived, 'Paul' felt more at ease, especially as he knew Paddy was still to come. He noticed that 'Peter' was very

cautious in her company and his foul-mouthed rhetoric suddenly
dried up. He knew that Colleen Connor came from a good,
solid IRA family. All the checks had confirmed she was reliable,
dedicated, and had shown her ability to kill in cold blood when
she'd been asked by the Derry commander to walk into a Belfast
pub and take out Billy McGinn, a Unionist paramilitary. McGinn
was not that big a fish. It had been a test for the young Connor,
and her reward was now being played out in this Ealing safe
house. Her notes had said she had a 'violent temper' but he had
seen none of this.

Maybe once, before the facial scar, she was a good-looking girl
who wore make-up and dressed in skirts and blouses rather than
the worn denims and old woolly jumper she wore today. Her hair
would benefit from a combing and her Dunlop tennis shoes had
seen better days, but at least unlike 'Peter' she was odour-free.

Paddy arrived ten minutes later. Unusually for him, he wasn't
smiling.

'OK. The 4Ps are here. I am "Paul". This is "Peter". This is
"Pamela". And this is Paddy. Paddy, you're very very welcome.'

Paddy nodded, nervously.

'Paddy has very particular skills that we are going to need as
he is extremely familiar with the venue, which has now been
chosen as the location for an attack. This is the team. Behave
like a team. Or else suffer the consequences.'

He paused, to let those words sink in, then began to brief
them properly.

'OK. We now have more information about the mission. We
have the target and we have the location. We will be taking out a
senior government figure who we know will be staying in Paddy's
hotel, four days from now.

'"Peter". Your specific instructions are these. We want a device
that will take out one individual in one hotel bedroom. What
we don't want is any casualties apart from the target, who is a
fifty-two-year-old white male. There will be serious repercussions
if we take down half the building and if any civilians are killed.
We only want to eliminate the target. OK?' 'Peter' nodded.

'The explosion will need to take place at exactly twelve

midnight this Saturday. That day we'll all meet here – except you, Paddy – at seventeen thirty hours, when I will go through the procedure once more. You two will then get the train into Paddington Station from Ealing Broadway at eighteen hundred hours. When you arrive at Paddington at around eighteen twenty-five, you will sit and wait for Paddy, who is a porter at the hotel, so he'll be in striped trousers, a waistcoat and tails. As you wait, you will both keep checking the notice board which is on the platform at the foot of the stairway leading up to the hotel for a note that says "*Grandma, ring home. Urgent. Pete and Pam*". Paddy, you'll place this note once the target has both checked into his room and then left his room, somewhere around eighteen thirty hours. This will signify a GREEN action. If for any reason Paddy doesn't place the note by nineteen fifteen, a quarter past seven, the event is off and you both jump on the next train and shoot off back home.

'This note, if pinned on the notice board, confirms that the target has both checked into the hotel and, more importantly, has left his room. You will then wait for Paddy who will meet you at the bronze statue of Brunel, the guy who built the station; you can't miss it, at the bottom of the stairs. Paddy will then take down the notice, which is a signal for you both to follow him, without making any verbal contact, and then Paddy will lead you to the bedroom.

'"Pamela", at approximately eighteen forty hours, when the target is out at a dinner, Paddy will show you exactly where to position the leather briefcase containing the device. Therefore, "Peter", we need a five-hour-twenty-minute delay mechanism to catch him at midnight when he returns to his room and starts sleeping with the fairies.

'I'm asked to tell you that twelve sticks of "jellies", about six pounds, wrapped in shrapnel is suggested, which will fit nicely in a standard brown leather briefcase which, "Pamela", you will purchase, place in the explosives and later set the timer with "Peter". And "Pamela", make sure you buy two almost identical second-hand leather briefcases. You'll hide one of these on the way in, so that "Peter" is seen to be carrying one on the way out, once you've planted the device.

'It's his job to manufacture the device and your job to plant it. Paddy will help you with this once you get into the room.

'You should both be finished and out of the hotel by eighteen fifty hours at the latest and back on the train to Ealing Broadway.

'OK, one final thing. You'll be carrying a briefcase not a duffle bag so, "Peter", you need to be dressed in a suit with a collar and tie, and "Pamela", you need to look businesslike. If you both dress like you are dressed today it'll look like a couple of bloody tramps have wandered into the hotel with a big sign that says *"We've got Irish accents and a fucking big bomb in our briefcase."* So you both need to smarten up.

'Are there any questions?'

'Peter' asked, 'What if I don't have a suit?'

'Paul' reached in his pocket and pulled out a wad of cash. He peeled off three £20 notes and passed them over. 'OK, go and get one, and make sure it's plain and dark so you don't stand out like a bleeding rock star.'

He emphasized his earlier point once more: 'We only want this one man taken out, nobody else. So we need the device that will do that.'

'Not a problem. I've got several ready-made for that.'

'Good. We don't want or need anyone else to be hurt. This is a prestige target and we want it done cleanly. The Brits already know we can do general targeting. We want this to be so specific that every single one of them will brick themselves once it's happened.'

'Does he have close protection?' asked 'Peter'.

'He does – and more so in his new role. But we know he likes to get to bed early, and so we want the explosion set for midnight. Paddy has been working as a porter at the hotel for a number of years so he knows his way around.'

Paddy nodded.

'OK. Can we get to the stuff that matters?' asked 'Peter'.

'It all matters. Get the slightest thing wrong and it all goes wrong. You of all people should fucking know that,' said 'Paul'.

'What's that supposed to fucking mean?' snapped 'Peter'.

'Enough,' said 'Paul'. 'Simmer down and shut up.'

He continued: 'If the path is clear, Paddy will let you into the room with the master key. Now ... this is a moment of possible vulnerability. Sometimes, one of his protection team will sit outside the room all day and all night. Other times, they will all be needed when he is out. We have staked out different hotel stays by the target, and others on the same security level, and it is frankly fifty-fifty. And when the target is sleeping, sometimes they have someone outside the door all night, other times they just check from time to time. It's all a bit hit and miss.'

'Fucking amateurs,' snorted 'Peter'.

'Up to a point.'

'So what do we do if someone is there?' asked 'Pamela'.

'You walk on. Paddy has a stand-by room ready on the same corridor. He puts you in there like you're just another couple checking in for a nice romantic weekend.'

'That'll be the day,' said 'Peter'.

'And how do we know when we can go into the target's room?' asked 'Pamela'.

'Paddy will let you know. These guys think nothing of him coming and going and checking everything is OK.'

'Sounds like this is not as drilled down as it could be,' moaned 'Peter'.

'It is as drilled down as it can be,' replied 'Paul', irritably. 'Who said something as big as this was going to be easy?'

'Why can't we just take the protection guy out?'

'Because he is not the target. And the target might suspect something is up if he arrives at his room and his cop is lying dead because you got fucking blood-hungry.'

Paddy spoke for the first time. 'My guess is when the target is out, his whole team will be out.'

'I don't like guesswork,' retorted 'Peter'.

'This is not a perfect plan,' admitted 'Paul', 'but it's as good as we have got right now. If the room is protected all night, we call it off and try again another day. But you will need no more than half a minute to get in there and do what you have to do.

Paddy shows you in, lifts the mattress at the side of the bed closest to the door, and there is a little compartment ready-made for you, just big enough to hold a briefcase. I know you don't like guesswork, "Peter", but I am guessing it's going to happen, provided we all hold our nerve. We know the target will be there. We know he will be leaving the room empty for a few hours. We know he will be in bed by, probably, eleven at the latest. A bomb timed for midnight will make him wish he had never been born.'

'So come on,' said 'Peter'. 'I'm not keen on guessing games. Who the fuck is it?'

'Paul' allowed himself a smile.

'We owe the general tip to Paddy, and we owe the specific groundwork to Paddy. Paddy – tell your good friend "Peter" the news.'

Paddy held on to the secret a few seconds more, his eyes almost demonic in the intensity with which he was looking at 'Peter'.

'Merlyn Rees.'

There was silence for a few seconds. 'Peter' smiled. Colleen let out a little 'yes' sound, and clenched her fists tightly.

'You fucking serious?' she asked. 'The newly appointed Secretary of State so-called for Northern Ireland?'

'Paul' and Paddy nodded in unison. 'He's used the hotel where Paddy works before. We knew he was booked in, we knew he was shadow Secretary of State, likely to become Secretary of State if Wilson became Prime Minister. And it's fucking happened. Sometimes, the gods shine on those who deserve their bounty, eh?'

'So we are taking out the new Northern Ireland Secretary in his first week in the job?' asked Colleen, barely able to take it in.

'Indeed we are. And one of the reasons we cannot be a hundred per cent sure of his security arrangements is that is what he is by the time we strike, and he is going to be better protected than he is now. But we still think this is totally doable.'

Martin Kelly had felt exactly the same excitement when he had returned to Belfast two days earlier to be briefed. But this had been mixed with shock on discovering that the Great Western

Hotel was the location of the target. For he knew through Toby Wilkins that his football team would be staying there on Friday in advance of their match against Chelsea. He knew too, not least from the night they had spent together in Norwich earlier in the season, that Toby tried to stay at the same hotel as the team. As his commander filled him in on the detailed reconnaissance work that had been done by Paddy in advance of 'a hit this weekend', 'Paul' – now very much Martin Kelly – had been trying to conceal his anxiety, and his desperate desire to hear that it would not be on Friday night but on Saturday night that the attack would take place. He had never been more relieved than when he heard the words 'midnight Saturday night/Sunday morning'. Win or lose, the team and most of their supporters would be well on their way home by then.

'Paul' oversaw the departure of his small active service team: Paddy first, heading off to do a night shift at the hotel, then 'Peter', heading back to Dartford to refine the device he was sure would be perfect for the operation, and finally 'Pamela', a big smile on her face, her disfiguring scar more prominent than ever.

'How you feeling?' he asked her as he led her to the back door.

'Happy,' she replied. 'Fucking happy, and excited as hell.'

'Good girl. Let's me and you drop "Pamela" for a moment. Colleen, my name is Martin Kelly . . . your father would be very, very proud of you if he knew what you were about to do.'

'If it wasn't that it went so badly the last time I tried it, I'd give you a bloody big kiss,' she said.

'I won't be needing that,' he said, smiling. He opened the door, and saw Colleen Connor disappear into the West London gloom, both of them confident that the next time they met, it would be to celebrate a murder that would have folk singers of the future writing ballads in their honour.

Club captain Wilf Moore knew that what he was about to announce, after Tuesday morning's brutal fitness and stamina session, would annoy his teammates, several of them intensely.

But the manager had insisted, and so far as he was concerned, that was that.

'OK lads, listen up, will you. First the good news. I reckon once we have totted up all the extra commercial stuff that the Cup run has brought in, we're looking at an extra several hundred quid per man – and before you say a word, Brownie, I am including the whole squad in that.' Loud cheers from most. Sulky shrugging from one or two.

'Now the bad news. We are behind schedule on our charity days, and the gaffer has promised we will do a squad visit to the children's wards at the infirmary tomorrow.' Loud groans from virtually everyone.

'I know, I know, it is a pain, but let's just do it with a smile on our face, get some good pictures in the papers and make a few kids happy when they're ill, eh?'

Taffy Rees was fit to explode.

'Fucking hell, Mooro, they're supposed to give us three days' notice of these fucking outside appearances. My kid brother is coming up from Wales and we're supposed to be playing golf. Why should I let him down?'

'We'll be in by half two and gone by four.'

'Bollocks to it. Three days' notice. You can fucking count me out.'

'Well, you know the gaffer's rules. If it is a squad event, then anyone who misses it gets fined twenty-five quid.'

'You can have fucking fifty,' said Taffy. 'I'm not coming.'

Inevitably, David Brown was next to charge in.

'Did you point out to the gaffer we have a fucking big game on Saturday?' he asked.

'I don't think the gaffer needs telling that, Brownie. But you know how seriously he takes the role the club plays in the community and he thinks with all this focus on us right now, this will show us in a good light.'

'I'll tell you what will show us in a good light – us beating fucking Chelsea, and that is less likely if we are shagged out from traipsing round picking up kids' fucking germs in a hospital.'

'Brownie...' protested Mooro.

'Don't fucking Brownie me. I've got a hospitality package at Redcar races tomorrow and if you take twenty-five quid off me for going, I'll have the fucking PFA all over you.'

'OK, Brownie, I'll tell the boss you and Taffy are not coming. You can argue about the fines with the gaffer yourself. Is everybody else available?'

He took the silence as confirmation, and thought the matter was closed, until Ronnie Winston chipped in.

'Mooro,' he said, 'the lads have got a point, and I just wonder if you think it is worth me having a word with the gaffer. I had no idea about this. It's not ideal preparation, is it?'

'Hear fucking hear,' said Taffy.

Mooro, who knew how important it was to maintain a united front between management and captain, snorted his contempt.

As Winston went off to 'have a word with the gaffer' – though it later emerged he merely said some of the players were pissed off at having to do the visit – Mooro sat down and reflected that his position too was likely to be under threat if Gordon was fired. He was very much Gordon's man, not the fastest or most skilful of defenders, but someone who had real leadership qualities. He knew as well as anyone that Winston didn't – he had just shown it once more. He was a Number Two thinking he could be a Number One. Mooro, whose legs were beginning to go anyway, thought that maybe it was time to think about a move to a Division Two or even Division Three club. It was the first time that prospect had entered his head, and as a one-club man who had come through the ranks, he knew what a wrench it would be.

He knew also, however, that virtually every dressing room in the country was like this. Football-mad kids who had grown into football-mad men. Largely uneducated, mostly from the rough end of town. It had been a fight for all of them to get this far, because so many working-class kids wanted the life they had, so most had learned how to look after themselves, especially on the field.

Most professional footballers came from ordinary backgrounds. Their siblings and school friends worked in factories, or on building sites, or in supermarkets. It seemed crazy to those people that footballers could complain about anything, let alone a hospital visit to brighten up the life of a child. But in truth, though the tough background of a lot of these players made them street smart, it didn't prepare them well for the pressures that fame, wealth and success brought them. That might be a problem most fans would swap for their humdrum existence, but it was a pressure nonetheless.

Mooro didn't know what he would be if he didn't have this community of men to be with, day in, day out. Some he liked, some he disliked, but it really was a community, with its rules and habits and oddities that few outsiders would ever understand. He had seen stacks of players come and go, but there was always the same dressing room mix at the end of whatever transfers were made in or out.

You'd find the great sprinter, the dribbler, the header, the tackler, the long-distance runner, the motor mouth, the leader, the follower and the genius. You would also find the gambler, the problem drinker, the incorrigible womanizer – there would be several of those – the born-again Christian, the snappy dresser, the brainy one, the quiet one, the loud one, the shy one, the boastful one, the spender, the tight-arsed saver, the cynic, the comedian who was funny, the comedian who wasn't, the hard man, the moaner, the hypochondriac. Most players had more than one label, but there was usually only one clear candidate for each type. Mooro wondered whether in most dressing rooms there might be the poofter one too, unable to admit it in the anti-'queer' football culture, which would ensure relentless ribbing by players was matched by vicious chants from the terraces. Mooro wasn't alone in thinking the Prof, unmarried and with never a sign of a girlfriend at club events, might be 'one of those'.

When the players gathered for the trip to the hospital, wearing club-crested tracksuits, they were briefed on the coach by commercial manager Pete Leadbetter, who had brought along three large boxes of kits, pictures, programmes, rosettes, key-rings and pens for the players to give out to the children. Rees and Brown had gone ahead with their threat not to take part, and had been warned by Gordon they faced a fine. The only other absentee was Jules Pemberton, who was having treatment on a back strain.

With the team cynic David Brown at Redcar races, and golf-aholic Taffy Rees out on the course with his brother, the bitter mood of yesterday had gone. Over half of these players had their own children themselves, and so were easily moved by some of the stories they heard. They behaved well and posed patiently for photos, both for *Courier* snapper Vicky Meredith and for parents and other visitors who had been tipped off the team was coming. Only Marland and Kilbride even came close to disgracing themselves, excessively flirting with the prettiest of the nurses on the ward. But Mooro would later report to Gordon that the trip had been a big success, and the words of encouragement from patients and parents alike ahead of Saturday had made them feel good.

24

SCOOP

Charlie Gordon had travelled to the hospital with the players, but told them this was very much a players' event, and he had meanwhile gone to the office of the children's ward sister Sadie Blake. He had organized the visit through her, and they agreed to meet for a coffee while the players did the rounds. She kissed him on the cheek after closing the door behind them, and he pulled her close to him and just held her, tightly, for a few seconds.

'I take it from that that you're missing me... or missing female company?' she smiled, pulling herself free to put the kettle on and spoon instant coffee into two plain white mugs.

'Aye, it's not been easy, especially these past few weeks.'

'I've seen.' Sadie was not a football fan, but you couldn't live in this town and not be aware of the pressure her former boyfriend was under.

'So if you lose on Saturday, you're out, is that right?' she asked.

'So they say.'

'You'd better win then.'

'Exactly.'

It was odd how neither his wife nor Sadie had ever really been into football. Then again, does every doctor's wife have to be interested in medicine? Does every pilot have to have a wife who loves flying? Footballers are unusual in that they so often take their families to see them at work. But Sadie, during the two years they had been together, had never been to a match; never asked to, never been asked. So it was no wonder she looked a little surprised when he asked her: 'Do you want a ticket for the match then? I've got a few comps.'

'Oh my,' she said, 'you really are missing me.'

'I'm missing having anyone I can talk to about how much I'm struggling right now.'

He had gone there with the intention of saying the dread words 'I think I have an alcohol problem', but when it came to it, and she asked 'Struggling with what?', he found himself pausing for a few seconds, then saying: 'You know, the pressure, all the talk of getting the sack.'

'I'm working on Saturday, Charlie.'

'Ah, OK, not to worry. Just a thought.'

The kettle was making slow progress. He heard from outside a siren blaring as an ambulance rushed to Accident and Emergency. It brought back memories, and Sadie knew him well enough to know what they were.

'It's not easy for you coming in here, is it?'

He shook his head.

'Do the players know that's why you wanted them to come?'

'I doubt it. One or two of the older ones maybe. None of them were with us when Alice died and I was still a player. You know, when we came in the ambulance, it never crossed my mind she wouldn't come out alive.'

'You will never get over it, Charlie, you have to accept that. But the hurt will continue to ease with time.'

'You must love your job, Sadie, all the good you do for people.'

'Hey, listen, you do good too, you know, it's just different. We ease pain. You give a lot of pleasure to a lot of people.'

'When we win.'

'In your game there have to be winners and losers.'

'I guess so.'

'Mine too.'

She went to pour boiling water onto the coffee, added milk and sugar, and took the cups over to him.

'You haven't got a drop of something to liven it up, have you?'

'I might be able to find you some pure alcohol from the pharmacy, but otherwise, no,' she said sternly.

'Sorry, I shouldn't have said that.'

'It does mean you've managed to remind me of the two reasons things didn't work out with us, Charlie.'

'Football and booze.'

'Exactly. Football and booze.'

Again, he found himself wanting to say the words 'I think I might be an alcoholic', but they wouldn't come. Instead he said, 'I hope the kids get something out of the visit today.' She saw through the diversion.

'Charlie, can I ask you a question?'

'Of course.'

'How much are you drinking?'

'Oh, you know, pretty much the same as when you were with me. Wine with dinner, the occasional whisky before bed.'

'Are you sure?'

He paused and, on seeing the real concern in her eyes, he found his filling with tears, and then sobbed, two loud, convulsive sobs which felt like they would rip his chest apart, through which the words finally came: 'I'm drinking too much, Sadie, it's out of control, it's out of control.'

She went to put her arms around him, and it made him sob all the harder.

For Charlie Gordon, Wilf Moore and Graham Smith, their public duties for the day did not end with the hospital visit. Wednesday evening had long been in the diary as the date for the monthly fans' forum with management and players. Gordon and Mooro were regulars. Other players attended on a rota basis and today it was Smudger and David Brown, who arrived five minutes late after his day at the races (conveniently avoiding any greeting by Gordon). Stan Moffitt had also hoped to attend but had been detained in Manchester at a business meeting, so Matthew Stock stood in.

Generally the tone of these meetings was set almost entirely by how well the team was performing in the League, and more importantly, how the team performed in the last match. But with

Chelsea looming, Gordon was hoping there would be more focus
on prospects there, less on the massacre by Leeds.

The meeting was chaired by Toby Wilkins, the president of
the supporters' club, and when finally the two hundred and fifty
people were all settled down in the Alan Cross Suite, named
after the manager who was in charge when they won promotion
to the top flight, he opened up in a way designed to ease the
pressure.

'Manager, can I maybe ask the first question before we open
things to the floor ... How has it been for you and the players
this week? You must be so conscious of the interest in this game
on Saturday.'

'Thank you, Toby, and thank you everyone for coming. What
a turn-out tonight. Hands up who's going to the match on
Saturday?' Most of the hands went up. 'Hands up who has not
been able to get a ticket?' Maybe forty or fifty hands went up.
Two of them belonged to a young boy in the front row, and a
woman Gordon assumed to be his mother.

'You, son, what's your name?' Gordon said, pointing to the
boy.

'Graham,' he said.

'Is that your mum, Graham?'

The boy nodded.

'And can I ask your mum something, Graham? Mum, if
Graham had a couple of tickets, would you go with him?'

The boy looked at his mother, clearly as big a fan as the boy,
who nodded enthusiastically.

'OK,' said Gordon, reaching into his inside pocket. 'A friend
of mine I was hoping would come to the game has to work on
Saturday. She works at the hospital where the players have just
done a visit to see the sick kids. Graham, come up here, son, I
want you to have her tickets, and enjoy the game.'

Graham, who was ten but looked younger, walked to the stage,
his hands clasped to his face in excitement. Gordon noticed Don
Robinson smiling, scribbling furiously, as Vicky Meredith leapt
forward and asked the boy to pose for a picture standing by

Gordon, who was being cheered as though he had just headed a goal from an inswinging corner.

'Well, what a way to start proceedings,' said Toby Wilkins, and when he added 'but you didn't really answer my question' there were friendly groans from the audience who felt Gordon had answered the question perfectly by making a young boy's day, his month, his year, his entire childhood even.

'No, fair enough,' said Gordon, silencing the noise from the audience. 'Fair point, Toby. I know how much this match means, and it means so much to me and to the players. We let people down on Saturday, no doubt about it, and these players know there has to be a reaction. We have to play as we know we can.'

'Mooro, would you like to add anything to that?'

'Well first of all, Toby, I want to say that if we do get a win, I want young Graham there to come with his mum and join the celebrations. That was a wonderful moment, gaffer, and it reminded us what football is all about. I can only echo what the gaffer said: we are not where we want to be in the League, but we are one game away from a semi-final and two games away from Wembley. Have no fear. We will be up for it.'

Commercial manager Pete Leadbetter brought in David Brown as the next question was being asked, Brownie mouthing 'sorry I'm late' to Gordon, and then to the audience, then taking a moment to look quizzically at Smudger Smith's dramatic new permed haircut.

'My question is for Smudger,' said an overweight middle-aged man who Toby introduced as 'Goldie', presumably on account of the fact he had golden hair before it went thin and grey. 'Do you have nightmares about Chopper Harris, because I know I bloody would?'

The audience laughed and applauded and Smudger laughed too.

'He is a very good defender. He is a very hard tackler. But I've played him before and I'd say if I had a quid for every time I got past him, and he had a quid for every time he put me onto the gravel, I'm quids in.'

David Brown broke in with a double-edged observation. 'And

don't forget the last time DD played against Chelsea, for Spurs, he got a hat-trick. One day he's bound to get one for us, so why not Saturday?'

Smudger came in again. 'Also, I'm hoping with this new hair-cut Chopper won't recognize me and he'll think he's marking Brownie.'

Brownie chipped in again. 'To be serious for a second. I play in behind Smudger. He is younger and he is faster than Harris. Chopper is getting on and his legs are not what they were. My money's on Smudger to leave him for dead.' The audience applauded both the bravado and the team spirit.

Toby called an elderly man at the back, who stood, tapped the microphone to make sure it was working, breathed in por-tentously, and said: 'Mis-ter Gor-don ... kindly explain to me ... how can any player be worth one hundred and thirty-two thou-sand pounds, and can you and the director on the panel tell us whether DD Marland has justified that outlay?'

Gordon looked at Stock, who indicated the manager should answer first.

'He made a great start, scored on his debut, and since then, yes, he hasn't scored, but he has created chances and I have been heartened by his attitude in training. As for the fee, I'm afraid there is a market for players, and if you want the big players, you have to pay the big money. I wish it wasn't so, but it is.'

Toby motioned to Matthew Stock to add his tuppenceworth.

'As a board, we really have to be guided by what the manager wants. I'm sure DD himself wishes he had done better, but as the manager said, he has shown quality before and I am sure he will do so again.'

Gordon gave him the kind of stare he used to give centre-forwards trying to push him around at corners and free-kicks. But Toby, perhaps primed by Stock, or maybe by Robinson, followed up: 'And Mr Stock, there has been some speculation before that if the chairman decided his time at the club had run its course, you would like to be chairman. Can you confirm that?'

Again, Robinson's pencil was taking down every word.

'I really don't think, Toby, that a few days before a big Cup tie is the time to be talking about the next chairman, any more than talking about the next manager or the next player to come in or go out. So I really don't want to go there, other than to repeat what I have said before – it would be the biggest honour of my life. But like I say – no vacancy.'

This time, Stock surely felt the heat in the Gordon glare. The manager knew that just by raising the prospect of 'the next manager' – nobody else had – Stock had put it on the agenda. And when the director slipped him a note, on which he had scribbled 'Sorry, that came out wrong', Gordon had to maintain all his discipline not to write back, 'You two-faced little shit.'

The next question was from a young woman, Matilda Devonport, who asked very directly: 'Mooro, why do we never seem to score from free-kicks and corners? You're the captain, why don't you ask Ronnie Winston to get the team back in the afternoons and do more practising?'

Wilf Moore looked taken aback by what he saw as a technical question, especially as it came from a girl.

'Good question, Matilda. The thing is, I don't think there is any science to this. We do practise corners and free-kicks, we practise them a lot, but what you can't do is practise against the teams you are going to be playing. But I hear what you're saying, and maybe we need to do more on the training ground, and maybe do things a bit differently.'

'Manager?' asked Toby.

'Good question, good answer,' said Gordon.

The mood among the supporters was good. Nobody got personal, nothing was asked they couldn't deal with, and Toby did a good job shutting down the wafflers and making sure the evening kicked along, Gordon having been clear he wanted the players to be out of there and off home no later than nine o'clock.

'OK, ladies and gentlemen, I'll take the two last questions and then these gentlemen have to leave.'

The first question, from a teenage boy, raised a laugh.

'I would like to ask Mooro where he bought that shirt. And does he have a spare one?'

Mooro pulled the collar forward and tried to read the label.

Knowing as he did that it was handmade by one of his Savile Row shirt-makers, he pretended he couldn't see it.

'All I know is if I did have two, I would give the second one to you. But I don't, and with that photographer there, I am not stripping.'

Some of the women shouted out, 'Oh go on, Mooro,' and he acted all bashful and shy.

'Final question – the gentleman at the front, with the dark-blue tie.'

A man in his late thirties or early forties with jet-black hair and a bushy moustache giving him the look of a secondary school headmaster stood and waited till all eyes were on him.

'Thomas Sutton, *Daily Mail*. Question for the manager. Sorry to raise this in this forum but my calls to Mr Moffitt and Mr Finley have gone unanswered, and Mr Kilbride would not speak to me when I went to his home.'

Gordon knew what was coming, and he barely heard the rest of the question as he tried to remember how they had persuaded the *Courier* not to run the story about Killer and Abigail Partington.

'So I would like to ask for a comment on the photo we have of Michael Kilbride leaving the Park Hotel in Crainton in the early hours of a week last Sunday with a seventeen-year-old girl who works at this football club. Have you looked into this, and what if any action are you taking?'

All eyes turned to Gordon, not least Mooro's, Brownie's and Smudger's, and Don Robinson's, who doubtless worried his credibility would be hit with his colleagues if another paper ran the story.

'Yes, I have looked into it, and no, there will be no action. The reason, Mister – was it Sutton, did you say? – the reason, Mister Sutton, is that you are not the first paper to have this photo sent to you, and as the other papers who had it have managed to establish, you have a picture, but no story. And I intend to say nothing more than that, because I am the manager of a football club which has a massive game on Saturday and nothing, not even your desire for a headline, is going to get in the way of that.

So thanks for your question, and above all thanks to the real supporters who have come here tonight and reminded me and the players just how much this club means to you, and why we go into this game determined to do everything we can to give you – all of you, but especially young Graham there – a day out in London you will never forget.'

And with that the audience stood as one and applauded.

'You're dead right,' Brownie whispered to Mooro. 'He's still fucking got it.'

Gordon told the players to leave by the entrance behind them so they were not swarmed with autograph hunters who would tire them out even more with their chat. As he shepherded them out, he heard Brownie saying to Smudger, 'Killer's going to get battered for this in the morning... fucking kiddie-fiddler.'

'Brownie,' said Gordon, a step behind him, 'not a fucking word. Your day at the races cost you twenty-five quid for the children's ward at the infirmary. One fucking word to Killer, and it's another twenty-five, OK?'

'OK, gaffer.'

'Smudger, you too, you hear me?'

'I hear you, gaffer.'

'Now get home, and sleep.'

As Gordon turned back, aiming to get himself a drink and mingle with the fans, he noticed Matthew Stock signing the autograph book of the young boy to whom Gordon had given his comps. Then he noticed the man from the *Mail* talking to Don Robinson, and he decided he would get a drink elsewhere. He left in time to see Mooro getting into his Ford Cortina.

'You did well there, gaffer.'

'Thanks, Mooro.'

'What about that Matthew Stock though? What's his game?'

'I think you know the answer to that, Mooro. A Number Two who thinks he's a Number One. Football is fucking riddled with them.'

'Yeah.'

'Anyway, you get home, Mooro, I'll see you tomorrow. Not long now.'

*

On arriving home in Dartford Seamus picked up the mail, mostly junk, from behind his front door, walked straight to the fridge, grabbed a bottle of water, and strode purposefully to the tool shed beyond the trio of large rhododendron bushes at the bottom of his tiny, overcrowded garden. He felt like having a proper drink, but he needed his wits about him, and so had decided on the train home that last night's four bottles of Guinness would be his last drop of alcohol until Merlyn Rees was on his way to the morgue. If they pulled this off, he would even offer that ignorant bastard 'Paul' a celebratory drink and hopefully never see that scar-faced bitch again.

He binned most of the mail, then flicked through the rest, mainly bills he had no intention of paying given they were sent to his pseudonym who could cease to exist come Saturday night, and he would be on the move to his next address with his next identity.

The one letter that did attract his attention, however, was one with a St Albans postmark. He had never been there, knew nobody who came from there, and so assumed it was the letter from Search & Reunion telling him they had not been able to find his father. Instead, it suggested they might well have located him after all.

> *Dear Sir,*
> *Thank you for all the information you provided to us. We*
> *believe we may have located the person you are seeking,*
> *though he does not currently share your name. We cannot*
> *at this stage give you any further details. As we explained*
> *at the outset, once the initial searches are made, the fees for*
> *our services rise if contact is made. Also, we would need to*
> *approach your blood relative to establish whether he wished*
> *to have a meeting. I hope this is helpful and I await your*
> *further instructions.*

'Jesus,' he muttered to himself, taking a swig from the bottle of water, then deciding he needed something a little stronger to take it in. Just one bottle of Guinness from the six-pack in the fridge; he could still operate at full capacity with that inside him, and with his mind racing now, just when he needed it to be calm, a drink would settle him down. He had almost been hoping it would say their hunt had been unsuccessful, then he could just focus on the job in hand, and leave the hunt for his father for a rainy day. How weird would it be to meet him, the man who made you, yet you had not a clue what he looked like? Would he want to hug him, shake his hand, or wring his neck? Did they look alike? Was he a supporter of the cause? Did he still have an Irish accent? Would he feel any guilt or shame at leaving his wife to raise a small baby alone? What would he say when he asked him, straight out, why did you leave and break my mother's heart, you bastard?

He walked back to the kitchen, the garden now shrouded in darkness save street lighting at the front of the house throwing shadows across his patchy lawn. He took a bottle of Guinness from the fridge and returned to his shed. He tried to crack open the bottle on the edge of his wooden workbench, but it came only partly away, and so he removed it with his teeth, then took a long, slow swig before turning to the serious task in hand.

He had all he needed. Taping twelve sticks of gelignite together was straightforward, but the next stage was trickier. It was as he sealed the plastic bags and taped them around the gelignite sticks that he noticed that in opening the bottle he had cut his lip. A droplet of blood fell onto one of the shrapnel bags.

'Fuck,' he said, cursing himself for having gone back on his vow not to drink until Sunday when the job was done.

He had a tiny mirror in the bottom drawer of his cupboard and on examining it realized the cut was minuscule and he could staunch it merely by sucking on his lip. So he continued to seal the bags and strap them to the jellies.

The timer device was the final piece, and in many ways the most important. His preferred option of the several used by the IRA was the Smiths Combat pocket watch delay timer. He had several in the second drawer from the top, mainly from Woolworths. He had been trained in timer setting by Hughie Murphy, who was widely viewed as the best in the business, but who lost an arm in a shooting two years ago. Determined not to lose his skills, the Army Council asked him to train the next generation, and Seamus was his star pupil.

To most who knew him well, Seamus was seen as crude, rude, ignorant and usually in dire need of a wash. But with Murphy now disabled, he was without peer at this. He had learned at the feet of the master, and surpassed even him. Though not to his face, some of his superiors called him 'the genius'.

Still angry with himself, he poured the remnants of his Guinness into a flower pot, chided himself for a final time, told himself to 'Fucking concentrate, you dick', and got back to work. He removed the watch glass and snipped off the second hand. He then carefully clipped the minute hand, leaving the hour hand as the longest of the revolving fingers. He stuck a piece of tape on the glass of the watch at the ten o'clock position and drilled a small hole towards the centre so that the hour hand would pass underneath it, when it moved across the hole above.

The circuit would be completed when the hour hand reached ten o'clock and touched the wire, which had been fed through the drilled hole onto the watch face. He then replaced the glass onto the watch and removed an inch of plastic coating from a piece of electric wire, doubled the end back and pushed it through the hole he had made in the glass, taping the wire in place. The ten o'clock position was chosen as a safety precaution just in case the hour hand loosened and slipped forward, as it ensured that the bomb would not detonate before it was touched by the hour hand completing the circuit below the drilled hole. The *real-time* on the watch would be ignored. A bomb intended to explode at midnight would need to be primed at 6 p.m. and set six hours before the ten o'clock position, at 4 p.m. Complicated at first, but he'd manufactured these timers on a dozen occasions and hadn't failed yet.

The other end of the wire was then connected to a five-volt battery with two terminals via an electrical detonator, which was then placed in the middle of the sticks of gelignite. Once the hour hand touched the wire, the electrical circuit would be completed and the bomb would explode.

He placed this safely, ready to be activated on Saturday night.

When he left his shed just after midnight, among nuts, bolts, screws, ball bearings and all the paraphernalia of the death he intended to inflict upon the Rt Hon. Merlyn Rees, a bottle top with a speck of blood from his lip lay on the floor.

25
STATISTICS

Thursday 7 March

Charlie Gordon managed to get himself showered and shaved and feeling reasonably OK, despite the hangover, in time to get to his breakfast meeting at the Tudor Manor Hotel. There was no sign of DD, and the hotel assistant manager, Kevin, one of Gordon's snouts, confirmed his star forward 'had company'. Gordon shook his head, and walked through to the breakfast room, ignoring the glances coming his way.

His voice was rough and deeper than usual, and he quickly ordered black coffee, orange juice and water as he waited for his guest to arrive. He had slept only fitfully, despite the half-dozen or so whiskies he knocked back while watching a recording of Chelsea's recent game against West Ham, sent by a friend taken on a home movie camera.

He had had his recurring dream of losing Alice in a crowd, this time on a busy ferry crossing. He saw her at the bow of the ferry, ran towards her, then the crowds came in, like they always do, and when he fought his way through, she was gone. On waking, he had one of his 'why me?' moments – no woman to share his bed, his only child dead, his mother barely able to know who he was in the last months of her life, his job on the line. It's a wonder he didn't drink even more, he said to himself as the waiter brought over his coffee.

He had already had a little tot of whisky in the car, just to calm his hands, and between them, the whisky, the black coffee and the orange juice helped bring him back to life. Not that the thoughts got any better. There was too much going on that he had to worry about. Why was Alfie Ruse, DD's agent, so keen for a meeting on Friday night in London, and what was he saying about DD not being right to play? What if Jules Pemberton really was injured this time? Would the *Mail* publish anything about Killer? Should he play Taffy Rees or would Walter Graham, an old head, be more stable? Would DD finally get another goal? Should he even think about bringing back Nuts, who had responded well and worked hard after being dropped? And then, inevitably, he reflected on what was for him the biggest question of all: was he two days away from the sack? He could see across the restaurant an elderly man reading the front page of a newspaper, filled with pictures of Harold Wilson's new Cabinet and a recent IRA bombing, while the back proclaimed 'Gordon's last chance'.

Maybe, he thought, maybe not. He had many times in recent days visualized the meeting with Moffitt – who knows, it might come immediately after the match on Saturday – and whether he could bring himself to say the single word '*Poulson*', and whether, if he did, the colour on the chairman's cheeks might change. It was not his style to play dirty in the boardroom game, but he had the rest of his life to think about. If he lost this job, might it be his last?

His guest was ten minutes late already, and though he was happily using the time to get himself going, he didn't like unpunctuality. He wouldn't have dared being late at that age.

It was twenty past when George Munro arrived wearing jeans and a white T-shirt. The receptionist brought him through, they shook hands, and Gordon passed him the menu. Gordon had not had a cooked breakfast in weeks – he never bothered at home and on the mornings of matches in hotels he always felt too stressed to eat – so he told his guest he was 'going for the full works'.

'I'll just have toast and coffee,' said Munro.

Gordon knew little about the young man beyond the fact that

he was director Geoffrey Raymond's son-in-law. He seemed so young, though. Gordon would have had him down as last year in senior school maybe. Or was that just another sign of ageing? Jealousy too, that this slight, skinny, odd-looking chap with curly hair could have a nice wife, and Gordon, an international footballer and now a top manager, lived alone and spent most nights with a glass for company.

Gordon liked to believe he was not as averse to new thinking as a lot of managers of his generation, but also he felt that in agreeing to the meeting he might get more support from Raymond in the event of a boardroom split about whether to sack him. Also, it was interesting that at the fans' forum, that young woman had made that point about their inability to score from corners. She was right.

'How's Geoffrey?' he asked, his mouth full of sausage and brown sauce.

'Very excited. Even Mrs Raymond is going on Saturday, first time this season.'

'What about you?'

'No. I've got a friend at Granada TV and he lets me go in there and watch all the tapes of recent games. That's how I do my research.'

'So who's your team, George?'

'I don't have one. I just love watching to analyse. It's easier if you're not emotionally involved.'

'So these new computer things can win me matches, can they?'

'No. But they can help. If you have more and better information about the other team than they have about you, who does that help?'

'It helps me. But I still need human beings to do what they have to do.'

'Exactly. But you will perform better with better information, and so will they.'

Gordon had been on FA courses, including one hosted by England manager Walter Winterbottom who had sketched out a number of different tactical formations on a giant blackboard:

4-3-3; 4-4-2; or the 5-4-1 defensive system that transformed into 3-3-4 on the counter attack. That was about as scientific as it got, and most people in football – as Matthew Stock had demonstrated when Raymond raised the issue of computer analysis – baulked at the new, let alone the revolutionary. Gordon was more open-minded, recalling two of his mother's favourite trilogies – 'You need to meet three people to find one that's useful,' and 'You'll have three ideas before you find one that works.' What number would George be, he wondered?

'Come on, George, what can your machines tell me that I don't already know?' said Gordon, pushing his cleared plate away.

'It's not about the machine. It's what you do with the information you put into it and get out of it. I can't tell you how to set up a team or decide if a player is worth a hundred thousand pounds. What I can do is give you a whole stack of *probabilities* in certain situations based on the statistical analysis of hundreds, thousands, of matches. You don't have to agree with me, but the fact you're here tells me at least you're prepared to listen.'

'I'm all ears, son.'

'OK,' said Munro, pushing his cup and plate to one side. 'Are you familiar with card-counting?'

'Assume I'm not.'

'Card-counting is what happens when someone with a great memory remembers, out of four or five packs of cards, which cards have been played, so he can predict more accurately what cards are left in the pack. But wait a minute, I hear you thinking, card-counting is illegal in casinos, isn't it?'

'You hear me wrong,' replied Gordon. 'As I understand it, it's not illegal, but if a croupier who is trained to spot card-counters feels that a player is indeed counting the cards, they will find an excuse to call in security and ask the player to leave the building.'

'OK, correct. I knew you'd know about card-counting. Hilarious, isn't it? And why do they do that?'

'Because the casino, which always has the odds stacked in its favour, feels the good card-counter has an unfair advantage.'

'Exactly, Charlie, exactly. Is it OK to call you Charlie, or do you prefer Mr Gordon?'

'Charlie's fine.' He was warming to the boy.

'I'm talking about giving you the kind of advantage a card-counter gets, but without anyone having the power to ban you. I can give you the information you need to instruct your players what is the likelihood of their success in certain set situations. Surely that will give you an edge.'

'Go on then, give me examples.'

'OK. You're the manager. You build the squad, you select the team, you have a lot of control over that. Correct?'

'Well, I am restricted by budget and availability but yes, I have a lot of say in that.'

'Then you oversee training sessions and you can decide what these sessions entail, yes?'

'Yes.'

'Then three o'clock comes, and how much control do you have then?'

'My team talk, my leaders on the field, my instructions from the sidelines.'

'Most don't even look when you're waving your arms around. They can't even hear you. You can't tackle, dribble, shoot. They do it, and you are reliant on their skill, their judgement, *their* instinct. They have good days, bad days.'

'OK, I kind of agree so far.'

'So you agree that the time you have the least control is the time you need it most. It's crazy.'

'But you still haven't told me how your machines can help.'

'You're going to have to shift your thinking on this, Charlie. I repeat – the computers can't do anything. But you can do something with the information they provide. Can I ask you a question, Charlie?'

'Of course.'

'How many corners have you had in all matches this season?'

'I have no idea.'

'Why not?'

'Why should I?'

'I'll tell you why. Do you know how many goals you have scored from corners this season?'

'Not many, I know that.'

'None is the answer, Charlie, zero, not one.'

'I know what none means.'

'You have an average of 6.8 corners per game and you have scored from none. Arsenal have had an average of 5.2 corners per game and scored 1.3 goals per game from corners.'

'They have big central defenders and big forwards who are good in the air.'

'Maybe, yes. So do most teams. But they must be doing something right that you are doing wrong. The statistics can help you assess what it might be.'

'How?'

'When the ball is in open play, we are agreed, you lose control. It is all down to the players. But in any situation we call a *set-piece*, a kick-off, a corner, a free-kick, a throw-in, there are three different approaches you can take. Firstly, you can let the players decide what to do and leave it entirely up to them. Secondly, you can put your wet finger in the air to see which way the wind is blowing and just leave it to Lady Luck. Or, thirdly, you can instruct your players *exactly* what you want them to do in a range of specific controlled circumstances.'

He paused to take a mouthful of coffee to let the point sink in. He swallowed it down, then looked Gordon in the eye.

'OK. Let's cut the crap, cut to the chase... when you have a corner, who decides what to do with that corner?'

'Dipper on the right, Smudger on the left.'

'Why them?'

'Because they take the corners.'

'Why?'

'Because they are good at crossing the ball.'

'But are they good at making decisions?'

'They are good at getting the ball in the box.'

'But you haven't scored a single goal from a corner all season.'

'You can't blame them for that.'

'No, I blame you for not changing things. What was it Einstein said about the definition of madness – doing the same thing again and again and expecting a different result?'

'Are you saying I'm mad?'

'I am saying a corner is a moment when *you* can have control, but you have ceded it to players who may be good at crossing a ball, but aren't good at analysing what they do. With the corners you have had this year, based on the national average, the ratio of corners to goals, you should have had 7.6 more goals this season. Think of the difference that makes to your League position.'

'But when we get a corner, there's thirty-odd thousand people screaming. I'm fifty-odd yards away. Am I supposed to get a megaphone out and tell them what to do?'

'No. But you make sure they know what you want them to do, according to the circumstances. I mean, let me get this straight, Charlie. When there's a corner, do you just leave it up to a player like Graham Smith, who's even younger than I am, to make his own mind up on which type of corner he's going to take? While you are sat there in the dugout, fifty-one years old, thousands of games under your belt, powerless. I don't want to be rude, but to me, that is fucking madness.'

Gordon was not used to being talked to like this by anyone, let alone someone so young.

'Charlie, listen to this very, very carefully. Let me give you a piece of information that will make you a corner-taking card-counter. If you listen, absorb, and adapt, I reckon you'll get between seven and ten more goals over a season.'

'OK, I'm still listening.'

'Charlie, sorry if I am being too direct but if you let these inexperienced, overpaid football stars take control eventually they will get you the sack, as they'll continue to make the wrong decisions, which are based on their instinct, rather than probabilities based on your directions. So... there are basically four types of corner: the driven corner either long or short; the inswinging corner; the outswinging corner; and finally the short corner. Agreed?'

'Uh-huh.'

'Which of those do Smith and Temple favour?'

'Outswinging.'

'Correct. Sixty-eight per cent. Fourteen per cent inswinging. Twelve per cent short. Six per cent driven low.'

'You've counted them all?'

'Every single one of them goalless. But not just yours. Let me give you a big fat fact, Charlie. Based on actual goals from actual corners taken over the past four years, a team is *twice* as likely to score from an inswinging corner as from an outswinging corner. Let me put that in terms Smudger and Dipper might understand – you *double* the chance of scoring from an inswinger compared with an outswinger.'

He asked the waiter for a pen, and began to scribble all the relevant numbers of his analysis of their corners on the back of the menu, to prove his point.

'So, Charlie, with this information at your fingertips, why would you let any member of your team ever take an out-swinging corner again?'

'What about short corners?'

'Once a short corner is taken it's just like entering back into normal play. The odds are just the same as if you cross the ball from normal play. Of all four options this is the worst, as it rarely results in a goal, or at least not from the crossed-ball element of play. There are other tactics and moves you can add on to a short corner that can deceive the opposition. But generally you should *never, ever* take a short corner.'

'So how do you explain the fact that more corners are scored from inswingers?'

'It's about how things look rather than how they are. A goal headed in by a centre-forward from an outswinging corner looks good because he has to rise above the defenders, meet the ball perfectly, change its trajectory with power and speed. But all too often, the pace and spin from the cross makes it hard to control which is why so many headers end up going over the bar. An inswinging corner, aimed head height at the near post – it *can* look good if a forward gets ahead of the defender and flicks it into the net, but more likely you'll see a scrappy goal, scrambled in during a goalmouth mix-up, sometimes the result of the ball being flicked on by a player positioned specifically at the near post, and then the goal is scored by someone coming at speed in behind him in the centre of the area. But these scrappy goals count exactly the same as a majestic bullet header. And Arsenal have scored lots of them and you have scored none.'

Gordon sat back, nodding. 'I see.'

'It is so obvious, Charlie, but nobody is doing it. You managers are no better than your stupid wingers. You just keep on doing the same thing, wet finger in the air.'

'OK, I will try telling them to do more inswingers.'

'Don't just try. Tell them. Make them. We've only done corners. I can help you with free-kicks, throw-ins, penalties. I have the stats on them all.'

Gordon settled the bill, then walked his young adviser out to the car park.

'One thing, George, we're both agreed we are talking about human beings. What happens if they don't follow my instructions?'

'Immediate substitution, plus fine them a week's wages. It doesn't matter if it's in the first ten minutes; pull the idiot off. You're the manager, if they don't follow what you say they have to be punished, just like you get punished when you get the chop.'

Gordon shook his hand, and thanked him.

'Good luck on Saturday,' Munro said. 'And by the way, if you get a penalty, Bonetti will dive left. Believe me.'

'You sure?'

'Seven out of ten sure, which is better than fifty-fifty. Based on fact not finger in the air, Charlie.'

Gordon sat quietly in the car for a few minutes, reflecting on what he had just been told. The boy had made a big impression on him. Maybe it was time to go with youth as his guide.

That thought, and another youth who had made an impression on him, was still in his mind when he arrived at the

training ground and called in George Brady, who had watched
the reserves game against Stoke City on Tuesday. They had won
3–2 and he knew that two of the goals had come from corners.

'George, who took the corners that led to the goals against
Stoke?'

'Little Willie Buchanan.'

'Describe the corners he took.'

'What do you mean? He crossed the ball in, the first one was
a header at the near post, hit the bar, came out to Dusty Miller,
got there ahead of the centre-back, whacked it in. Nuts scored
the second one: corner from the other side, bit of a melee, fell
out to Nuts on the penalty spot, half-volley.'

'Were the corners inswingers or outswingers?'

'Christ, now you're asking. Why?'

'Think.'

Brady nodded to himself a few times. 'Inswingers. Yes, definitely, first one near post, second one a bit deeper. Definitely
inswingers.'

'Thanks.'

Next he called Willie Ormond at the SFA training camp in
Largs. He was out on the training pitch but Gordon agreed with
his secretary that he would be there to take a call at 6 p.m.

When he called, Ormond was full of praise for Gordon's young
star.

'I've not seen him much myself, Charlie, but all I am hearing is
good. And from the bits I have seen, I would say he is as skilful
a young player as we have.'

'Good stuff, glad to hear. And how does he seem up top?'

'His head? Seems good.'

'I'm thinking of taking him with the squad to Chelsea. Do
you think he'd be ready?'

'Look, Charlie, you know him better than I do, but from what
I have seen and heard he is not far away. He has been anything
but out of his depth here.'

'So, hold on, Willie, you're not thinking of picking him for
your game?'

'No, I don't think so, but I want him to go to the game and

I'd have him in the dressing room, maybe on the bench as a non-playing sub. Can't do any harm. Do you want me to drop a wee hint about Chelsea?'

'No. But maybe I should have a little word, just check in with him.'

Ormond explained that the players were in the restaurant, and he suggested Gordon call back in half an hour.

'I'll get the boy lined up to take the call.'

'That's great, Willie, thanks for all your help.'

When he phoned back, he spoke briefly with Ormond again, who then passed him onto Willie Buchanan.

'Hey son, how's it going?'

'Good, gaffer, really good. Training's been terrific, really enjoyed it. Kenny Dalglish and Andy Gray are both here. And I've been doing shooting practice at Alan Rough.'

'How's it feel wearing the Scotland gear?'

'I think you know the answer to that, gaffer.'

'I do, son, I do. Now, tell me, I've got some good news and I've got some bad news. So which would you like first?'

'Oh, I don't know.'

'I always think it's best to get the bad news out of the way first.'

'OK, give me the bad news.'

'I want you to come back down south first thing.'

'What? Just leave?'

'Yes.'

'Oh.'

'And the good news is ... I want you in the squad for the Chelsea game.'

There was silence on the line. But he could feel the emotion Willie Buchanan was feeling. He could sense Willie Ormond enjoying the scene too. It was for moments like this that Gordon loved his job so much.

'You still there, Willie?'

'Yes, gaffer, I am.'

'So what do you say to that?'

There was another long silence, then Willie finally replied: 'I say I will never let you down, gaffer.'

'That's good to hear. I'll see you in the morning.'

26

BUCHANAN

Friday 8 March

Come the Friday before a big match, it was all about the waiting game. There was a training session in the morning, but they tended to be light, low-key, uneventful. Gordon's main aim was to avoid any silly injuries and make sure everyone understood the planned tactics. They did a bit of work on throw-ins and free-kicks, while Taffy Rees and DD Marland practised spot-kicks with Jock Johnson. Friday's training normally finished with a five-a-side match with the worst player being awarded the yellow jersey, which he had to wear the following week.

By then, Charlie Gordon was knocking off a few interviews, local and national. There was predictability to the questioning, but these had to be done. Was he worried about being sacked? Did he think they could win? What kind of game was he planning? Had his relationship with Chelsea manager Dave Sexton improved since their touchline-slinging match two seasons ago (which Gordon had forgotten)? Then questions always about the big names on the other team ... how big a threat was Peter Osgood? Had he heard Charlie Cooke was a doubt because of injury? Was there a better goalkeeper than Peter Bonetti in the League? He would make sure that his answer to that one – yes, Jock Johnson – found its way back to his number 1.

Normally he would discuss team selection with Ronnie Winston and George Brady, but as the players filed in from training, without saying a word he handed Winston a sheet of paper with the team for Saturday.

'Pin that up, will you?' he said, Winston's face creasing with surprise and then anger that Willie Buchanan's name was among the twelve.

'I thought we normally talked about things like this?' he said.

'Sometimes I have to follow a hunch. This is one of those times. Nothing to discuss.'

'But Willie is in Scotland.'

'He's on his way back. He knows.'

Winston turned on his heels and went out.

Buchanan arrived late morning, still wearing his Scotland tracksuit top. Gordon called him in.

'What a week you've had,' he said. 'You deserve it, son.'

'Thanks, gaffer. So, er, do I still help Cockie pack up the team coach?'

'Yep, only when you've made your first appearance in the team do those responsibilities finish. Now,' he added, 'how is that young lady of yours? And how did your mum and dad take the news?'

'She is fine,' he said. 'My parents were a bit shocked at first, but Catriona came over with her parents and by the time they'd had a couple of drinks, and we told them we were getting married, it wasn't as bad as I thought it was going to be.'

'You're a man now, son. That's why you're coming with us. Now get in that dressing room, and enjoy every minute today and tomorrow.'

Rain was forecast, so in addition to his little suitcase with a change of shirt and underwear, Gordon decided to take the old cream-coloured raincoat, stained and with the middle button missing, which had led to Brownie calling him 'Colombo' – behind his back – after the scruffy TV detective. He took a quarter bottle of Bell's and slipped it into the inside pocket, first taking a tiny sip.

As the players took their places on the coach, waiting on each seat was one of the lunch boxes Magic Rowland had fetched from Yannis's café. With a long drive ahead, it made sense to eat en route rather than at the club, or by stopping at a service station where they would be bothered by fans. Yannis provided the lunch for free in exchange for four tickets, and for this one Gordon had told Magic to give him six. The Greek café owner was just as generous, filling the boxes with chicken legs, ham and salami, cheese, tomatoes, fruit, bread and crisps.

Magic's other catering job was to call in at the off-licence four doors down from Yannis, and pick up four crates of beer, four bottles of champagne and a half-bottle of whisky for the gaffer. The whisky he would give to Gordon when they reached London. The beer would be shared around on the long trip home. Whether the champagne got drunk depended on the result, and until that was known it would be packed into the hold, along with the skips of kits, boots, massage and medical equipment.

Players and managers tended to like routines at this stage of the week, and they all had their own little ways of greeting Dermot Cochrane as he sat waiting to drive them south. Mooro always shook his hand. Dipper liked to ruffle his curly hair. Dougie Jones and Dermot had an advanced banter relationship, so that when the player walked up the first step, the driver said: 'Fuck me, Jinkie, I can't believe he's still picking you. David Webb is going to have your bollocks on a plate.'

'Hey Cockie, do you know why they call Peter Bonetti "The Cat"?'

'I feel sure you're going to tell me, Jinkie.'

'He's the only member of the team who can lick his own bollocks. You can't even see yours, you fat Irish bastard, and what's with the stubble, you look like a fucking tramp.'

It was as the players already on board were laughing at this – some of them anyway – that Willie Buchanan stepped nervously onto the coach. With all the players now on, Dermot took the microphone and announced that the toilet was not in service and he was growing a beard that he wouldn't shave off till they won another game.

'You mean you just took a big fat Irish dump, Cockie,' shouted Jinkie.

There was no guide for how a young debutant should behave,

but Willie had decided to go on last so as not to make the mistake of sitting in someone else's seat. He opted to sit in the readers' section in the middle of the coach. Norman Nulty, whose chances of getting back in the starting line-up had taken a further backward step with Buchanan's elevation to the bench, sat alone behind the Prof, Walter Graham, the player Willie was replacing on the bench, who was settling down to read *The Rise of the Roman Empire*. But as they had walked out from the changing rooms, Gordon had whispered to Willie, 'The Prof is a grown-up. He'll help you settle in.'

He had not even had time to call Catriona and tell her the news. But he knew she would be pleased, and proud that he had taken her advice, dug in and fought back against the bullies, and had this reward. Mooro had told him they couldn't remember an apprentice who had shown balls like it. And even Brownie, when he knew that Willie had made the team, dialled down on the piss-taking.

'Got to love the way you Jockos look after each other,' he said. 'Teacher's fucking pet or what?'

Seeing the empty seat alongside the Prof, Willie said: 'Prof – sorry, Mister Graham – do you mind if I sit here?'

'No problem, son, and call me Prof.'

'OK, thanks, Prof.'

'Now you're not going to talk all the way, are you? I'm a reader.'

'What are you reading?'

'I only read about three subjects: Kings and Queens of England, Presidents of America and Emperors of Rome. On this trip I'm studying the Roman Emperor Augustus. Outside my love for football, I find these people fascinating and they all have one thing in common: they are all fucking dead – and I'm not.'

'The Queen and President Nixon aren't dead,' said Willie.

'That's a fair point, son. It'll be good to have another brain on the coach.'

'Sorry, Prof, I promise not to talk much. But why do you read about all these dead people?'

'OK. Give me a date between 1066 and today.'

'What?'

'Just think of any date. Yep, shout one out.'

'I don't know... 14–15.' He chose Catriona's and his house numbers back home in Forbes Street.

'Willie, you couldn't have picked a better year in all of history.'

The Prof had a slight speech impediment: his S sounded like a whistle, so it sounded like hissshtory...

'You see, in 1415 we annihilated the French. Our King was Henry the Fifth, he took an army over to Harfleur, there was a long siege' – sssheege – 'and battle, he took the fort but lost most of his men and a lot of his survivors were sick. He decided to take what was now his small army to Calais before sailing home. On the way the French army, more than twenty thousand men, intercepted him. We were down to six thousand, mainly sick, knackered, full of dysentery. Now then, what do you think happened? Well, we overpowered them at a place called Agincourt, Willie. "*Once more unto the breach, dear friends, once more; or close the wall up with our English dead... Cry God for Harry, England, and Saint George.*" I know you're Scottish, son, but I tell you, when Shakespeare is writing your speeches for you, you know you've made it in history.'

'But how does that help you be a better footballer?'

'All knowledge is good, son. But listen, what if the boss sent us out with words like that before the game? Inspirational, eh? Talk about leadership! We had six thousand, they had twenty-four thousand, and we won the day.

'Willie, these are my last words before I get stuck into Augustus. Life is about choices. We make hundreds of them every day. The gaffer made a big choice today, you over me. Now you have big choices too, and one of them is this: when you travel to away games should you talk about wine, women and song; play cards; read a trashy paper or a porn mag; or treat the coach trip as a travelling university of life? The choice is yours, son. Now shut the fuck up, and good luck tomorrow!'

There was a bigger than usual gathering of fans at the gates to Summerton Manor as the coach finally set off for London, just before 1 p.m. The lunchtime radio news was leading with yet more bomb-blasts, one in Whitehall and another at the Old Bailey. The newsreader interviewed a senior police officer who said that though nobody had yet claimed responsibility, it was almost certainly the work of the IRA. Nobody was hurt but it created chaos in the capital, and added to the security worries about high-profile weekend sport events.

As the newsreader turned to the latest development in the Watergate scandal, David Brown shouted from down the coach, 'Cockie, turn that bloody radio off or change the bleedin' station, will you? I don't want to hear about your immigrant relatives blowing up my country.' Dermot switched to Radio One, where DJ Tony Blackburn introduced 'Tiger Feet'.

Brownie settled down with his card school friends then, after an hour or so, he and Smudger Smith had a go at doing the *Daily Mirror* crossword.

'Hey, young'un,' he shouted over at Willie Buchanan. 'I see you're sitting in the brains section, so can you help with a cross-word clue?'

'Sure.'

'Seven down. Postman's bag.'

'How many letters?'

'Fucking thousands!' and the cards section erupted with laughter as Brownie cast out his imaginary rod and reeled in another big one.

Willie took it on the chin and answered back, 'Is it the type of letter you wear on your head, Brownie?'

'What are you talking about, young'un, you don't wear a letter on your head,' said Brownie.

Willie immediately struck back. '*You* could, Brownie, you could wear a French letter... because you're a dickhead.'

Now there was even louder applause amid the laughter. Even Brownie nodded his respect. The Prof, his eyes remaining firmly on his book, raised his right thumb and whispered, 'Well done, son.' Then Brownie came over and grabbed Willie by the throat in mock anger.

Willie pretended to launch a fishing line, shouting, 'Brownie, I think I've landed a fucking *monster*!'

Charlie Gordon was listening carefully as the charade unfolded and grinned to himself as he popped another mint in his mouth. 'The boy is learning to swim,' he whispered to George Brady across the way. Winston was staring out of the window, still sulking at not having been consulted about Buchanan's inclusion in the travelling party.

Halfway down the M1, the first demand to stop the coach came from Dipper.

'Cockie, stop at this services, before I piss my pants.'

'Don't listen to him, Cockie,' shouted Mooro, 'keep going till the next services.'

'Cockie, if you don't stop I'm going to piss in your bag.'

Cockie ignored the comment then turned his head towards the manager and quietly asked, 'What do you think, gaffer, this services or the next?'

'Go for the next one, Cockie,' said Gordon.

Twenty miles on, Dipper led the way as most of the players got out to stretch their legs, have a pee, stock up with sweets and crisps.

'Can I get you anything, Prof?' asked Willie of his neighbour.

'I'm fine, son. I'm less than halfway through my Emperor's forty-odd years in office.'

Willie Buchanan made brief phone calls to Catriona and then to his mum Mairi, who sounded like she was about to cry when he passed on his good news, and asked if they should try to get down overnight.

'Would we be able to get tickets, Willie?'

'I don't know, Mum. Do you want me to find out?'

Most of the thousands of supporters would head down by coach and train tomorrow, but the service station had a good smattering of fans who couldn't believe their luck on seeing the players walking in. DD, Mooro, Jules and the manager got the biggest gaggles of autograph hunters, but Gordon noticed one or two stopping to ask Willie for his signature, and smiled at the young player's evident embarrassment.

They had reached the outskirts of London when Gordon passed a note to Winston, whose job it was to tell the players who they would be rooming with. Usually he tried to deliver this mundane news with a bit of humour and panache, as on the last away game, when he invented a new TV show, 'Roomtime', announcing the pairings with one-liners. This time he just read the names. Jock and Doug Jones. Killer and Mooro. Taff and Brownie. Jules and Smudger. DD and Nuts. On he went, leaving Willie and the Prof, youngest and oldest in the squad, to last. It was classic Gordon management.

The other players thought it odd to put an ousted player with his replacement, but Gordon knew – and had already seen – he needed DD and Nulty as friends fighting for a place in the team, not enemies, just as he wanted Willie to learn from the Prof about how to handle setbacks.

The players never seemed to notice the second rear-view mirror above Dermot's head on the inside of the windscreen. It was there not for Cockie, but for Gordon, so he could see down the coach, and he had been watching Willie closely, seeing where he sat, who he talked to, how he handled the banter; whether he had a bit of fight and sparkle in his eye, or was overcome with nervousness. Long before they reached London, he had decided that Willie was ready, if he needed him.

By now Radio One was pumping out David Hamilton's afternoon show, with the DJ chattering away about the chances of 'I'm Always Here For You' by The Choirgirls knocking 'Billy Don't Be A Hero' by Paper Lace off the top of the charts by Sunday, together with regular news, weather and travel updates. The terror attacks were still making the headlines, with the IRA having admitted they had carried them out; but the top sports story was a trailer of the big game at Stamford Bridge and doubts over the fitness of Chelsea winger Charlie Cooke. Dave Sexton was quoted as saying the Scottish international would have a fitness test in the morning. Gordon knew the whole thing was a ploy, one he played often enough himself.

'Don't listen, Killer,' shouted Gordon, standing so his left-back could see him. 'He'll be playing all right, and I want you tackling him in your dreams tonight.'

'He'll be too busy dreaming about young girls with big tits,' said Brownie, only to get a fierce glare from his manager. Brownie put up his hands, much in the same manner as he did after a foul, knowing he had gone over the top but pleading innocence nonetheless.

At last the coach pulled up outside the Great Western Hotel, next to Paddington Station. Barriers had been erected to hold back a few dozen fans waiting in the drizzle, and porter Paddy O'Connell stood ready with umbrellas to keep the players dry for the few yards from coach to lobby. Gordon stayed in his seat, waiting for Brownie to pass him.

'You were sailing close to the wind there, Brownie.'

'Honestly, gaffer, I wasn't thinking about the girl in the photo. It just came out. Don't fine me for that one, please.'

'Just make sure all your fucking hatred and anger is fuelled at Chelsea from now on in.'

'Yes, boss. I will. Thanks.'

Willie Buchanan was last on, last off. As he filed past Gordon, the manager asked him how he had enjoyed the journey.

'A lot, gaffer, a lot. I'm really grateful.'

'Hey, son, nothing to be grateful for. You're here on merit.'

'Thanks, boss.'

If only they were all like him, thought Gordon, as Willie stepped down and went to retrieve his bags from the luggage hold. He accepted he had a bias for Scots, but he couldn't help thinking the boy was the real deal. Even as the thought passed through his mind he watched as Jules Pemberton used an umbrella to poke Smudger Smith in the backside, and DD Marland flicked Dipper Temple's ear. It's like herding children, he said to himself as he waited till they were all inside, took a slug of Scotch, then walked off the coach to be greeted by Paddy, and handed over his usual crisp note for keeping him informed if any of the players were up late, went out or had visitors.

27

HEIST

Friday 8 March, late afternoon

The hotel had a special cordoned-off parking place for the team coach, and once all the players were off, Dermot Cochrane parked up, checked in himself, then went off in search of a new key-cutter. He never used the same one twice.

He was in Room 501. He removed the key from the ring, and the heavy plastic slab to which it was attached, complete with address and phone number of the hotel printed on the side. He slipped both into the inside jacket pocket of the club suit he so liked to wear.

He left the Great Western via the side entrance and made his way down Praed Street. The last time they were here, he had noticed a new shoe-repair shop about a quarter of a mile past St Mary's Hospital. It was close to six o'clock, and he worried it might be closed, but when he arrived, the sign outside confirmed that they had what he was looking for and as he stepped into the shop, flicking his almost-done Embassy Regal cigarette into the gutter, he removed the key from his jacket pocket.

The cobbler's white jacket, splattered with boot polish and leather shavings, had seen better days. The shelves behind the counter were filled with brown paper bags, pairs of shoes all labelled up ready for collection. The smell was not dissimilar to a dressing room, he thought, minus the mix of aftershaves. He also sold a huge variety of wallets, bracelets, handbags, key-rings, ornaments, and cups and saucers displaying the Union Jack, and as Cochrane walked in, two Japanese tourists were buying a Union Jack teapot with a picture of the Queen in the middle of the flag.

'Yes sir, what can I do for you?' asked the cobbler when finally the Japanese had counted up their change, and gone.

'Can you cut me a copy of this key please?' he asked as he scratched the stubble on his chin.

'Want to wait, or go get a cup of tea and come back?'

'I'm happy to wait.'

'OK. I have a couple of shoes I need to resole, then I'm with you.'

'Ah, OK, I'll pop back then.'

'No problem.'

He walked, aimlessly, in search of the next key-cutter, for the next visit, and found it just the other side of the Edgware Road. He made a note of the shop, the address, and drew himself a little map of directions from the hotel, then went back to fetch his newly cut duplicate for Room 501.

Back in his room, he retrieved his briefcase from under the mattress, placed the new key on one of the spare hooks and wrote on a tiny piece of sticky paper, *Friday 8th March; Great Western, 501*. He then took from another hook the key of the room he intended to target tonight, 427.

First, though, he had to establish it was not a room being used by anyone connected with the club. That was easily done. Regular staff at the hotel knew he was the coach driver, and even if they didn't the club suit made it obvious he was a part of their party. So when he asked for a list of all the rooms where members of the team were sleeping, the receptionist was more than happy to provide the information he needed. And as she wrote it all down, while looking at a register in front of her on the desk, he could see himself that Room 427 was booked under the name Angela Chessington.

It was now time. He went briefly back to his room, changed out of his club suit into his own clothes but retained his collar and tie, poured himself a bottle of beer he had brought down in his overnight bag, and quickly drank it to try to calm his nerves. He then had a vodka from the minibar, then another, and as he stood up, ready to go down to the lobby to start, he knocked over the glass, which broke into several large pieces. He put them in the bin, resisted the temptation to have another drink, then went downstairs, carrying his M&S bag and his sports bag inside. Nuts and Killer were on their way back from a walk. DD was talking to some friends. First, he spent a minute or two watching the lifts, then went to the house phone, to the side of the reception desk. He called Room 427, and there was no reply. He spent another couple of minutes watching the lifts, had a brief chat with George Brady who was going out for a walk, then called the room once more. Again, there was no reply. All good.

He went to the gents to have a pee, wash his face and calm his nerves, returned to the lobby to make one last call to the room – again no reply – went to the lifts and waited until all three were down on the ground floor. He quickly sent two lifts to the ninth floor. As he jumped into the third lift, which was empty, he pressed the button for the fourth floor. Still haunted by the day he nearly got caught at the Nottingham Hilton, Paddy massaged in a thick fingerful of Brylcreem and ran a brush quickly through his curly locks, pasting his hair tightly to his scalp. He pulled on a pair of black-rimmed, thick-glassed spectacles on arrival at the fourth floor and sent the lift up to the ninth floor. He quietly made his way along the deserted corridor and began his count to one hundred and fifty. He pulled out the key to Room 427, briefly remembering his stay there some months previously when they lost two-one at Spurs. Ten, eleven, twelve . . . he knocked on the door and shouted, 'Room service.'

There was no reply so he put the key into the lock, opened the door and silently stepped through into the darkness. Sixteen, seventeen, eighteen . . .

Up until the moment he switched on the light, the room was all quiet. As the brass chandelier illuminated the room he heard screams from the double bed, where two naked women had been locked together fast asleep in each other's arms. One, a brunette, leapt up and grabbed a pillow to cover her breasts. The other, a blonde, screamed at him.

'What the hell are you doing in here, get out, *get out!*' she yelled in a strong Irish accent.

His hands raised in apology, Cochrane started backing his way out of the room, mumbling excuses... terrible mistake, wrong room, so sorry to disturb you... trying to speak in his best southern English accent, and nearly knocking off his glasses.

He switched off the light, and scuttled out. As he closed the door, his heart pounding, he could hear the two women suddenly erupting in gales of laughter, one of them saying, 'Oh my God, Stella, did you see his face?' which at least suggested they wouldn't be complaining or calling the hotel manager. Still, he could feel himself sweating all over his upper body. Thank God the corridor was clear. Still carrying his M&S bag he chose the stairs, not the lift, as the quickest route back to the toilets on the ground floor. As the time passed, his tension eased a little, and later he was able to enjoy the fact he had stumbled across two attractive naked women, their bodies and the state of the bed, strewn with sex toys and discarded lingerie, suggesting exhaustion after hours of afternoon sex.

This was only the second time in five years that something like this had happened, but it made him wonder if he was taking too many risks. But what more could he have done? Three phone calls. Either they were asleep or they just decided what they were doing with each other was more interesting and more important than any phone call was going to be.

He went up to his room, opened his briefcase and replaced key number 427 back on its hook, writing simply 'lesbos' on the little note he Sellotaped beneath it. He also placed his black-rimmed glasses in the briefcase. But despite the scare, he knew he would be trying his luck again soon. It was like falling off a bike or a horse, he said to himself. Got to get back in the saddle quickly, but make sure he didn't get recognized.

After washing the Brylcreem from his hair and returning to his thick bushy curls, he then shaved off his stubble and went downstairs to join Gordon and his backroom staff for dinner, in a corner of the team room, next to the bar, set apart from the players, who tended to be much quieter on the eve of a match. It was a sign of how much Cochrane was accepted as part of the club furniture that he was allowed into this inner sanctum. Gordon liked the fact that Cockie had a fund of anecdotes about his Irish childhood that had nothing to do with football, but also his handful of caps as a schoolboy rugby international meant he could bring a different perspective – not to mention hilarious drinking stories. Though he was heavily overweight now, a sporting past was written on his face, and the broken nose and scars over the eyes were badges of credibility in this company.

Charlie Gordon liked his routines this close to the match. Once dinner was over, he would do a little tour of the players' tables, and without ordering them to bed, he would perhaps talk about what was on TV, or remind them how important it was to sleep well, and in dribs and drabs the players would disappear to their rooms. Sometime between half past nine and ten, he would then lead his backroom team to the bar, where Paddy O'Connell would have made sure their usual table was reserved. Ronnie Winston would order drinks at the bar, putting them on the club's account. Gordon liked to have Magic to his right, Winston to his left, Brady opposite him, and the rest could take the places that remained. Gordon actively discouraged talk of tomorrow's match now. It was more an opportunity for the ex-pros to reminisce about games, goals and escapades with girls.

'Come on then, Ronnie,' Gordon kicked off, 'who was the best player you ever played against, and why?'

Though Winston was still smarting from the snub of not being consulted about Buchanan, he took it as a good sign that Gordon had asked him to get the ball rolling.

'I dunno, boss, sounds too obvious but Bobby Moore, I'd say. We had them in the Cup once, and he was just so fucking cool it was ridiculous.'

'Slow runner, fast thinker,' chipped in George Brady.

'Exactly. I reckon over a fifty-yard sprint, or a ten-yard sprint, I could have had him. But he just seemed to read the game better than anyone.'

Cochrane was a fully fledged member of this football banter and reminiscence club. 'You putting yourself in the same breath as Bobby Moore, Ronnie – do me a fucking favour. I saw you at Bradford City – you'd put on so much weight, they had to stitch two pairs of shorts together to get your fat arse in.'

'At least I've retained my good looks. Your face looks like a road map, you ugly Irish bastard. Shaving off that stupid stubble makes you even fucking uglier.' It was all said in good humour and no offence was taken. They were all just killing time before a few hours' sleep, more time-killing tomorrow, then the match.

George Brady and Charlie Sinclair always had a little side-bet about how long into the conversation they would be before Gordon would claim superiority for a Scottish player over any English player being mentioned. Today, Brady had gone for 'first drink', and Sinclair for 'third drink'. With Bobby Moore the player being discussed, the only British footballer ever to lift a World Cup, and glasses from the first round close to empty, Sinclair thought surely Brady had lost. But Brady knew never to underestimate Gordon's one-eyed Scottishness.

'Bobby Moore was a great player, and I can see why you said he was the best you ever played against. But you never played against Jim Baxter, did you? He was the best for me, by a mile.'

'Oh, here we go,' said Magic, 'the story of the 1967 game at Wembley.'

'Indeed,' said Gordon. 'So much for you lot being world champions. April the fifteenth, 1967, less than a year after you'd beaten the mighty West Germans – dodgy goal mind you, that shot from Hurst was never over the line—'

'Yeah, yeah, yeah,' said Magic, 'at least we were in the bloody tournament. Your lot didn't even qualify.'

'This was the Home Championship, the decider, and I am telling you, Jim Baxter showed you lot up. He was juggling the ball at times. I remember Bobby Charlton looking like he didn't know what was going on. Absolute master-class. England 2, Scotland 3, which basically made us world champions.'

'It doesn't matter how many times you tell it, gaffer,' said Winston. 'We won the World Cup, you didn't, and when we are all dead and gone everyone will remember we won the World Cup and nobody will remember you winning by the odd goal in five the year after in a nothing match.'

'Law, Lennox, McCalliog... their names will echo down through the centuries.'

As the laughter rose, Charlie Sinclair slipped a pound note across the table to George Brady.

As he glanced to his left, Cockie noticed that the two women he had disturbed in Room 427 were seated at the bar, drinking cocktails. He nearly froze and quickly rushed off to the toilet.

'I'll get the next round in,' said Charlie Gordon, 'I need to loosen up my knees. Who wants what?'

He caught the eye of the blonde, who had a thick Irish accent and who smiled at him on hearing his Scottish accent when ordering the drinks.

'You're a long way from home.'

'You too,' she said. 'Stella McCafferty, Enniskillen.'

'Charlie Gordon, Glasgow.'

'Lovely to meet you, Stella.'

'And this is my friend Angela.'

Angela Chessington turned, smiled, shook his hand and on seeing the club crest exclaimed excitedly, 'I told you that was Charlie Gordon, Stella.'

'Yeah, we're playing Chelsea tomorrow.'

'I know,' said Angela. 'I've watched your progress in the Cup with great interest. I'm on the board at Bristol City and we could do with a manager like you, if you ever fancy a change.'

'You going to the game?'

'No, Stella and I are just having a quiet weekend away together.'

'That's nice. And what business are you in?'

'I'm in property,' said Angela.

'And I'm in sex shops,' said Stella, laughing.

After Charlie took the drinks back to the table, this time it was Stella saying, 'Did you see his face when I mentioned sex shops?' But Charlie had registered the name Angela Chessington, thinking he might be ringing her up early next week.

Head porter Paddy O'Connell kept an eye on Gordon's party, made sure they were being properly looked after and not bothered by other guests. Because of their Irish ancestry he and Dermot Cochrane got on well together but the head porter didn't seem to be his usual self. He was nervy, less assured than normal. Something was clearly troubling him, but Cochrane had enough worries of his own to try to find out what.

28

CONFESSION

Saturday 9 March

It was part of Charlie Gordon's ritual that none of the staff were allowed to go to bed before he did, but tonight he let them off, Alfie Ruse having left a message with porter Paddy O'Connell that it would be past midnight before he made it to the hotel. So the manager sent them all off at half past eleven, and sat alone nursing a large Scotch.

There were still a few residents in the Kingdom Bar, including a group who had been to see a musical and were singing, badly, some of the hits from it. Gordon was feeling tired, constantly checking his watch, and asking Paddy when he came through whether he had heard any more from Alfie Ruse. He wondered whether this was the last time he would ever stay here, the last time he would have anything to do with the friendly Irishman. If they lost, would Stan Moffitt try to sack him immediately? He felt the likeliest scenario was lose the game, get home, then get summonsed to the club after an emergency board meeting on Monday. But could he face the humiliation of a long coach journey back, knowing that he was a dead man walking, and knowing the players knew it too? At least he knew that Moffitt would not be on the coach home, as he and Gloria were planning on staying down in London for the weekend, although it was possible he'd decide to hold an emergency board meeting on Sunday, he supposed.

He knew he had had too much to drink already, and he was already thinking ahead to the morning, and how he would need to throw up before facing the day. How he would have to gargle and talk to himself in his room so he could get his voice in working order before going down for breakfast with the team. The Scotch had both mellowed and darkened his mood; darkened it in that he could no longer see a way to winning tomorrow, nor a way of avoiding the sack; mellowed it in that he had decided that playing the Poulson card against Moffitt was not the right thing to do. It wasn't his style. Why stay somewhere just because you have something to hold over your boss? When your time was up, it was up. No, he mused as he took another sip, if they lost tomorrow, that would confirm the season was a failure, and he would deserve to lose his job. Poulson was a sleeping dog that was nothing to do with results on the field, and he should let it lie.

As so often when on his own, he reflected on one of his mother's little homilies. 'To be happy in life, Charles, you only need to get three decisions right. Who are you going to lead your life *with*? That's about family, marriage, friends, who you work with. What are you going to lead your life *in*? That is about your home, your car, your clothes. And finally: What are you going to lead your life *for*?

'That is the most important,' she said.

Although Charlie had cocked up numbers one and two, he had tried his best to stay true to the third part of his mother's trilogy. Truth, honesty and integrity mattered to him. It was why he wouldn't try to use the Poulson scandal to protect himself against the sack.

Paddy O'Connell brought Alfie Ruse over just before half past midnight. With his dark-brown overcoat, trilby hat and leather briefcase all spattered with rain, he apologized for being so late, and said he couldn't stay long as he had kept the cab waiting for him outside.

'You've time for a drink, surely?' asked Gordon.

'Yes. Paddy, I'll have a Scotch and ginger, with ice.'

'Anything to eat, Alfie?' asked O'Connell, who knew the former player turned agent well.

'No, I've had dinner, thanks, Paddy. Just the drink then I'll be off.'

Gordon and Ruse had played together at Preston, and even if Alfie had not stayed in the game as an agent, they would almost certainly have stayed in touch as friends.

'You're looking well, Alfie,' said Gordon. 'You did the right thing not going down the management route.'

'Tell me about it. I wouldn't have your job for all the Scotch in Scotland. It's bad enough looking after a handful of players; a whole squad would drive me round the bend, let alone having to deal with bloody directors.'

Paddy O'Connell arrived with a tray, two large Scotches, a bottle of Canada Dry and an ice bucket. Alfie Ruse bubbled in the dry ginger, added a few cubes of ice and then took a small sip from his glass.

'And what about you, Charlie, how are you, really? Looks like you are heading for the chop if you lose tomorrow.' He lifted his sleeve and looked at his watch. 'Or should I say today?'

Charlie knew Alfie understood football so there was no point bullshitting him by pretending he thought they would win. He just said, 'If we have a good day, and they have an off day, we can win it, certainly get a draw and take them back to our place. But yeah, I'm in a tough situation right now.'

'You still doing that lucky white shirt thing you used to do when we were roomies?'

'Yeah. Fucking daft or what? Never change a winning shirt. I've been getting through plenty this year.'

'You remember that time we won five games in a row? Christ, you stank then.'

'Is that why you gave the ball away at Leicester?'

'My God, you've got a memory. Yeah, it was Leicester, wasn't it? Ended the run.'

'One shit pass from you and I finally get to change my shirt.'

They paused to take a drink, then Ruse said: 'Looks like my boy's not bringing you much luck. What's going wrong?'

'DD? Fuck me, I wish I knew. Dream start, and since then, it's just not happening.'

'Is he missing home? Missing his wife?'

'If he is he has a funny way of showing it. Shags himself silly all over town.'

'Yeah, you're never going to stop that. But he did it at Spurs, didn't stop him playing well.'

'If things don't turn soon, I'll have to think about putting him on the bench and giving Nulty another go ... if I'm here, that is.'

Gordon asked if he wanted another drink, but Ruse said he needed to get going soon. 'So let's get it over with, why I wanted to see you.'

He clicked open the golden clasps on his leather briefcase, reached inside and pulled out a plain, white, bulging A5 envelope, unsealed.

'If I recall, Charlie, we agreed to share two and a half per cent of one hundred and twenty-five grand, so there's sixteen hundred in twenties in here, which includes an extra little drink for you. I sure hope DD will start to come good for you very soon, Charlie.'

Without even looking inside, Charlie placed the gift down the back of his trousers, pleased that there was no writing on the envelope, which meant he could write on it later that evening. He had no need to count the money; his old teammate would have ensured that the amount was exact.

Alfie Ruse stood up, finished the last of his whisky, put on his overcoat and hat, and picked up his umbrella from the adjacent table. He then clicked his briefcase shut and gave Charlie an affectionate hug and a soft kiss on his cheek. There was an unexplained bond between ex-professional footballers, a brotherhood, a trust, a feeling that was hard to explain to outsiders.

Alone once more, Gordon sat back down, scratching away at his right ear. He finished the last of his neat whisky, wondered about having one for the road, but then, pleased with himself, fought the temptation and retired to bed, thinking it might not just be his last night in the Great Western, but his last in football.

*

In normal times, Paddy O'Connell preferred night shifts. But these were not normal times for the head porter. He was trapped in a situation from which there was no easy escape. He knew the IRA were planning an attack on the hotel tomorrow night. He knew that if it subsequently emerged that he knew, but did nothing, he could face a long jail sentence. He also knew that if he told a soul, he would be kneecapped at a minimum, more likely murdered. It was little wonder he lacked the *joie de vivre* that Charlie Gordon and co. saw as one of the reasons for their regular visits to the Great Western. It wasn't that he hadn't looked after them with his usual care and attention, but he knew he was emanating the nerves he was feeling – more than he had ever felt them about anything in his life before. The reason he was so good at his job was because he was streetwise, and a good reader of people. So how, thanks to his love of Irish music and his falling a little bit for Margaret, had he dug himself in so deep that he feared for his freedom if he didn't tell the authorities, and he feared for his life if he did?

He was a practising if not entirely observant Catholic, and insofar as he had strong views on the question of the North, and where it should lie, he was an Irish Republican. But he knew that a majority in the North favoured staying in the UK, and he was a democrat as well. It was more a romantic attachment to Republicanism that he held than a deep-seated political commitment, especially when he moved to England and settled down with his wife Elsie in Fulham. He had spent his early days in Hollywood, North Belfast, where both Catholics and Protestants lived side by side. But when his family moved across to the Ballymurphy Estate in West Belfast, he became much more politically aware. He realized there were two communities, and little or no trust between them. And he also realized it was hard not to take sides. Protestant families were living in the face of the violence breaking out, and the sectarian fights. He found himself having to take part, but not particularly enjoying it. It was one of the reasons he finally set off for London.

As the weeks and months rolled on, the hatred increased and Protestant families from the Springmartin Estate would come across the divide to watch the violence and disorder unfold. Barricades would be constructed and burning lorries, buses, cars, vans and taxis would light up the night sky. The air filled with the stench of burning rubber and every now and then the fireball of an exploding petrol tank was met with loud cheers. To add to the pungent aroma of conflict, tear gas from the grenades that the Royal Ulster Constabulary rained down on the rioters. By dusk even more lorries had been hijacked and driven to the estate by IRA members, who then set them alight to provide new barricades for the rioting yet to come.

Initially the police would scour the area in their armoured cars, speeding through the narrow streets, firing seemingly at random then more deliberately when under street lighting. Paddy and his family knew when the real trouble was beginning; his father would say, 'Listen carefully, when you can't hear the police, it means the others are coming.' He was often right. With the street cleared and in darkness, Unionist arsonists would invade the area and systematically burn down some of the houses. It was a pattern that he had experienced many times before. In the distance they could hear the noise of a growing, advancing crowd. It was horrifying to see his father in panic. Paddy was desperate to go to the window to watch what was happening but his father forbade him to leave his cover under the upturned settee. As the noise of cheering, shouting and gunshots grew closer, Paddy's apprehension for himself, his father and his three older sisters changed to outright panic and he would often wet himself.

When the noise slowly passed by, their father allowed them to creep upstairs and look through the skylight, where they could see flames rising from the streets nearby. His father would then lift Paddy above the heads of his sisters and tell him, 'If you hear gunshots from both sides of Ballymurphy, it means we are fighting back. As long as that is happening, it means we'll not be driven out of our home tonight. We'll just stay here and pray.'

On walking to school the next day, with fear still in his heart, and his eyes still bleary from lack of sleep, he vowed one day to seek revenge. But again, it was a vague threat, not the visceral commitment others in his midst now had to fight back against soldiers, police, Unionists, anyone who ruined their lives in the name of the Queen.

After marrying and living in London for the last twenty-three years, in September 1973 Paddy, a regular on the Irish pub music scene, was invited by a friend to a meeting at an Irish pub in Islington. It soon became clear that the social group they met were members of the IRA London recruitment arm, who were contacting locals with Irish connections who might have sympathies with the Republican movement. They were nice enough guys, and after two or three more meetings Paddy was put on a stand-by role, if and when needed, for example handing out leaflets and newsletters at Tube stations. He continued to attend regular get-togethers, which moved around London from pubs in Chiswick to Highgate to Vauxhall, with the last one in the back room of an Irish pub in Shoreditch. The nights were also great social gatherings, all fuelled with Irish humour and song. These people became his newfound friends. One of them, Margaret, became his lover.

After six months or so, he realized this was not really about social life. Firstly, although he was accepted into the fold, he was not trusted. But this applied to anyone and everyone. At times, Paddy was certain that he had been followed, and on occasion the followers wanted him to know it.

Secondly, he overheard two of his new friends talking about what had happened to one of their former comrades who had been found to have talked at work about these meetings. On his next visit home to Belfast, three men collected him, took him for a short ride in a car, made him get out and kneel; then fired a single bullet into the back of his head. No trial, no appeal, no leniency, no prayers, just business.

By now, O'Connell was in too deep. When he was told of possible attacks on mainland England, focusing on London, he had no way of extracting himself. Each of them was told that the time when their assistance would be needed could be days, weeks or months or maybe never. But they were all on call three hundred and sixty-five days of the year.

Also, when he had thought these groups were more social than political, he had mentioned, sometime in late 1973, his role as porter at the hotel at Paddington Station. He also mentioned that on regular occasions government ministers stayed at the hotel, sometimes using false names. He also explained their arrival via the tradesmen's entrance and the top-secret security process to get the government ministers and MPs into the bedrooms.

He was given the number of a private London telephone line and asked to ring with the name of anyone associated with the British government who was staying at the hotel, and the date. Over the last two months Paddy had made several phone calls, naming different MPs who were booked into the hotel, but no further action had followed. But when he passed on the news that Merlyn Rees had booked in again, under a new pseudonym, unsurprisingly there was a little more interest from his IRA friends. Rees had easily regained his seat in the election, and then like everyone else in the country had watched and waited to see who was going to be able to form a government out of one of the closest results the country had ever known. Then the following morning, a week before O'Connell was due to be looking after his favourite visiting football team, he was told by hotel manager Jim Studdard that Rees was going to be staying at the hotel on the evening of Saturday 9 March. He would be booked under the name Thomas Buckley. Studdard then added, 'If Wilson ends up as Prime Minister, this guy will probably be Northern Ireland Secretary, because he is the shadow right now. So we will have all that special protection palaver. But you've dealt with that before now.'

'No problem.'

So Paddy O'Connell made a fourth call to the secret number. This time he was invited to a meeting at a house near Ealing Broadway Station on Tuesday 5 March, the day after Wilson was finally confirmed as Prime Minister, and the day Rees was appointed Secretary of State for Northern Ireland.

When he saw the two men and the woman already gathered to hear what he had to tell them, he knew he was in with the big boys, and it scared him, though he tried to hide it.

They went over every last detail of the booking process, the entrances that would be used, and any information he had about Rees's planned movements. O'Connell had been told the minister would be arriving around six, going out for a dinner shortly afterwards, and was expected back no later than eleven because he had an early start the next morning. One of the three, named Paul, wrote everything he said in a brown notebook, though he appeared to know more than Paddy already. By the time he left, O'Connell was in need of a visit to church. He was petrified.

He took the Tube to Fulham and walked to Our Lady of Perpetual Help in Stephendale Road. He sat in his usual pew, the one he had used every Sunday for the past twenty-three years. What in heaven's name had he got himself involved in? What had started as a few friendly Irish get-togethers that made him feel connected with home could end with him being involved in the murder of a prominent politician. No doubt those others he'd met at the safe house would vanish into thin air, and he would be the one left at the Great Western Hotel to cooperate with the police investigation into the murder of an MP – and not just any MP, but the new Secretary of State, after the Prime Minister himself, and the Queen, probably the biggest target the IRA could hit. The Northern Irish Catholic porter; who else would be able to get a bomb into a fifth-floor bedroom undetected? Paddy O'Connell – even his name was enough to put him in the frame.

Also, he had come to like England, and the Brits. Even the soldiers he once hated, they were all probably retired by now; like he would be, in just a couple of years, but the chances were he would spend that time either in a coffin or in a jail. The church was freezing cold, but he felt a hot sweat rolling from his shoulders down his back.

He picked up the church newsletter which lay alongside the Bible, and in which Father Landrigan liked to publish his sermons. Paddy had been there two weeks ago and had already heard the one he now read, which seemed to speak to his current predicament.

'The dignity of man rests above all on the fact that he is called to communion with God,' Paddy read. 'This invitation to converse with God is addressed to man as soon as he comes into being. For

if man exists it is because God has created him through love, and
through love continues to hold him in existence. He cannot live fully
according to truth unless he freely acknowledges that love entrusts
himself to his Creator.'

How was the killing of a British MP going to improve the
quality of his life? What would it do to his wife Elsie if he was
caught up in it? *'Week by week we listen attentively to God's word*
so as to know him and love him,' Father Landrigan had said.

He noticed an elderly woman leave the confessional and,
assuming a priest was there, he strode over and entered the small
booth, just as Father Landrigan – for he it was who had heard
the old lady's confession – was leaving through the other side.

'Father,' said O'Connell.

'Yes, my son.' The priest resumed his place, and slid open the
small wooden screen.

O'Connell had been hoping it would be one of the junior
priests who would not necessarily know him. Father Landrigan
recognized him by his voice.

'Paddy, what is it that brings you here? I cannot ever remember
you coming to confession.'

O'Connell said nothing. He had confessed regularly as a young
man, but just as he was about to recite the well-worn words
'Forgive me, Father, for I have sinned', he found they wouldn't
come to his lips, for his mind was a torment of questions. Had he
sinned? Nothing bad had happened. All he had done was pass on
some information about an MP. But he had done that before, and
nothing came of it. So did his sinning depend on the outcome?
If Rees was killed, and he played a part in that, he accepted he
was a sinner. But what if at the last minute the plot was botched
or aborted, and Rees got away, and nobody was hurt – was he
then really a sinner in the same way?

'Father,' he said, 'if I may be about to sin, do I ask for forgiveness now, or wait till the sin is committed?'

'Ah! Interesting. In the mind, it may be the sin has already
been committed.'

'But what if I then do not commit the sin, and no harm is
done?'

'Nor is harm done if you ask for forgiveness for having at one point thought you might have committed the sin.'

'Like getting retaliation in first?'

'No. I would say more like topping up your insurance scheme with God.' He smiled at his own comparison. 'Do you wish to tell me, my son?'

'I do, but I feel I can't. I fear for my own safety if I do.'

'But there is nothing to fear from telling me in this box, my son, you know that.'

Should he mention Merlyn Rees by name; should he mention the IRA; should he explain the panic his father went through when he was a small boy on the Ballymurphy Estate? What if Father Landrigan, for all the sanctity of the confessional, felt he had to step in to save a man's life? He knew that when a person unburdens his soul and confesses his sins to a priest in the Sacrament of Penance, a very sacred trust is formed, and the priest must maintain absolute secrecy.

But what if Father Landrigan told him that rather than say a few Hail Marys, he should go to the police? But if he followed that route, it would be him losing his life, not Merlyn Rees.

'I have been helping the IRA,' he said.

'Ah. But is that of itself a sin? There are many who think the IRA cause is just, that they are more sinned against than sinning.'

'Do you think that?'

'Well, I do, in many ways I do.'

'So when they kill innocent people, that is not a sin?'

'I did not say that. I said I felt they had a just cause, and were sinned against. Of course taking the life of another is a sin. Thou shalt not kill. Have you killed anyone, Patrick?'

'No.'

'Have you helped kill anyone?'

'Not exactly.'

'But you could? You might?'

'Yes.'

'My son, you will be in my prayers. I am sure you will settle this in your mind, the right way. God has you in his heart.'

Paddy hurried out of the church, and by the time he had

reached the bus stop he realized tears were streaming down his face.

'Are you OK?' a friendly West Indian lady asked him, as she waited for her bus.

'Sure, I'm fine,' he said. 'Just been to a funeral.'

'Aw, they're in heaven now,' she said, picking up two huge grocery bags as she saw her bus come into view.

Though the rain was falling lightly, he decided to walk and try to gather his thoughts sufficient to calm himself as he contemplated the next few days and what they might bring.

29

SEDUCTION

Saturday 9 March, early morning

As the old grandfather clock behind the Great Western Hotel reception desk chimed nine o'clock on Saturday morning, a tired DD Marland was leaving an envelope with two complimentary tickets for his sister and her boyfriend to collect later on. It was a busy time, with people checking out, and though normally he didn't like queuing, he was happy enough to be standing behind a sweet-smelling, auburn-haired woman, in her late twenties or early thirties he reckoned, wearing a tight pair of black jeans which showed off the kind of backside he would never tire of studying, even after the remarkable night he had had with Patrizia Moretti.

As the woman handed in her key, she said simply, 'Room 427, Chessington, can I settle up please?' No doubt sensing the attentions of someone behind her, she turned, and he smiled.

'Ah, DD Marland,' she said.

'The one and only,' replied Marland, spreading his arms.

'And if I am not mistaken, the scorer of that one and only goal at Everton, since they paid all that money for you.'

'Ooooh, well I never, a pretty woman who knows her football. What a rare bird you are.'

'Maybe if your form carries on like this, I'll end up signing you. Angela Chessington, director, Bristol City.' She shook his hand, then turned back to the receptionist.

'I'm sorry, Mrs Chessington, but the bill has been settled in full, including the two bottles of Bollinger. And a note has been left for you.'

'Oh my,' said DD, 'did Mrs Bristol City have a secret male admirer in her room?'

'No,' smiled Angela as she tore open the envelope, 'female.'

She removed a small white card and read it, careful that the irritating Mr Marland couldn't see the words. It read, '*Some people live a lifetime and never find themselves. You are now free; and all your bills are paid. Thanks for a wonderful day and night, all my love, till next time* ♥ *Stella xxx.*'

Sadly it would have to be destroyed, she thought, but well away from this arrogant 'superstar'.

'Good luck today,' she said as she picked up her bag and headed for the door. 'The way you've been playing, you'll need it.'

Once he had left the tickets for his sister, DD went to join Jules Pemberton and David Brown who were busy eyeing Angela Chessington as she walked to the hotel exit.

'See her, you've no chance there, Jules,' said DD. 'She bats for the other side.'

'You're full of shit, DD,' said Jules.

'I'm telling you, she just told me.'

Brownie laughed. 'That's her way of telling you she's not interested, you knob.'

'I could convert her,' said Jules. 'Half an hour, that's all I'd need and she'd be batting on our side.'

They went to the team room where breakfast was being served. Gordon insisted all the players ate together, and liked them to eat porridge on a matchday, though he himself went for the full English breakfast, and he allowed players who couldn't stomach porridge to have a couple of poached eggs on toast. The mood was always fairly subdued, as they started to turn their minds ahead by six hours. The banter levels tended to drop at this stage. Once breakfast was over, Gordon liked them all to gather in the lobby just before ten and go for a stroll in Hyde Park, which was five minutes away. Of course there was a risk of fans spotting them and asking them for pictures and autographs, but it was rare they were mobbed. So much else was always going on in London, and there were so many tourists who wouldn't have a clue who they were. It was all about killing time, and keeping the players calm.

Gordon noticed that Marland had arrived a few minutes late for breakfast, and also that he had barely eaten. He wondered if he was coming down with a heavy cold. So when the striker asked the manager if he could be excused from the walk, he knew something was up.

'Why?' asked Gordon.

'I didn't sleep so well. I just reckon if I could get a short nap now, I'll be sorted.'

'You can get a nap after the team walk,' said Gordon. He then went to find Paddy O'Connell to find out if DD had had visitors in the night.

DD had gone to bed at the same time as everyone else. He was sharing with Nuts, who was continuing to hide his anger and depression at being excluded from the starting line-up. He found DD's arrogance a bit trying, but they got on well enough. Both came from south London, DD from Dulwich and Nulty from Wimbledon. Both had been married for around four years and neither had children, even though they'd both been trying. Their big disagreement was in music. DD was a Beatles fan and Nuts preferred The Rolling Stones.

After dinner on Friday evening they'd walked down Praed Street together and later watched TV till about half ten, when Ronnie Winston was doing his rounds to make sure everyone was in their rooms. DD waited almost an hour, till he could tell from Nuts's deep breathing and gentle snore that he was fast asleep, before slipping on his tracksuit and making his way up the stairs to Room 627. There was always a risk of bumping into Gordon or one of his staff, but he had already rehearsed his line: 'Which room is Magic in? I can't sleep, got a headache, need an aspirin.' And he was deliberately walking in his bare feet so nobody would think he was heading out for a night on the tiles.

Patrizia quietly opened the door, and ushered him in.

She had a bottle of champagne on ice, and poured two glasses.

'I know you shouldn't be drinking before a match,' she said. 'But champagne doesn't count, surely?'

'Right on both counts,' he replied.

He had done a little research about Patrizia before their meeting and clearly there had been plenty of men in her life. The only one who appeared to be a reasonably regular fixture was the new Chelsea owner Bernie Yaakov. If DD's brain had matched the size of his sex drive, that might have aroused just a little suspicion as to why she had wanted to meet up with him in her hotel room on the eve of such an important tie against a club owned by the man often described as her 'on-off boyfriend' or, in some cuttings, 'mentor'. But given the prospect of having sex with this mature, gorgeous woman, his brain was less engaged than his groin.

They both knew, the second those champagne glasses clinked against each other, where this was leading. Even if Patrizia was doing this as a favour to Yaakov, DD had the body of a top athlete: long muscular legs, slim hips, wide shoulders, a strong, firm back, clear skin and bright eyes – all the things she liked in a man. And he was young, handsome and eager.

It was as she poured a second glass that he took her arm with one hand, removed the bottle with the other, and pulled her towards him. As they kissed, he quickly had one hand undoing her bra, the other sliding inside her jeans, and part of him was thinking, 'I want this, I want it now, I want it over with and I can get back to my own room and get some sleep.' But she clearly had an entirely different strategy. Hers was to keep him at it for as long as she could.

'Not so fast, DD, not so fast. This is going to be so good, let's not rush it.'

She slowly, perhaps ten seconds per inch, unzipped his tracksuit top, kissing every part of his flesh as it emerged. She stood, took his hand and led him to the bed. But as he tried to pull her on top of him, she pulled back and began a long, slow striptease, occasionally leaning forward to touch the bulge she could see forming beneath his tracksuit bottoms. First her jeans, then her knickers, then her shirt, then her bra, she removed them and used them to caress his chest and arms. Once she was naked he sat back and studied her body. Her large, firm breasts, slim waist and long legs with – this surprised him given she was a fair bit older than him – not a wrinkle in sight.

She leaned over and removed his tracksuit bottoms. But again, as he tried to grab her towards him, she pulled back, stood and went to fetch the champagne. She took a swig from the bottle, then went to kiss him and let the champagne flow from her mouth to his. Then she poured a trickle from the bottle over his chest, his stomach and his thighs and took what seemed like an age to DD – just desperate now to get inside her – to lick it off. Even then she wasn't finished. She gave the bottle to him, rolled over and instructed him to pour it down her spine, and do the same to her.

'I want you now, Patrizia,' he said.

'No, not now,' she said. 'Turn over.'

She produced a lavender massage oil that he recognized from the package her friend Stella had sent him, and began to massage him slowly, deeply, all over his neck, his shoulders, his back, his buttocks, his thighs, his calves and his feet. When she asked him to turn over, he was becoming desperate with desire.

'Please,' he said, 'just climb on me, now.'

But she smiled, poured massage oil onto his chest and kept the agony going.

When, finally, she climbed on top of him, he was ready to explode, but again she knew how to slow him, calm him, keep him going.

'Shall we stop for half-time at forty-five minutes?' she laughed. 'I can even squeeze some lemons on you.'

'No way, no way,' he said. 'I'm not stopping for anything or anybody.'

But by the time he finally exploded inside her he looked at the bed-side clock, and it was almost half past two.

'I thought I was going to die,' he said afterwards.

'I wouldn't do that to you,' she said.

'I need to get back to my room,' he said. 'The gaffer has his spies out all night. He'll kill me if he knows I'm here.'

'In which case it's safer to stay a while yet, DD. Anyway, the second time is always the best,' and with that, she began to kiss his neck and chest and work her way down to his thighs and arouse him again. And when the second time was done, she decided that in fact it was the third time that was always the best.

It was ten to six when he finally left her, and she picked up the phone to leave a message for Bernie Yaakov... '5.50 a.m., he's gone. Thanks for all you taught me.'

Norman Nulty was woken just after 6 a.m. by the sound of the shower, but then DD went straight back to bed, and seemed to be immediately asleep. By the time Nuts was showered and tracksuited and ready for breakfast and the team walk, DD was still asleep. He nudged him awake.

'Are you OK?' he asked.

'I'm fine. Didn't sleep much.'

'So I see. Well, come on, you better get your arse in gear.'

'Yeah, I will. I'll have another shower and see you downstairs.'

He left his complimentary tickets for his sister, flirted with a lesbian who was checking out, downed three cups of coffee at breakfast, tried to get out of the team walk, failed, then came back to see if Patrizia was around, but she was gone. Probably for the best, he thought, as he went to his room and tried to catch a nap before the team talk and lunch.

Not for the first time, when Nuts went to pack, he asked him if he was feeling OK as he was looking pasty. Not for the first time, DD lied, and said he was feeling fine.

30

MATCHDAY

Saturday 9 March, morning

Gordon liked all timings to be round figures on match day. Breakfast at nine, walk at ten, return at eleven, team talk and light lunch at twelve, leave at one, arrive half one, pitch walk at two, kick-off at three.

Walter Graham had been an inspired choice of room-mate for Willie Buchanan. The Prof was one of life's grown-ups, Gordon knew that. He was a team player, who understood that not everyone could be picked for every game. He also had enough self-awareness to know that he was a good, solid, reliable squad player who would never play for England, never win Player of the Year, but who could turn out wherever and whenever the gaffer asked him to, and not let him down. How many times, in the programmes at away games, in the 'meet our visitors' section, had he seen himself described as 'a useful member of the squad', 'a utility player', or 'often used as regular substitute'? But the game gave him a living, he knew his place, and at least he was universally recognized as the best-read member of the entire club set-up, if not the whole game in England.

So what Charlie Gordon knew in putting him with Willie Buchanan was that the Prof, even though he'd lost his place on the bench to the boy, would give him nothing but support and encouragement. And so it proved to be.

'Which bed would you like, Prof?' asked Willie as they'd carried their bags into the twin room.

'Hey, son, I'm a non-playing travelling squad member, you're on the bench, so you choose.'

'Oh, OK. I'll have the one near the window. You sure that's OK?'

'Positive.'

The Prof had known Willie might find it hard to sleep, so he had taken him for a walk after dinner, partly to tire him out, and as they lay in bed, the lights out at eleven, he told Willie deliberately dull stories about his own early days as a pro, and after half an hour or so he could hear the unmistakable sound of sleep coming from the back of the young winger's throat.

Walter was up and about when Willie woke, just after seven, and suggested they go for another walk. They ended up sitting in a café inside Paddington Station, just watching the thousands upon thousands of people go by. They noticed some wearing Chelsea colours, others wearing their own. They noticed too that the newspapers, the front pages still filled with either stories of the IRA bombing campaign or the post-election political jousting, were dominated on the back by their Cup quarter-final. Charlie Gordon's worried, lined face stared out from a paper being read by a young man at the next table.

'This time tomorrow,' said the Prof, 'that could be your face on there, celebrating a winning goal, and the gaffer will be safe. Imagine that, Willie.'

'It's hard to. I still can't believe I'm here.'

'Well, you are.'

'My mum and my dad and my girlfriend are on their way down from Aberdeen, they set off at five o'clock this morning. How do I get them tickets, Prof?'

'Did the gaffer not mention comps? We're all supposed to get a couple at least.'

'No.'

'Leave it with me. You just concentrate on getting yourself ready for the match. Just three you need, yeah?'

'Aye. Mum, Dad and Catriona, my girlfriend.'

'I'll sort it.'

'Thanks, Prof.'

He asked the Prof to wait five minutes while he went to buy something. Ten minutes later, after a visit to the station bookstore, he came back with a present, which he gave to a clearly touched Prof. 'You said you only study Roman Emperors, American Presidents and English Kings and Queens. I hope this is allowed. It's just to say thanks for helping me so much on such a big day for me.' The Prof removed the book from its bag, and smiled as he saw the cover, a picture of Mary Queen of Scots, and the title *Scotland's Monarchs*.

As they walked back to the hotel, Willie asked the Prof if he thought Gordon would be sacked if they lost.

'I think so. That's why we need to win, or at least get a draw and take them back to our place.'

'Do you like him?'

'I do, yeah. It's not an easy job, you know, what with dealing with directors and fans who think we ought to win every time we go out; and players, well, you've seen what players are like. Not easy.'

'Yeah, he's been good to me.'

'You'll never forget him, you know. Nobody forgets the first manager who gave them a chance. I just worry what he would do if he didn't have this in his life. No family. I'm not sure he has that many friends. I can't see him playing golf or fishing. He'd just mope around all day drinking more and more. It'd bloody kill him, if you ask me.'

'I'd better get on that back page then.'

'Yes, you better had. "Young Willie's lifesaver for Gordon". That's a lot better than all these "last chance saloon" headlines.'

'What if he doesn't put me on?'

'He will, Willie. He'll find a way.'

It was another veteran, goalkeeper Jock Johnson, who latched onto Willie on the team walk. Willie was pleased to hear another Scottish accent.

'How you feeling, son?'

'Yeah, fine thanks.'

'Slept OK?'

'I slept well.'

'That's good. Half the battle is sleep before a big game like this.'

'The Prof was nice, really helpful.'

'Good guy. Funny though, isn't it, this could be my last ever FA Cup game, and it's your first.'

'Let's make sure it's not the last then. What a way to go if your last game was at Wembley.'

'That's what I like, son. The optimism of youth.'

'So what are you going to do when you retire?'

'Well, I reckon I can play another couple of years in Scotland, and then I'm writing a book. I've already got the title.'

'Which is?'

'*Goalkeepers are Different*. May as well go with the flow of what people think. Most outfield players think we're insane. I think it myself at times, when I'm diving down where I know some giant centre-forward's boot is going to be, or when some thug is there with the specific order to shoulder-charge me into the net at the first corner. Also, Willie, you can make all sorts of mistakes out on the wing, a centre-forward can miss a sitter, and provided he scores sometime soon, it's forgotten. But goalkeepers, if you drop a clanger and it costs you the game, you never hear the end of it. Better than working though, Willie, never forget that. Better than being a miner or a bus driver or a welder or working in a shop. Never ever forget that, son.'

Charlie Gordon used to enjoy pre-match walks as a player, and he enjoyed them even more as a manager. There was no physical benefit, unless you counted the help a bit of fresh air can give you. It was all psychological, the coming together of a group of people who were hours away from having to perform as a team. They'd trained all week together, argued and bantered and joked around, had the tactics drilled into them; but now it was just about knowing each other, trusting each other, wanting to look at the next guy and say, 'There is nobody I would rather have in my team than him.' It was that mindset that meant someone like

Killer Kilbride could positively hate someone like David Brown, but as they strolled around the park, could turn to skipper Wilf Moore and say, 'Fucking hell, Brownie looks up for it.'

The effect of everyone wearing the same tracksuit was of course going to draw attention to them, and anyone who followed football knew immediately who they were. But it was also to separate them out from everyone else, including their own fans. We are us. This is the team. Nothing and nobody else matters.

Gordon also liked these walks for the opportunity they gave him to have little one-on-one chats, to emphasize a point about tactics or an opponent, and with Mooro to go over the game plan and also the things he was planning to say in his team talk. Gordon knew from his time as a player that managerial team talks sometimes went in one ear and out the other. If you heard the same thing again and again, it became dull, and you didn't listen. If it was too new and complicated, you didn't take it in properly. But he also knew the players could sense when the manager had really put some thought into what he was saying, and then they would listen. At least he did as a player.

Gordon had grown both to like and respect Wilf Moore since making him captain, and he knew how important this Cup run had been to him. Wilf had played in two previous quarter-finals and one FA Cup semi-final during his time at Newcastle, but he had never played in a Cup final at Wembley, which remained one of the great ambitions for most professionals.

At twenty-eight, and with a recurring knee injury, Mooro knew that this was probably his last chance of leading a team out of that famous tunnel into the most iconic football arena in the world, beneath the Twin Towers. Two wins, that was all it needed.

Mooro knew that Gordon took his views seriously, but nonetheless, thinking the line-up had been settled when Ronnie Winston had pinned it to the dressing room notice board yesterday, he was taken aback when the manager asked him, 'Do you think I should stick with the team I announced yesterday?'

'You worried about young Willie?'

'Far from it. I'm worried about DD.'

'DD?'

'Been up all night.'

'On the piss?'

'And shagging.'

'Oh Jesus, you'd think he'd be getting enough at that hotel during the week.'

'This was literally all night.'

'How do you know that? Have you got cameras in our rooms or something?'

'I've got my sources.'

He told him of the phone call he got this morning, but didn't tell him it was from Alfie Ruse, his old teammate turned agent to the players, and adviser to Chelsea owner Yaakov. Ruse said he'd not been able to sleep, knowing that Yaakov was doing the dirty on his old mate, and he let him in on how Bella Luca's manager, as requested by Yaakov, had targeted DD for the specific purpose of shagging him senseless on the eve of the match.

'How do you know Alfie isn't making it up so you'll drop your star player?'

'I thought of that. But I've got my second source, the head porter. He has confirmed it, that DD moved rooms and didn't go back to his own room until daylight. And I've got my third source... just fucking look at him.'

Mooro looked at DD, walking a few yards behind them. He did indeed look pale and exhausted.

A young woman jogged by in a pink tracksuit. David Brown pretended to chase her, and she laughed over her shoulder as she sprinted off. Dermot Cochrane, who always joined them on the team walk, was quick to comment, 'Fucking hell, Brownie, I hope you move faster than that this afternoon. You looked like my Auntie fucking Mabel chasing the milkman.'

'What frame of mind is Killer in?' asked Gordon.

'You're not dropping him too, are you?' retorted Mooro.

'No, just interested. I'm still getting grief from Partington, like it's my fault his daughter can't see a player without spreading her legs.'

'He'll be fine, boss. He's been quiet all week but he's up for it, and he knows that the Cooke injury talk was bollocks. Don't worry about him.'

'OK. Well, I'm going to deliver the news to DD. One other thing though, Mooro. When I do the team talk, I am going to be giving very, very specific instructions about corners. I'm shaking things up a lot. And I want you to make sure it fucking happens, OK?'

'OK, boss. What is it?'

'I'll tell you all at twelve. But I want you to listen very, very carefully.'

He let Mooro walk ahead, slowed until DD was alongside him. 'How you feeling, DD?'

'OK.'

'You sure? You look fucking rough to me.'

'No, I'm good. Didn't sleep great, but I never do before a big game.'

They walked on in silence for a few yards, then Gordon said, 'DD, sometimes a manager has to make tough calls, and I'm making one today. I feel this game needs Nuts, and as you two have never played together, I'm playing him with Jules up front.'

'So where do I go?'

'You're not playing. I'm not dropping you, I'm resting you. You look to me like you need a rest. Do you understand me?'

DD said nothing.

'You travel with us to the ground, you stay with us, you travel home with us. You reflect on your priorities in life, and on Monday, if I'm still in the job, we'll have a chat, OK?'

Again, DD said nothing. He knew that Gordon knew. Or else, what was that about 'priorities'?

'You're a good player, DD. But even good players don't always play well. I am making the call that if I pick you today, you won't play well. My call. Live with it. Learn from it. And be at the team meeting at twelve, or else call your pal Alfie Ruse and ask him to find you a new fucking club.'

He then walked straight over to Nuts, who was ambling along with Dipper.

'Nuts, can I have a word?'

'Yes, boss.'

'Alone.'

Dipper walked on.

'You're playing today.'

'What?'

'I said you're playing. Up front, alongside Jules.'

'Why?'

'I've been impressed by how you've handled yourself and I just think this game is better for you than DD.'

'Thanks, boss.'

'Never mind thanks, you've deserved it. Ronnie was telling me about Thursday and how you asked for some of the youth team to do an extra session after everyone else went home. I like that, Nuts. I like that a lot.'

'I won't let you down, gaffer. Promise.'

'OK. Well, keep it to yourself for now, just start getting your head in the right place, OK?'

'I'm there, boss, I'm already there.'

Isn't it strange, Gordon thought to himself as Nuts walked on ahead of him, how the same human being could look so different, one minute apart, purely because of a single piece of information, a single choice made by another human being?

Ronnie Winston had been watching Gordon move from player to player, and, seeing him now alone, came over to join him as the party strolled on.

'How do they seem to you?'

'Good,' said Gordon. 'Really good.'

'Yeah, me too.'

Gordon knew that his Number Two was in one of those strange dilemmas that often surfaces in football. On the one hand Ronnie wanted the team to win because that's what he was paid to help achieve; but on the other hand if the team lost today there was a very good chance Charlie would be sacked and a fair-to-reasonable chance that he would be offered the manager's job, and so fulfil a lifelong ambition. Gordon could hardly complain. He remembered that time he was with the Scotland set-up before a wartime international against England,

and Matt Busby went down after a bad tackle in training. Gordon must have been the only Scot on the planet hoping the injury would see Busby ruled out of the match, and he might get a call-up. There was nothing different in what Winston was hoping for now. He thought he was in a win-win situation. Gordon had always felt Winston was a Number Two, and one of the reasons was that he lacked the intelligence to see he could also be in a lose-lose situation.

'Any changes you're planning?'

'Not sure yet. One or two I'm mulling over. We'll see. I'm going to head back now and prepare a few notes for the team talk. You make sure they're all there on time.'

Gordon knew he shouldn't, but he positively enjoyed the discomfiture Winston so evidently felt at his sharpness, and his obvious concealment of selection plans.

Gordon was usually last in for his team talks. He would wait for the players to gather, and then stride in, confident and strong. He wanted everything about this to feel different. So instead of retiring to his room to make notes, he went to the Brunel Suite, sat down at the chair which stood behind the table at the front, and stared out at the twenty or so chairs that would soon be filled with the muscular backsides of the men whose success or failure would decide his future.

He never read his team talks. But he did make notes, and tried to get them on a single piece of paper, which he would then leave lying on the table as he stood to speak, often marching around the room as he did so.

The players began to file in at five to twelve, surprised to see him there. He didn't look up, he carried on writing, shuffling papers. It meant that the players arrived and sat down in near silence, save for the occasional cough, the shuffling of feet, the moving of a chair, or the sound of Gordon's pencil across the page. When he heard the clock strike twelve, finally he looked up.

'Is everyone here?' he asked Winston.

'Yes, boss.'

'Good.' He stood, walked to the front of the table, and pointed at Graham Smith.

'Smudger, what's the biggest game you've ever played in?'

Smith looked flummoxed, but eventually muttered something about his debut against Manchester City.

'This is bigger, Smudger. Hands up who has played for their country?'

Half a dozen hands went up.

'This is bigger than any game you played for your country. Do you know why?'

Nobody answered.

'I'll tell you why: because if we win this game, I am telling you, we will go on to win the FA Cup. And if we win the FA Cup, twelve names, the eleven who start and the sub who comes on, your names will be remembered for ever. Not just in the books, but in the hearts and the minds and the voices of people who love this club. And do you know something, that includes people who aren't even born yet.'

He looked around the room, his gaze settling on the young Scottish apprentice. 'How old are you, Willie?'

'Seventeen, boss.'

'There is a child who will be born in seventeen years' time, and by the time he starts supporting this club, you'll have retired. But his dad, who is at this game today, he will make sure that child knows your name, knows that Chelsea away in the sixth round was when Willie Buchanan made his first trip with the first team, and that was the day our 1973/74 season turned around and we went on to win the Cup.'

He paced around for a while, silent, for thirty seconds maybe, said nothing. Thirty seconds sounds a short time. It is when you're a goal down in injury time and the referee's whistle is about to blow. It's not when you're in a room, waiting for someone to speak.

'So listen, you boys, you men, can make history. If we don't win this game, we don't win the Cup. Win this game, and we can, and I believe we will, and long after I'm gone from here, men will sit in pubs and say, go on then, name that Charlie Gordon team that beat Chelsea when everyone wrote them off, and they went on to win the Cup.

'So your names will echo down through history ... Johnson, Dyson, Kilbride, Rees, Moore, Brown, Temple, Nulty, Pemberton, Jones, Smith and Buchanan.'

He paused again, scratched his ear – another long silence to let the team news sink in, as eyes shot around and DD Marland had to sit there and bear it. Gordon caught him out of the corner of his eye; he was staring down at the floor. Nuts just looked straight ahead of himself, refusing to meet the eyes of those looking at him, who wanted to share what must have been a great moment.

'Willie,' Gordon said, breaking the silence. 'Are you nervous, you might be needed today?'

'Er, yes, a wee bit, yes.'

'Good. A wee bit is good. Nuts, are you nervous?'

'A lot, boss, a lot.'

'OK. We need to bring that down a bit.' A little laughter eased the tension, but then Gordon cranked it up again.

'How many of you have read a newspaper these past few days?'

Most put their hands up.

'So what is the most common thing you've read about?' Silence. 'Come on, I know the fucking answer, there is no need to be shy.'

'That if we lose,' said Smudger, 'you'll get the sack.'

'Correct. But let me say something about that ... this isn't about me. It's about you, and it's about this club. I know we have had a poor season. But I know we're not a poor team. I know you are good players. I know Chelsea have good players too. But I know you can beat them. I know that. I know you all inside out. Apart from the Prof, who has been here since Julius fucking Caesar's time, I bought every single one of you. You're my team. And when you're good, you're as good as any team I've played in or managed. So be good, today. Be your best, today, and we win. And if we win this, I am telling you, we win the FA Cup. You get your hand on a medal and you show it to your grandkids in years to come and you may not remember a thing about all the games on the way, but without winning them, all of them, that medal never gets in your hands. You don't get to show your grandkids FA Cup medals, you just take them to the swings like every other fucking granddad.

'That's why today is momentous. And there is no better feeling than the one you will get today, at quarter to five, if you've played your guts out, given your all, left blood out there, yours or theirs I don't fucking care, and you've won, and those thousands of fans on their way south as we speak are so happy they'll look back on this as one of the best days of their lives. OK?'

The players nodded or murmured their assent.

'Hands up who's got family and friends at the match?'

Almost all hands went up. Willie's did not.

'Willie, Prof told me your mum and dad and your girlfriend are coming. Tell them to come to the players' entrance at half past two. I've got tickets for them. OK?'

'Thanks, boss.'

'Thank the Prof. And next time, ask me yourself.'

Another pause. Another stalk around the room.

'So are we ready?'

Nods. Murmurs.

'I said are we fucking ready?'

Shouts of 'Yes!'

'Good. Now I have one final thing to say, and I want you to listen, very, very carefully. It's nobody's fault but mine, OK, because I should have done this long ago. But did you know we have a record for goals scored from corners worse than any team in the League, all four divisions, apart from Plymouth Argyle and Bradford City? I don't have time to go over all the reasons, but I do know we have to make changes. So Dipper, Smudger, it's no criticism of you, it's a criticism of me, but you're not taking corners today. If we win a corner on the right, Killer, you cross the fucking pitch from left-back and you take it – left foot, inswinger, not too close to the keeper, but you're aiming at the near post area – and Jules, Nuts, Mooro, Brownie, one of you is going to get that fucking ball first. Do you understand me? Do you all fucking understand me? Good.

'Now, if we get a corner on the left, Clutch, you get over there and you take it – right foot, inswinger, same place but this side of the goal. OK? And the same big bastards get in there and win it at the near post. Dipper and Smudger, you cover for both of them when they are taking these corners. And let me stress, this is an order. Not a suggestion. Not an idea. It is a fucking order. If anyone disobeys me they will be immediately substituted. I'll say that again. Listen carefully. If anybody doesn't follow these instructions you will be *immediately* substituted.

'Wilf, you make sure it happens and that everybody understands what is expected of them. OK?'

It had certainly been a team talk like no other. When he asked if there were any questions, there were none, so he instructed them to go to the team room for tea, toast and jam, the traditional pre-match snack, then to go to their rooms to change from their tracksuits into their club suits, pack their bags and be ready for a departure at one o'clock on the dot. The players filed out as silently as they had come in, and Winston went with them, doubtless to stir and tell the players the new plan for corners and the late team changes were nothing to do with him. It is why he could never be a leader, Gordon mused to himself. He didn't know what a difficult decision was. If he thought the players would respect him because of his sidling up to them, he was wrong.

Only DD Marland felt uninvolved in his teammates' renewed feeling of respect for Gordon.

By the time the players were gathering in the hotel lobby, ready to load their bags onto the coach, journalists from national newspapers were hanging around trying to get a few quotes, there were supporters inside and outside, and on the TV in the bar Barry Davies was interviewing supporters and some of the celebrities who followed Chelsea as part of the pre-match build-up. All but the most diehard were predicting a Chelsea win.

When Gordon saw Willie Buchanan talking to a group of people in the corner of the lobby, he strode over. 'Is this your family, Willie?'

'Yes, gaffer. This is my mum and dad, and this is Catriona.'

Gordon shook their hands, said they should be very proud of him, and then took an envelope from his pocket.

'This will save you a trip to the players' entrance. These are your tickets for today. Walter Graham said he didn't need his, and one of them is a spare from David Brown. Enjoy the match. And if you're anywhere near me, don't be shouting at me to get Willie on early.'

'It's just great that he is in the squad,' said Mr Buchanan.

'I think he'll be doing more than just making up the numbers,' said Gordon.

As he walked off, Catriona took Willie's hand and squeezed it hard.

'Just enjoy every second of today, Willie.'

'There's going to be forty odd thousand there, Catriona. The biggest crowd I've ever played in front of was at that schoolboy international at Falkirk. There were barely two thousand there. What if I mess up?'

'You won't. Or else he wouldn't have picked you. It's just the same with forty thousand as with one. Two teams, one pitch. You'll be fine.'

'OK, son,' said Mrs Buchanan, 'we'd better go now and leave you to it. Good luck.' His dad hugged him, Catriona and his mum kissed him, and they filed out to join the dozens of supporters now held behind crush barriers near the team coach, where a TV cameraman was waiting to record the players leaving for Stamford Bridge.

Stan Moffitt had arrived now, and made a point of telling Gordon he was staying down for the weekend. He was taking Gloria, a big Bryan Ferry fan, to a Roxy Music concert at the Albert Hall after the match. Was it a way of signalling to the manager that he did not, contrary to all the press speculation, intend to sack him if they lost this afternoon? Or was Gordon reading too much into everything now? Stewart Finley was also there, and handed the chairman his room key, having already checked in Stan and Gloria Moffitt (who would arrive later) and settled their bill on the club account.

At one o'clock prompt, the team coach had everyone on board and Dermot Cochrane steered carefully through the throng of fans and began the relatively short journey to Stamford Bridge.

To Gordon's irritation, given his usual approach to non-essential people not being allowed on the bus, the plan was to make the return journey to the Great Western Hotel later purely to drop off Stan Moffitt, before taking the team home.

It was a nice enough afternoon, forecast to be clear for the rest of the day, and warmer than was usual for this time of year. So Gordon threw his dirty raincoat on the rack above his head and sat down, the chairman choosing to sit next to him. Maybe, Gordon thought, he would just whisper the sack to him on the coach ride back to the hotel later. He smiled, but then said to himself, 'Come on Charlie, no negative thoughts, just think of winning,' remembering that last night he'd decided to let the Poulson sleeping dogs lie. He looked in the rear-view mirror that allowed him to see the length of the coach, and he was pleased at how quiet and calm everyone seemed to be. The card players were not even playing as a new boxed pack sat in the middle of their table. This really was a big game.

With Moffitt sitting right alongside him, Gordon was eating more mints than usual. He'd had a Scotch before the team walk, another before the team meeting, and an extra large one in his room afterwards, partly as a reward for what he felt had been one of his best team talks in ages. But now he was starting to sweat.

'Cockie, can you turn down the heating, it's like a fucking sauna in here,' he asked as he scratched his ear.

Without response, Cockie obeyed. On matchdays he stayed quiet.

'What time's Gloria getting down, Chairman?' Gordon asked.

'She'll get to the hotel about half four. I can't stand Bryan bleeding Ferry but if it keeps her happy...'

'Yeah, at least you've got one to keep happy.'

'If you had a wife, Charlie, you wouldn't have so much time for the team.'

'Guess not.'

'Got to get something today, Charlie. I'm not sure I can take Labour back in power and us out of the Cup in the same week.'

Gordon smiled. He could see DD staring aimlessly out of the window, doubtless wondering where it had all gone wrong for him. However good last night had been with his latest fancy piece, any pleasure was surely outweighed by the pain and humiliation he was feeling now. Willie Buchanan and Norman Nulty had both gone to the loners' section at the back of the coach. Neither of them spoke a single word on the entire journey, but Gordon knew they were loving every second, and every thought of what lay ahead.

With the football team and all their fans and hangers-on gone, the hotel quickly went back to normal. But for Paddy O'Connell there was no normal right now, only fear. That fear was exacerbated when he was called to a meeting to go over the service for the VIP who would be staying with them that evening. The newly appointed Northern Ireland Secretary was only a few notches down from the Prime Minister and the most important Cabinet minister to stay at the hotel for twenty years. They were used to high-profile politicians staying with them, particularly those who represented seats in the West Country, but Rees was very much man of the moment and, as the various police visits had made clear, on a par with the Prime Minister in terms of security considerations at this volatile time for government.

O'Connell knew that the minute this briefing was over, he had to inform Paul, who would then inform the rest of the cell. Just as they had a codename, so did Rees. He was booked in as Thomas Buckley, and his stay was known as Operation Lioness. He was expected shortly before six, and would be driven to the main tradesmen's entrance, where Paddy and a protection officer would greet him and the protection team travelling with him. They would be taken up via the service lift, and all other lifts would be held on the ground floor until the protection team confirmed he was in his room. The same procedure, in reverse, would be carried out when he left for dinner. Also, O'Connell heard that if anything Rees hoped to be back in the hotel even earlier than they had expected, one of his policemen reporting that he was exhausted and as the dinner tonight was not a significant one, he hoped to slope off early.

As O'Connell went back to his bread-and-butter work – being

nice to guests, telling them where they could run or walk, how to get tickets for the sold-out shows, which were the nicest restaurants in the area – he was beginning to feel ever more nervous. Yes, he felt his father had had a horrible life on the Ballymurphy Estate. But he had passed away eight years ago and would get no benefit from his son's actions today. And yes, he was broadly sympathetic to the aims of the IRA, but not if it meant going to jail and not, frankly, if it meant killing someone. Merlyn Rees had stayed at the hotel before, including with his wife, and he'd always struck O'Connell as a genuinely nice man. What on earth was he doing getting involved in a plot to kill him?

But involved he was, and in a few hours' time he would have to invent an errand that a guest was insisting only he could fulfil. His fellow unit members were so different to the people he first got to know when he went down this 'Irish community' route, with a few social nights in Islington and Hammersmith. They represented everything that he felt was good about the exiled Irish, the craic, the laughter, the love of a good Guinness and a good sing-song. The trio he had been drawn into were simply cold-blooded killers. The fear that now enveloped him was worse than anything he had ever felt, even when his father held him and hushed him to be quiet as the rioting Unionists ran rampant through the streets where they lived, encouraged by the Brits. This time he was the one with life and death in his hands. He again briefly considered telling the police what was happening, telling them where he would be heading, and letting them bust open the meeting so that Paul and co. were arrested. But that way lay certain death for him. He was facing a truly horrible choice: someone had to die, but was it to be him, or Merlyn Rees?

31

CHELSEA

Saturday 9 March, early afternoon

'Now now, Brownie,' Gordon chided as he spotted his midfielder flicking a V-sign at the Chelsea fans hurling abuse at the coach.

'Cocky bastards,' said Brownie. 'Look at them, arrogant fuckers.'

There was something a bit superior about fans of the big London clubs, but Gordon said, 'Ignore them. There is only one way to bring them down to size.'

There were huge crowds outside the pubs near the ground, and mostly the mood seemed good-humoured. That annoyed Gordon and his players even more, though. It suggested they had already decided they were in the draw for the semi-final.

'Just use it all, lads,' Gordon shouted up the coach. 'Use it all.'

For the last quarter of a mile, the coach had a police escort to help Dermot nose his way through the crowds and draw up a few feet from the players' entrance. The last hundred yards or so were driven at a crawl as the number of fans getting dangerously close to the coach grew, but Cockie had anticipated this and the team arrived in good time.

There were a few hundred fans of both teams, and a handful of police and stewards, all kept behind security barriers. Cockie switched off the ignition, opened the automatic door, and was first down the steps to open the luggage compartments for Magic,

George Brady and Charlie Sinclair whose job it was to unload the skips.

Some managers liked to be first off. Gordon liked to be last. He liked to see his players file off, he liked to see how they reacted to the antics of the fans, the boos, the cheers, the demands for autographs, the questions from journalists. He could see their moods and their characters that way. Brownie always smiled if booed. Dipper couldn't see an autograph book without stopping to sign it. He also noticed that it was Willie Buchanan who was being shouted at by the journalists. So the news had got out. It would be a player telling an agent who told a journalist. Willie looked startled, but just carried on, saying nothing as they tried to get his reaction to being selected for the number 12 shirt.

There were more police and stewards than usual on duty, it seemed to Gordon as finally he followed Stan Moffitt off the coach and into the stadium through the players' entrance. It was something of a tradition at the club that the players went straight out to look at the pitch, while Magic and co. set up the dressing room, and this time Gordon followed them. The stands were virtually empty, just smatterings of early arrivals. The centre of the pitch and the two goalmouths were bare, not a blade of grass in sight, and Jock Johnson groaned on testing just how hard the ground was in the six-yard box. But there was plenty of green down the wings and it was clear that the whole pitch had been rolled flat earlier that morning. The groundsman had decided on simple stripes, each the width of his mower. The light-green grass as he mowed away; the dark-green when he mowed towards. The pitch, which was ever so slightly cambered, had a well-worn surface. It would look good on TV.

'Pitch is OK for this time of year, Brownie,' said Wilf Moore.

'Apart from the middle. No wonder they play down the flanks.'

'Good old ground though. That fucking East Stand, you'd get vertigo up there.'

'Yeah, fucking near broke the bank though. They're in a right old mess financially.'

'Let's hope we make it worse.'

David Brown was slowly slipping into a zone that only he could create for himself before a big match. He was getting his head focused and strangely his personality changed from the sarcastic piss-taker everyone hated into a true team player.

Willie came over.

'Thanks for giving me one of your comps for my family, Brownie,' he said.

'The gaffer made me,' he replied, smiling. But then he took Willie by the shoulder. 'You just drink in every second today, because it's a big day in your life and it'll be gone in a blink. And if we win, on Monday, I'll bring in my shirt and you can sew some fucking buttons back on it, you little git!'

'Deal.'

Brown then crouched down on his haunches and ran his hand through the grass and soil beneath, to weigh up whether to wear studded boots or rubbers. The pitch was soft from the spring rain and there was no doubt he would wear studs today. Not only would this give him a better grip on the pitch, but they would inflict more pain if he went over the top in a tackle. As he stood up, stretched his back and took a deep breath, he said to Mooro, a few yards away, 'Everybody looks up for the game, Wilf, especially Nuts, I've never seen him so focused. What's got into him?'

'Maybe that's the best thing DD has done – got Nuts going again.'

Clutch, Jock, Dipper, Jules and Taffy were grouped together on the edge of the eighteen-yard box at the Shed End, where more supporters were arriving. Smudger was chatting with Killer and Walter Graham as they flicked idly through the match programme.

By the time they strolled back into the dressing room, Charlie Sinclair, Magic and George Brady had carried in all the gear from the coach and were laying out the strips under the pegs. The main skip contained three complete sets of team jerseys, all the players' boots and rubbers, towels, slips, socks, shorts, shin pads, and a wide range of tools should studs need changing. There was also a bottle of whisky in there. Not everyone did, but quite a few of the players took a swig just before running out to start the match. For some it calmed nerves. For others, it fired them up. It also helped Gordon feel better about his own regular trips to the gents to take a slug from his own bottle.

In another skip, Magic Rowland had all the medical equipment that might be needed in the event of Joss Partington, club doctor, being called in to deal with a serious injury.

Willie Buchanan had been taken aback by the size of the stands, and also how small the pitch seemed compared with how he had imagined it was going to be. He decided to keep himself busy by helping Magic unload the skips and hang the shirts in numerical order around dressing room hooks from one to twelve.

Alone of all the players Dougie 'Jinkie' Jones never stepped out onto the pitch before the kick-off as he thought it brought bad luck. Instead he read the match programme cover to cover, and everyone knew not to interrupt him.

Charlie Gordon was disappointed to see that referee Jack Taylor had been given the game by the FA refereeing panel. Taylor had given two penalties to Leeds United the previous Saturday and seemed to hold a grudge against Clutch Dyson. He would no doubt be pissed off that the club had appealed against his sending off, even if he knew the reason. But perhaps mentally Taylor would think he owed the club a favour and today he might balance off the bad decisions he made last week in the League game? Taylor was walking around the pitch with his two linesmen, all three proudly dressed in claret FA blazers, navy blue slacks and FA ties.

This was also a massive game for these officials too. Referees were becoming almost as well known as some of the players and managers and one or two were making a good living on the after-dinner circuit. Fame came in strange packages for these officials: if they had a great game they'd be inconspicuous, nobody would even remember their names; on the other hand if they made a massive error or the game was decided by a highly dubious decision, their name was plastered all over the Sunday papers. Some loved it. Luckily Jack Taylor wasn't one of them. But Gordon would still rather it had been someone else.

Just before two o'clock, Chelsea assistant manager Ron Suart and Ronnie Winston walked down the corridor to hand in the team sheets to the referee. Taylor met them both. As he studied the players listed on both teams he commented, 'Well, I've been reading for two minutes and I haven't spotted one good player yet. Have you both got the reserve squad out today?'

Suart and Winston both pretended to find it funny, then walked to their respective dressing rooms to hand over the opposition's team sheet to their manager. It was the first that Chelsea manager Dave Sexton would know for sure that Marland was dropped. He knew all about Nulty. Earlier in the season he had tried to buy him for £75,000. He knew nothing about Buchanan and quickly had Suart contacting a few scouts.

The Chelsea team was largely as expected, though Sexton was giving a game to young Ray Wilkins. That didn't make it any less intimidating to see the names down in black and white as Gordon read over the sheet of paper. Scratching his ear, and sucking on a mint, he read, 'Bonetti, Boyle, Dempsey, Harris, Swain, Webb, Cooke, Hollins, Wilkins, Baldwin, Osgood, sub. Hudson.'

'OK, lads, Chelsea team pretty much as we expected. Nothing to worry about.'

The away team dressing room was quite subdued as each of the players enacted his own individual build-up to the game. Some players would sit and read the match programme till 2.45 p.m. and then rush into their kit, while others would stand naked and jog on the spot. Most had a set routine driven by superstition, which dictated which boot they would put on first or in which order they dressed: shorts, socks, jersey, boots or similar. Some, including one or two who hadn't been inside a church for years, whispered prayers to themselves. Others cracked jokes to fight off their nervousness. At least one, usually two or three, would feel better after forcing themselves to be sick in the toilets. These pre-match nerves and superstitions were rarely discussed.

On the whole, players felt it brought bad luck even to admit they were superstitious.

Jules Pemberton was always first to have Magic massage his legs with wintergreen liniment, which would be followed by a tight strapping on both ankles. Once the wintergreen had been smeared over twenty-four thighs, it was impossible to smell anything else in the room.

David Brown, who was now approaching thirty-one, liked to sit waist deep in a piping hot bath. This loosened his muscles and joints, which, as with many players who had survived to that age, were affected by the early symptoms of osteoarthritis. Jock Johnson was in full kit but barefoot as he bounced a ball against the wall in the shower area next to the dressing room.

By 2.45 it was possible to hear the noise from the capacity crowd through the walls and roofs that separated them. Gordon nodded to Ronnie Winston who then went round getting all the players to sit down. The manager had his own superstitions too. One was to wash his hands and dry them on a club towel before his final team talk. Then there was his lucky white shirt, feeling tight these days what with his expanding girth and collar, but it still gave him that little extra confidence as he looked around and prepared to speak. Even the Prof had commented on how good his team talk at the hotel had been, so all he wanted to do was cement those thoughts in the players' minds. 'That was your Agincourt time,' the Prof had said to him, which was not bad considering he had been dropped.

He was back scratching his right ear now, which was not so much a superstition as a nervous tic. But again, he spoke well, the stain on his jacket unnoticed.

'Gentlemen, Brownie was right. They are cocky, arrogant Londoners. Listen to the crowd now. Do any of them think they can lose? Does Dave Sexton think he can lose? Bonetti, Boyle, Dempsey, Harris, Swain, Webb, Cooke, Hollins, Wilkins, Baldwin, Osgood – do they think they can lose? Do they hell. Cocky, arrogant and smug. But being cocky doesn't win matches. Being arrogant doesn't win matches. What wins a match like this is what lies in your heart. Courage. And give me the hearts of

Johnson, Dyson, Kilbride, Rees, Moore, Brown, Temple, Nulty, Pemberton, Jones, Smith and Buchanan – give me those hearts against these cocky, arrogant bastards any day, any place. The place is here, the day is now, and today, against all the odds, you will be victorious.

'I know this because I can read people and for the last twenty-four hours I have watched each one of you, and noted your every move. I have seen victory in your eyes, in how you walk, in how you think, in how you prepare. Today you will not be defeated.'

He paused and stopped for effect. Circling round the room, he looked into each of their eyes to let the importance of his message sink in.

'My playing days are long gone and I am reaching an age I don't like, and every day my past failures come back to haunt me. I too played in games like this and if you want the truth there were times when I really fucked up. On occasions, I wasn't prepared to put myself on the line for my teammates; I chose natural skill before undying effort. And I was wrong. I still hate myself for it even now, thirty years later. I was a good player; you can read about all that in the record books. But I could have been a great player, if I had done all the things I know I should have done. In 1950 I won a Cup medal with Villa. But 1952, we had Stoke in the fifth round, and I fucked up. I got cocky, I got arrogant, I didn't do the basics, I gave away a goal. I think about that every day. I didn't play as well as I could have done. If you play your best today, all of you, we will win, believe me.

'You know something, lads, there is a strange sense of pleasure being beaten to hell by a storm, when you're travelling on a ship that isn't going to sink. This team is the ship, my ship, and we are not going to sink. We will weather the storm and continue our journey. But, I am sorry to warn you that the victory will not be won without some sacrifice and to achieve our goal some of you will need to leave not just sweat, but blood on that field. This game will be a battle against a great team who will try to hurt you by inflicting pain to steal the victory from you and your grandchildren's grasp. And I know you will not let this happen. Because you know your offspring are watching you from their life in the future. And when they ask for you to recall the score, you will simply reply, we won.

'That, and nothing else, is all that matters. Now go and make yourselves and your families proud.'

As Gordon finished, the room was initially silent and his mouth was dry. He could do no more. He was now desperate for a drink. As he turned and walked into the shower area to wash his hands again, and sneak a final pre-match slug, his players rose as one and roared a cry of defiance and hope, then came together as a team into the middle of the dressing room, hugging and wishing each other good luck, hairs standing tall on their necks.

The next sound they heard was the referee's bell summoning the teams to the tunnel, which brought another roar from the players. Gordon went to stand by the door, shook each man by the hand as they left, remembering to remind Mooro, Dipper, Smudger, Killer and Clutch of the new plan for corners. Along the short walk to the tunnel there were stewards, club officials, people working for BBC Television. Half a dozen ball boys in Chelsea tracksuits and bibs handed out balls to the players for the two-minute kickabout before the whistle. Some balls were white, some brown, some were plain, some had the new diamond pattern stitched in them. Clutch made sure to get one of the balls. That was his final superstition: carry the ball out under his left arm, then once he had crossed the touchline onto the field of play, kick it goalwards with his right foot.

The referee had the match ball, tested to make sure it was the correct size, perfect weight, exact pressure and ideal consistency for a game of such magnitude – namely he had lifted it to his chest between his arms and pressed it hard with his two thumbs on either side of the ball.

For most games, the teams came out separately, but the FA had asked that today, led by the referee and linesmen, they should walk out side by side, for effect, as if it were the Cup final already. This gladiatorial arrival into the Chelsea Colosseum brought a massive roar from both sets of supporters.

The sun was breaking through as Chelsea's match announcer read out the two teams. Each name was received with a roar and as always the most skilful, the goalscorers, and the most violent hitmen got the biggest and loudest receptions. Ron Harris and David Webb, Peter Osgood and Charlie Cooke were definitely the Chelsea favourites. Amid the booing that greeted the announcing of the away team could be heard loud cheering by the travelling support as the names were read out one by one, the loudest cheer saved for Norman Nulty. He waved to them in acknowledgement.

With the day's first extended blow of his whistle, referee Taylor called the two captains into the middle of the field for the traditional handshake and coin-toss. This would be the only time all day that Ron Harris would show any civility to an opposing player. Wilf Moore arrived, shook his hand, then Taylor handed him a silver half-crown. Mooro tossed it high in the air, Harris shouted 'heads' and all three of them looked down to see the Queen, face-up on the barren centre spot.

Harris chose to defend the Shed End in the first half, so they would be attacking that way in the second half. As the referee signalled for the players to change ends Willie Buchanan, who had been out for the warm-up, quietly jogged off to the dugout to sit with manager Charlie Gordon, Ronnie Winston, George Brady and Magic Rowland. He looked, without success, to see if he could spot his parents and Catriona in the crowd.

The sun was now bright in Jock Johnson's eyes and he was wearing a cap for the first time since September. Wilf Moore and David Brown exchanged a few words of encouragement with Clutch Dyson and Taffy Rees and the familiar 'W'-formation started to take shape. Wingers Graham Smith and Frank 'Dipper' Temple were already getting some mainly good-natured abuse from the Chelsea supporters with warnings of the consequences of any squabbles with David Webb or, even worse, with Chopper Harris, who had the reputation of being the dirtiest footballer on the planet. As the referee prepared to blow his whistle, and Smudger stood at the point where the touchline meets the halfway line, a fan shouted out, 'Chop-per's gon-na get ya!' and another went further: 'Stay away from him, Smith, or you'll wake up in Chelsea infirmary with a size-nine boot wedged up your arse!' Smudger glanced over with a nervous smile, which prompted shouts of 'you soft bastard'.

32

KICK-OFF

Saturday 9 March, 3 p.m.

The kick-off, bang on three o'clock, produced the biggest roar of the day so far. After all the hype and the waiting, all the nervous excitement for fans and players alike, finally it was under way.

Norman Nulty tapped the ball to Jules Pemberton, who slipped it back to Brownie. Gordon had given strict instructions that he wanted Brownie to blast it as far upfield as possible to give Chelsea a throw-in deep in their own half. But the Chelsea front line were at them like rockets and David Brown needed to feign clearing the ball and dribble around Peter Osgood before firing the ball into the far corner for a throw-in. Ron Harris threw the ball to David Webb who tapped it back to Peter Bonetti to give him an early feel for the new leather. Bonetti bounced it a few times, took a few paces forward and kicked it upfield.

So began ten minutes of intense Chelsea pressure, around 35,000 home supporters urging them on, and they were unlucky not to take the lead from a Cooke cross in the third minute, which Osgood headed over the bar when it looked easier to score.

'Tighter, Mooro, tighter!' screamed Gordon from the dugout.

From the goal-kick Jock Johnson launched the ball back towards the Chelsea half but Kenny Swain and John Dempsey linked well to move the ball to John Hollins, who clipped it to Webb before Rees could get near him. Webb played it wide to Cooke who beat Kilbride to the touchline and clipped in a wicked cross which Mooro headed out but only as far as Wilkins who volleyed it inches over the bar. The Chelsea fans started to smell an early goal.

Again Jock Johnson blasted a goal-kick upfield, and again the ball came straight back towards him. Again, they played through Cooke – Gordon began to wonder if Dave Sexton somehow knew about the troubles Killer was having in his marriage, and was deliberately targeting him. Cooke played a one-two with Hollins to get round Kilbride, crossed the ball. This time Osgood's header was on target but Clutch was there on the line to head it away, and Brownie kicked it out for a corner.

Webb, Swain and Harris ambled up the field to add bodies and pressure in the visitors' goalmouth. Cooke floated the ball into the middle of the box and Swain headed the ball goalwards as he climbed all over David Brown. Luckily the referee had seen it all and after he blew his whistle for a foul, the Chelsea team leisurely jogged back into position, clearly very content with the way things were going. After fifteen minutes Gordon heard a supporter behind the bench shouting his name, and asking: 'Any chance of a match being played here, Gordon? Takes two fucking teams you know.' It brought a cheap laugh.

As if to provide the answer, from the free-kick came a move which led to the first remotely serious threat on Bonetti's goal. Jules Pemberton brought the ball down on his chest and despite Swain pressing him from behind, he slid it wide to Smudger Smith who went around David Webb before getting in a good cross towards the penalty spot, just where Gordon liked it. Norman Nulty ran on to the ball, beating Swain to it, but blasted the ball straight at Bonetti. Gordon punched the top of the dugout.

'Fuck,' said Winston, 'three feet either side of him and it's a goal.'

'He's looking sharp though,' said Gordon. 'Left Swain for dead there.'

But back came Chelsea, and after twenty-two minutes came the inevitable. John Hollins pushed left, took a long crossfield

pass from Cooke, fooled Clutch into thinking he was going to
the by-line, pulled inside and floated over a cross which Osgood
headed down, and though Brown was first to it, he could only
stab it to the edge of the box, from where Ray Wilkins blasted
it past Johnson. The long-haired seventeen-year-old then ran past
the prone Johnson to pick the ball up from the back of the net
and kick it into the visiting supporters in celebration, just before
his teammates arrived to jump all over him. It was nothing less
than Chelsea deserved.

As the players ran back to set up for the kick-off, Sexton was
on his feet, urging them, 'We go again, we go again, let's kill it
off by half-time!' Gordon on the other hand felt flat, anxious,
and stayed put. The Chelsea pressure was now relentless with
balls flying into the goalmouth from all angles. Only Johnson was
really covering himself with the kind of glory Gordon had talked
about in his team talks. Osgood was hungry for goals and had
another chance go begging on the half-hour when he slipped the
ball past Brownie, chipped Johnson but saw the ball land on top
of the bar. But there wasn't a single person inside that stadium
who didn't think he would get his name on the scoresheet the
way he was playing. Moore and Brown were starting to look
and feel their age. Osgood was hard as well as skilful and while
going for a Charlie Cooke cross his flailing arm crashed into Wilf
Moore's face. Jack Taylor stopped the game for Magic Rowland
to run on carrying his little medical bag. After washing away all
the blood with his wet sponge Magic could see that the nose was
fractured at the bridge, towards the left eye. Magic managed to
move the nasal bone back slightly but the blood was gushing out.

'No way I'm coming off, Magic.'

'Understood. All I can do is plug it with cotton wool to try
to stop the bleeding. So keep the sponge and keep going till
half-time when I'll get the Doc down from the boardroom to
check you out.'

Magic jogged off as Jack Taylor came over for a quiet word
with Moore. 'Are you OK to carry on, Wilf, or do you want the
sub on?'

'I'll be OK, ref, but watch that fucker Osgood, will you? Every time we're in the air, his arm or his elbow is into me.'

'I hear what you're saying,' Taylor replied, jogging on, then restarting play.

There was no respite. It was all Chelsea. After thirty-five minutes a flowing move involving Webb, Cooke and Wilkins saw Osgood through one-on-one with the goalkeeper Jock Johnson who, as the big centre-forward rounded him, dived to tap his ankles and bring him down. Penalty no doubt, no one argued, probably Osgood would have scored anyway. At one-nil, Gordon felt if they could hang on to half-time, he could get them fired up and playing better in the second half. At two-nil though, the way Chelsea were playing, the odds would be heavily stacked against them.

As the Chelsea fans gloated, there was a little tussle between Charlie Cooke and Ray Wilkins over who should take the penalty and seniority won. Cooke, though he knew and liked Johnson from their times together with Scotland, couldn't resist a little kidology, pointing to the spot in the goal where he intended to put the ball, knowing Johnson would know he was just playing games with him. As the whistle blew Cooke walked away from the ball, turned quickly and took three quick paces before smashing the ball to the left of Johnson, who guessed correctly, somehow got his fingertips to it and tipped the ball onto the post, and it bounced out for Kilbride to clear it for a corner. The defenders all shouted their praise of Johnson but then quickly had to focus on defending the corner, Mooro organizing them to man-mark all who came into the box. They were still in the game.

From the short corner Wilkins whipped the ball into the box but nothing came of it and everyone took a breather as Jock Johnson waited for the ball to come back from the ball boys and placed it on the six-yard line for another goal-kick.

Jules Pemberton and Norman Nulty had been virtual spectators for most of the game. That Ron Harris was yet to punish Graham Smith was purely the consequence of the fact that Smudger had seen so little of the ball, and though Frank Temple had got round John Boyle a couple of times, he was immediately blocked off by the covering central defenders. The reality is that Chelsea were playing football the way Gordon would love for his team to play it.

As half-time neared, Magic was on again, this time after Kenny Swain, perhaps remembering what Brownie did to him last time the sides met, went in for a crunching tackle, leaving Brown writhing in agony holding his ankle. He rolled down his sock to reveal a deep gash just above the foot that was bleeding heavily. After a couple of minutes Magic had patched it up and the game continued with more Chelsea pressure.

John Hollins was playing as well as Gordon had ever seen him play, and making Taffy Rees look average. He played a one-two with Baldwin, which left him free on the wing. He skipped around Clutch Dyson and sent over a pinpoint cross to the near post, which Peter Osgood reached ahead of Mooro, and headed into the roof of the net for Chelsea's second goal. Behind him, Gordon could hear the Chelsea fans asking if they could hit four, five, six. 'Might as well go home, Gordon!'

Again, Dave Sexton was up on his feet, urging his players to keep going for more. 'Let's kill 'em off!' he shouted at Charlie Cooke, strolling back to his own half.

After thirty-nine minutes Norman Nulty was wide on the right wing tempting John Dempsey into a tackle. As the two of them fell to the floor, with the ball somewhere underneath them, Boyle and Webb dived into the sprawling legs and started to kick at both the ball and Nulty's shins. Within seconds three more Chelsea bruisers had joined in and soon Wilf Moore and David Brown were also in the melee, which resulted in a few punches being thrown. Both Ronnie Winston and Chelsea's assistant manager Ron Suart were on the pitch trying to separate the players while the referee was talking with his linesman before calming things down and deciding that a dropped ball should restart the game. Tempers were raised as Norman Nulty waited for Taylor to drop the ball. As Taylor prepared for this, Ron Harris ran over from the other side of the field to take part in the dropped ball, accompanied all the way by loud cheering from the Chelsea fans.

As Taylor dropped the ball Harris blasted it against Nulty's legs and then followed through so that Nuts fell to the floor. David Brown ran over to remonstrate with Harris, who pushed him. Brownie pushed back, harder, then David Webb joined in and before long all three were on the ground, as others ran over to join in. Taylor blew his whistle frantically but nobody was listening.

From nowhere Michael Kilbride quietly arrived on the scene. He waited his moment and, with the referee looking towards one of his linesmen, he jumped two-footed into the pack of six or seven fighting players. Dave Sexton screamed at the referee to take action, but he had seen nothing. Kilbride quietly jogged back across the park to his left-back position, to be greeted with roars of abuse and a few missiles thrown on the pitch by fans who had witnessed his every move. Stewards moved onto the pitch to remove the coins and bottles that had been thrown, and then crouched down facing the crowd.

When finally order was restored, and the referee had managed to separate the feuding players, only Ron Harris was still lying on the ground, holding his private parts and screaming in pain.

'Fuck me,' Gordon whispered to Winston. 'Killer's only gone and kicked Chopper in the bollocks.'

'Well, you did say we'd need courage today,' said George Brady.

Harris eventually stood, to huge cheers from the home crowd, but then within seconds he was back on the ground. This time it was the away fans cheering, and returning the earlier chants of 'you soft bastard'. Harris could not continue. A stretcher came on, and he was taken off the pitch then off to hospital, home fans applauding, away fans cheering.

Harris's departure meant Sexton was out on the touchline again, asking David Webb to be captain, and rearranging the line-up so Hollins slotted in at right-back and substitute Alan Hudson went into midfield. For very different reasons, both managers wanted half-time to come soon.

Three minutes before the interval Wilf Moore, the front of

his jersey discoloured by the blood leaking from his damaged nose, started a good move, probably their best move of the first half, down the right flank. Moore to Rees, Rees to Smith, Smith rounded Wilkins and switched play to Dipper Temple who with his trademark move dipped his right shoulder, sending John Dempsey the wrong way, and while making his way to the by-line, he clipped over a great cross for Jules Pemberton who beat Swain in the air, and hammered in a header which Bonetti gracefully tipped over for a corner.

In the heat of battle, and amid the noise of a huge crowd still at boiling point over recent goals, fights and skirmishes, Frank Dipper Temple forgot Charlie Gordon's instructions – his order – about the way corners should be taken. Temple collected the ball from behind the goal, ran to the corner flag, failed to hear Mooro shouting at him to leave it and drop into defence, failed to see Killer sprinting over from left-back. Instead he raised his right hand, aimed for Jules with an outswinger and then watched as Webb confidently headed the ball clear and play continued. Killer, halfway towards the corner flag, was now out of position. Wilkins played the ball to Cooke, who had a free run towards goal but thankfully chose to shoot from distance and the ball flew wide.

Gordon was now on his feet. He told Willie Buchanan to warm up. He told a stunned Ronnie Winston to inform the referee that he was making a substitution. He then pointed angrily at Frank Temple and summoned him over. Only when Gordon said, 'I told you, any disobedience of the order on corners, immediate substitution – you're off,' did Dipper realize what he had done. 'I just forgot,' he spluttered. 'I'm sorry, gaffer, just one more chance,' but Gordon was determined to make an example of him. From the directors' box Stan Moffitt looked on shaking his head, wondering what on earth was going on. The journalists who packed out the press box were asking each other what the hell was happening, and who this boy Buchanan was. It was all especially baffling because Gordon had not even waited till half-time. Forty-three minutes, and he subbed a recognized player for a virtual unknown, and beyond those who had been at his team talk in the hotel, nobody knew why.

As Temple reached the bench his temper got the better of him. He shouted, 'Fucking ridiculous!' clear enough for the opposing bench and hundreds of fans to hear, kicked a water bottle which almost hit George Brady in the head, and flung the tracksuit top Magic was offering him to the floor in disgust.

'Go take a bath and calm down, Dipper,' said Gordon, angry that his authority was being so blatantly challenged.

'Bloody hell, boss, I didn't think, it was the heat of the moment. It's a battlefield out there.'

'Next time you probably will *fucking think*. Go and get a bath.'

As Dipper made his way off the field, Charlie Gordon had a quiet, fatherly word with Willie Buchanan who was obviously nervous about entering the cauldron of a violent match against some of the best players in the game. 'Willie, look me in the eyes. Son, the next fifty minutes will change your life. Don't be scared, you are faster and more skilful than any of these Chelsea players, just use these two minutes to settle in, then in the second half, you show the world what you can do.' Instead of a pat on the back he ruffled Willie's hair, and sent him on for his first-team debut.

When Jack Taylor blew for half-time, Gordon disappeared down the tunnel and found Dipper sitting beneath his peg, still in his kit, still sulking. Gordon went over and ordered him to take a bath, and said that if he didn't he would be fined a week's wages. He went to take a pee himself in one of the cubicles, knocked back a large swig of whisky from the bottle inside his jacket, then went back to the dressing room, where Magic was working his way around the walking wounded. Mooro and Brownie were his main concerns. Broken noses were painful but Mooro had played on with worse, and with fresh wadding up both nostrils, a couple of painkillers and a fresh shirt, he was ready to go. David Brown had a nasty gash but the team doctor was there to put in a couple of stitches, bandage it, and then as Brownie sat with an ice pack on it, he felt up for another forty-five minutes, though he knew as well as anyone how hard it was going to be to come back from two-nil down.

Jules was complaining about his back, but a good rub with some placebo cream would put that right, and apart from some minor cuts and bruises everyone else seemed OK. Michael Kilbride sat quietly in the corner of the dressing room tightening his boots and waiting for the manager to speak, after which he would slip off to the toilets for a quick smoke. Morgan Rees turned and said to him, 'Bloody hell, Killer, you've nearly assassinated the hardest man in football. I don't think anybody saw it except me. Where did that come from?'

'Fuck knows. Not looking forward to playing them next season, mind,' and he laughed.

'All on camera too, pal. *Match of the Day* will be playing that one again and again. The day Chopper's bollocks got rearranged. Fucking brilliant, Killer.'

'Cheers, Taff.'

Charlie Gordon had returned from the shower room, having washed and dried his hands once more. He scratched his ear before he spoke, and if he was worried about the scoreline, he didn't show it.

'Gentlemen, we are still in this game, and for that I want to thank Jock. Jock, we owe this score to you. That penalty save was magnificent and it was not the only great save you made.' Other players echoed those sentiments. Jock nodded his appreciation.

'They are a good team, this lot, and once they'd gone one up they started kicking, and I'm proud of you all that you fought back like you did. Killer, if I'm asked about your assault on Ron Harris, I'll say I didn't see it. But between these four walls, I totally disapprove of violence, obviously, and I am fucking proud of you.' The players laughed as Brownie started a little chant – 'Kill-er, Kill-er, Kill-er' – and several joined in.

'Now, they are in there right now, saying more of the same – we're in control. But two-nil is a difficult score for any team to preserve as whoever scores the next goal often wins the game. If we get one, we'll get two, even three, believe me.

'Now, I know you were surprised I took off Dipper, who was

playing well. And I understand why he forgot what I said about corners. But an order is an order and a threat of punishment has to be carried out and to be taken seriously. Any corners, Killer and Clutch take them, Willie and Smudger drop back to cover. If you disobey I'll drag you off the field even though I've used the sub.

'Two changes I want to make. Smudger, swap wings with Willie and both of you get as many crosses in as you can. Nuts, I want you to drop ten yards short of Jules. Dempsey and Webb are a good pairing when they are next to each other, so we need to split them up. Now it goes without saying, if we concede another goal early on, we could be in trouble, so Mooro, stay very tight at the back.'

Gordon then paused and slowly looked at each one of them intently. 'Now go out and make some history.'

With that the referee's bell could be heard again signifying the end of the ten-minute break. Killer rushed into the toilets for another quick twenty-second smoke as a siren could be heard outside the ground – an ambulance taking someone to hospital. He so hoped it was Chopper Harris.

Chelsea were now playing towards the Shed End and the majority anticipated an easy victory, especially when substitute Alan Hudson smashed a right-foot shot against the left-hand post after fifty-three minutes. Willie Buchanan at this stage was still nervously awaiting his first real touch of the ball. He'd received a couple of passes from Taffy but had had to quickly pass the ball back or risk getting scythed by David Webb. The Chelsea pressure increased and Wilf Moore and his defenders were under siege, desperately protecting their goalmouth. Charlie Cooke, in Gordon's view the best player on the pitch, was now becoming an even bigger threat as defenders' legs got tired and he ducked and weaved his way through Rees and Dougie Jones who were both dragged deeper and deeper into defence.

Osgood continued to put himself about in the box, and when he slid into a tackle with Clutch Dyson he immediately realized his mistake as Dyson coolly picked himself up and gave Osgood one of his famous *you're going to pay for that* glares, which looked even more threatening when flashed with the black eye he was still nursing, a present from Eddie Gray in the Leeds game. Ten minutes later the debt was settled when Osgood found himself on the pitchside track with four red stripes down his calf from Dyson's studs. Jack Taylor had no alternative but to book Dyson who took the caution with a nod to Osgood without complaint; all square.

The crowd hurled abuse at Dyson. A few threw coins or toilet rolls. Dyson casually lobbed a toilet roll back towards the Shed.

It was thirteen minutes into the second half before Willie Buchanan got his first real touch of the ball in space on the right touchline. Jock Johnson rolled the ball out to Michael Kilbride who pushed it forward to Taffy Rees. As Baldwin lunged in to tackle, Rees shoved him off, looked up, and hit a crisp thirty-yard ball to Buchanan who was alone on the wing. He comfortably brought the ball down with his instep, and his running action and close control suggested confidence and skill not often associated with a seventeen-year-old. He effortlessly ghosted past John Hollins before picking up speed and pushing the ball fifteen yards past John Boyle. Although he'd given Boyle three yards' start his burst of pace got him there first and he managed to keep his balance even though Boyle tried to chop him down from behind. Rather than fall and win a free-kick Buchanan fought hard to steady his balance, keep his feet and keep the game flowing as Taylor allowed play to continue. On reaching the by-line he found time to look up and chip the ball into the centre of the goalmouth where Pemberton rose to bullet a header into the top corner of the net, well out of the reach of Peter Bonetti.

The away stand erupted. Having spent the half-time break reflecting on how they had been outclassed, and lucky just to be two down, now they were right back in it. They also sensed that the kid from Scotland might have some real potential. The scouts who watched hundreds of matches and travelled thousands of miles would be thinking the same thing.

Chelsea appeared rattled from the kick-off when Nulty sprinted at Charlie Cooke who was slowing the game, hanging on to the ball before moving it back to John Dempsey. Nulty's endeavour paid off and he won a throw-in fifteen yards inside the Chelsea half. This show of effort from Nulty inspired the rest of the team as he, Rees, Kilbride and Dyson all pushed ten yards forward. They sensed the Chelsea players were starting to lose their composure.

On sixty minutes the game was halted briefly when a drunken Chelsea fan ran out of the Shed End and charged at Michael Kilbride, clearly looking for revenge for the attack on Harris. He swung his fists but luckily for Killer the alcohol had hindered the fan's coordination so the blows were easily avoided and four orange-coated stewards ran on to apprehend him. They were within a yard of catching him when he reached the perimeter advertising signs and threw himself head-first into the Shed End crowd who broke his fall and helped him to vanish, while shouting abuse at the stewards. The police moved in but the offender seemed to have been lost in the melee.

Once play started again Jules Pemberton and Norman Nulty began to gel well together. Nulty was often unmarked when he dropped back into the deeper position as Gordon had instructed and he could see where the ball was most likely to break. In addition he was helping out in midfield, and after a goalmouth scramble following a corner, he was responsible for a clearance off his own goal-line. His extra stamina training was obviously paying off.

With most of the Chelsea attacks still going through Cooke on the right targeting Kilbride – now being booed every time he touched the ball – Tommy 'Clutch' Dyson had had a relatively quiet afternoon. With Harris off injured, Dyson was without doubt seen as the hardest player on the field, and he was not averse to finding opportunities to show it. After sixty-five minutes, Osgood headed a long throw from Bonetti wide to the wing. Alan Hudson, who'd found himself on the left flank, picked up the ball and interchanged a couple of short passes with John Hollins. Norman Nulty had chased back again and got in a good tackle, which nearly won him the ball from Hollins, but it broke free fifteen yards from David Webb and Kenny Swain – and fifteen yards from Clutch Dyson. It was a classic fifty-fifty-ball situation. All three players sprinted to the ball and they all arrived at the same time. None of them took the risk of being the last person into the tackle and all three left the ground two yards from the ball, launching themselves above the ball and into each other's shins, ankles and knees, which were always vulnerable on these occasions.

A sickening crunch was heard, even above the noise on the terraces, and Taylor ran over frantically blowing his whistle while trying to work out who if anyone had committed a foul, or, if all three had, what he should do next. As he did, Clutch was up on his feet and he began to run down the field with the ball leaving the carnage of two prostrate bodies behind him. Webb was rolling around holding his knee, and Swain was lying perfectly still holding his right shin, which indicated a far more serious injury. Webb was lucky he was wearing shin pads to cushion the blow but Swain's shin pad had been ripped off in the tackle and blood was flowing from his leg.

On hearing the referee's whistle Dyson came to a stop and slowly made his way back to the scene of the assault, tapping the ball between his feet as he walked. Dave Sexton and Ron Suart were going wild on the touchline, as was the whole East Stand as they watched the Chelsea physio attend to Webb, while Magic Rowland ran on to ask if they wanted him to see to Kenny Swain.

On reaching the stricken players Dyson said, 'What the bleedin' hell did you blow the whistle for? Another twenty yards and I could have got a shot in!'

Jack Taylor was still flustered by the incident and responded quietly, 'Clutch, don't fuck about, you're lucky I've not sent you off for this.'

Clutch rolled the ball onto his right instep, flicked it into the air, caught it, and lodged it under his arm.

'For what? We all went in fair and square for the tackle and I came out with the ball. This game's called football not fucking netball. I can't help it if somebody picks up the odd scratch in a tackle.'

Jack Taylor was not so understanding. He was still panting

from the twenty-five yard run he'd made to get to the scene. 'A bloody scratch? Somebody nearly got fucking killed.'

By this time Webb was back on his feet limping badly as the feeling returned to his shinbone. Swain was helped up by Hollins and he also limped around to see if he was fit enough to keep playing after Magic had bandaged his leg. Both physios jogged off the field and Taylor signalled a dropped-ball restart at the point where the three-way tackle took place. Dyson left it to Taffy Rees. Clutch slowly walked back to the right-back position smiling a little as the East Stand crowd showered him with abuse. A couple of irate Chelsea supporters tried to get onto the field to confront him, but this time the stewards were quicker, held them back, and then got the police to eject them. Meanwhile the away fans were singing, 'Who needs Ron Harris when you've got Clutch Dyson?'

A string of Chelsea attacks followed and they got the ball in the net for the third time, but it didn't count as Osgood was judged to be offside. Now it was the linesman getting all the abuse. As the game went on it looked very much like Dave Sexton had told the Chelsea team to keep it tight at the back and hold out for a 2–1 victory, which was a risky tactic.

Buchanan had seen little of the ball since making the first goal, but on seventy-five minutes, Brownie floated him a long pass which he took down expertly; but he did not have it fully under control when he felt the full force of David Webb's body as he crashed into him and they both ended up on the gravel track. Webb said nothing as they both stood up. He just glowered at Buchanan. Blood started to trickle from the shale scar on Webb's hip, but he ran back, unconcerned. One of Webb's metal studs had left a red stripe down Buchanan's thigh and ripped his sock, which was now around his ankle. He was starting to resemble the Burnley winger Dave Thomas whose rolled-down socks had become his trademark.

Buchanan took the throw-in and Jules passed the ball back to him with Webb ready to pounce again. But this time Buchanan had the time and the confidence to tempt Webb by showing him the ball; like a cat with a mouse, like Stanley Matthews with

Tommy Banks, drawing him into a tackle he never had a chance of making. As Webb fell for the bait Willie skipped around him and shot off up the field ready to take on John Dempsey who he easily rounded after stepping over the ball to send him the wrong way. The ball just seemed to stick to Buchanan's boots as he progressed down the wing and again clipped a great ball into the box. Kenny Swain was closely marking Jules Pemberton this time and neither won the ball cleanly as it ricocheted from Jules's head onto Swain's shoulder and then out towards the edge of the box.

Norman Nulty was ideally positioned just outside the eighteen-yard box, watching and waiting for his moment to pounce. As the ball fell from the Pemberton-Swain clash, he ran towards it, got there before John Hollins, and smashed the ball low past Bonetti from fifteen yards. Remembering Wilkins' celebration in the first half, Nuts retrieved the ball from the net and kicked it into the crowd. Then he ran towards the bench where Ronnie Winston and George Brady were hugging each other, and Charlie Gordon was smiling up at Stan Moffitt.

Gordon then turned to see how Willie Buchanan was reacting to the goal. Nuts scored it, but it was very much Willie's goal. So would he encourage the fans' applause for him, or would he return into a huddle with his teammates and share the moment with them? Gordon was delighted to see that Willie's celebratory instinct was to jump into the pack of bodies that had piled onto Norman Nulty in celebration of a great team goal. Amid the euphoria Charlie Gordon was beginning to realize that young Buchanan had the chance of being a top, even world-class player and his gamble on the first-half substitution had proved to be a good one. As he looked to the sky it might have seemed that he was thanking the Lord for this good fortune, but he was a non-believer. He was quietly reminding himself to thank Geoffrey Raymond for introducing him to a scruffy, spotty-faced young kid in a plain white T-shirt.

As they reassembled for their sixth kick-off of the day, the Chelsea back four began to argue about who should have been picking up Nulty; no one took the blame. It was back to all-square at 2–2. So much for Dave Sexton's 'kill it by half-time' game plan. Ron Suart stood helpless with the look of a player-turned-coach who wished he was back on the field in his full-back position. How well Charlie Gordon knew that feeling. But their day had been and gone. The future was now in the hands of talents like Wilkins and Buchanan.

There were only five minutes left on the clock when Charlie Cooke beat the offside trap and found himself one-on-one with goalkeeper Jock Johnson. Only yesterday George Munro had sent Gordon a note saying that in a one-on-one situation, when a forward breaks away with only the goalkeeper to beat, dribbling around the keeper gave an attacker twice as good a chance of scoring than shooting. Thankfully, Cooke shot. Johnson saved, though he conceded a corner.

Nothing materialized from Chelsea's outswinging corner, Dempsey heading well wide for a goal-kick. Jock Johnson put the ball down for what he hoped would be his last touch of the game. A replay was looking likely when a tired Jack Taylor again looked at his watch.

From the goal-kick Pemberton rose above Dempsey and headed the ball wide to Buchanan, who dribbled to the by-line before Webb caught up with him and pushed the ball out for a corner. It would surely be the last corner of the game.

Remembering Charlie Gordon's instructions, Michael Kilbride ran from his left-back position across to the right wing to take the corner kick. As he stood against an advertising hoarding in the corner of the pitch, some Chelsea fans tried to hold Kilbride back but soon stewards were on hand to push them back into the terraces. This created even more noise as Killer realized that he only had three paces to the corner flag, again reminding him that Stamford Bridge was one of the most intimidating football grounds in England – not only could you touch the supporters, you could also smell their breath. As he curled the ball into the near post with his left foot, the angle was perfect. Bonetti was stranded at the back post and didn't have a chance to get near the ball as a dozen bodies blocked his way. Moore, Dempsey, Swain, Brown and Dyson all frantically challenged for the ball in the air and as they crashed into each other, no one got a clean head to it.

The ball pin-balled around and hit Kenny Swain's knee before bouncing between Pemberton and Webb whose flailing legs could neither score nor clear the ball. In the midst of this melee, Norman Nulty appeared from nowhere and toe-poked the ball, which seemed to take an age to cross the line, but with Bonetti grounded, and nobody left behind him, cross the line it did. It was a scrappy, untidy goal scored by a man who was quickly regaining his scoring touch. But it counted just the same as Jules's bullet header and his earlier brilliantly timed drive. The away supporters were now rampant and songs about playing at Wembley could be heard as the Chelsea players desperately tried to get the game restarted, and the referee tried to bring the goal celebrations to an end.

Taylor told Moore and Webb that there were two minutes of added time left to play. Chelsea kicked off and immediately made their way down the field, Sexton screaming from the touchline, over and over, 'Get the ball in the fucking box!'

He stamped in frustration when Charlie Cooke chose to dribble the ball around Michael Kilbride when it would have been easier for him to cross it. Killer got his foot to the ball, tapped it to his left and smashed it deep into the East Stand for a throw-in. It was good fortune that long-throw expert Ian Hutchinson hadn't played today. He was still blighted by injuries, which included two broken legs, a broken arm, a broken toe and persistent knee trouble. But today it was a mere bout of 'flu that had kept him out of the team.

So David Webb took the throw-in, which reached the six-yard line, and in the centre of a cluster of bodies Wilf Moore's blond head and blood-stained shirt was seen rising above them all to head the ball out for a corner. The away fans were whistling for the game to end. Charlie Gordon was screaming for the final whistle. But the referee allowed the corner to be taken. Charlie Cooke crossed in another outswinger. But it was too near the keeper. Jock Johnson ran out to catch it, and then collapsed to the ground, keeping the ball safely beneath him. Surely that was it. Johnson bounced the ball twice, three times, four times, then ran to the edge of the box, and as he kicked it into the London air, Jack Taylor blew his whistle, and sent several thousand away fans into a delirium that had not seemed possible an hour ago.

Somewhere in the crowd, Malcolm and Mairi Buchanan were hugging each other. Catriona was close to tears as she watched Willie being hugged and embraced by his teammates. He had made two of the goals, and made the corner that led to the winner, and he had made her feel prouder than she had ever felt in her life.

Michael Kilbride was the first to throw his shirt into the away supporters who had travelled down hoping and praying for a moment like this. Others followed. A few Chelsea fans came onto the pitch looking for trouble, but the police and stewards quickly got them under control. Wilf Moore shook hands with a number of Chelsea players as he quickly made his way to the dressing room to allow Magic Rowland and Joss Partington to assess his broken nose. Charlie Gordon strode directly to Dave Sexton, who despite the obvious pain he was feeling gave his heartfelt congratulations; and later, as the party atmosphere started to develop in the away dressing room, the Chelsea manager sent in the case of champagne he had planned to give to his own players.

As the champagne was sprayed around the room, and players who minutes earlier could barely walk or run because of injury now danced around naked as though they were children without a care in the world, Stan Moffitt and Matthew Stock came in to offer their congratulations. Brownie immediately drenched both of them with champagne. But just as Gordon had been strict with his rule about corners, there was another rule he needed to enforce now.

'Stan, it's a great win and it's great to see you, but you know the rules, no directors in the dressing rooms. I'll see you in the boardroom for a celebratory drink in about fifteen minutes, and you can congratulate the players on the coach to the hotel.' Sheepishly, and annoyed, the chairman and his would-be replacement walked out.

As the door closed, over in the corner Joss Partington and

Magic looked like they were re-enacting a scene from *MASH* as the walking wounded waited their turn to climb onto the treatment table. In another corner Willie Buchanan sat quietly still in a dream after being showered not just with champagne but with praise from all his teammates. Gordon knew within ten minutes of putting him on the field that the kid was going to be a great player; he could smell it.

DD Marland, in collar and tie, was quietly shuffling around the room congratulating his teammates, as yet unaware that thanks to Gordon's old friend Alfie Ruse, and head porter Paddy O'Connell, the manager knew exactly what he had been up to all night. Gordon led a simple life built on a solid foundation of honesty, integrity and humility all blended together with a big helping of friendship. And again his principles had paid off, when Alfie Ruse decided he could no longer hide from his friend and former teammate the cynical plan of Chelsea owner Bernie Yaakov to use his lady friend to wear out an opposing player. This simple repayment of previous favours had won Charlie the game today. Nobody would know why he had chosen to leave DD Marland out of the team, but one day, in a quiet smoky pub in the heart of Glasgow, Charlie planned to share a whisky and Canada Dry with Alfie Ruse, to say thanks. And whether DD learned from the episode would dictate whether he turned his talent into something meaningful, or joined the long list of footballers who almost made it to the top.

As the noise settled down, David Brown stood naked on the treatment table, and raised a toast to Michael Kilbride. 'Gentlemen, will you please raise your glasses to the dirtiest fucking player in the history of football. Chopper Harris is now in hospital walking to the toilet with his bollocks in a brickie's wheelbarrow. If he's very lucky, his next shag will be on Boxing Day, so please show your appreciation for football's favourite silent assassin, Michael "The Hitman" Killer KKKIIIIILLLLL-BBBRRRIIIDDDE!!!!!!!!!!!'

The dressing room again exploded and Killer was showered with champagne as he sat quietly in the corner embarrassed by the adulation, protectively cupping his lit cigarette in his left hand.

Jock Johnson was happy with his game and appreciative of the praise from his manager. Taffy Rees, Dougie Jones and Smudger Smith had also performed well, and Frank Temple had now cooled down and acknowledged his mistake. The manager had got it right. The game was won by an inswinging corner, which had created a scrappy goal. If Dipper had stayed on the pitch, making his own decisions, the game would have been lost. Through the next week Charlie Gordon would work hard with Frank Temple, as he knew that he would need him later as the season came to a close. He also made a mental note to send both young George Munro and director Geoffrey Raymond a case of champagne as they had both played a major role in today's victory.

Charlie Gordon, Jules Pemberton, Norman Nulty and Michael Kilbride were all asked by the BBC for an interview after the game for both *Grandstand* and *Match of the Day*.

When Kilbride was asked about the incident with Chopper Harris he simply replied, 'I just went in for the ball,' prompting a smile from the interviewer.

John Motson added in his report that the statement from the Chelsea hospital suggested that Ron Harris would be 'kept in overnight for observation', and Motson asked Killer if he had a message for Ron.

'Please pass on my good wishes to Chopper for a speedy recovery. Any one of us could have got hurt in the incident and Ron was just unlucky it was him.'

At shortly after six o'clock the skips were loaded, the interviews were finished, the stadium was empty and the coach was ready to leave Stamford Bridge.

Willie sat next to 'Professor' Walter Graham who hadn't featured in the game but who had been among the first to congratulate the young man on his debut.

'You had a great game today, son. But remember this, football is a two-day wonder; by Tuesday morning it's all forgotten about, and you then have to concentrate on the next game and do it all over again. So enjoy the weekend and don't get carried away. Football fame is short-lived. And if you need a reminder of that, take a look at the back seat right now.'

There, all alone, no doubt feeling he ought to be sharing in the happiness but unable fully to do so, was DD Marland, the most expensive signing in the club's history, who had missed out on their greatest game of the season so far.

Willie was still in a daze. His appearance on the field was nothing like what he had expected. 'When we were two-nil down, I thought there is no way I'll get on, and when Dipper took that corner, I'd forgotten too that he wasn't supposed to. So when the boss suddenly says, "Warm up, son, you're on," I honestly couldn't believe it. Maybe it was best like that, I had no time to think.'

'You did well, son. Those first two goals, you made them, no doubt.'

On the way out of the stadium a string of journalists had tried to interview him as he helped load the skips onto the coach. Even though he had played an important part in the victory, Charlie Gordon had insisted that he help tidy the dressing room and support Charlie Sinclair.

'I can't wait to ring my girlfriend.'

'Did you see her?'

'No.'

'That's the thing about crowds. They can all see you, but you can't see them.'

'I felt them though. I felt them supporting me. I didn't feel nervous at all, not once I got the first touch behind me.'

The coach was scheduled to drop chairman Stan Moffitt at the Great Western Hotel. Moffitt had been planning to meet his wife Gloria, take her for a quick dinner and then go straight to the Roxy Music concert at the Royal Albert Hall. But during the match, the Chelsea club secretary had taken a call to pass on the message that Gloria had slipped getting into the taxi outside their home and sprained her ankle badly. She'd had it X-rayed and had no broken bones, but was told to rest and hadn't made the trip to London after all.

Stan Moffitt decided he would pick up his clothes from the Great Western, leave his tickets for Roxy Music with the head porter – who'd looked after them so well – to do with as he pleased, and then get back on the coach to head home with the team.

A historic win had mellowed even Charlie Gordon, who, having earlier been a bit irritated at having to give the chairman a lift back to the hotel, because it meant breaking his own rule about having no directors on the bus, now grabbed the microphone and announced to his players: 'Lads, we have to make a little detour back to the hotel so the chairman can pick up his stuff and head back with us. So there will be a short interlude, and given how brilliant you have been today I suggest I buy you all a drink in the Fountains Abbey pub on Praed Street and then we can set off again at half seven, and we'll stock up with fish and chips before we hit the motorway.'

'And I'm paying!' announced Moffitt, to cheers from all around the coach.

33

TEMPTATION

Saturday 9 March, early evening

At a few minutes before six o'clock Merlyn Rees arrived in an unmarked car at the tradesmen's entrance behind the Great Western Hotel to be met by head porter Paddy O'Connell. Rees had stayed at the hotel a couple of times before but this was his first time as Secretary of State for Northern Ireland, and so he had a protection officer in his car, and three more in the car behind.

'Good evening, sir,' said Paddy in a quiet voice, for the first time ever not making eye contact with a hotel guest. 'Please follow me.'

Rees turned to his driver and instructed, 'I'll be back in twenty minutes, keep the engine running to keep the car warm.'

O'Connell guided the minister to the service lift, a bodyguard ahead of them, and another behind. They took the lift to the fifth floor, and walked down the empty corridor to Room 501, which had been reserved for Rees. O'Connell led him in, switched on the lights, and showed him where everything was. Rees threw his small overnight bag on the bed and switched on the TV, keen to catch the news, but also the football scores. Though a Leeds fan, he said he had a nephew, Morgan Rees, who was playing in the big game at Chelsea today.

'What was the final score?' he asked O'Connell as he was leaving the room.

'Chelsea lost three-two, sir. Sounds like it was a real battle. They were here last night.'

'I know, I heard that on the radio but missed the result. I was hoping they might have the goals on the news.'

The mention of a relative totally unconnected to politics made O'Connell feel even worse about the mission in which he was now involved. Rees was just a human being, the same as him, although doing a very different kind of job. Everything about him suggested he was a nice guy, yet he was about to go downstairs and make a phone call to the safe house in Ealing and utter the simple words '*Just to let you know Patricia got home safely.*' It was clear the bodyguards had no suspicion whatever about the porter. It was clear too, and this was the coded significance of the word 'safely' in the message, that the room would be unguarded when Rees went out for dinner, as Paddy had ascertained the minister's entire protection team would be going with him. They hung around in the corridor while he showed the minister around. He then said he would be waiting for him in his office ready to escort him back to his car. All he or his bodyguards had to do was to ring the extension on the card, which he handed him along with the room key, Room 501.

It was 'Paul' who answered O'Connell's call, and on hearing the words '*Just to let you know Patricia got home safely,*' he said, 'Great to hear, give her our best,' and put the phone down.

It was the cue for 'Paul' to call 'Peter' and 'Pamela', waiting at a phone box at Ealing Broadway Station, and say, 'All on. See you back here later.' He had with him three flight tickets to Belfast City Airport from Heathrow, Gatwick and Manchester. Three drivers, all IRA sympathizers working in London, were on hand to drive to the respective airports. Two suitcases in the back of each car contained the terrorists' only possessions for what would be a longish period of lying low.

'Peter' and 'Pamela' had both dressed as smartly as either of them had dressed for years: him in a dark suit, blue shirt and red tie and her in grey skirt, plain cream blouse and navy jacket and carrying a worn brown leather briefcase. He had a second briefcase inside a sports bag. They'd had to endure an unmelodic busker singing Terry Jacks' 'Seasons in the Sun' to an audience of none just outside the station entrance. The words *Goodbye Papa please pray for me, I was the black sheep of the family* made Colleen wonder what her father Frank Connor would think of her now, fighting the cause, the Irish cause – his cause.

They made the entire Tube journey in an awkward silence. He hated her with a passion; she scared him and the sooner he could get away from the bitch, the better. They exchanged neither looks nor words all the way to Paddington. Each knew their instructions well and luckily no further dialogue was needed. Within ninety minutes they would be back at this station, out of these stupid clothes and then on their way to Belfast. Job done...

By 6.20 p.m. the train had arrived at Paddington. They slowly walked through to the main station platform, to the foot of the stairway leading up to the hotel where they found the notice board. 'Peter' checked that the notice '*Grandma, ring home. Urgent. Pete and Pam*' had been pinned up. It had. They then moved over to the bronze Brunel statue to wait for Paddy to take down the notice.

At 6.23 p.m., Merlyn Rees was washed, shaved and being escorted to the service lift by Paddy O'Connell and two bodyguards. The porter had been told to observe whether one of the bodyguards stayed outside the room, and report that information to 'Paul' as soon as the minister left the building. Neither of them did, exactly as expected. One bodyguard got into the front seat of Rees's car, the other joined his colleagues in the car behind. O'Connell said to the bodyguard in the front, 'Call me when you're leaving the dinner and I will come down and open up again.'

'OK, no problem. It'll be half ten latest.'

Then Rees shouted through from the back of the car, 'Can you organize me a wake-up call for half past six.'

'Yes sir, no problem,' said O'Connell, his voice weak.

As the two-car convoy drove off, Paddy felt almost sick with anxiety and self-hatred. Nonetheless, he then hurried down to the station platform.

At 6.30 p.m. as planned he took the two drawing pins out of the brown cork board, folded the paper notice and put it in his trouser pocket.

As Paddy took down the notice, 'Peter' reached into the briefcase and carefully pushed in the self-winding hand to set the Smiths Combat pocket watch in motion. The timer was set to delay until midnight. It was always a tense moment, but he'd been there before, and had a hundred per cent hit rate with his delayed timer explosives. His hands were steady. He smiled, pleased there was not even a trace of sweat on him. Below the timer lay six pounds of gelignite, a dozen sticks of explosives wrapped with bags of shrapnel.

He now just wanted this to be over. A loner, he felt uncomfortable in these clothes and in this company. Suits reminded him of funerals, especially the funeral of his wife and young son. To his mind, Secretary of State for Northern Ireland was as Establishment as it got, and he stroked the briefcase tenderly, telling himself that when that device inside went off at midnight, his revenge would be advanced if not complete. He also knew he would have to lie low, and that would give him time to find his father.

They then followed Paddy to the room.

As Paddy moved across the platform a young receptionist asked him, 'Did you find her?'

'Sorry?'

'Did you find her?' she repeated.

'Did I find who?' Paddy replied, puzzled.

'The old lady who has to ring home. And who's Pete and Pam?'

'Oh yes, everything's fine. I took the two youngsters to ring their grandmother at the hotel recep''on, she's fine. Now, I've just got to check something at the service lift.'

He called the lift, the three of them entered, and button five sent them on their way to the fifth floor. Paddy, dressed in his porter's uniform, checked the corridor was clear and led 'Peter' and 'Pamela' to Room 501, which he unlocked with his master key.

As they entered the room 'Pamela' turned to Paddy and simply said, 'Where?'

Paddy lifted the mattress, and beneath it was a ready-made space in the bed's wooden frame. 'Pamela' placed the briefcase carefully into it, Paddy remade the bed just as carefully, 'Peter' took the second identical briefcase from his sports bag and handed it to 'Pamela'. They looked around, nodded to each other, and left the room. When back in the lift, Paddy pressed the button for the ground floor. They came down, he escorted them to the same side door used by Rees, and without any goodbyes, off they went. Paddy O'Connell looked at his watch. It was 6.38 p.m.

At 6.45 p.m. Cockie turned down Praed Street and parked the team coach directly outside the Great Western Hotel, to the delight of a group of fans who just happened to be passing by.

'OK, lads,' said Charlie Gordon. 'This is not a three-line whip. If any of you want to stay on the coach and rest, no problem. But if any of you want a quick pint on the gaffer, follow me to the Fountains Abbey.'

The cheers suggested there would be few if any staying on the coach. 'Back on the coach by seven fifteen, then. One minute later and it's a twenty-five-pound fine.' Now came a chorus of boos, but it was all the kind of good-humoured team stuff Charlie Gordon had loved all his life.

'I won't be long, Charlie,' said Stan Moffitt. 'I just need to pack, and phone home to make sure Gloria's OK. Shall I see you at the pub?'

'Yeah. You can get the second round, then we can hit the road, OK?'

'Sounds good.'

One of their supporters had a copy of the *Saturday Pink*, the front-page headline proclaiming 'WHAT A COMEBACK – supersub Buchanan turns things around'. Charlie Gordon took it to the young Scot and said, 'Save that for your mum's scrapbook, son.'

Willie looked up at him, then down at the paper, and said,

'Are you sure I should be coming to the pub, boss? I'm only seventeen.'

'Come on, son, I'll stand you a shandy. Don't forget you're Scottish!'

He walked into the bar, where the club's Devon and Cornwall supporters' branch, waiting for a train back to Plymouth and Truro, could scarcely believe their eyes as the manager and most of his players walked in. Gordon ordered himself a large Scotch, a shandy for Willie, and opened a tab for the whole pub.

He knocked down his whisky, ordered another, and shouted to his players, 'Fill your fuckin' boots, lads, but be on that coach at quarter past seven.'

Only Walter Graham, a strict teetotaller, remained on the coach, using the quiet to rest his eyes, knowing he had a few hours of reading ahead of him. Cockie made his way outside and lifted the vertically opening door to the storage compartment in readiness for the chairman's luggage. He climbed back in the coach and sat alone behind the wheel reflecting on his failed attempted robbery the night before. Room 427, lesbo lovers. What a disaster. He could laugh to himself about it now, and he would hit it next time, maybe if they reached the final; if not they had Arsenal away last game of the League season. But he hated leaving these trips empty-handed.

Moffitt was down in a matter of minutes. He just had a couple of light bags and a suit carrier, and Cockie packed them away for him.

'So where is this pub they're all drinking dry?' he asked.

'It's the Fountains Abbey,' said Cockie. 'Down there on the right.'

'I think I can hear them,' the chairman laughed, and set off.

'Don't forget, Mr Chairman, we're leaving at quarter past seven, sharp.'

He looked at his watch. He had twenty-three minutes to wait. Obviously he couldn't drink, not when he had such a precious cargo to take home. As he went to close the hold, he saw his beloved key briefcase packed in between the kit and the medical skips. 427 might have been a disaster, he said to himself. But what about 501, where he had stayed last night? Was the gaffer's sudden desire for a drink-up perhaps a sign, certainly a stroke of luck, that meant he didn't have to go empty-handed after all? Serendipity.

'Prof, are you staying on the coach?' he asked Walter Graham.

'Yeah, not moving from here, Cockie.'

'Can you just keep an eye on things then? I've just got someone I need to see. Won't be long.'

'No problem.'

He went back to the hold, flicked open his briefcase and took out the key to Room 501. His heart was now beating fast. He shut the briefcase, then picked up a sports bag lying on top of the now empty food containers.

The head porter, Paddy O'Connell, had now come out to see why the team was back at the hotel. Cockie said to him they were all having a drink in the Fountains Abbey, and added: 'Can you keep an eye on the hold for me, Paddy? I'm just going for a dump before we head back. Are you feeling OK, Paddy? You look pale.'

'Not a problem, Dermot, always a pleasure to work with you guys. So glad you won. And very nice of Mr Moffitt to give me his Roxy Music tickets. I've just made a young American honeymoon couple very, very happy. Yep, I'm feeling OK, just been working too hard I guess.'

Dermot could feel the obsession's grip tightening as he walked through the hotel lobby, then went to the house phone on the reception desk and dialled Room 501. No reply. He would normally dial at least twice over a ten-minute period, but he didn't have the time. He had to strike now. He rang again, let it ring eight times, then made for the lifts. He had no time to wait for all three lifts to become available but noted that lift number 1 was at the seventh floor and number 3 at the sixth. He walked into lift number 2 and pressed the button to the sixth floor, then walked down a flight of stairs, and straight to the room where last night he had slept so fitfully after his Room 427 'lesbos' cock-up. The corridor was empty, so he took out the key for 501, tapped on the door, said 'Room service', and on hearing nothing, opened the door and walked in.

He quickly opened his sports bag and laid it on the bed. He could feel his heart pounding. There was a suit hanging in the wardrobe. No way he could take that. There was a ten-pound note on the bedside table, a pair of cufflinks and a few coins, which he scooped up and dropped into the bag. The bathroom made clear it was a man sleeping alone, and nothing worth taking apart from an electric razor and a leather shaving bag. He was already into the forties on his counting, and his pulse was beginning to race, so he left them. He jumped onto a chair and examined the top of the cupboards – nothing. He ran his hands between the pillows, and inside the pillowcases, where once he had made his biggest ever cash discovery. Nothing. He was up to seventy-two now as he picked up a pair of slippers and a small alarm clock. He looked under the bed. Nothing but a pair of discarded socks. He then lifted the mattress, and ran his hands underneath. He felt a crack in the wooden frame, lifted the mattress a little higher.

'Bingo! You fucking beauty.'

He took the briefcase from its secret hiding place under the bed, and tried to flick it open. A combination lock made that impossible, for now, but he would work it out in his Aladdin's Cave immediately he got home. Whatever is in there must be valuable, he thought, for the occupant to go to all that trouble. Cash? Diamonds? Even though he never spent or sold what he stole, he got a bigger kick the more valuable the theft. He was up to ninety-four in his counting, and knew he would get nothing better than this. But then he noticed a bottle of House of Commons whisky hiding behind a bedside table. It had been signed by Harold Wilson no less. Definitely worth having. He stashed the bottle and the heavy briefcase into his sports bag, now at one hundred and twenty-three in his counting, zipped up his bag and began to make his journey back to the coach. He switched off the light and in the darkness removed his gloves. He opened the door with one glove, carefully wiping the door handle, which he'd used on the way in. He then slipped the gloves into the side compartment of the bag. The corridor was still empty.

Job complete, taking deep breaths to try to calm himself, he walked cautiously down the stairs, so as not to bump into anyone in the lifts, and lit a cigarette to calm himself a little more. He then headed out through reception to load his bags onto the coach.

He could feel his pulse hammering inside his head. He lived for this feeling, and for the calm that would follow once they were halfway up the motorway, and he could visualize the panic and the fuss as the theft was reported and nobody ever gave a thought to the little Irish feller who drove the coach of that team that just beat Chelsea in the Cup.

Cockie climbed inside the hold to rearrange a few of the skips and bags. He then put both his key briefcase and the one he had just taken from Room 501, which was really heavy, inside his sports bag. He packed them in the far corner, so that everything else would be taken off first when finally they arrived back at the training ground, before he made the last part of the journey to Cochrane's yard, where he would stash his latest theft with the hundreds of others in his collection. He then slammed the doors shut.

As Cockie arrived at the pub, to remind Gordon he had said they would be leaving at 7.15 sharp, Killer Kilbride was on the phone to his wife, asking her if she thought Harris was a good name for their baby if it was a boy.

'Harris?' she asked.

'It's just a thought,' he said. But he could tell from the reaction it was not one she shared.

Overhearing the conversation got Willie thinking about the name of the child Catriona was carrying. He would be barely eighteen when he became a dad, but he felt she was mature enough, and that he would grow into the role, just as he had grown into the role of footballer today.

He took Cockie to one side, and asked him, 'Do you think it

would be really naff, if we had a boy, that I named him after the gaffer?'

Cockie sighed. 'Charlie Buchanan?'

'Yeah.'

'What about Gordon Buchanan? Makes it less obvious.'

'That's a great idea. I hope Catriona likes that. I'm sure she will.'

'And at least you won't have to raise him on an apprentice salary, son. You are going places, believe me.'

Gordon settled the bill, which, once he had added a big tip, went into three figures. The players said goodbye to the West Country supporters, then they all headed back to the coach. The only one who missed the 7.15 deadline was the manager, who had allowed himself a final double as he paid.

'That one's on the house, Charlie,' said the landlord who, as a Tottenham fan, was thrilled they had knocked Chelsea out of the Cup. 'You're welcome here any time.'

As he finally climbed up the steps of the coach, the players were chanting 'Fine the boss, fine the boss, fine the boss', which Gordon took in good heart as he sat down beside Stan Moffitt.

'Come on, Stan,' he said, slapping the chairman on the thigh, 'be honest with me now: if we had lost, was I a goner?'

'Charlie, we didn't lose. We fucking won, and it was all down to you. Just enjoy it, and let's look forward to the draw for the semis.'

The smell of a kebab Wilf Moore had bought on the way back from the pub was wafting down to the front.

'Put your fucking shoes back on, Mooro!' shouted Cockie.

'I'm fine with it, Cockie. The best thing about a broken nose is you can't smell a thing.'

Nuts was reading aloud from the report in the *Sporting Pink*, especially loudly when it got to the description of his goals, though he carefully avoided the references to him being recalled to replace an 'out of form DD Marland'.

Once the manager and chairman were settled, Ronnie Winston walked up and down the coach just to check everyone was back. Was Charlie Gordon being a little paranoid when he noticed the embarrassed eye contact Ronnie made with Stan Moffitt? Was there a hint of 'Tomorrow's meeting cancelled – till further notice'?

As the coach pulled out, and they were waved off by Paddy O'Connell and a few supporters who had followed them from the pub, Cockie switched on the radio, and turned it up full blast when their match report came on, John Motson's words regularly cheered by the players as they relived the day.

'*At two-nil, thanks to goals from Wilkins and Osgood, the Blues must have thought they were cruising to the semi-finals. And how must Charlie Cooke be feeling tonight? Man of the Match for many, but his missed penalty...*'

'It wasn't fucking missed, I fucking saved it!' shouted Jock Johnson.

'One Jock Johnson... there's only one Jock Johnson,' sang his teammates.

'*Even so, nobody could have predicted the second-half comeback,*' Motson's report continued.

'The fucking gaffer did, Motty, you numpty,' shouted Mooro.

'*But nobody counted on the skills of a special young talent seen for the first time today, a tiny young Scot...*'

'Oh Willie-Willie, Willie-Willie-Willie-Willie Bu-chan-an!' chanted David Brown, the man whose bullying had almost driven Willie home, now standing and leading the singing of his name.

Motson was now winding up for a big finish.

Buchanan, who reminded so many of us of a young Willie Morgan or Dave Thomas, even dare we say it a young George Best, made the first two goals by making older and much more experienced Chelsea players look, frankly, foolish, and he forced the corner that led to the winner, as scrappy a goal as you will see from Norman Nulty, who poked the ball past Bonetti, in the last few minutes. But nobody cared how scrappy it was. It was the winner in a game that will live long in the memory, and not just for the goals. There were several bookings, but amazingly none for an incident in which Ron Harris of all people was stretchered off after what looked like a deliberate kick in the most delicate area of all by left-back Michael Kilbride, who claimed afterwards he was only going for the ball. I think he might have meant balls.

Motson's little joke prompted a new chant to go up, to the tune of 'We'll Support You Evermore' . . . 'Kill-er Kil-bride, Kill-er Kil-bride . . . kicked the Chopper in the nuts . . . kicked the Chopp-er in the nuts!'

Cockie turned to Gordon and said, 'First decent chip shop I see, gaffer? Or crack on a bit?'

'Tell you what, Cockie, let's get up nearer the start of the motorway first.'

Fish and chips was the staple diet for modern footballers on the way home from an away game.

Morgan Rees meanwhile was singing one of the two songs he knew, Tom Jones's 'Delilah', and though everyone joined in the first time, by the second it was down to half a dozen, and by the third Cockie turned on the microphone and announced, 'Unless someone shuts up that tuneless fucking sheep-shagger, I'm not stopping for fish and chips.'

Charlie Gordon asked George Brady if he would go down the coach and ask Frank Temple to pop down to see him.

Still angry, Dipper made his way down to the front, hoping nobody would notice him, but David Brown shouted, 'Dipper, tell him one good thing that came out of today's game was that they've no need to wash your strip – as you weren't on the field long enough to get a bleeding sweat on.'

Gordon had asked Stan Moffitt to sit across the way so that Frank Temple could join him.

A subdued Dipper Temple slouched down in the seat next to his manager.

'Frank, I want to apologize to you for any embarrassment I've caused you today. You are a terrific player and you still have a good career ahead of you. But today you made a mistake and I needed to make my point, not just to you, but also to the rest of the team. When you lads are out there on the field, there's not much I can do to influence the game apart from the instructions

I give you regarding set plays. It's essential that you follow my instructions and the *only* option I have, if you choose not to listen to them, is to substitute you. I've nothing else open to me.'

'I understand. I was just, you know ...'

'Of course I do, and I have no problem with you being angry at being hooked. I want players desperate to play. I don't want you ever to forget how you felt being taken off today.'

'I won't.'

'Learn from it. I saw in the programme against Forest when you were the "player profile", you said you want to be a manager one day.'

'I do, yeah.'

'Well, two things to say to you. One, being a manager is about the tough decisions not the easy ones. But two, by the time you are a manager, you are going to have a whole mass of data and information to help you make the big calls. That's what I did today, I just didn't have time to explain it all. I'm going to do that on Monday. But there is a young lad I know, he couldn't kick his way out of a paper bag, but I am going to ask the chairman if we can hire him, and I want you to sit down and learn from him when you do your badges. OK?'

'OK, gaffer. Thanks for that.'

'No problem. And don't forget, Dipper, when fans recite the team that beat Chelsea in the FA Cup in 1974, you're on that list. You played your part. Now go and tell Taffy to have a fucking sleep.'

The rain had started to fall by the time Cockie eventually spotted a decent-looking fish and chip shop on the Finchley Road. Most of the players were hungry even though they had filled up with sandwiches immediately after the match in the players' bar. They'd even eaten some of the food reserved for the Chelsea team who were all still in the home dressing room, probably trying to figure out what had gone wrong.

'My treat, don't forget,' announced the chairman, who grabbed an umbrella and ran in with Magic, who knew exactly what to order.

*

Was there any group of people, Wilf Moore thought to himself, quite like a professional sports team? Maybe in the military you would find groups like this, or an orchestra perhaps, but anywhere else? He doubted it very much. There were coaches all over the country right now transporting groups of men almost identical to this. They wouldn't all be as happy as this group. Hardly any of them would. But they would have known happiness, like they had all known sadness. It's just that every team he had ever played for, from when he was a young kid starting out with Hartlepool, it was like this. There were clever ones, stupid ones, funny ones, dull ones, happy ones, sad ones, laid-back ones, neurotic ones.

He had, rarely for him, wandered to the loners' section of the bus, and was sitting alone in the middle of the back row, DD Marland sleeping – or pretending to sleep – on the row in front. He was not a big drinker and the two and a half pints at the pub had quenched his thirst, but also made him feel tired, and a bit sentimental. He often was. He loved a good cry at a film.

As often happened when he was feeling happy, he thought of death, his own and that of others. He wondered how many of these guys would come to his funeral if they were still alive, and how many of their funerals he would go to if he was still going. What a morbid fucking thought to be having when you've just led your team in knocking arrogant, cocky Chelsea out of the FA Cup! But no, it wasn't morbid. It underlined how close they were to each other.

If the gaffer died, yeah, we're all at that one I think, he said to himself. Maybe not DD, unless he gets himself in gear and learns the boss was right to drop him. Dipper will be hating him now too, but he knows he owes him a lot. I reckon the Prof would get a good turnout. He is a real team man, keeps himself to himself, but we all know we can count on him. Look at the way he is mentoring that young lad from Aberdeen, making sure he knows he did well but also making sure he keeps his feet on the ground. There's a few that would be there at mine, for sure, he assured himself. What was it Killer had said when they were celebrating in the dressing room, and Brownie had toasted him? 'Never mind me, the player we should be thanking is our fucking skipper. He is a leader of fucking men.' That meant a lot to Mooro, sitting there now with his nose all bandaged up.

Brownie – what about Brownie? I mean, there's not one of us, from Jock the oldest to Willie the youngest, who hasn't had reason to curse his fucking tongue and his nastiness at training, and his moaning, whining all day long, Monday to Friday. But he showed it again today, didn't he? He's a special sort of player, so I reckon he would get a good turnout, too, and we'd all stand around telling stories about what a bastard he was, but we did like him, because when it came to matchday he was there for you, always. Clutch is the same. Horrible to play against, great to have on your team. Killer Kilbride, he's a strange one, but my God he has written himself into legend today. That tackle on Chopper Harris we'll be talking about for the rest of our lives, including in his eulogy. Yeah, we'll all be there for that one. Smudger Smith, not the brightest, totally under Brownie's spell, both of them thinking nobody knows about their bloody racing scam when everyone does and one day they'll surely get done for it, but he's a good lad basically, just easily led. Taffy, he's one of those players who is a lot brighter than he lets on. He never talks about politics, but his dad is the leader of a council in Wales, and his uncle is a Labour MP. But once he is out of the game, he'll be gone. Dipper, he is bright, which is why he has taken today so badly. He'll be a coach one day, no doubt about it. Jules – you'd reckon on him dying young what with all his supposed illnesses and injuries. He's a parody, but in a good way. I'll be at his funeral if I'm still here. Jock, he's the oldest by a few years, and I know it'll mean a trip to Scotland, but he's another one. A top man. Goalkeepers are weird, of course they are, but if it hadn't been for him we'd be relegated by now and we'd have lost today by six or seven.

And what about the young debutant Buchanan? We've all watched his incredible skills in training, but for him to walk out in front of 40,000, just before half-time when we're losing two-nil, and turn the game around into victory shows a special type of magic. He has a wonderful career ahead of him if he stays injury free, and who knows, he might end up a manager himself one day.

Yeah, this is a good bunch, Moro concluded. I reckon DD is the only one who isn't really part of the team yet, and if the gaffer gets the time, he will be. All this time we spend together, home and away, ups and downs, wins and losses, training and matches, and on the best day we've ever had as a team, I'm sitting here thinking how many fucking funerals I'll have to go to. Weird. But it's what a team does to you. You don't want to let it go. You want it to be part of you, to the end. Then add up all the different teams we have all played for in our time. The football family. There's something in it.

Look at old Cockie there. How many miles has he driven us? How many times has he told us how lucky we were to win? He'll definitely get a big turnout. Magic, Charlie Sinclair – Christ, the whole town will come to a stop when Charlie goes. He's been there all his life. Then poor old Magic whose wife Anne has had depression all her life and is now losing her marbles too. He is going to have to give this up soon to become a full-time carer, and it will break his heart. Magic's release is his job.

Ronnie Winston was one he wasn't sure about it. All things to all men. Not to be trusted.

Not a patch on the gaffer, even if he thought he was.

34

REES

What with the detour for Stan Moffitt, the drink in the Fountains Abbey, the traffic getting out of London, the slow service at the fish and chip shop, and now the driving rain, Dermot reckoned they were well over an hour behind schedule, and falling further behind. The rain had started just after Peterborough and was now falling so hard, Cockie was having to reduce his speed by around ten mph. The wipers were going at double speed but still he was finding it hard to see clearly. Then came a stretch of road where night repairs were being done, and they were soon moving at a snail's pace as the orange and white striped cones filtered the three lanes of traffic into one.

'Whose fucking idea was the M1, Cockie?' Brownie shouted down.

'You can always walk,' yelled Cockie. 'You can't run, that's for sure.'

The coach still smelled of the vinegar from the fish and chips they'd had earlier. Around half of the players were dozing now. This was the really dull part of the week, though a lot more bearable after a win.

It wasn't long before some of the players were shouting down the coach to Cockie, hoping that the boss would hear their requests.

'Cockie, stop at the next services, I need a pee.'

'Cockie, when are we stopping? Those chips were shit, I'm bloody starving.'

'Cockie, Killer will give you his win bonus if you stop at the next services.'

At first, these all went ignored. But as they increased in volume and intensity, Cockie turned to Gordon, who himself had had a little doze after he and Stan Moffitt ate their fish and chips side by side, speculating on who they would get in the semis, Gordon hoping for a return to the ground where he had played most, Villa Park, one of the neutral grounds used by the FA for big matches.

As the demands for a stop increased Dermot Cochrane said to the manager, 'What do you think, gaffer? I reckon we have about an hour to go, which gets us to the training ground just before midnight. Shall I stop or shall we head for home?'

Charlie was drifting in and out of sleep, with his chairman sitting quietly alongside him staring out into the rain. A stop, given how hard it was to shepherd this lot, especially after they had been drinking, meant a minimum of an extra half-hour. Gordon also knew that he would have a busy day tomorrow, analysing the match, starting to think about their next opponents once the draw was made, and also fielding calls from pressmen.

'Just keep going, Cockie, otherwise it'll be the middle of the night before we get home.'

Cockie reached for the microphone.

'Gentlemen, and Brownie, I have discussed the travel arrangements with your manager and chairman and I am instructed to tell you all to *shut the fuck up!* Just because you've had a lucky victory today, against a far better side, you should be thankful that you're all nearly home. If I'd been manager today I'd have left at least three of you lazy buggers in London and told you to make your own way home. So the message is, will you all please stop pestering your magnificent Irish driver?'

It brought on a fresh volley of good-hearted abuse from five or six frustrated travellers. As the coach was only moving slowly through this single-lane chaos, David Brown walked down the aisle and gently massaged Cockie's scalp with a combination of salt, pepper and vinegar left over from dinner.

'Cockie, you smelly Irish immigrant bastard, get this bleeding coach back home or next time I'll rub your fucking bollocks with Deep Heat.'

On his way back to rejoin his applauding teammates, he apologized to Stan Moffitt. 'Oh, sorry for the bad language, Chairman, I thought you were asleep.'

'Now you can see why I prefer to keep the coach a director-free zone,' a jaded-sounding Gordon said to his chairman.

At 11.17 p.m. Colleen Connor was walking through Belfast City Airport to a waiting car. For all the talk of extra security, there had been next to none beyond the usual luggage scanners at Heathrow, and she didn't see a single police officer or Customs man as she went through after landing. It felt good to be back. She knew she could say nothing to anybody about where she had been or what she had been doing. But all that she wanted was for news to reach her father, Frank, still with four years of his sentence to run, that she had been involved in the killing of the Secretary of State for Northern Ireland. This was Colleen's way of bringing some sort of closure to the events that led to her family being broken up. She would return to the empty house just off the Shankill Road and await instructions for her next mission. As she waited to hear the news of Mission Accomplished, and watch the politicians and the securocrats scrabble around pretending they had everything under control, and trotting out the usual clichés that accompanied any and every attack they made, she was sure her IRA family would reward her in some way and her influence within the organization would significantly increase, once the world absorbed the news that Rees was dead.

At 11.20 p.m. Seamus Laughlin was just outside Kendal in Cumbria. He had returned to the safe house and been handed his ticket from Manchester to Belfast, but once he was on his way, he made his own change of plan, and told the driver to keep heading north. He had already booked himself into a hotel in Windermere. He would be up early the next morning and would continue by taxi up the M6, and at 10.30 a.m. he would board the Stranraer–Larne ferry on his way home.

Stranraer had been the place he took his wife Sinead and their young son Tom, before the shootings that ended their lives and in many ways destroyed his. He remembered how they walked as baby Tom slept. Sinead and he would sit in the Galloway hills and he would stroke her flame-red hair as she told him of her childhood, her love of horses and her parents' support of the IRA movement. Only once had he mentioned his own father to her, as to him his birth father barely existed.

He knew that his unilateral change of plan would not go down well with the hierarchy in Belfast, but he cared not. He would say he was worried he was being followed and that first and foremost he needed to protect his own safety.

At 11.30 p.m. Martin Kelly was also on his way back to Armagh; he had not told Toby, who had been hoping Martin would join him in the away end at Chelsea earlier in the day. He was happy they had won. But he had no choice; he had to follow instructions. He intended to blend back into the underground homosexual scene in Armagh once he could get out of these ridiculous clothes and shave off his irritating stubble. He would ring Toby over the weekend to say that his mother had been taken ill in Derry.

At 11.35 p.m. Merlyn Rees was in a deep sleep in his hotel bedroom. He had arrived back at 10.45 p.m. and Paddy O'Connell was there to meet him and his protection team at the service entrance. The moment his car pulled up, the heavens opened and the piercing rain nearly cut through the umbrella that Paddy O'Connell was holding to shield their VIP guest from the downpour. The Minister looked tired, but said the dinner had been 'enjoyable as these things go'. He said he was glad to be getting to bed, and reminded O'Connell he would like a call at half past six. O'Connell nodded. Knowing as he did what was going to happen in just over an hours' time, he could barely bring himself to speak in the presence of such a palpably nice man.

'I still haven't seen the goals from the Chelsea match,' he said.

'It's been on telly, you've just missed it.'

'Shame, I must send a message to my nephew Morgan. I'm so proud of him. We all are. I might just have a nightcap and see if it's on the news.'

O'Connell showed him into his room, switched on the lights and then turned on the TV.

'Thank you,' said Rees.

He then stopped, felt his pockets, and said, 'That's odd. I'm sure I left some money on the bedside table.'

'Are you sure?' asked O'Connell, thinking how fucking stupid are those IRA boys to draw attention to themselves with a bit of petty crime?

'I must have taken it with me. I just don't know. Anyway, time for bed. Thanks for all you have done to make my stay pleasant and safe.'

The politician's politeness made O'Connell feel even worse. He then showed the bodyguards their rooms on either side, and made his way to the lift. He suddenly realized he had said 'good-bye' rather than 'goodnight' to Rees. Once inside the lift, he had to hold one hand with the other to stop himself shaking. He was already imagining being locked up in Paddington Green police station, which is where the anti-terrorism branch was based, and being grilled again and again about what he knew.

He carried on as normally as was possible, given what he knew was about to happen. He made a note to himself to be in the lobby close to the front of the hotel before midnight, just in case the explosion was more severe than expected. He knew from his meetings in Ealing that the aim was to kill Rees alone, but there was something in that 'Peter's' face that made him think he would stop at nothing once he got the bit between his teeth.

35

LAZYBONES

Saturday night, 11.45 p.m.

Once the road opened up to three lanes again, and the rain eased, Cockie could pick up speed, and once he was cruising at sixty-five miles an hour, he reckoned a half past midnight arrival at Summerton Manor might be possible. It was now a quarter to midnight. On the grass banking to the left, highlighted by the coach's headlamps, a sign stated 'Services, 3 miles', and yet again there was a chorus from the players to stop.

'Come on, gaffer,' shouted Smudger, 'you're the one who got us on the piss, and it's not our fault Cockie has broken the fucking toilet.'

Dermot turned to Gordon once more, hoping he would instruct him to drive on. As he neared home, he became more and more excited at the prospect of opening the briefcase he had found in Room 501. When they had set off, in his mind's eye he was planning to break it open tomorrow, but now he had decided, late though it was, that he would give himself that thrill tonight when he took the coach back to the depot. He had the cash to add to his cash supply, the cufflinks for his cufflinks pile, and the whisky signed by the Prime Minister could go either in his alcohol section, or possibly memorabilia. He would decide later. In any event, it was the briefcase that really mattered. That was where the biggest thrill would come from, he knew it. Must be cash, he thought, for someone to go to the trouble of carving out a space to hide it beneath the mattress.

Charlie Gordon looked at his watch. It was eleven minutes to midnight. He then looked out at the dark and the rain outside.

'Cockie, keep going, we'll be home in thirty minutes. If we let them off now it'll add an hour to the journey and they'll all get wet through.'

He then slipped back into his half-sleep.

His mind drifted back to his childhood in Scotland and his early days as an apprentice at Rangers under Bill Struth who managed the club for thirty-four years between 1920 and 1954. Struth was one of the most successful managers in Scottish football history, amassing eighteen League championships and ten Scottish Cups. In his early playing days Charlie dreamed of one day matching his hero's success. Even on days like today, he knew that dream was gone.

His mind also wandered to the time he made his debut for Scotland, the great games he had played for club and country, the Scottish caps and that massive celebration on the night they beat England at Hampden Park. He was a fit, handsome young man then.

He started to remember the early days of his marriage to Florence and their beautiful daughter Alice. He could now see her clearly, aged five, standing there in her new navy-blue school uniform, holding her favourite doll, which she had christened Mrs Lazybones.

'What do you think, Daddy?' she would tease him. 'I'm a big girl now, aren't I?' The trouble is, she never became a big girl. She was taken too young, and he'd never got over it, and he knew he never would, no matter how many games he won, no matter how many bottles of whisky he emptied.

Dozing fitfully, as he pictured Alice in his mind, he could hear her calling him Boss, stood in the middle of a football crowd, shouting to him from a distance. 'Boss, Boss...'

'Boss, boss, please can we stop, I'm dying for a pee.' As he opened his eyes, Alice was gone. It was Dougie Jones stood in front of him, his hands covering his crutch, pleading with him for a pee stop.

Gordon also needed one now, and so he relented.

'OK. Cockie, next services.'

Dougie went back to his seat accompanied by applause.

It was 11.53 p.m. as Cockie steered his coach into the A1 services car park.

'Ronnie,' Gordon said to Winston, 'tell them they've got exactly fifteen minutes. Anybody later than that gets fined twenty-five quid and also gets left behind.'

Dermot Cochrane guided the coach as near as possible to the entrance to the shops, which left a forty-yard dash through the rain to get to the toilets and refreshments. Everybody apart from Charlie Gordon, Dermot Cochrane and DD Marland, who was fast asleep on the second-back row, left the coach to take advantage of the unscheduled break.

'Charlie, do you want anything, chocolate, crisps?' Stan Moffitt asked.

'Maybe some Trebor mints if you see them, Chairman.' Charlie remembered he had a couple of miniature whiskies left.

Some of the players ran, some walked and some limped across the tarmac into the service station.

Willie Buchanan was the last to leave, in his shirtsleeves.

'Woah, Willie, you'll catch your death of cold. It's pouring out there.'

Charlie Gordon stood to reach up to the luggage rack and pulled down his old cream-coloured raincoat.

'Here, Willie, put this on, son. David Brown'll take the piss but you can handle that now. I don't want you sat in bed with 'flu if I need you for the semi-final.'

Willie Buchanan reluctantly put the coat on, knowing it would dwarf him, and ran off into the rain, not bothering to do up the two buttons that remained intact.

At four minutes to midnight, the coach was empty of everyone apart from Gordon, Cockie and a sleeping DD. Suddenly Gordon and Cockie noticed Norman Nulty sprinting back to the coach.

'Need to wake up DD,' he said. 'Not good if he feels excluded.'
'You're a good man, Nuts. Plenty would leave him to rot.'

Nulty went to the back of the coach, shook DD awake, and told him the rest of the players were having a quick snack and they wanted him to join them.

They left the coach and ran back to the service station together. It was 11.57.

Dermot Cochrane sat behind the wheel with the engine running to keep the coach warm for the players' return. He turned to Charlie Gordon. Gone was the endless banter he'd had with the players. He was serious now.

'Great win today, gaffer. You deserved it. And there is no way they can get rid of you after that.'

'I certainly hope so, Dermot, it's been a tough few months. I've got a feeling we can go all the way after that.'

'And you've found a gem in young Willie. Even I can see that.'

'Yep. He really is.'

Charlie Gordon stood and rummaged through his battered case to fish out the bulging unsealed envelope he was looking for. It was the package that Alfie Ruse had given him last night in the hotel bar, his cut for the DD transfer. He picked it up and placed it on the seat next to him. He then pulled out his notebook and tore out a blank page. He asked Cockie if he could borrow a pen. Cockie handed over an old Bic pen he had by the dashboard.

Slowly Gordon wrote:

'Hope this helps, love as always, Mrs Lazybones.'

He again rummaged through his pockets, this time pulling out two hundred pounds from the various fines he had collected through the week. He added it to the £1,600 bundle. After inserting his scribbled message, and the handful of banknotes, he sealed the envelope then wrote on the front:

Children's Wing Fundraising Appeal
c/o Sister Rachel Winterbottom,
Rimmington Hospital

He then stuffed it back into his jacket pocket. He would post his anonymous donation, like all the others he had made over the years, when he drove past Rimmington Hospital on his way to the club tomorrow.

Job done, he thought, thinking he now deserved those last two miniatures as he waited for the players to come back.

'Oh shit,' he muttered, realizing they were in the pocket of his raincoat, which he had given to Willie Buchanan.

'Won't be a second, Cockie,' he said as he skipped down the steps, looking for Willie Buchanan. His alcoholic urge drove him into the lashing rain.

He found Willie making a phone call, his girlfriend having just arrived home. He was reliving every second with her, and Gordon felt a shared sense of happiness, hearing Willie describe his emotions as he had been called into action late in the first half. He motioned to Willie that he needed his coat, and the youngster, who moments earlier had had Brownie asking him 'When did you decide to become a tramp?', was more than happy to hand it over.

It was 11.59 now, and Dermot Cochrane was alone on the coach. He thought about nipping out, but it was cold, rainy, his jacket was in the hold, and he was enjoying the silence. He could see some of the players inside the services, and he thought how lucky he was to have these people in his life. He thought back to those times he visited Martha the Blackpool psychic, black mesh dress, long burgundy fingernails and black mascara, quietly sitting in front of those thick velvet curtains. She never told him life would be as good as this, chatting to a great manager and ferrying around as good a bunch of lads as anyone could want to work with. He was Dermot Laughlin then and could picture her now as she rose and left the room with his ten-shilling note in her hand. Then he shivered, as he thought about the heavy briefcase stored below, and recalled that same shivery feeling when she had told him never to steal. 'If you do, you will be broken into small pieces.' It was the last thought he would ever have.

David Brown and Graham Smith were heading back to the coach, chatting about next week's race meetings, when the explosion ripped through the air. They both ducked down, and then as he rose Brownie noticed that the coach was nearly in two pieces and was ablaze, and the two vans next to it had also caught fire. The large door from the coach's storage compartment had smashed through the windscreen of the car next to them. Luckily there was no one inside.

Brownie ran back inside, screaming, 'It's the fucking coach, it's the fucking coach, the fucking coach has gone up!'

Gordon ran towards them. 'Cockie, Cockie's in there!' Then as he reached the entrance to the service station, flames now fifteen feet high, shrapnel firing off in all directions, he knew there was no way Cockie was coming out alive. The rest of the players joined them and slowly began to walk around the scene of growing devastation. The coach was already on its way to becoming a skeleton.

Charlie Gordon noticed Willie Buchanan alongside him. An old football player, possibly coming to the end of his magical life in football, and a phenomenal young player who had the potential to be one of the greatest players of his generation. What if? What if Willie had stayed on the coach? What if, when he left the coach, Gordon had not given him his coat? What if he had not felt that burning desire – need, even – for a drink, and so leave the coach and go in search of the coat? Without that, he'd be dead, with Cockie. Willie saved his job, and now he'd saved his life. And how could he be an alcoholic when it was his drinking that got him off that coach and into the safety of the gents, where he slugged down those two miniatures?

He turned and noticed that Charlie Sinclair was shaking, and in tears. Mooro was consoling him, and muttering to himself, 'It's my fault, for thinking about funerals.' For the rest, they stood rooted to the spot, thinking it could have been them. Out of nowhere police cars, ambulances and fire engines arrived, as dozens of people ran out of the service station thinking it might be next to explode. Stan Moffitt called Stewart Finley to tell him the news and ask him to order a fleet of taxis, and contact the insurance company.

*

When midnight came and went without incident, Paddy O'Connell had no idea what to do next. There was no Plan B. An abortive mission had never been contemplated, let alone discussed. For all he knew the device could explode at any moment.

The sixty minutes between midnight and 1 a.m. seemed to drag on for ever as he busied himself around the hotel reception area waiting for the sound of an explosion, but it never came. The young couple he had treated to Roxy Music tickets came back just after one, and regaled him with what a wonderful time they had had. Then two o'clock, then three o'clock, then five o'clock all came and went without a murmur. He thought about going up to the room to knock and check that Merlyn Rees was OK, but that in itself would cause attention – why shouldn't he be OK, it was the middle of the night? Once the bomb did explode he would be asked to explain exactly what he was doing that night, so he had to be careful that he wasn't seen to be anticipating an event. Of the four members who made up the unit, he alone would still be on the scene of the crime by the time this place was flooded with police and other security services. As for those 3Ps, he would never see them again, for sure, and he doubted they were still in the country. 'Paul' and 'Peter' especially – they were real pros, real Provos.

At half past five, before the sun rose, he sat down with a cup of tea and looked out through his tiny office window into the rainy early morning darkness. Praed Street was empty except for a queue of taxis with their orange lights looking for business. He made a decision: he decided to do nothing. Just to carry on as normal, and forget about everything that had happened over the last few weeks and months. For nothing to have happened meant that something had gone wrong. But it was not for him to know what it was, and nor should he care.

By 6.30 a.m. Paddy O'Connell was back home in Fulham with his wife. He felt much calmer than a few hours earlier. As he switched on the morning news he was both mystified and terrified. There was no news of a bombing in London. But there had been a bombing on a service station on the A1, in the north of England. It was the team coach he had waved off less than twelve hours earlier. He imagined the worst, then felt a strange surge of relief as the newsreader said: 'The driver, Dermot Cochrane, was killed, but manager Charlie Gordon and all the players, who were eating at the service station, are alive and unhurt, though in shock.'

Epilogue

BACKFIRE

Monday 11 March

On his arrival back in Northern Ireland, Seamus let himself into the empty safe house that had been rented for him. His job was to do nothing for a few months, and to be noticed by nobody, before slowly getting back into everyday life. There were some bottles of Guinness in the fridge, so he clipped the top off one bottle with his teeth and opened his duffle bag, which contained some food and the rest of his worldly possessions.

He had listened to the radio and television reports over the last two days and was baffled as to how their plans had not materialized. Merlyn Rees was on the TV news on Sunday lunchtime, condemning the attack on the coach of the football team, and saying that had it not been for the good fortune of them stopping at the services, this would have been the worst footballing disaster since the Munich air crash. The bomb was planted safely enough. So who the hell moved it? Someone must have informed the police. But who? Maybe that fucking stupid porter.

His mood wasn't much helped by the news of the other bombing either. It sounded like one of theirs, though nobody had claimed responsibility. Yet the only victim was an Irishman, the guy who drove the fucking coach. Big deal. It would have been brilliant to take out a whole fucking football team. That would spread terror like wildfire. But something obviously went wrong there too. What kind of inquest must the Army Council be carrying out, he wondered? If they started the day thinking they were taking out the Northern Ireland Secretary and a First Division football team, and all they got was a fucking Irish coach driver?

So much for the images that had kept him going these last few months of him being hailed a hero, his name entering the history books as one of the great Republican freedom fighters. At this rate he'd be lucky to avoid a few punishment beatings.

His mail had been shipped from England to a private PO box address in Belfast, and driven to him by a courier in anticipation of his arrival at this new address, his old life in Kent for now behind him, and after a day or two he finally got round to opening the handful of letters that had been waiting for him on the dusty kitchen table.

One of them was from Search & Reunion, the St Albans charity he had asked to help locate his real father. He opened it. It had been written last Wednesday.

We are pleased to inform you that your biological father is indeed the person we had suggested he was when we last contacted you. We have made contact with him and we are pleased to tell you that he has indicated he would be happy to meet you. He lives in the North of England, and can be contacted on the telephone number below. He owns his own coach company. He changed his name from Laughlin in 1961, and is now called Dermot Cochrane, known as Cockie to his friends.

Seamus picked up the phone and, excited, called the number at the bottom of the page. There was no reply. Then, as he replaced the receiver, he suddenly realized why the name Dermot Cochrane had rung a bell.